DARREN O'SULLIVAN is the No.1 best-selling author of psychological thrillers *Our Little Secret*, *Close Your Eyes* and *Closer Than You Think*. Formerly an actor, theatre director, and teacher, Darren was accepted onto the Faber & Faber novel writing programme in 2015. After completing their extensive six-month training, his debut was born. Darren lives in Peterborough where he's currently writing his fourth dark and unsettling novel which is due for publication in 2020. Darren loves to chat to readers and spends too much time on twitter, you can find him on @darrensully.

Also by Darren O'Sullivan

Our Little Secret
Closer Than You Think

Praise for Darren O'Sullivan

'An immensely talented new author'
John Marrs, author of *The One and When You Disappeared*

'Engrossing, compelling and twisty from the first page to the
shocking ending. This book grabbed me and didn't let go'
Michele Campbell, author of *It's Always the Husband*

'Unique and utterly compelling. This twisty
psychological thriller will chill you to the bones'
Gemma Metcalfe, author of *Trust Me*

'A stellar and original concept, brilliantly executed.
The final chapters had my heart in my throat!
O'Sullivan is certainly one to watch'
Phoebe Morgan, author of *The Doll House*

'I was gripped by this taut and emotional thriller.'
Louise Jensen, author of *The Sister.*

'I thought it was absolutely brilliant – really fast-paced,
and packed full of action.'
Lisa Hall, author of *Between You and Me*

Close Your Eyes

DARREN O'SULLIVAN

ONE PLACE. MANY STORIES

HQ
An imprint of HarperCollins*Publishers* Ltd
1 London Bridge Street
London SE1 9GF

This paperback edition 2019

First published in Great Britain by
HQ, an imprint of HarperCollins*Publishers* Ltd 2019

ISBN: 9780008348236

MIX
Paper from
responsible sources
FSC   FSC™ C007454
www.fsc.org

This book is produced from independently certified FSC™ paper to ensure responsible forest management.

For more information visit: www.harpercollins.co.uk/green

Typeset by Palimpsest Book Production Ltd, Falkirk, Stirlingshire
Printed and bound in Great Britain by
CPI Group (UK) Ltd, Melksham, SN12 6TR

To Helen,
because time is the most precious gift,
and one you have given me

Prologue

Daniel

Sheringham

5th January 2018

Breathe.

Just breathe.

That was all I had to do. And yet it was impossible. Lying on the ground, the cold seeping through to my back and chest, I stared up at the sky. Unblinking. A sheet of nothingness stretching in all directions. Flat and smooth and devoid of anything I could identify with, devoid of anything I could latch hope onto. Just grey. I looked anyway, for something, anything that meant there was more. My eyes stung, I needed to blink. But I didn't dare. I knew if I did, my eyes might not open again. And grey was better than the black of what was surely to come.

Ironically, grey was the colour that made up my past, made up who I was, made up my memories. I had fought against it, now it was all I had left. The only thing to hold on to. Grey was a friend all along.

Breathe.

Just breathe.

The pain was too much, the knowledge of what was coming next too constricting. I knew I would pass out soon. I could feel it creeping up my arms and legs. A stillness as my extremities conceded defeat. The blood flowing from my body was unstoppable, it came from too many places. My life was leaking out, a millilitre at a time, forming a pool in which I lay. It warmed the concrete around me, inviting me to relax, to accept. And it didn't hurt, it didn't matter.

I wasn't scared of what was next, part of me knew it was inevitable. It didn't even matter where I went once I died, all that mattered was that life would continue. The storm would end, spring would come. Summer would burn and then winter would return. It would do so for many, many years. There would be laughter and love. There would be success and change. There would be children growing to become adults who would have their own children one day. Then there would be peace as it came to an end, only to be replaced with another winter, another summer forever and ever.

I was just a very small part of a much bigger picture.

I was just a single paintbrush stroke on a canvas that was the entire world. A single small stroke of paint. One that was never very vibrant or colourful. More shading than subject.

Just before I closed my eyes for the final time there was a small gap in the grey, just enough for me to see beyond it. A small space of the brightest blue I had ever seen. Pure. Untouched by the past five days.

And that bit of blue, it told me everything would be okay, for the one person that it was all for.

And that was what mattered.

ONE WEEK EARLIER

Chapter 1

Daniel

Stamford

29th December 2017, 7.48 a.m.

A long time ago I was told that the moments that were truly important in life were the moments we carry forward and recall on our deathbeds. Things like the perfect sunset. The moment we fall in love. A passing of someone dear.

As I lay in my bed, I was doing exactly that, as coming from the room next door was the sound of Thomas and Katie, talking and playing together. Their voices were my two most favourite sounds. Katie said something I couldn't quite make out, but whatever it was it made Thomas laugh and I couldn't stop myself from smiling. I wanted to join them. But not yet, first I would use my senses as I had been taught.

It was a doctor who told me to let my subconscious take over when it mattered. A doctor who was one of the many I had fifteen years ago in the days, weeks and months after I woke up in a hospital bed. But he was the only one I would never forget. He was the one who first told me what had happened and helped me understand my life had re-begun. He helped me make sense of the facts. I was a broken body that didn't know where it was. A broken body that didn't know its name. A broken body whose even more broken mind couldn't comprehend that it once had a past that it may never see again. Its memories, my memories, like all memories, were tiny bubbles that contained joy and happiness, sadness, fear. Only mine had all been popped.

Our conversation, the one that helped to save me from the pit of despair I was in, came on a grey February morning. I was sitting staring out of the window nearest my bed, trying to find a reason to carry on and he, doing his morning rounds, approached. Noticing I was lost in thought he asked me what I saw. I told him I saw drizzle and darkness, before looking away from the window back to nothing in particular.

'What about the trees?'

'What about them?'

'What do you see when you look at them?'

Sighing, I looked outside again, to humour the doctor, thinking if I did he would go away and leave me alone.

'They look dead,' I said, holding his eye. I almost followed it up with a comment about how they were lucky, but stopped myself. The doctor sat on the end of my bed and looked outside. I watched him, wondering what he was doing. Doctors usually rushed in and out. I didn't blame them retrospectively, I was intolerable to be around. I waited for him to say something, but for a long time he just sat, looking out of the window, a small smile on his face. The silence was too much.

'What do you see?' I questioned.

'The same as you at first glance.'

'So then why ask?'

'Because I wanted to see how hard you looked.'

'Doc, you aren't making sense. If you don't mind, I want to be left alone.'

He looked at me, the smile unmoving and nodded.

'Before I do, Daniel, humour me once more and look again

6

at the trees, but this time, look closer. Focus on the tree tops. Look at the way they are moving in the wind. Look at the very tips of those branches. What can you see?'

Reluctantly I did what he said and looked again, having to hide my astonishment when I focused on where he told me to. The trees may have looked dead at first glance, but as I focused I saw their tips starting to show the signs of sprouting buds that would become leaves eventually, they would attract birds who would nest and raise families. As he spoke, I could almost smell the sweet scent a sapling gives off in spring. But I didn't remember any springs, or summers, or autumns. Only winter, the one I watched from my window. I learnt that the small act of stopping to let my senses work properly helped me see something wonderful that was always there, and the morning wasn't quite so dreary anymore. As he left my hospital room, he told me that if we embraced the stillness from time to time, we captured the moment entirely. His final words to me were that letting myself see the small things that really mattered wouldn't help me remember my past, but it might just help me have a future. That day, I knew I could learn to hold on to the precious moments that were to come in my life. Things I would experience going forwards, and they could be wonderful if I let them, despite not knowing anything about the past. Shortly after that moment with the smiling doctor I was told I would be going home soon. I never saw that doctor again.

I have had several moments in the fifteen short years that I can remember where I have done exactly that. I stopped, I became still, and in doing so I made sure those moments were branded permanently in my mind so that no matter what might happen I would never forget them. Moments likes the two occasions I have fallen in love. The first time to Rachael – the memory feels traditional, sweet, and is almost as far back as I can remember. Two people who were nervous and excited. Full of possibilities. That first kiss suspending me above myself. I didn't know then, but that first kiss would eventually lead to another wonderful moment when Rachael told me I was going to be a dad. A box presented to me, inside being a positive pregnancy test, a card and Baby-gro. Tears that fell and warmed my cheeks. Her smile, unfiltered.

The biggest moment of all is reserved for the day my son was born, six years ago. Although it feels like six minutes. His tiny body helpless and defenceless. His beautiful little head that fit perfectly in my palm as I carried him towards his mummy who lay on the operating table post-caesarean. His cry, his voice. As I carefully moved towards her, his eyes found mine and changed everything I assumed I knew about myself.

But there is also the second time I fell in love, more recently, to my Katie. Our meeting and dating coming from a place that was wiser, but no less powerful.

I might have had more of these moments in the years before 2003. But I would never know. Mum prefers never to speak of the time before the accident; it's not important, she tells me. I know that they're memories that she doesn't want to relive and I'm not interested in finding out about them, not when I have no way of remembering. She's more focused on the man I am now – on rebuilding my life after what happened. She has spoken of my kindness though, my ability to love others and to jump into situations too quickly. Sometimes I will catch her staring into space and I just know she's recalling another time, another me.

In some ways, me losing my past was harder for her – she had to mourn for the man I once was without mourning at all, and I knew, despite how much I wanted to know about the me before, that if I asked her outright, she might break her silence, spilling the bottled-up emotions she held on to for my benefit. Something I couldn't do to her; she has been through enough. So I left it alone and focused on the now and the future. Which was Thomas and Katie.

From his bedroom I heard Thomas tell Katie what Santa had left him at Mummy's house, before asking her to build a tower from the Lego my mum had bought him. His voice was followed by the crashing sound of hundreds of plastic blocks being poured onto his bedroom floor. It wasn't the words spoken or the sounds of Katie and Thomas building that would form into a lasting memory, but the context.

The woman I loved and the boy who meant more than anything else in the world to me had formed a relationship that didn't need me to mediate. I wasn't required for them to play and talk. I wasn't needed for them to know and care for one another. And, with what I had planned for the new year, Katie and Thomas caring for one another in such a way was essential.

Katie still thought I was asleep. I knew because she was speaking in her quiet whispery tones despite Thomas not lowering his voice at all. Truth was, I'd not really been asleep since just after 4 a.m. A dream, my dream, waking me early. The same one I had been having for over a year. The one of the accident that took away my memories and the life before.

Slipping out of bed I tiptoed towards Thomas's room. As I stepped in, I allowed myself a moment to enjoy the sight of them sat next to each other, him leaning into her as they built some sort of tower that stood about eighteen inches tall. Katie saw me first as Thomas was concentrating on his building task, and she smiled, looking from me to Thomas before resting her chin on his head. Her eyes told me everything. She was happy that he let her be close, she was content. After just over a year, he was treating her like part of his family. She mouthed a good morning to me, and I mouthed it back before turning my attention to my fixated boy.

'Morning, Thomas.'

He looked up at me, a smile spreading across his face.

'Daddy, look at the robot Katie and me made.'

'Wow, did you two really make this?'

'Yep.'

'All by yourselves?'

'Yep.'

'That's amazing. You are both very clever.'

'Well, Thomas did most of the building, I just helped where I could,' Katie said, focusing on Thomas as she spoke.

'Well then, I'm even more impressed. Bit of a clever one, aren't you?'

'Am I?'

'Yes, look at your robot. I doubt there's anything you can't do. Are you two hungry? Shall I make some breakfast?'

'Not yet, Daddy.'

'Okay, no rush.'

'What time are you meeting Will today?' Katie asked, her smile shrinking, morphing into a tight one that she always held firmly in place when she was trying not to be worried about how I would feel after seeing my therapist.

'Not till 2.30, so we can take our time this morning.'

'Do you want me to come?'

'No, it's okay. I'll drop Thomas back at his mum's earlier than usual this week.'

'Daddy, can I stay up here and play a little longer? I want to build a racing car.'

'Of course you can. Do you want me to help?'

'No. I want Katie to.'

'You want Katie to?' I said looking once again to my girlfriend, not even trying to suppress my smile.

'Right, I'll leave you two to it. I'll be downstairs, come down whenever you're ready.'

Once downstairs I flicked on the kettle before sitting at my kitchen table. I quietly drank my coffee and looked into my garden as the lazy sun forced its way over the horizon and listened to them talk above my head. Thomas laughed, his infectious giggle making Katie laugh as well.

10

Not knowing my past is a huge part of my present, and the questions that remain unanswered about me will be ones I will carry forever. But, listening to my son and my love playing in a bedroom above me, I let myself believe that the questions I had, the scars I carried, wouldn't be the future of me.

The future was now. The future was upstairs and everything about it was definitely real.

Chapter 2

Daniel

Stamford

29th December 2017, 3.18 p.m.

It turned out I didn't need to take Thomas back to his mother's early after all, as Katie suggested that they went to the park to play whilst I met up with Will. Then we could take Thomas back to his mum's together. Before I could say anything, Tom was putting his shoes on to leave.

'Are you sure, Katie?'

'Of course. We've not spent this much time together before.'

'Honestly, it doesn't matter if we take him back.'

'Dan, honestly. It will be fine. I love your little boy. I want to spend some time alone with him.'

'Katie, come on, let's go!' Thomas said, pulling on her jumper and away from me.

'Right, you need to wear a hat and gloves, it's freezing out there today,' she said playfully whilst trying to wrestle his coat on. I asked if she needed a hand, but she told me she was fine.

I had known Katie for two years. She had known Thomas for just over one, and after kissing them both I watched them walk out of the house without me for the first time. It felt good and weird all at once.

With the house quiet, I got myself ready and drove to Will's for our session. The hour we spent together mostly followed the same routine as usual; we talked about how I was feeling, I told him about how I remembered the taste of blood in my mouth, and the pain of a broken bone.

'Have you told anyone about this?' he asked.

'Yes, my mother.'

'But not Katie?'

'No, not Katie.'

'What did your mum say?'

'She laughed and told me I had been watching too many action movies.'

He agreed; it was my imagination faking memories. I knew the term for it, confabulation. It was common for people with my condition.

Before I left we scheduled our next meeting to be just after the Easter weekend. But he told me if anything new happened that I wanted to talk through, he was always on the end of the phone.

In the car on the way back I let myself reflect on my chance encounter with Katie; I often did so after seeing Will. I guess it was because with Will we spoke of a past I didn't know, but thinking about how Katie and I met, that was from a past I did and our memories, our past, helped me suppress the knot in my stomach that sometimes swelled.

Pulling up on the side of the road by the park, I could see the two people I loved the most in the distance. He was climbing the ladder to the top of the slide and Katie stood close by, her face glowing in the cold weather. As I walked towards them I took it all in. The crisp winter air, the sound of the breeze creaking through the limbs of the exposed trees. Thomas's laugh over it. Her laugh. Bright and unreserved.

13

Thomas saw me approaching and waved. I was expecting him to run over for a cuddle, but he was so wrapped up in playing that he carried on running from the slide to the swings, dragging Katie with him. He climbed into the bucket seat and asked Katie to push him. It warmed me despite it being so cold that the frost had not melted from the night before. I watched them, not wanting to interrupt for a few minutes, and then I glanced down at my watch and sighed. It was nearly time to go. It would be getting dark soon. But I didn't want to move, I wanted to stay in this moment forever. The cold air, the warm laughs.

Thomas shouted for Katie to push him harder, although she was clearly pushing with all of her strength. He was swinging so high it made my stomach turn. Each time he swung into the air I was sure he would shoot off the seat and fly ten feet into the air before hitting the frozen floor. I felt my muscles in my legs ready to spring, my arms ready to catch. He was screaming and for a moment I saw a flash of something from before. It was dark, almost pitch black, a woman's scream echoed, her shrill bouncing off a low ceiling, and I was running, hard, and crashed through a door.

As quick as it landed it was gone. It took me a moment to realize he was screaming in glee and she was smiling and making rocket noises behind him. He was fine. They both were. Katie looked at me, a quizzical expression on her face. She had seen my reaction. I smiled weakly at her, trying to assure her that everything was fine. No doubt another moment of confabulation; I had seen something similar on the BBC perhaps, and mistaken it for a memory.

I turned my attention back to Thomas, shaking the last of the adrenaline that shot into my chest. I looked at his hands wrapped around the freezing chains, and his feet dragging across the ground each time he passed. It amazed me how big he was getting. Time moving at a pace that I couldn't keep up with, changing him from a defenceless baby, to a gabbling toddler, to a little boy

14

with his own mind and ideas and plans for who he wanted to be. Thomas shouted he was going to be sick and the swing slowed down, being grabbed from behind by Katie to help the process.

I watched as he jumped off and, grabbing her hand, he dragged her to the roundabout to push him on it. She smiled over at me and I smiled back. She was good with him and looked so happy. I wanted to get up and join in, but it was important for them to have their time alone.

There was no doubt that Katie and I had a future together. I had known it for just about as long as I had known her, despite not wanting to admit it at the time. She was kind and thoughtful, and her laugh lit a fire. When she learnt about my condition she didn't judge, she didn't ask questions. She accepted it, and me. She offered patience when I occasionally forgot a word, and she would soothe me when I woke from a bad dream as the crash haunted me. Because of her I had pieced together some small moments from the boy I once was. We discovered that when I was drifting to sleep she could ask me questions and occasionally things would lift from my subconscious. She wrote them down and sometimes I would recall what it meant. If only for a moment. When I had my lightning bolts of recollection of past moments, she waited until I was ready to say what I had seen. Her patience and understanding were more than I felt I deserved at times.

As Thomas continued to scream for Katie to spin him faster and faster, I let myself picture a future with us three in it, just for a second, until it was broken by Thomas running over to me, dizzy and smiling from ear to ear.

'Daddy, did you see how fast I was spinning?'

'I did,' I replied, smiling back.

'Come and spin with me.'

'Thomas, darling, it's time to start heading back.'

'Do we have to, Daddy?'

'I'm afraid so. But don't worry, next weekend will come quickly, and we will have the whole weekend together to play games and go out for yummy food. How does that sound?'

'Can we go ice-skating?'

'We can even do that.'

'Will Katie be there too?'

'Would you like her to be?'

'Yeah.'

'Yeah?' I said grabbing my boy and hugging him tightly. 'Well, let's see what Daddy can do.'

I took his little hand and the three of us started to walk towards the cars, Thomas pausing to grab hold of Katie's as well so we could swing him between us. With the sun setting behind us, our shadows were stretching out over the frosty ground. The three of us, hand in hand walking together.

Back at our cars I gave Katie a kiss and told her I wouldn't be long. She and Rachael knew each other and got along well. We often met up with her and her new husband, Sean, for dinner. She liked him too, as did I. As hard as it was to accept that Rachael had moved on, at least it was with a decent man who Thomas really liked. After they had first met, Sean called me to talk about how he wasn't trying to replace me in Thomas's life. Like he had replaced me in Rachael's.

Thomas was nearly four when we, actually *she*, decided it was best for us to separate, for the sake of our son. It had broken my heart. More because I wouldn't be with Thomas night after night. But we both knew it would be the best thing for him in the long term. No courts would be involved. I could talk with Thomas whenever I wanted and we still came together for big events, like birthdays and Christmases, even after she had married Sean. We did it for Thomas at first, to make sure he didn't feel like he wasn't loved because of love breaking down in other places. But now we did it because, despite everything, we were friends. That's why the five of us would all be seeing in the new year together, as a giant family.

Although Rachael and Katie got along, Katie didn't come with me to drop Thomas off. She said it was time for his mother and father to catch up, to make plans for the coming week and ensure things ran as smoothly as possible for him. The little things like this made it easy to love her.

As I unlocked the car, Thomas let go and ran back to Katie to give her a hug. His little arms wrapping around her waist. Katie kissed the top of his head and then smiled at me, the kind of smile that made me want to burst. He said goodbye and ran back over, climbing into his car seat. Katie mouthed that she loved me, and I mouthed it back. She blew me a kiss, got into her car and drove away. I watched her disappear down the road.

Chapter 3

Daniel

Stamford

29th December 2017, 3.41 p.m.

'All strapped in tightly.'

'Yes, Daddy.'

'Great, shall we take you home, little man?'

Getting into the driver's seat I looked at Thomas through the rear-view mirror, watching him smile at the other children who were now playing on the swings he had been on. Content, I began the ten-minute drive back to Rachael's house, the sound of the radio playing quietly above the hum of the car. I wanted to talk about Katie, but it took me a few minutes to work out how. If I appeared too nonchalant he might think his view, or my feelings, didn't matter, and they both did, very much. If I went in too gung-ho it might freak him out. I took a deep breath.

'Thomas?'

I waited for a response, one that was not forthcoming, as Thomas was so wrapped up in people-watching through the car window. So, I turned down the radio, which lifted him from his trance.

'Thomas, I want to talk to you about Katie.'

'What about her?'

'Did you enjoy spending time alone with her today?'

'Yes, she's great.'

'What else do you think about her?'

'What do you mean, Daddy?'

Pausing for a moment, I thought about the best way to answer.

'I mean, well …'

'What do you think about her, Daddy?'

Thomas's question caught me off guard and, knowing I needed to be honest, I pulled over into a layby, put on the handbrake and turned to be eye to eye with my son.

'I care about her a lot.'

'You mean you love her?'

'How would you feel if I did?'

'Well, Mummy loves Sean.'

'She does love Sean, very much.'

'Then you should love Katie.'

'Should I?'

'Yes, Daddy. I don't like thinking of you on your own when Mummy has Sean'

'Thomas, you don't ever have to worry about me, okay? I'm fine.'

I looked into his big green eyes. I could feel him really caring. He was such a bright, bright boy.

'I'm more than fine,' I said. 'Are you really okay with the idea of Katie and me?'

'Of course, Daddy. Can we go home now? I'm getting hungry.'

I laughed. 'Before we do, can I ask you a really big question, one I want you to answer as honestly as you can. And don't worry about what I might feel, this question is about how you feel …'

'Daddy, if you love her, you should marry her.'

I smiled at my wonderful, intelligent boy, who in that moment looked at me with a wisdom beyond his years. I could feel myself welling up with pride.

'You're a brilliant boy, you know that, right?'

'Uh-huh, can we go now?'

'Of course, darling. Let's get you home.'

Turning to face the road again I started the car, turned the radio back up, and drove the rest of the way to Rachael's in silence, like nothing had happened. When we arrived, Thomas unfastened his seatbelt, jumped out of the car and ran to his front door, ringing the bell repeatedly until Sean answered. Following behind with his coat, I shook Sean's hand.

'Hello, mate. Good week off?'

'Yes thanks, Sean. Went far too quickly though.'

'I hear that.'

Thomas ran down the hallway into the kitchen, shouting to the entire house. 'Daddy is going to get married.'

'Really?' said Sean, trying to hide his surprise.

'I haven't asked her yet, just wanted to know how Thomas felt.'

'Well, he seems fine with it. Congratulations in advance,' he said, patting me on the shoulder. 'Come in, mate. Rach would love to hear.'

I chuckled to myself. I hadn't even picked up the ring I'd been eyeing up – a single stone in a clasp that allowed you to see the diamond from all angles.

'Sure. As long as I'm not interrupting.'

'Of course not.'

Stepping into the house I had to take off my coat; the central heating was on high as Rachael always liked. Sean shut the door and gestured for me to walk to the kitchen. As I stepped into the kitchen Rachael stood back from her long embrace with our boy and Thomas walked to the fridge, opened it and buried his head in there to search out something to eat. He emerged with a Frubes yogurt, held it in the air to wait for the nod to say he could have it before running into the living room where Sean had gone, no doubt to give me and Rachael a moment. I ruffled Thomas's hair

20

as he passed me. Once we were alone, I leant on the counter and smiled at Rachael. She looked tired. I knew her well enough to know what that meant.

'Tough time at work?'

She laughed and lowered her head. 'Am I that easy to read?'

I didn't say anything but waited. Rachael wasn't one to be pushed into talking. If she wanted to say, she'd say. If not, I'd not ask. A few seconds was usually the timeframe for us to either move on or discuss it further.

'Just a patient of mine. Terminal. He blamed me for him dying today.'

'He's just …'

'I know, I know, he's angry. He's afraid. I know he didn't mean it. But it's still hard to hear.'

'I bet.'

'I'm sure he will be calmer tomorrow. He'll probably apologize and then we can focus on making sure his transition is as dignified as possible.'

'I don't know how you do it.'

'Sometimes I don't know either. Speaking of which – how is Katie's dad?'

'No change really.'

'Is she okay?'

'I think she's coming to terms with it now. I guess that's all anyone can do, right?'

'Yes. Anyway, Thomas has just told me. I hear congratulations are in order?'

I couldn't help but laugh and feel embarrassed. I hadn't planned it enough in my head for it to be said out loud. I needed to know what Thomas felt before I let myself go that far. She read my mind. She often did.

'He's clearly happy about it.'

'It seems so.'

'So, when?'

21

'I haven't worked that out yet, soon. Are you all right with this?'

'Of course. I'm really happy, Daniel. You deserve someone lovely.'

Rachael stepped towards me and gave me a hug, warm and safe. A hug that had changed in context, but never affection.

'Thanks, Rach. Are you all good though?'

'Yeah, I'm fine. Like I said, tomorrow is another day.'

'It is indeed. Well, I'd better be off.'

'I'll see you out.'

Leaving the kitchen, Rachael followed. I leant into the living room where Thomas sat watching the start of Pixar's *Planes* with Sean.

'Bye, Sean.'

'See you soon, Daniel. Congratulations again, you know, for when it happens.'

'Thanks, mate. Bye, Thomas.'

'Bye, Daddy,' he said, unable to take his eyes off the screen.

'Thomas, come and give your daddy a hug,' said Rachael from the doorway.

'Okay.' He got up and wrapped himself in my arms. His hugs were the best part of any day.

'I love you, little man.'

'Love you too, Daddy.'

Putting on my coat I opened the door and turned back to Rachael, who crossed her arms as the cold air flooded in.

'I mean it, Daniel. I'm really happy for you.'

'Thanks, Rachael, it means a lot.'

'She's lovely. You two are really good together.'

'Can I call later, to say goodnight to him?'

'Of course you can. Are you two still coming on Sunday?'

'Yep, we're looking forward to it. Is there anything you want us to bring?'

'A bottle of wine wouldn't go amiss.'

'That goes without saying.'

'Then no, just you and Katie. Sean is doing dinner. God help us!'

'I heard that!' Sean shouted from the lounge, feigning hurt. 'I'm in trouble now!'

'Well, worst case, I'll order us a takeaway.'

'I heard that too, Dan! Have a little faith, you two. I'm like Gordon Ramsay.'

'I don't doubt it,' I called into the lounge.

'Do you and Katie want to come over for about eight? If he hasn't burnt the house down, of course,' she said in a conspiring whisper, but still loud enough for Sean to call back that we were both so charming.

'Eight sounds perfect. And not a word to Katie about … you know.'

'Of course. When are you going to pop the question?'

'Some time in the new year.'

'I'm really happy for you, Dan.'

'Thanks. See you Sunday,' I said before calling out, 'Bye, Sean. Bye, Thomas.'

'See you, mate.'

'Bye, Daddy.'

I kissed Rachael on the cheek and walked back to my car, shielding my eyes as the setting sun blinded me and gave everything a soft orange glow. As I drove away, Thomas waving at me from the window, I let myself picture the moment I got down on one knee, imagining the look on Katie's face. I couldn't wait. 2018 was going to be a good year for us, for all of us. I could feel it.

23

Chapter 4

Daniel

Stamford

31st December 2017, 7.44 p.m.

I sat on my bed fully dressed, waiting for Katie, aimlessly scrolling through the posts on my Facebook newsfeed and trying my best not to think about the dream that had startled me awake early this morning.

It was the same as usual. I was in a car. But I don't know what kind, or where I was. It was dark. Bright lights of a large van or lorry blinded me, and then I was rolling over and over and over until I stopped upside down. Blood dripped from my head, pooling onto the sunroof. Someone was shouting. I tried to move but couldn't; I was trapped. Panic began to bubble up in my throat as I fought against the constraints of the seatbelt. No matter how hard I tried to get out, I couldn't. Just as I thought any hope of me getting out was gone, just as I had believed that I would die in the car, a hand reached in and dragged me out. I couldn't see the person. They didn't have a face, it was just a blur.

They pulled me far enough away from the car that I would be safe, talking to me, but I can never remember what they said.

The car goes up in flames and I can feel the heat on my face, it is singeing the hairs on my arms as I'm still that bit too close. The person looks at me and tells me to run.

That was what usually happened in the dream, give or take. Sometimes I climbed out of the wreck. Sometimes I was the one in the van or lorry smashing into the car. But I was always bleeding, and someone was always talking to me in sentences I couldn't process, except for that one word – 'run'. Their voice sounded like they were screaming underwater. Last night's had something new though – something I hadn't dreamt before – but it was just on the edge of whatever held on to dreams and stopped them coming forward with clarity. I could almost touch it. However, try as I might, I couldn't quite touch it. I'd been wracking my brain all day to work out what the new thing was, frustrated with myself for not being able to see it.

I desperately wanted to talk to Will about it. To have his professional mind analyse what I had seen, but it was New Year's Eve and I couldn't call him, it would be selfish. So instead, I clutched my hand to my phone to stop it from shaking.

My Facebook timeline was full of comments about how hard or wonderful or heartbreaking the year had been, and how 2018 was a fresh start. As clichéd as that was, I felt it too. At some point early into 2018 I was going to ask my girlfriend, who was meticulously applying her eyeliner, to be my bride. We would then probably plan our wedding and honeymoon. Maybe even begin talking about children. A brother or sister for Thomas. Life could change in a heartbeat, so the prospect of an entire year and what change would come was almost too exciting to digest.

'I'm nearly done,' Katie called out as she moved on to applying mascara.

'No rush, darling, we've still got time,' I replied, despite it being close to eight. She smiled at me through the wardrobe mirror and continued applying. I watched her in the glass. I loved the way she pouted whilst she stroked the mascara brush delicately upwards. And how she needed to lean back from the mirror after to look at her handiwork because she refused to wear glasses despite being slightly long-sighted. She caught me looking and I saw her cheeks blush a little, a smile spreading on her face.

'What?'

'Nothing, darling. I just like looking at you.'

'You're hopeless.'

She was right, I was hopeless and I didn't care. Getting up I took the necklace that she was struggling to clasp under her hair and clipped it together. A delicate silver chain with a pearl attached. A gift from her father. Once it was secured I stepped closer and held her shoulder, placing a kiss on the space between her neck and collarbone. She smiled, but I could see a sadness in her eyes as she looked at the pearl.

'We can get up early tomorrow and go see him a day early if you want? I don't have to drink tonight.'

'No, it's okay. Dad isn't good in the mornings anymore.'

'If you change your mind, I'm happy to stay on the soft drinks.'

'Thank you, Dan, but it's fine.'

'Do you want to try and ring him?'

'He'll be asleep now. I'm sure he doesn't really know what day it is today. If I call and he is by chance awake, it will remind him. I think I'd rather he wasn't aware. Does that make sense?'

'Yes, it does.'

I understood. If her father was aware that it was the start of a new year, he would also be aware it was likely, almost certainly in fact, his last on this earth. His cancerous body in its last stages of fighting the disease, a fight he was always going to lose. And although he never said it out loud, with each visit – the ones where his medication was just enough to manage his pain but not so much that he was completely out of it – I could see that he wanted it to be over. So did Katie who, like her father, wouldn't ever say. It killed me to see her quietly hurting as she fixated on the pearl. But there was nothing anyone could do. It was life, it begun, it ended and all we could do was make sure we had enough wonderful little bubbles floating with us when it was our time to pass.

Turning Katie around, I looked into her deep-brown eyes and watched as her pain lifted.

'Are you all right?'

'Yeah, I'm fine, thank you,' she said before leaning in and kissing me softly. 'How do I look?'

'Perfect.'

She smiled and kissed me once more, this time less softly. A smacker landing hard on my lips before she turned to check her make-up one last time. 'Shall we go?'

'We could be a little late?' I said, sliding my hands down her shoulders and onto her hips, pulling her closer.

'And why would we be late when we are both ready?' she asked.

'I don't know … but I can think of a reason,' I replied with a cheeky wink.

'Has that ever worked for you?' she laughed, wrapping her arms around my neck.

'I'm about to find out.'

I kissed her neck just under her left ear, the small patch of skin where I knew she loved to be kissed. With my lips placed there I listened as her breathing became heavier and she placed her hands on mine, moving them across her stomach, resting them just under her belly button. I kissed her lips, at first softly then, as she pressed herself into me, with more intent. Lifting up her dress I placed my hand back on her hip, my thumb sliding under the elastic of her underwear and, lowering myself, I slid them down her thighs before placing a kiss close to where I could feel heat. She pulled me back up and pushed me onto the bed, undoing and pulling down my jeans before climbing on top of me.

'We are going to be so late, Dan.'

'Not that late.'

'Oh, I see.'

'In fact, probably only a few minutes.'

'A few minutes, wow, you know how to spoil a girl.' She laughed, smiling as she leant in and bit my lip. 'You'd better not smudge my make-up.'

Chapter 5

Daniel

Stamford

31st December 2017, 10.17 p.m.

Even now, I'm shocked at how natural it feels to be with Rachael and Sean. The conversation never faltered as we talked about everything grown-ups could with a six-year-old buzzing around them. In the background Alexa, Sean's Amazon speaker, played song after song, most of which I hadn't heard in a long time and some being completely new to me despite Sean telling me they were hits back in the day. We had already eaten together, Sean's cooking actually surprising me and Rachael. Probably Katie too, but she was being polite by suggesting she trusted his chef's abilities. Rachael announced he could start cooking more often and I saw him smile proudly.

'I didn't doubt you for a second,' Katie said when Rachael and I expressed our surprise that the food was edible.

'Thanks, Katie. This is why we're friends.'

After we had eaten I played on the floor with Thomas, building a Scalextric track that covered most of the lounge. Sean helped move the furniture to create more space and to make tunnels from sofa cushions until, between the three of us, we had entirely turned the room upside down.

Katie and Rachael chatted as we played. I couldn't hear their conversation clearly, but I heard Katie telling Rachael about her father. Rachael, being a nurse for as long as she had been, spoke comforting words about what the staff would be doing for him in his final months. Most of the time I wanted to be by Katie's side when she was talking about her dad to give her a shoulder, comfort. But I knew in this instance to let them chat and so focused on Thomas. Rachael knew what she was talking about and I liked that Katie felt comfortable enough to talk about it with her.

With the track complete and the cars placed on the start grid we flipped a coin to see who would race against Thomas first. Sean called heads, and heads it was, so I moved to let them begin the miniature Formula One course of our design. As I went to pocket the £2 coin, Thomas asked for me to do the trick he always loved seeing.

'Coin trick?' asked Sean curiously.

'Daddy can make a coin vanish. He's a magician.' He said the last part in a whisper.

'Now then, I would also like to see that.'

'Really?'

'Sure, who doesn't love a bit of magic?'

Standing, I rolled up my shirt sleeves a little, so they were resting on my forearms, and in my best magician voice I declared I would make the coin in my hand vanish before their very eyes. Thomas started giggling in delight and Sean made a 'woooo' noise, indulging in my silliness for Thomas.

'As you can see, I have this £2 coin. Would anyone in the audience like to hold it to make sure it's real?'

'I would!' Thomas said, jumping to his feet, knowing what was to come. 'It's real,' he continued before handing it to Sean who also confirmed the coin was, in fact, real. Taking the coin back I pushed my sleeves up over my elbows and, holding the coin tightly in my grasp, I shook my hand and asked Thomas to blow on it before rubbing my fingers into my palm, dissolving the coin. Both Thomas and Sean applauded and I took a mock bow like I was on the stage at the Royal Variety before sitting back on the floor beside them.

'Where is it? Where is it?' Thomas begged, looking in his hair, behind his ear and in his socks.

'It's gone, Thomas, it's gone forever,' I said mystically.

'No, it always comes back,' he said, searching through Sean's hair also.

'Okay, how did you do that?' Sean asked and, responding in my best magician voice again, I told him a master never reveals his secrets. Thomas was still frantically searching both himself and Sean for the coin. It was time for the finale. Looking up, I made a face as if about to sneeze, and said as much, drawing their attention. As I did, I shot the coin back into my hand as if I had just sneezed it from my nose. Thomas erupted in laughter and Sean gave me a fresh clap for my showmanship. I handed Thomas the coin, telling him he could put it in his money box.

'This is the only reason he indulges my magic now. Somehow, I do all the work and Thomas keeps all the money,' I said, making Sean chuckle. 'Right, now that's over, let's see you two race so I can defeat the winner.'

'No way, Daddy. I'm like Lewis Hamilton.'

'Oh really, we'll see about that,' declared Sean, positioning himself to begin. As the race began and Thomas shot into a commanding lead, Sean looked towards me.

'Okay. You have to tell me. How did you do that trick?'

'You want me to explain it?'

'Yes, no. Just where did you learn how to do it?'

'I have no idea. I've just always known it. Recovering from my accident I had a lot of time to kill, and was always bored. I discovered I was pretty good with my hands and then when I

31

knew Thomas was on the way I decided to learn a few tricks, so went to our friend YouTube. I picked it up so easily that I guess it's something I did before.'

'Well, handy to have.'

'They are good for parties.'

Thomas crossed the finish line in a triumphant first place and Sean and I took turns to race Thomas for another half-hour, but Thomas proceeded to beat both us adults, despite us actually trying.

Thomas tried to stay up with us to see the fireworks, but his little body gave in just after eleven. Rachael and I carried him to bed, like we used to when he was a baby. We changed him into his pyjamas, tucked him in and, because he had stirred, I sat on the floor beside his bed and read him a story as Rachael stroked his back until we watched him close his eyes. We did it all without needing to talk, our instincts guiding us seamlessly. Once he was asleep we both kissed him on the head and went back down to join Sean and Katie who were mid-conversation as they tidied the carnage we had created in the living room. Katie was telling Sean a funny story about how much of a tomboy she was as a kid. Sean was sitting with tears of laughter in his eyes as she talked about the day she was locked in an outdoor bin cupboard after getting in a fight with Cary Gorgon, the local bully from her childhood. I had heard the story before but couldn't help joining in with Sean's laughter when she spoke of how her father found her, fingers poking out of the ventilation holes in the cupboard door, nose bleeding.

Once the lounge was tidy, we went into the kitchen and Sean opened a fresh bottle of red and topped up mine and Katie's glasses before filling his. Rachael's glass was still full. I felt the energy shift in the room as he exchanged a glance with her. The air around them became charged with anticipation.

'There is something we want to share with you two,' he said, his tone formal and nervous.

'Is everything all right?' I asked, looking first to·him then to her.

'2018 is going to be a busy one for us,' she said, a smile drawing across her face. 'We're having a baby!'

Katie squealed in delight and leapt up, giving Rachael a hug. I too rose to my feet, first offering a handshake to Sean that turned into a hug. We then swapped, and I told Rachael I was truly very happy for her.

'How long?' Katie asked.

'It's still early days, about ten weeks. We haven't told anyone yet as we are waiting for our twelve-week scan, but we had to share it with you. Once we've had the scan we're going to tell Thomas.'

'I'm so happy for you both,' Katie said again hugging Rachael. I raised my·glass and toasted to the start of the next chapter. Which was echoed by Rachael, Sean and Katie.

As the clock ticked closer and closer to the new year, we talked about everything and nothing at all, the discussion always coming back to Sean and Rachael's news about their baby, until just before midnight. Rachael opened the back door which led to their conservatory and turned the TV on to BBC1 which was showing a live performance of a disco band called Chic. I hadn't heard of them, but they were fantastic to watch at a New Year's Eve party.

Outside, over the Stamford night sky, the fireworks had already started with a display coming from Burghley House, the sixteenth-century country house that famously hosted the Burghley horse trials. From where we were, we could watch both the live fireworks above our heads and the ones coming from central London. As the countdown began, the fireworks outside intensified and grabbing hold of Katie, I held her as we counted backwards from ten.

We brought in the new year stood out in the cold garden watching the night sky light up from the neighbours setting off their own fireworks and the official ones happening down the road, our faces illuminated with the reflection of the bright colours. I could smell the potassium and gunpowder on the air from the fireworks, a familiar smell that I secretly liked. Somehow it reminded me of being younger.

None of us wanted to speak. The moment felt so real, so easy. The four of us together should be a complicated existence but it was effortless.

Then a song came on, wafting through the patio doors, reaching us outside. It was one of the many being played by Sean's new toy. This was one I didn't think I knew, but as the guitar riff started, something washed over me. The gunpowder smell intensified, as did the explosions of fireworks. I saw myself high off the ground looking down. The wind whipped around me as fireworks lit the sky above and I was filled with a sense of panic, a fear of being caught. I remembered a feeling of adrenaline filling my body as I ran.

Then there were words painted on a road sign that shot in front of my face. I could read the letters but couldn't make sense of the words; it wasn't English. The sign vanished and I was on my knees, covered in soil, somewhere else. A crow cawed somewhere nearby. The sound of fast-moving water was around me. It vanished and then I was with my father. I could see his face. I knew it was him from the photos my mother had of us all on her mantelpiece. The man who was permanently absent both in my life and in my mind. He was so clear I felt I could reach out and touch the stubble on his cheek. I heard his voice. Gravelly and deep. He told me to wait where it all began. Wait for him to return. It was all coming at me in flashes, like a jigsaw I needed to put together. It was overwhelming and like nothing I had experienced before.

Katie touched my arm, shaking me from the images that were attacking my peaceful fog. As I focused back on the present Rachael and Sean were oblivious. Her head on his shoulder, both contained in their own bubble of happiness. No doubt both thinking about their baby.

'Dan, are you okay?' Katie looked at me, worry clouding her eyes. I released my grip on her arms, aware that it had tightened far more than I had intended it to.

'Yes, yes I'm fine.'

'You just saw a memory, didn't you?'

'I don't know. Maybe.'

'What happened?'

'I'm not sure. It's probably nothing.'

I reach for my wine glass to take a sip, my hand shaking a little as I did.

'Tell me anyway.'

'Later, this night is about those two,' I said gesturing to the soon-to-be parents.

'Okay,' she said, understanding. 'Let's talk about it tonight when we're home. Promise?'

'Of course.'

I pushed my troubled thoughts away and made myself continue with the evening. Once the firework display was over we made our way back inside and chatted for about an hour more before we could see Rachael getting tired. I went upstairs to give Thomas a kiss on his head and he mumbled dream-like words in his sleep that had no true form. We said our goodbyes, congratulating Rachael and Sean again and thanked them for a great night before we began our fifteen-minute walk home through the town centre that was full of happy revellers, most of them wishing us a happy new year. We left High Street and turned onto Maiden Lane that cut through to Blackfriars Street where St George's Church stood, uplit and majestic. The quiet lane offered a chance for us to talk uninterrupted, so I told Katie what I saw when the song came on.

'I've not seen anything so vivid before. Usually it's just a flash of one thing but I saw so many different things. I heard my father. I'm sure of it. It was his voice. And those words. I can remember them, but I have no idea what they mean.'

I spelt out the letters that I could still see in my mind and Katie struggled to understand them too. The arrangement wasn't something either of us knew.

'Try Google,' she suggested. I wasn't sure why I hadn't thought of that already. Punching the letters in there was an immediate hit. It stopped me in my tracks.

'Dan, what is it?'

'France,' I said, my confusion clear in my voice.

'Sorry?'

'Those words, it's the name of a place in France.'

MONDAY

Chapter 6

Daniel

Stamford

1st January 2018, 7.31 a.m.

Following my vision, I pushed my concerns for professional boundaries out of the way and messaged Will, saying something new – something big – had happened. He responded within a few minutes telling me he would call later. I could barely contain my excitement, and fear, as Katie and I spent the morning looking into the French town I had seen, the name flashing past my eyes whenever I closed them. A place called Auvers-sur-Oise. It was a small town, unremarkable aside from the fact that it was a popular destination for landscape painters. Amateurs had been going for hundreds of years to paint the view. The pictures of the town online didn't look familiar, they didn't coax anything else out of the blank space in my mind. We even did a Google Earth Street View, and still there was nothing about Auvers-sur-Oise that I recognized.

But seeing the name so clearly in my mind had to mean something; the image was too powerful to not be part of my past, part of the man I once was. I messaged Mum, asking her to come over, and waited for her to reply. Katie and I looked at Auvers for clues for hours, speaking of little else, until my head hurt so badly I needed to lie down. No matter what we tried, no more memories came back to me.

When I woke, Katie was packing her bag. Her eyes were puffy and red. She had received a call from the hospital as her father had taken a turn and she was advised to come down as soon as she could. I started to get a bag ready too, but she told me she would drive by herself. I protested but she told me it would be good for her to spend time alone with him.

She left just after two o'clock and as I watched her drive away towards the A1, I couldn't help but feel guilty. I should have been driving her, I should have been holding her hand as she coped with the forthcoming loss of her father. But I understood, she had to do this alone. I didn't know her father, it would be wrong for me to be there. So, home by myself, all I could do was wait until Will called.

It was just after four, as he'd promised, when he called. In our brief chat I told him what happened at Rachael and Sean's. He asked me what specifically was happening in that moment and I mentioned the smell of fireworks and the song that was playing in the background that triggered the montage of broken images.

'Yes. Sounds and smells can play a huge role in recalling memory. Especially smells.'

'But I've smelt fireworks before?'

'Perhaps the combination of both was what triggered the memories. Perhaps, Daniel, this is the progress we've been waiting for.'

'Do you think?'

'Before we get excited, talk to your mother. Tell her the things you saw and mention the French town you recalled. All of what you experienced might not be true. But some could be, and if so, that's promising.'

Mum finally replied, apologizing for the delay, telling me she was out with friends for the day and she would be over in half an hour. I needed confirmation from her of what I had seen so that I could get a sense of what was true and what was confabulation. I didn't want to get my hopes up until I had that conversation. But Will's final words – 'that's promising' – made it impossible not to. By the time Mum arrived I had paced around my lounge so much I was sure the carpets had worn thin. I didn't ask how she was or make her a drink before launching into what I experienced. As I motored on, she only spoke to ask me to slow down.

'Sorry. I'm trying to keep calm.'

'I understand.'

'Mum, is any of what I've just said true? Is any of it actually from my memory?'

'Yes, some. Your dad's voice for a start. How you described it is exactly how I would.'

'What about the digging? The sense of being high on a building?'

'I don't know about those things, they sound like something we might have done on a trip somewhere? The building could be a castle we visited perhaps? Nothing springs to mind but I'll check when I get home.'

'Check?'

'My holiday scrapbooks. When we went away each year I kept a scrapbook of the holidays. Something to look back on.'

'You've kept holiday scrapbooks? For how long?'

'Every trip we've ever taken.'

'Including holidays before my accident?'

'Yes.'

'Why haven't you shown me? They could have triggered something years ago! You know I used to ask about pictures all the time. You always said you never took any.' I couldn't keep the anger from my voice.

'I thought about showing you, many times. But I didn't want you to be upset reading about things you couldn't remember. Every time you see a picture of you from your childhood, I see how much it hurts you. Our holidays with your father were magical times, Daniel. Some of the best. I didn't want to rub them in your face.'

I understood her logic, but I couldn't stop my annoyance. In the early days when things were bad, Mum had been there on the countless nights I cried myself to sleep. She had held my hand when I had my many panic attacks. She had stayed patient when my frustration spilt over as rage and I broke things in her home. Despite it being a symptom of a head injury, I still felt ashamed of how I was all those years ago.

'Mum, I'm stronger now. I'm okay with it now. I can handle that there are some things I cannot control. Things I may never know. You're right, back then it would have caused more harm than good. But not now. I think it will help. I'd like to read about me as a kid.'

'Then we'll find an evening and we'll do it together.'

'Thanks, Mum. What about the French town? Does that mean anything?'

'Maybe, I'll have to check. We often drove to the south of France for our holidays, sometimes stopping in small French towns along the way – time to soak up the culture, your dad would say. It's possible we visited Auvers. Again, it'll be in the scrapbooks if we did. We'll know soon enough. Whenever you're ready.'

I had mixed feelings about what we had discussed. Part of me was excited to know if it was real, that it wasn't made up, my brain wasn't playing a cruel trick on me. Another part felt hollow as I ticked off what I could take from the flashes. I saw my dad and learnt of a French town but as for the other things, I was none the wiser as to what they meant.

'Mum, what do I do now?'

'I guess you carry on. Find more songs from the same time-period and wait for more memories to come.'

'Do you think they will?'

'I think that over the past year you have remembered more and more. And who knows, maybe it's like a snowball rolling down a hill. Now it's started, it will pick up speed and grow bigger and become unstoppable.'

'I hope so, Mum.'

'Me too,' she said, but with some hesitation.

Sensing that I needed time alone to process what was happening, Mum made her excuses to leave, promising me she would dig out the scrapbooks and have them ready for when I came over next. I joked it would probably be tomorrow, half meaning it.

After Mum left, I tried to call Katie a few times but her phone went straight to voicemail. At just after 11 p.m. my phone rang.

'Katie? Are you okay?'

'Yes, sorry, it's been a rough day.'

I wanted to ask if her father was all right, but I already knew the answer.

'Can I do anything?'

'No. I'm going to have to stay here for a while.'

'I understand. Shall I come down?'

'No, it's okay.' She sounded exhausted.

'Katie, please. I want to be there for you.'

'I just …' She hesitated, and I could hear in her voice that she needed me there.

'Let me be there, I want to be.'

'Thank you,' she said conceding. Her voice was tired, the edges of her words wrapped in sadness.

'I'll get a few things together now.'

'No, there is no point tonight. Come tomorrow.'

'Are you sure?'

'Yes, it will give me something to look forward to.'

43

'Okay, Katie, I'll come first thing. Is he comfortable?'

'Yes.' She stopped, catching her breath, unable to finish her sentence. 'He knew it was New Year's Eve after all. And I didn't come and see him.'

'Don't, you did what you thought was best for him. He knows that.'

'Maybe.'

'Darling, you can't beat yourself up over it. He knows how much you love him. Focus on that.'

'Thanks, love. I can't stay on the phone long. Cheer me up, what did Will and your mum say?'

'That doesn't matter right now, you're the one that we should be focusing on at the moment.'

'It does to me, please.'

I took a breath. 'Mum told me that some of it's real.'

'That's fantastic! And Will?' she replied, her voice tired but still I could hear her smile in her words.

'He said that the fact it was more than one memory was really promising.'

'Oh, Dan, I'm so happy for you. I needed to hear that.'

In the background I heard another voice speaking to Katie, a male one. I couldn't make out what was said but she let out a tired sigh.

'I've got to go; Dad is awake.'

'Of course, go. I'll be here. Call me whenever you want, okay?'

'Okay. I love you.'

'I love you too. If you want me there before tomorrow morning, I can come.'

'I know, thank you.'

'Bye, Katie.'

'Bye.'

The line went dead and I stopped to think about Katie for a moment. I couldn't imagine keeping it together if I was by my mum's side as she died. Katie was a stronger person than I was.

44

And I wished I was with her with my arm around her, keeping her upright when she was ready to fall. Tomorrow couldn't come soon enough. Thinking about her in a dark, quiet hospital room, the only sound being the machines keeping her dying father alive, I felt embarrassed that my past mattered so much. Putting my phone on loud in case she called me in the night, I sat in front of the television watching nothing until I fell into a fitful sleep.

Chapter 7

Daniel

Stamford

1st January 2018, 11.47 p.m.

I was back in the car. In the dark. Bright lights of a lorry blinded me, and then I was rolling over and over and over until I rested upside down, blood coming from my head, the same place it always comes from. Dripping onto the sunroof. Drip, drip, drip. Then someone was shouting. I tried to move but couldn't. A hand reached in and dragged me out. This time I was able to see who it was coming to my aid. It was my father. He spoke to me, telling me to run. Telling me to go to the place where it all began. I got up and ran as fast as I could away from the car. I couldn't get caught, I knew I couldn't be found. I didn't know why. As I ran, the world went dark. A thick smoke enveloped me, blinding me. In my hands was a rope. There was an explosion above and I began to fall. As I hit the ground I expected it to be hard, like concrete. But it wasn't. It was long, soft grass that cocooned me. A caterpillar waiting for its metamorphosis. After I wriggled free I sat up next to a river bank, the water fast moving, a tree shading me from the sun.

* * *

I snapped awake, my heart pounding, sweat sticking my hair to my forehead. The dream again, and again it had evolved. I looked over to where I thought Katie would be. Her side of the bed was empty. It took me a moment in my post-dream state to remember why she wasn't there. She was in a hospital ward down south.

Slowing my breathing, I swung my legs off the bed onto the cold wooden floor. I was glad in a way that Katie wasn't with me while this was going on. She worried a lot when I woke with a dream. She asked a lot of questions, wanting to help decipher them. She would write down in the book any words that jumped out and then try to connect them to something else I had said or done in my sleep. Katie had enough on her plate without having to manage her boyfriend who was, by definition, mentally unstable.

I reached over and picked up the book. Skimming the contents I could see the same phrases repeated over and over. Grabbing the pen that was clipped to the top I wrote down that I saw my father and the dream had ended with me on a river bank. Getting out of bed I went into the bathroom to splash my face with water. The bathroom light hurt my eyes and as they adjusted I caught my reflection. I was pale. I expected that. Every time I dreamt I felt sick after. That and my scar always hurt as if dreaming about cutting my head gave me the psychological symptoms. Lifting up my hair, I looked at it. Faded, but still very noticeable, fortunately hidden below my fringe most of the time. My eyes were bloodshot and heavy. Wrinkles were beginning to set in around them, fine, but they were definitely noticeable as was the odd fleck of grey hair. Getting older worried me, mainly because I couldn't remember being young.

From my place in the bathroom, I heard the phone beside my bed start to ring. It was the middle of the night. It must be Katie, calling to tell me that the thing that we were dreading had happened, or was about to. Moving quickly to the bed, I fumbled to pick it up. I expected to see Katie's number on the screen, but it just flashed as unknown, probably a hospital landline. My breathing was quick and nervous as I spoke.

'Katie?'

The line was quiet.

'Hello?'

Still no response, but I could hear someone on the other end.

'Hello? Katie? Can you hear me?' I said again, a little louder.

'You need to listen to exactly what I have to say.' The voice was male, deep. It wasn't one I recognized.

'Sorry, who is this?'

He didn't respond.

'I think you have the wrong number? I'm going now.'

'I don't think that would be a good idea.'

The statement left an eerie silence. The force with which he spoke made me pause, but after a few moments I pressed on.

'What do you want?'

'I've waited a very long time to have this conversation with you.'

'I'm sorry, but I really don't—'

'A long time ago you took something that didn't belong to you.'

'What are you talking about?'

'I want it back, Michael.'

'My name isn't Michael, you have the wrong number.'

He laughed. The sound was menacing and full of intent. He spoke like he was toying with me. His voice was calm and measured, it was clear that he had done this before.

Then my tired mind caught up with me and I relaxed a little – there was only one feasible conclusion; 'Is this some sort of sick joke? Matty, is that you?'

'This is no joke.' There was not even a hint of humour in his voice.

I placed my hand on my pillow and screwed a handful of it up in my fist. My knuckles turned white. 'Listen to me. I don't know anything about taking something from anyone. If you call me again I'm going straight to the police.'

'I wouldn't if I were you.'

His comment fired something inside, an anger I hadn't felt before, yet it felt normal. Like a song that I'd not heard in a very long time, but still knew the words to.

'Are you threatening me?' I said, getting to my feet. I pushed my shoulders back, stood up straight, and planted my feet. It was as though I were ready for a fight.

'Just giving you some friendly advice.'

'I'm hanging up now.'

Just as I moved the phone away from my ear, I heard him speak again. One word that snapped me from anger to terror. The name of my son.

'Thomas is a handsome little boy, isn't he?'

My entire world shifted under my feet as I could feel panic rising up in my throat, its white heat burning until it blurred my vision. This man threatening me filled me with rage, and in saying Thomas's name, he made me feel afraid, like a child lost.

'He's safe, so is Rachael. For now.'

'What?'

'Michael, you have something I want. I have something you want.'

'Who is this? Rob? Stop pissing around, would you?' I clung to the hope that this was just a joke.

No sooner had I said that than the phone pinged against my ear and, looking at the screen, I saw there was a new text message from an unknown number. I saw it was a multimedia message and once I opened it, everything changed. The image I looked at knocked me backwards and I had to grab the wall to stop myself from falling. It caught my breath and pulled it out from my chest, crushing my lungs as it did.

I could feel my heart pounding, blood rushing through my ears, my lips tingling. The picture was of Rachael. She was gagged

49

with her hands tied behind her back looking at the camera, terrified. In the picture I could see a wheel arch that you would find in the back of a large van. Beside her, in the shadows of her body, against the camera flash, was Thomas. He looked asleep, almost peaceful. I thought I was going to pass out.

'Does it look like I'm pissing around?'

'Who are you?'

'That doesn't matter.'

'What have you done to them?'

'Nothing. Yet.'

'Have you hurt my son?'

My question was answered by silence.

'Please, please let them go. If you want me for something come to me, take me, just let them go, please, please let my boy go home.' I was grasping at anything I could. This had to be a horrible joke, surely? Things like this didn't happen outside of movies.

'As I've said, Michael. I will, when I get back what is rightfully mine. There is an easy deal on the table here.'

'Please, don't hurt Rachael. I'm begging, please don't hurt them.'

'Give me back what is mine and I won't.'

'But I don't – I have no idea what you're talking about. I've never taken any—'

'I know I don't have to tell you this.' He cut me off. 'But if you call the police, the next time you'll see your family is on the news when they're dragging their bodies out of a river.'

'Please, I don't understand, I—'

'You have until Friday.'

And then the line went dead.

TUESDAY

Chapter 8

Rachael

The Garage

2nd January 2018, 12.09 a.m.

We had a lovely New Year's Day together as a family. We went to the seaside and ate fish and chips in the freezing cold. All three of us wrapped in coats, gloves and scarves, Sean and Tom skimming stones into the sea until it was so cold we gave up and drove home. Then, we watched TV, Tom had a bath and finally Sean and I got into our own bed and talked about what we'd need to do to the house before the little one comes, until, at just after nine, excited and exhausted from the late night and sea air, we turned off our lights and went to sleep.

At ten Sean was sound asleep and as I rolled onto my side, trying to curb my excitement long enough to join him in the land of dreams, I heard something downstairs, like the sound of a coat being dropped. Then it happened, it happened so fast.

They came into our room, two of them. One a very large man, one smaller, both in balaclavas, and before I could shout out the large one dragged me off the bed by my ankle and dropped me like a ragdoll. My instincts taking over to protect my stomach as

I landed meant I hit my head on the carpeted floor. I saw Sean, dazed from waking to the horror, trying to fight the other one. He was hit hard and toppled over the side of the bed, the small one falling on him as the fight continued. I also tried to fight, not to escape but to get into Tom's room and protect my baby. But the man was too strong. He pinned me down and pressed his knee into my back, his weight crushing my ribs. He was forcing my hands behind and upwards with such violence I thought my shoulders were going to come out of their sockets. I could feel tendons pull and I felt a muscle, one in my rotator cuff, tear. I wanted to cry out, instead I bit my lip to muffle my scream. I didn't know what was happening, or why it was happening to us and I hoped Tom hadn't woken. I pleaded he wouldn't hear the noise of our struggle and come into the room. I prayed they didn't know he was there. I held my breath until the pain died down before mustering the energy to escape and get to Tom, but I couldn't move, my captor was too heavy.

Then I saw him, my child in the arms of the smaller man. There was no sign of Sean. With my face pressed into the floor I strained my eyes to look at my baby. His arms were swinging by his side, his legs limp; he looked asleep but there was no way he would sleep through what was happening. For a moment I thought he was dead but then I saw his chest rise and fall. I tried to shout for help, but a wide hand came from behind and pinned my voice in.

'If you make a noise, it won't end well,' he said, his voice deep and commanding.

I nodded helplessly and, as he hauled me towards the stairs, I looked for Sean, but I couldn't find him. The man dragged me downstairs, the tops of my feet banging on each step as he did. I tried to beg for them not to hurt Tom. Arms bound behind me, I was thrown into the back of a van. Tom was already laid down inside and I scrambled to him. I tried to wake him by rocking his body with my head, but he was unresponsive.

'What have you done to him?'

'He's been sedated, he'll wake up soon.'

The van then drove off calmly, like nothing had happened. I struggled to see anything; the darkness around me complete. The only thing I could hear was the hum of the engine and the sound of my short and sharp breathing which I was fighting to control.

My hands and lips tingled, and I knew that if I didn't calm down I would soon pass out. I shook my head, shook away my fear, taking control of my jagged breathing, trying to focus on details. First there was a sharp left out of my road, then after about thirty seconds a sharp right, then uphill. I could picture Waitrose on my right. Panic began to creep in as I knew we were driving out of Stamford.

The van drove for about two more minutes in a straight line. Then it turned right and slowly bent back round to the left before the road became louder as we merged with the A1 southbound. From there we could go anywhere. We were on the A1 for what felt like forever in the dark, before coming off again, first left, then right then over a roundabout.

After some time – I wasn't sure how much – we stopped and I heard them talking, three voices, arguing in hushed tones. A door opened and slammed shut. Then, the back door swung open and a man who wasn't either of the two I had seen before stepped in. He took a photo of me, the flash blinding me as he did. He caught my eye, I couldn't see his face, but I knew he was smiling under his balaclava as he closed the door. The slam woke Tom suddenly. He looked at me and I knew, from years of being a nurse, that the drugs still had hold.

'Mummy?'

'It's okay, darling, everything is okay.'

'What's going on?'

'We are on a little trip, that's all.'

'I don't feel very well.'

'You've had a really deep sleep, you'll feel better soon. Come here, baby, come lay on Mummy.'

Thomas lay on my lap, closing his eyes again. I wanted to stroke his hair, but couldn't free my hands to do so and it broke my heart, forcing me to hold my breath because I knew I would cry if I did anything else. And I couldn't cry.

As the van drove, streetlights lit the inside through a tinted vent in the roof. A beam of light would quickly flood through like a Mexican wave. I looked towards Tom and when I could see, I noticed his breathing became deeper, his head heavier as he drifted back into a sedative-filled dream. I didn't know why we had been taken, but I knew that I couldn't let this impact who he became in the future.

Eventually, through the combination the light sweeping in and the adrenaline wearing off, I fell asleep too, my head resting on Tom's shoulder. I don't know how long I was asleep for, but I was woken by wide hands grabbing me, ripping the tape from my wrist, making me yelp. I was told to get up and walk. My right leg was entirely numb, making the simple task almost impossible to do. I picked Tom up, my hands hurting as the blood rushed back into them, and moved as fast as I could, dragging my dead limb behind me. Tom woke for a moment, and I saw one of the men start to twitch. What if he shouted out, called for help? Tom didn't know the rules. I calmly told him everything was okay and that I was carrying him to bed. As I spoke, I kept my eye firmly on the biggest of the three men who were escorting us wherever we were going. I told him without speaking that I would keep Tom quiet so he didn't need to.

'Nearly in bed, darling,' I repeated, to ensure he was content and asleep again. I wondered how long I could lie to him about everything being okay before he realized it wasn't. The man pushed us along the side of an abandoned building towards a half-open metal shutter. A small light was coming from within.

'In here,' he said shoving me towards the opening. The shutter was like the mouth of a monster that was about to swallow us whole.

Chapter 9

Daniel

Stamford

2nd January 2018, 12.12 a.m.

I grabbed my car keys, and, still in my pyjamas, I climbed into my car. I rang Rachael's mobile, my heart pounding so hard I was sure at any moment something would rupture and kill me on the spot. It didn't even ring, instead going straight to her voicemail.

'Hey, this is Rachael.'

'And Tom.'

'We can't get to the phone right now so leave a message after the beep.'

I hung up the phone and tried to call Sean's mobile. It too was switched off. Hearing his voicemail kick in, I swore loudly and pressed hard on the accelerator, my body and mind on autopilot. I nearly lost control a few times, I couldn't feel my hands properly. My fight or flight had kicked in and all I could think of was not letting the severity of the situation take over. If I fell apart, like I thought I was going to at any moment, I couldn't help Rachael. I couldn't save my son. Not being able to go to the police, I knew I needed to get to their house. The man on the phone's last words echoed in my mind as I made my way. I desperately tried to quieten the voice, but I was failing.

'If you call the police, the next time you'll see your family is on the news when they're dragging their bodies out of a river.'

It was like a broken record, over and over, and hearing it meant I could see nothing but an image of Rachael face down drifting in a current, Thomas close to her, their hands almost touching as they were carried away into the darkness. I needed to remove it from my mind. Slamming on the brakes, the car skidded before coming to a stop. I got out, staggered around the car and heaved beside the passenger door, and still the image held strong.

I crumpled, clutched my head in my hands, then hit the side of my head with a clenched fist and screamed at the floor, my lips touching the frozen ground until the image, and his words, were gone. The outburst momentarily lifted my adrenaline-fuelled thoughts enough to know that I needed to find something hiding in the grey parts of my mind. I needed to find something that could give me a clue as to where to start. I had something of his, he had my ex-girlfriend and my son. My wonderful boy. The image of her tied, and him drugged, in the back of a van caused my eyes to blur. I wiped them and brought myself back to the present. It was time to be proactive.

I had to breathe, just breathe, that was all I had to do.

Back in the car, I jumped a red light, not seeing it until it was too late to stop. Luckily there was nothing coming the other way – though I suppose there wouldn't be in the middle of the night. The last thing I needed was to be pulled over by the police for speeding or running lights. He told me, if I called the police they would be …

I still hoped it was a sick joke of some kind.

As I pulled onto their drive my headlights lit up the front door. It was slightly ajar.

I turned my car engine off, got out and walked towards the

house, looking to see if anyone was there as I quietly opened the door wider, flinching as the hinge squeaked. Once inside I reached for the light switch but thought better of it. I didn't know who might be in the house.

Quietly moving down the hallway, I stepped into the kitchen. There were some dirty dishes on the side and the fish tank's light was still on, the fish swimming around calmly, like nothing had happened. Turning, I looked into the living room. Nothing was out of place and my hope lifted slightly.

I walked up the stairs, stroking the wall with my right hand as it was so dark I couldn't see, but I was too scared to switch on a light and be confronted with the truth. The only light was coming from a dim lamp somewhere upstairs, creating hard shadows on the wall at the top. Once upstairs I was met with the truth of the situation and it forced the air out of my lungs.

In the low light I could see the signs of a struggle. The hallway lamp was on its side and bedding from both Thomas's and Rachael's rooms were scattered around the landing along with toiletries, some of Thomas's plastic toys and a small mirror. I could picture them being lifted from their beds, fighting, throwing whatever they could at whoever took them. Rachael screaming, begging. My baby boy crying, terrified. The image forced me to my knees and I cried until my lungs ached. My little boy, my defenceless boy.

Slowly I made my way into his room and looked inside. His wardrobe door hung off its hinges. His bed was flipped, the mattress cut open. Like they were looking for something; the thing that I was supposed to have.

His favourite teddy, a giant cuddly toy we had named Barnabas that I had got him for his first birthday, lay decapitated with its innards strewn across the floor. I began to make my way towards Rachael and Sean's bedroom. Looking through the doorway the first thing I saw was blood on the far wall. A lot of blood. Taking a breath, I stepped in. The television was smashed. The mattress had been torn to shreds, and as I stepped closer, I saw a hand lying on the floor between the bed and window, stained dark crimson. Sidestepping I looked around the end of the bed, the image making me choke on my own voice as I tried to scream. Sean lay there, staring back at me, in a dark, almost black, pool of his own blood. His hands were covered in it like he had tried to stop the bleeding. His head was forced backwards unnaturally. His throat was cut and the wound messy and uneven, like it had been hacked at rather than sliced. The wound was deep, so deep that I could see his exposed spine with the knife that had been used to do the unimaginable stuck in.

There was so much blood, so much violence. His chest was littered with more wounds, black holes through his ribcage. The wounds hadn't produced much blood, suggesting they were made after he was already dead. I couldn't count how many, possibly twenty in all. Each one dark and deep. I thought about the effort needed to do such a thing. It wouldn't have been a quick death. I prayed he'd passed out before he knew exactly what was happening to him.

I staggered backwards out of the room, unable to take my eyes from Sean, and I threw up on the landing. Each heave became more painful than the last as my stomach emptied onto the carpet.

I needed to get out, fast. I was shocked the police weren't already here, but then I thought about it; their house was detached, back from the road. Unless you were passing, which was nearly impossible because of it being set at the end of the close, you'd not hear anything from within. But it wouldn't be long before someone noticed something and called the police. I couldn't afford to be caught at the scene of the crime. I didn't have time. I staggered towards the stairs as my legs gave out from under me and I fell down them, hitting my elbow on the hard wooden edge of one close to the bottom. Pain shot up into my little finger where I had hit the nerve and I shook my hand until it eased. It took me a moment to get to my feet and, as quietly as I could despite the sound of blood rushing in my ears being deafening,

I left the house, closing the door behind me. As I wrestled my keys from my pocket I dropped them because my hands were shaking so hard.

I managed, somehow, to get into my car and start the engine, though I stalled it twice as I tried to drive away. I felt hot, on the brink of passing out, so I opened my window to let the cold air in and it slapped me across the face. It helped. I don't know how long I was driving for, but once I felt far enough away I turned off the main road and found a layby to park in. A few moments later, or maybe an hour, my phone buzzed in my back pocket. I looked at the caller ID, it came up unknown.

'So, now you've been to your old house do you believe me?'

They knew I was there. They knew I had just left Rachael's house. They had watched me arrive, watched me leave. They were somewhere very close by. I tried to recall if I saw anything or anyone outside when I got back into the car. But nothing came. Only the image of Rachael and Thomas in the van.

'Please, please don't hurt them.'

'Do as you are told, and we won't.'

Staring out of the front windscreen into the black nothingness of night I couldn't think, I couldn't focus. I didn't know what to do. Sean was dead, Rachael was tied up somewhere, and Thomas was unconscious beside her. Because of my past. Because they believed I had something that didn't belong to me.

'Don't hurt them, please.'

'You know what I want.'

I wanted to say to them I didn't, that I had no idea because of a car accident fourteen, nearly fifteen, years ago, but I stopped myself. If they believed it, and knew I couldn't give back whatever I took, would it mean Rachael and Thomas would die like Sean had? So I lied, hoping it wasn't obvious.

'Give me time, I will get it.'

'That's the spirit. I've left something in the glove box of your car.'

'Pardon?'

'Your glove box, look in it.'

I did as I was told and inside was an iPhone. One that wasn't mine.

'Take the sim card out of your phone and burn it. Then throw away your mobile, Michael, soon people will be looking for you. I will contact you on the new one.'

'Okay, whatever you say. Just don't do anything to them.'

'One more thing, Michael. Just so you don't think about doing anything to try and be smarter than us, we know Katie too.' He paused, knowing I would wait. When he continued, his tone was harder. 'We know where she is. We know who she is with, we know everything about her. Get to work. The clock is ticking.'

Chapter 10

Rachael

The Garage

2nd January 2018, 12.34 a.m.

With Tom asleep in my arms, the shutter slammed behind us and for around twenty minutes I was paralysed, holding my six-year-old whose weight was making my arms shake. Within minutes I could feel my skin cooling as there was no heat inside. Then Tom stirred, the drugs like a tide, freeing him momentarily before dragging him back under.

'Mummy?'

'Shhhh, it's okay, honey.'

I kept him close, his face buried into my pyjama top and I wrapped him in my arms as tightly as I could to try to use my body heat to keep him warm. It snapped me from my daze and I looked around, taking in the space. It was a single garage, sized about eight feet across and sixteen deep. A bed sat in the far corner to my left, a thin, stained mattress hanging off it like a damp flannel. Beside it, a lamp. I put Tom down gently on the bed before leaning down and switching it on, grateful that it worked. It only lit the room dimly, but enough. On the right-hand wall was a small portable radiator. Between the radiator and bed, a sliding metal door. I tried to open it but, of course, it was locked. Turning to face the way we had entered I wracked my brain, trying to find a way to get things to where they should be, us in bed, at home, dreaming. Shaking the thoughts from my head I moved to the radiator, and thankfully it worked too. We needed to warm up, and quickly. Our pyjamas were not designed for sub-zero temperatures.

I saw something poking out from under the rusting bedframe. Bending to reach for whatever it was I pulled out three old blankets. They smelt of mothballs and years of dust, but it was better than freezing. I lay one on the mattress and moved Tom onto it and wrapped him in the other two.

'You'll warm up soon, baby.'

'Mummy, where are we?'

I looked at him, at the fear behind his eyes, and I didn't know what to say.

'Mummy?'

I couldn't tell him the truth. I had to protect him from this. If he knew, he would panic, be as scared as I was, and I was frightened what would happen as a result. Somehow, I had to make it all seem like it was a game.

'We are on an adventure, baby.'

'An adventure?'

'Yes.'

'But I'm scared.'

'I know. I'm scared too. But that's a part of it.'

'Part of what?'

'A story, this is part of the story.'

'We're in a story?'

'Yes. Yes, that's it, this is the first chapter.'

'What's it called?'

I couldn't think so I looked around the room, trying to take in something that he would believe. I looked back at him, his sleepy eyes staring into mine, waiting for an answer.

'It's called, "Waking Up in the Unknown".'

'I like it.'

'We are the main characters.'

'Are we?'

'Yes, baby, me and you.' And Sean, I quietly whispered to myself, hoping he was all right.

'What kind of story is it?'

'An adventure.'

'It feels like a scary one.'

'All good adventure stories have a bit of scariness, don't they? Like, in …' I paused trying to remember the name of the story he had been reading that I had considered too grown-up for a six-year-old. '*Wolf Brother*. Our story is like *Wolf Brother*. Remember how scary that is at times'?'

'Yes.'

'And do you remember how it all turns out?'

'Happy.'

'Exactly. Now can you tell me anything that happens in that book that's a bit like this?'

I watched as Tom's fear was replaced with a curiosity, and he looked around the room, recalling from his favourite book.

'There's a bit where Torak is hiding in a cave?'

'Yes. Good, that's really good. Can you remember what the cave looked like?'

'It was cold.'

'Yes, anything else?'

'It was dark too. I remember a bit where he could hardly see.'

'You could say it was a bit like here, couldn't you'?'

Tom looked around the room, and after a few seconds his little face lit up with the idea of an adventure. 'Mummy, is this our cave?'

'Yes, darling, yes it is,' I said as relief washed over me. This idea might just work. It might just keep him oblivious to it all.

'Now, Tom, I need you to listen.' He stopped looking around the room and turned back to me. His eyes were bloodshot, the drugs still heavy in his system. It broke my heart and I had to swallow to stop myself showing it.

'This is really important. This is really important for our book.'

'What is, Mummy?' he asked, his little body shivering. I sat beside him and pulled him close to me again, my arm wrapped around him, rubbing it to warm him up.

'Someone might come in here, someone who is a baddy in our story.'

'A baddy?' I thought about the sheer size of the man who had pushed us into this space. 'A bear. Like the one Torak had to face?'

'The Bear is scary, Mummy.'

I turned to face him, our eyes coming together, and I could see fear in his, so I pulled the blanket over his head to make a hood as I spoke. I hoped this would take the intense edge off what I was saying. Hoped it would numb his fear and numb my own.

'Yeah, The Bear is scary. But remember, it's all a part of the story.'

'Okay, Mummy.'

'And if The Bear comes in, I want you to hide for me. Under the bed.'

'All right, Mummy.'

'And you must be really quiet so The Bear doesn't hear you.' I could see fear begin to creep back into my little boy. His face was so small under the mound of old blankets. 'Tom, remember darling, this is all a part of the story.'

'Why?'

'Because ...' I paused, looking around the room, its corners sharp and cold in the low light. 'Because in later chapters, you hiding is really important to us escaping from The Bear, like Torak did. Now, tell me. What do you do if The Bear comes?'

'Hide.'

'Where, Tom, where do you hide?'

'Under the bed. If The Bear comes I hide under the bed.'

'Say it again.'

'If The Bear comes, I hide under the bed.'

'Why?'

'Because it's really important to the end of the book?'

'Yes, exactly. Well done. Good boy, you're such a good boy.'

I leant in and kissed Tom on the head, his arms wrapping around me tightly.

'Now, darling, lay down, time to get some sleep. Tomorrow we start a brand-new chapter.'

'I'm still scared, Mummy.'

'It's okay, darling, close your eyes and count to ten, and it will all go away.'

'Can you sing, Mummy?'

He closed his eyes and I watched him for a moment, trying to think of something I could sing to him. Then it came to me. 'Everything's all right' from *Jesus Christ Superstar*. The same song I sang when he was a tiny baby, crying as his nappy was being changed. The same song I sang when he had a fever, ear ache and chickenpox. And now, the song that I would sing when we were kidnapped. As the words came out, the melody was scratchy, but it seemed to do the trick.

I could feel my eyes begin to fill with tears and looking at my baby, I could see him drift into a worry-free sleep. We had been taken. I didn't know why, I didn't know who by, and I didn't know if I could keep my baby safe from them. I didn't know if Sean was okay or if Daniel knew what had happened to us. But I couldn't focus on them now. Now I needed to focus on keeping Tom from harm and how I would get us out of here.

Chapter 11

Daniel

Barnack

2nd January 2018, 1.42 a.m.

I had sat paralysed for over an hour trying to work out what I had taken all those years ago. I thought about me being mixed up in something bad and couldn't see it. Was I a bad person? Had I been involved in scraps as a kid? Surely everyone has at some point, especially adolescent boys, but something like this? Something that created an unimaginable backlash? Something that meant two of the most important people in my world were now in danger? I couldn't get there and because I couldn't, I struggled processing the reality of what was happening. I fought with my memories, only seeing outlines of shadows as they hid from me, mocking me when I couldn't find them. I could almost hear them laughing. Taunting in their tones, 'You'll never know what you did.' It felt impossible to move. I wrestled with the grey spaces in my head, trying to pull something clear from it. But my past was like a bait ball, circling quickly, and changing direction before I could grab hold, confusing me. Yes, I'd managed to grab small moments in the past year, lots coming in the last week, but there was nothing to suggest my past was caught up in something that was worth kidnapping for.

Something worth killing for.

The image of Sean's mutilated body was there with each alternate blink. Every other being Rachael and Thomas in the van. Blink, a dead friend. Blink, my child and his mother, her fear etched on her face. I tried not to close my eyes until I had no choice. My vision blurred out of focus, eyes stinging through forcing myself to blink as little as I could. My mind, empty. The shock setting in. Then, from a dark corner of it, I heard a voice, quiet and disrupted as it echoed from the deepest, darkest parts of me. It told me to start the car. Get moving. He sounded like a soldier in one of the war movies I loved. Another moment of confabulation. But it was right. Sitting and waiting for something to happen was not going to help anyone. There was nothing I could do for Sean, he was dead. But Rachael and Thomas needed me. Katie too. I wanted to call her, but her number, along with every other I had, was on my phone which was now broken. Foolishly, I had done as I was instructed without making a note of her number. So, going onto the Safari app, I logged in to Facebook and sent her a direct message. I told her to send me her number when she could. I told her to not leave the hospital, under any circumstances. After I hit 'send' I felt more in control somehow and I knew the first thing I needed to do was get rid of my car. The police would eventually discover Sean and when they did, they would see the struggle also, telling them Rachael and Thomas were gone, and then, they would want to talk to me. My registration plate would be the first thing they would look for after they had banged on my door and discovered I'd taken flight. That part would be easy to do. It almost felt natural to hide. Driving from the layby, I looked for somewhere discreet to leave it. Ideally, somewhere close to my mum's house. Then, I needed to speak to her, ask her questions about before 2003. I had to ask her about Michael.

Up ahead I saw an entrance to a lane which led to one of the many fields on the outside of Stamford, near Barnack. I veered off the road and drove for about a mile, looking for a gap in the wall that surrounded the Burghley estate where I could dump my car. It didn't take long to find one. Pulling onto the verge I turned off the headlights and carefully drove behind a line of trees.

I got out of the car and went to the edge of the road and looked back. The rear of it could still be seen, so releasing the handbrake, I pushed it further behind. I checked again, this time satisfied. From there I figured it was about a mile, as the crow flies, to my mother's, and at this hour, moving across the grounds of Burghley House, I was unlikely to bump into anyone. So, lowering my head I began running across the lifeless, frozen dirt, the cold air making it impossible to control my breathing.

My slippers made it impossible to run properly so I took them off and carried them. Within moments my bare feet were completely numbed, like two slabs of raw meat on the end of my ankles, but at least I could move quicker. After about ten minutes of running and stumbling, I stopped and doubled over to catch my breath, wishing I had looked after myself better in recent years. But I didn't let myself stop for long. Instead I ran onwards across the uneven, frozen ground until I tripped on a stone and hit the unforgiving earth face first. Dirt broke off from the frozen soil smearing across my face, my teeth knocking together. I could feel blood form and drip from my lip. But that didn't matter. I got up and started to run again harder and faster until my lungs screamed, and the uneven soil was replaced by tarmac.

In the street light I could see blood on my jumper. I wiped my mouth, and more blood came. Feeling my bottom lip with my finger and thumb I could feel the tear where I had bitten clean through it, but I ignored it, it wasn't my priority right now. Trying to move as quickly and discreetly as I could back down into the high street, I heard a car coming towards me and had to duck into The George pub's ancient archway that led patrons to the heavy oak front door. My brain immediately jumped to the conclusion that it was the police. But it wasn't, just some kids in a small Ford Fiesta, vape smoke, or possibly the smoke of a joint, bellowing out of one of the windows. I watched as they passed, talking and laughing, two girls in the back dancing to the loud music that seemed to power the small motor up the hill.

They didn't have a care in the world. Not one.

After they had passed and I could no longer hear the bassline of whatever track they were listening to, I stepped out of the shadows. The road, town and sky were all silent. Poor Sean hadn't been discovered yet. If he had, there would be more happening. Stuffing my hands into my pyjama pockets, and keeping my head low, just in case someone saw my muddy, bloodied face, I headed towards my mum's. Most of the houses were in total darkness but a few had upstairs lights on. One had light coming from the lounge and another from the window directly above. I saw through a gap in the curtains that it was a nightlight making stars on the ceiling. There was a baby in that house. Asleep, and warm. His or her parents safe in the knowledge that no harm would come to them. I hoped that would always be the case. Walking away I forced back a tear. There wasn't time for that now. I could cry tears of joy once I had them back.

A few minutes later I was at my mum's front door. I took my keys out of my pocket and let myself in, closing the door quietly behind me.

Chapter 12

Daniel

Stamford

2nd January 2018, 1.58 a.m.

Mum was asleep, I could hear her heavy breathing as I moved around the house. I looked up the stairs as some light spilled over the top, coming from her room. Her TV was still on but whatever programme she had been watching on catch-up had finished. I knew this because she had always fallen asleep this way, ever since I could remember at least. Quietly, I moved into the kitchen and pulled the door to. I turned on the light and it blinded me temporarily. I knew I needed to wake her up and talk about the things we never spoke of, but I also needed her not to get upset. She had to be able to think, remember something that would tell me what I had done. Seeing me in the state I was in wouldn't help. With the light on I could see myself clearly in the kitchen window. My lip was worse than I had thought and opening my mouth I could see I had also broken one of my front teeth. I ran a tea towel under the tap and pressed it on the cut. The cold water slapped against the exposed nerve sending white heat through my jaw. I wanted to cry out, but I took a deep breath.

Then something from the depths of my brain told me what to do.

Super glue.

I had no idea where the thought came from, and at first didn't know what it meant. But then I thought about it. Glue would stop the bleeding and cover the exposed nerve. I didn't know why I knew that. Rummaging through Mum's junk draw I found a small tube of it and going into the toilet under the stairs I pinched my bottom lip together and applied some. My hands shook as I did, the tube slipping in my fingers as my blood ran onto them. I continued to pinch for another minute and then let go. It seemed to work.

Opening my mouth I then applied some to my front tooth which hurt so much that my vision blurred. Using sticky, crimson fingers I rubbed it in, forming a layer over my broken tooth. I could feel my pulse throbbing through my whole face. Eventually it began to die down enough for me to look at myself in the mirror. I looked a mess, my skin covered in blood and dirt, but better than a few minutes before. I rinsed my face and looked again. It would have to do for the moment.

'Hello?'

Mum's voice called out from the top of the stairs, sleepy and on edge. A hint of fear bleeding through.

'Mum, it's me,' I called up, my words slurring as the swelling in my face had begun to flare.

'Daniel? Oh God, Daniel what are you doing? I thought someone was breaking in. Are you okay?'

I didn't know how to respond, instead I pretended I hadn't heard her and went into the kitchen and waited, knowing she would come downstairs. When she walked in, she stepped back, covering her hand with her mouth.

'Daniel, what's happened to your face?'

'Something's happened, Mum, something terrible.'

Mum came towards me to look at my cut, but I stepped away,

I didn't have the strength to keep my emotions in if she touched me.

'Daniel, what's happened?'

'Mum, sit down.'

She did as I asked, looking at me with tenderness and fear mixed in equal measure. I could see her holding her breath, waiting.

'Mum?' I began slowly, frightened of what I was about to ask. 'What's my name?'

'What?'

'What's my name?'

I saw a reaction in her. It was small but noticeable, my question had shocked her rather than confused.

'Daniel, we need to get you to a doctor.'

'I haven't got time.'

'What do you mean, "time"? Daniel, what's going on?'

'Mum, please, just tell me the truth, for once.' I sounded exasperated, desperate, my voice on the verge of breaking.

'I don't understand what you're asking.' She looked away from me, not able to meet my gaze. I struggled to hide my shock at seeing she knew something.

'Yes you do, Mum. You do, and I know it. I need you to tell me. What's my real name?'

'It's the middle of the night, Daniel, you're bleeding. Why does that matter?' she asked, standing and taking a step away from me, busying herself by digging out a first-aid kit from under the sink and putting it on the table beside us.

I couldn't look at her, I could barely get the words out at a whisper. I felt if I said what I said next any louder I would lose the fragile composure I was keeping.

'Thomas has been taken.'

'What?' She stopped and looked up at me, her mouth agape. As I spoke I did so slowly in an attempt to make it clear and hold my composure. But as the words fell from my mouth they came out as a sob.

'Mum, someone's taken my little boy.'

'What do you mean? Daniel, what do you mean someone's taken him?' Her voice became louder, started cracking.

'And Rachael. Someone's taken Thomas and Rachael.'

'Taken? What do you mean "taken"?' She turned frantic and fidgeted, her voice high-pitched and breathy.

'And they've told me they will hurt them unless I return something to them.'

'Who's "them", Daniel, who?'

'I don't know.'

'Daniel, you need to go to the police. Why haven't you rung the police?'

She stepped away to grab her phone, but I got up and stopped her, taking her firmly by the hand.

'Mum, they killed Sean.'

I watched the colour drain from her face, mirroring my own. As I spoke I did so at barely a whisper, as if by saying it quietly it might not be true.

'They said if I go to the police they'll kill them too.'

She tried to say something but just the sound of her breath escaping came.

'They said I have something that belongs to them. Something from the time I can't remember.'

Stumbling sideways, she sat down in her chair, her eyes unblinking and a million miles away from where we were.

'Oh God!'

'Mum, who was I?'

'I thought we had left all that behind,' she said to herself as she opened, then shut the first-aid box.

'Mum?'

She moved to put it away but stopped and then turned and placed it back on the table, her thoughts moving so fast it powered her body.

'I was assured your injury would give you a clean break.'

Grabbing a tea towel, she held it like she was about to dry up, but there were no plates on the draining board. With her back to me, she raised the towel up and buried her face into it.

'Mum! A clean break? A clean break from what?'

'Oh God, Daniel. I'm so sorry,' she said through muffled fabric.

'Mum, what's my name?'

'I thought, after all this time it was all behind us.'

'Mum, what is my real name?' I placed my hand on her shoulder, harder than I intended.

She turned and looked at me, resignation in her face.

'Your real name is Michael.'

The quiet hope that this was all just some sick joke or a bad dream had been destroyed. My name was Michael. The man on the phone wasn't lying. He wasn't confusing me with someone else. It meant I really did have something of his.

'Mum, why did you change my name?'

'It's hard to explain.'

'Try, Mum, try.' My voice rose as anger replaced my fear. 'You've been lying to me for as long as I can remember and now my little boy is missing. Rachael is gone and a good man is dead. You need to stop this shit and tell me what I was involved in.'

'Daniel, I don't know how to—'

I grabbed the chair beside me and threw it against the wall. One of the legs snapped off.

'Daniel, please, you need to calm down,' she begged.

'Calm down? They said I have until Friday to give back what I took from them. Friday. I don't even know what the fuck I took, Mum. Up until a few hours ago I was just Daniel, and now I know I'm someone else entirely, someone who took something from people who are prepared to kill to get it back. Don't you tell me to calm down! What was I involved in, Mum?'

'I don't know.'

'You must know. I don't have that part of my life, only you do. You have to know.'

76

I grabbed my mum by the shoulders and shook her. I could see fear rush into her whole body. A fear of me.

'What did I take?'

'I don't know. Honestly, I don't know. Please, Daniel, you're scaring me.' Tears were running down her cheeks, her eyes wide, her head tilting away from me.

I let go and stepped away, afraid my anger towards her would result in me doing something I would instantly regret. Pacing beside the table I reiterated what had happened; Sean was dead, Rachael and Thomas were missing.

'Mum, I need you to give me something. I don't know where my boy is, I don't know where they've taken my little boy. Mum, help me, please help me. Tell me something, please. I don't care that you lied to me. I just want them back.'

She got up to give me a hug, but I stepped away from her. She looked shocked but lowered her arms. I was angry. I was angry because I didn't know that my family would be put at risk.

'Mum, I don't have time, just tell me.'

She nodded and swallowed hard before talking, her voice delicate and lost. 'When we learnt you might not remember who you were, your dad insisted we kept it that way. He said it would keep you safe and the less I knew the better.'

'Safe from what?'

'I don't know, honestly, Daniel, I don't know.'

'But he does?'

'Yes.' She looked down at her feet, her shoulders rolling in, tired and defeated. I stepped towards her gently, placing my hands back on her shoulders again. Slowly she looked up at me.

'Is he likely to be involved in this?'

'I don't know, Daniel.'

'Yes or no, Mum?' I said quietly but through clenched teeth.

'He was mixed up in the same things you were,' she said, again looking away as if she was drifting back to the past. The past that was destroying my present. I shook her again, releasing her from the shock she was slipping into, snapping her attention back to me.

'Yes or no?!'

'Yes. But I don't think he took them.'

'But he would know who did?'

'Yes, yes he would.'

For the first time since the call, I felt like I had a sense of direction. I needed to find my father. He was either involved in this or knew who had taken them. In the back of my mind something fired. It made me feel defensive, cornered, like I knew my father was someone capable of committing a crime. I could feel my hand clench into a fist. I could feel myself wanting to hurt him.

'Where is he?'

She paused.

'Where is he, Mum?'

I could feel myself getting more exasperated. I knew she was trying to protect me, but I didn't matter. Protecting my family was far more important.

'Mum!'

'Chalfont. He has a house in Chalfont.'

'Where?'

'When we first married, before you were born, we bought a little two-bed in a place called Chalfont. He still has it.'

'And you know he's there?'

'Yes.'

'How? How can you be sure?'

I watched as she began to speak but stopped herself.

'Mum, how do you know?'

'Because … because we still speak from time to time.'

'What? You told me he was gone.'

'And he is. I promise, I've not seen him in years. Just, some-times he calls.' I had to move away from her, I was worried if I stayed so close I would really lose my temper. When I spoke I did so quietly, fighting to keep control of my anger at being lied to so often.

'When was the last time he rang?'

'It's been about a year. He usually rings around Christmas.'

'You speak to him … every year?'

'Yes.'

'And didn't think to tell me?'

'He insisted you two didn't speak. He insisted it was for your own good that you didn't know about him at all.'

'Don't you think that's suspicious?'

'I didn't. I don't. I mean, I don't know.'

'And he always rings around Christmas?'

'Yes.'

'But not this Christmas?'

'I just assumed he'd been busy.'

'And now my family has been taken.' I felt my muscles start moving, wanting to head for the door and leave. 'Where in Chalfont is he?'

'What are you going to do?'

'I'm going down. He needs to tell me what he knows.'

On shaking legs she left the room, assumedly to get a pen and paper from the telephone table. I turned my back to the room and looked at the window above the sink, catching my hazy reflection. My lip was swollen badly, as was the corner of my eye. I didn't recognize myself. Who was the man staring back? I was involved in something that meant it was safer to change my identity and hide the past. It explained the question I always had and never asked, for fear of the answer. Why none of my friends before the accident got in touch. Now I knew. My name had been changed, they wouldn't know how to find me. But still I didn't know why my mum and dad would go to such extremes. What had the man in my reflection been involved in?

Mum came back into the room, the address written shakily on a piece of paper in her hand. She gave it to me. She told me it was close to where I grew up, a place just outside Slough called Wexham. Until then, I thought I had grown up in Cambridge with Mum moving this way after my accident to help with my recovery. That was what I had always been told. I had never heard of Wexham. The place that owned all of my childhood. Strangely, I felt myself mourn the childhood I didn't remember. None of the stories that I had used to manufacture memories were real. None of them.

But now wasn't the time for self-pity. I needed to think of what I would do next. I had to go home, grab some cash from the bottom of my wardrobe. Mainly change, but some notes too. Then I remembered. Mum's holiday scrapbooks. There might be something in them that would help.

'Your books, Mum, did you get them out?'

'My holiday scrapbooks?'

'Yes, give them to me. I need to see them.'

'There are so many.'

'Give me the ones you had before I got hurt. When I was in trouble. And your car keys. Get them, and in the morning ring the police and say your car has been stolen.' Suddenly, I had a plan. My thoughts frantic, coming thick and fast as I fired information at Mum.

'What, why?'

'Because I cannot drag you into this.'

She looked at me blankly as shock began to wash over her. I shouted to snap her out of it.

'Mum, go! The holiday scrapbooks and keys.'

'Yes, of course, yes.'

She got her car keys and handed them to me but held on to one, connecting us.

'Daniel, I'm so sorry.'

'Mum, the holiday scrapbooks!'

She was in shock. And I knew my tone was harsh. But I didn't have time to waste. She left, retrieved three hardback yellow books and handed them to me. I wouldn't look now, despite wanting to. I needed to get to Chalfont first and speak to my father.

'I've got to go.'

'What are you going to do?'

'Get my family back.'

She leant in to hug me, but I waved her away. I was still too angry at her. Fifteen years of lies. Fifteen years, and although she was only trying to protect me, she'd put my little boy at risk by doing so. I walked to the front door, opened it and then turned back. She hadn't moved; she looked ten years older than when she came downstairs.

'Remember, Mum, ring the police in the morning. It removes your involvement.'

'But then they will be looking for it.'

'I'll dump it somewhere, I just don't want them thinking you've helped me. And don't say anything if you're asked about where I am.'

'But we should speak to someone.'

'Mum, if we do and they find out, it will put Thomas and Rachael in danger.'

'But who are they?'

'I don't know Mum. But I'm going to go to Dad's and find out. Just don't talk to anyone about this. Especially the police. Don't tell them I was here, don't tell them about Dad's place in Chalfont. Just tell them your car has been stolen, okay?'

'Okay, but why are the police going to be looking for you?'

'Because Sean is dead. Because Rachael and Thomas are missing and I've taken off in the middle of the night. Because I'm going to be their prime suspect.'

Chapter 13

Daniel

Chalfont

2nd January 2018, 5.31 a.m.

It had taken longer than anticipated to drive back to my house and grab the few bits I needed – hoping I wouldn't draw any attention to myself – before I started the drive to the address Mum had given me. Moving quickly, I had run upstairs two at a time into my bedroom and emptied the money tin that lived in the bottom of my wardrobe. It had around a hundred pounds inside. I had also grabbed the notebook that Katie wrote all my dreams in from her bedside table, just in case I discovered something that linked the dream world that had slipped out in my sleep to the nightmare I was living in now. Foolishly, so preoccupied with collecting the money and leaving quickly, I hadn't grabbed any warmer or more appropriate clothes. That annoyed me; it told me I wasn't as focused as I needed to be.

The drive down had been tough. I had to stop regularly. The image of Rachael's eyes, blindly staring back at the camera in terror and my little boy behind her, so still, so fragile, kept jumping out at me despite how hard I tried to keep it suppressed. It robbed me of my ability to focus on the otherwise easy task of driving.

I mounted a kerb or run a red light several times en route. My broken tooth began to hurt more than I thought I could bare, my lip throbbing with every slight gust of wind. My eyes stung as I fought to hold myself together and, in front of me along the A1, the tail-lights of the cars and lorries merged into one long red stream.

Inside, there was a quiet rage bubbling, targeted at myself. At a point when I needed to be inconspicuous and time precious, I was driving erratically, speeding more than I ever normally would. I had to get centred. I had to regain control. I ditched the car near a secondary school close to the address Mum had given me and walked the rest of the way through a sleeping street, lights off in all of the windows.

My mum's words echoed in my mind, reminding me that I was once a man called Michael. Someone who was mixed up in bad things. He was once me, and I didn't know who he was.

Checking the scrap of paper that had the address scribbled on it, I confirmed I had found his house. It was a small end-of-terrace. Two up, two down. Unremarkable. An old VW Passat sat on the drive. As I got closer I could see frost on the top of the tyres. Spider webs hung in the gap between the side mirror and the door. Moss grew along the bottom of the window. Not what I expected to see. I looked around, to my left, then right.

All was deathly quiet, deathly still, and although it was pre-dawn I didn't want to risk anyone being up early and seeing me, so I walked down the side of the house and tried to open the back gate. It was locked. Reaching over I could feel a dead bolt. It was stiff with rust but eventually gave. I closed it behind me and walked to the back window. Cupping my hands against the glass I could see a small kitchen leading on to an even smaller living room. Even through the glass I could see the dust that had settled over everything. It had been empty for a while. I didn't know what that meant. I couldn't stop my heart from sinking. I guess, part of me hoped if I found him it would be over.

I examined the back door. Its wooden frame held small panes of glass. Twelve in all. Single glazed. Decades old. On the inside I could see keys hanging out of the lock. I pressed on the pane closest to the handle, I could feel it move. Using Mum's car key I scored along the putty that held it in, first along the top, then the sides, then finally the bottom. Chucks of old dried-up sealant broke off. I pressed the glass again and it moved with more freedom. Putting the keys back in my pocket I pushed the glass in a little more and with my fingertips pulled on the wooden lip in which the glass sat, the point in the frame I knew to be the weakest as it was where two separate pieces of wood joined. And I knew that in an older door the adhesive was more than likely just as effective as the sealant. It broke away cleanly, barely making a noise. Once off it gave me a few millimetres in which I could slide out the glass. I then stuck my hand inside and unlocked the door before stepping in and closing and locking it behind me. I barely made a sound. And it had taken me less than thirty seconds.

Only once inside with the glass slid back into its frame did I stop to wonder how I had just broken into a house like it was a normal thing.

As I stepped into the dark kitchen I put Mum's scrapbooks along with Katie's notebook on the side and closed my eyes, listening for any movements coming from within. It felt empty, it felt like it had been empty for a long time. I wondered if it was intentional. Did my father disappear off the grid in preparation for what had happened? I opened kitchen drawers to find a knife just in case my instincts were wrong. Wrapping the cold handle in my grip I walked towards the door connecting the kitchen and lounge.

I began to skim over the room, sweeping my eyes from left to right, taking in the images, looking for things that seemed out of place. I saw a small shape out of the corner of my eye at the bottom of the steep narrow staircase. I thought it was Thomas curled up like he was in the photo. I felt a squeezing in my chest. I snapped my head back, to see it was just an old coat on the floor under a broken coat hook. But still, for a moment it forced the air out of my chest, making me double over to place my hands on my knees. Staring at the old carpeted floor, I refocused. I needed to find something to help me get my family back. I reached and picked up the old coat. It smelt old, unworn. Dust covered it, as it did everything. The cuffs were stiff. I hung it over the banister end and began walking upstairs slowly, only applying pressure to the carpeted steps with my toes. Less surface area, quieter tread. I pressed down before load-bearing each step, ensuring the floorboards didn't creak or move before pushing up to the next, careful to put my trailing foot in exactly the same place as I did my lead. I couldn't help but see how odd it was that my body moved in such a controlled way when my mind was seizing. I tried to slow my thoughts.

'Close your eyes, Daniel. Count to ten,' I told myself until I obeyed. It helped. The anxiety was contained, for now. To help, I decided to create a list, something I could action. Something that made it seem easy. It had just three points:

Find out what I took.

Retrieve it.

Get my family back.

I whispered it over and over again to myself in my head until it became part of my pulse. My new mantra. Just three steps and then this nightmare would be over.

Three small steps. It seemed so simple, and yet, not knowing anything about what I had taken some time before 2003 made it seem like an impossible task.

Once my feet were both firmly on the top step I paused, allowing my hearing to take over. The wind blew outside, a clock ticked to my right, my breathing calm like it came from the lungs of a different man. Nothing else. To my left was the doorway to a small bathroom, to my right were two rooms, one small, one larger. This was the one I stepped into. The most valuable things were kept in the rooms where people slept. Outside, a lamp post shined in, the room no doubt never being fully dark, its contents lit by the artificial amber light through thin curtains. The single bed, drawers beside it and a half-size wardrobe I could make out through my straining vision. It looked unloved, devoid of personality. The space had dust on the windowsills and on the tops of the furniture. It had been empty for a long time, as my instincts had suggested.

I dropped the knife on the bed and once again I scanned. It was unremarkable besides a small bookcase which was half hidden behind the wardrobe, with a handful of titles on it. As I approached, only one caught my eye. Whereas the others where all old and beaten, most showing the signs of being read more than once, the one that had my attention looked as though it had been barely opened. I picked it up. *The Handbook of Memory Disorders*. It was heavy, its dark-blue hardback cover suggesting it was expensive compared with the novels. I opened it. Six hundred and fifty pages of hard data and facts around a wide array of memory problems. Turing to the contents page, I saw that 'chapter four' was underlined. It was the chapter about retrograde amnesia. The introduction told me nothing new. I skimmed its pages and noticed that although it was in almost pristine condition, there were other markings on some of the pages; small pencil lines under letters. At the bottom of the page, there was another marking. Looking closely, I saw it was a name. It said Michael.

He knew I would come to his house. He knew I would take an interest in the book. I moved to the wardrobe and felt on top of it first; nothing. Then opening it I looked at what was hanging, a handful of T-shirts, jeans and jumpers. Ironed and in order. Like the rest of the house it was devoid of personality. It almost felt as if that was by design. Keep everything neutral, leave no clues behind. Dropping down, I ran my hand into the dark corners of the wardrobe base. In the corner, pressed into the wood was a book. Pulling it out I saw it was a *Learn French* book.

France, again.

I opened it and three photographs fell out. I held them up so the outside light could make the images visible. In the top one was two men, one older and bigger than the other. They were arm in arm smiling to the camera. The older wore a white vest and cut-off jean shorts, the younger in a baggy T-shirt with hair with a centre parting. It took me a moment to realize the younger of the two was me, arm in arm with who I now assumed was my father. We looked happy. I turned the picture over and in pencil it said, 'France 1999'.

Four years before my accident, a year when I was still Michael. I tried to remember being there with my father, but as hard as I tried, nothing would come. The darkness held firm.

I looked at the next photograph; one of him and my mum. I must have taken it. They were overlooking a view of a village. He had the same top on, so I assumed it was still in France. I tried to see that moment, and again, nothing came. When I looked at the third, however, my heart rate increased. It was me alone, smiling at the camera.

For a moment I could hear my mum's voice.

'Say cheese.'

'Cheese.'

'Let's have one of the pair of you.'

Then he came and stood beside me.

'This is it, Mickey, this is the place where it all began. This is the place that will change everything.'

'Smile, you two …'

The memory hit me harder than I thought I could take. I had to sit down. I couldn't breathe. It was so clear, so real. Like those I experienced on New Year's Eve. I had pulled another thing out of the darkness, and I knew without the need to check that this moment was entirely true. This was something I had done.

87

I hoped the more I found, the more I would get back and the more I got back, the closer I would be to my family being returned to me. I hoped my mum was right and now the snowball was in motion it would gather speed.

I was starting to think that somehow, this thing I was involved in, had something to do with France. I had seen it clearly a few times now. Maybe the picture in my hand was taken there – in Auvers, the place I had not been able to shift from my mind since seeing it. Auvers was somehow a big part of my life. It had to be, or I wouldn't be so drawn to it. So, the question was, could the thing I took all those years ago be there?

Could I have stolen something and hidden it in France, and could that be why I had heard my father saying that phrase? '*This is the place that will change everything.*' With his house being empty for some time and the French book, I wondered, could he be there?

Deep down, something was telling me that I needed to go there, to see if it conjured memories, if anyone could point me in the right direction. But, the idea of intentionally going further away from Thomas and Rachael made me feel sick. Regardless, France was important to my father and he either had my family, or he had the answers. But before I made any rash decisions to head to Auvers, I needed to go to Wexham, retracing the steps of where I grew up, hoping I might find something useful. Or something that would trigger more memories to float out of the darkness. Or so I hoped.

I also needed to read Mum's three yellow holiday scrapbooks. If France was important, they might give a clue as to why. I also wanted to speak to Katie. I checked my Facebook messages and she hadn't seen it yet. Before anything though, I needed clothes. Opening the wardrobe again I grabbed a pair of jeans, a T-shirt and a sweater and put them on. They were a little big on me, but they would do. Downstairs I grabbed the old coat and shoes, again too big, but better than my slippers. I had to tie the shoes tightly to stop them falling off my feet. Finding a car key on the small window ledge that was beside the front door, I grabbed the scrapbooks and notebook, left through the door I had entered, and walked towards the car. Just as I was about to open it I caught a man in my peripheral vision on the other side of the street to me. He was looking in my direction with a quizzical expression on his face. Despite my paranoia I tried my best to appear calm. Smiling, I gave him a small friendly wave, one that might trick him into thinking we had seen each other before, as I climbed into my father's car. Grateful that it fired up on the second attempt, I put it into reverse and made my way off the drive, before heading away from my father's house. The man watched me the entire time.

Chapter 14

Rachael

The Garage

2nd January 2018, 6.48 a.m.

I hadn't heard anything other than the sound of mine and Tom's breathing for hours, the last sound being footsteps walking away from just outside the door. They must have been there listening up to that point. Hearing me spin my story to Tom, listening to me sing. In the low light my eyes burnt. I hadn't slept, I didn't dare to. Instead, I watched my baby sleep, barely visible under the mound of dirty blankets. His breathing calm and light. He was in a deep slumber, the kind that frightened me when he was a tiny baby. His little body so still, so small. Seeing him like that was both soothing and heartbreaking. His peace was a small light that lived in the darkest of places. He was too young to know what we were facing. If I didn't keep my fear at bay, if I didn't stay smart, a step ahead, my baby would lose his innocence.

The only thing that was a saving grace to this nightmare was the fact Tom believed we were writing a story, an adventure that was about a little boy and his mummy who would eventually save themselves. I hoped I had the strength to continue plotting when he woke. But I wasn't sure I could, because in a story, things made sense, and here, nothing made sense. We were just a normal little family living our normal little lives. There was no reason why we would be taken, and hypothesizing through the long, cold night just fuelled the fear that circled over my head like a flock of vultures, their wing span so wide it blocked out the sun. I had to push it out, focus on the now, stay in the moment. Do it to keep my baby from feeling any of the emotion that I was. Whatever was happening, I had to keep myself together and make sure it stayed an adventure. Thomas and I were writing our own children's book, one with twists and turns. One with peril, but a peril that was important for the victory.

Or so I hoped.

I knew I needed to try to sleep. Without it I wouldn't be able to keep my head clear, but every time I did I'd see Sean and the way he fell when he was hit. I prayed he was okay, I prayed he was trying to find us.

Tom mumbled in his sleep and, reaching over, I stroked his mousey hair which settled him again. The longer he slept, the better. In his dreams he would be safe. In his dreams none of this would be real. I looked at the shape of his face. From the side he looked just like his father. A younger, softer version.

Would Daniel know what had happened?

Would he also be trying to find us?

I pushed it from my mind; whatever was happening outside this room wasn't something I could do anything about. But my heart told me yes, both Sean and Daniel were trying to find us, and they would. Until then, I had to do what I could.

Looking out of the small vent that led directly to the outside world I could see light begin to show; dawn was on its way. The sky that was black, was now blue. I guessed it was around 6 a.m., maybe a little later. I always struggle to judge winter dawns. Knowing Tom wouldn't stay asleep for much longer I lay beside him and closed my eyes. I just needed two hours, I could function on that much. With my hand resting on Tom's back I could feel him breathing gently and my body began to give. A sudden heaviness that worked its way from my extremities up my spine and into my head. The thin mattress felt somehow softer than before, as I began to drift.

Then I heard a voice, the words distant and muffled. The sound startled me, but I thought I was dreaming. It was quickly followed by a rattling of keys and still, for a second, I thought it was coming from the corners of my mind. A key went into a lock. It wasn't a dream. Someone was coming in.

Shooting up like I had been electrocuted, I grabbed Tom and woke him.

'Tom, Tom, wake up.'

He looked at me, then around the room in confusion. He then remembered where he was, and the fear came back instantly.

'Mummy?'

'The Bear is coming, honey. Remember, what did Torak do?'

'I can't remember.'

'Think, Tom, what did Torak do?'

'He hid.'

'Exactly, good boy. You must be like him now. Under the bed, not a sound.'

'Mummy, I don't want to.'

'It's okay, darling, this is part of the second chapter.'

For a moment the fear left as he remembered what I had told him. He looked around the room again, more curious than fearful.

'We're in chapter two already?'

The lock snapped.

'Yes, baby, now quickly.'

'What's it called?'

'It's called "Hiding from The Bear". Now go! You don't want to spoil the surprises in the next chapters.'

'Surprises?'

'Shhhh, darling, under the bed, right to the back. And not a word!'

Helping him crawl under the bed, capping the back of his head with my hand so he didn't catch it on the rusty bedframe, I heard a bolt slide open slowly, old metal grinding against old metal until it too snapped open. I grabbed one of the old blankets and stuffed it under the bed in front of Tom, hiding him entirely from view. Light flooded in, hurting my eyes, forcing me to cover my face. I heard steps coming towards me, the shape of a man. He wasn't big like The Bear or wiry like the one who smiled and looked at me in a way that made my skin crawl. This was the one who climbed into the back of the van and took that photo. He was dressed in similar clothing to the others. He had a balaclava over his head but was rounder, heavier. His dark sleeves were rolled up showing fat forearms that were covered in tattoos. On the back of one hand, a swallow, on the other five dots that looked like they should be on a dice. As he stepped in I could hear his heavy breathing, like he had been running, but looking at his shape I'd guess he had only had to walk to cause breathlessness. In his hand was a camera. Before I could speak he took a photo. My hand instinctively came up to protect my eyes from the flash. Then he looked around the room, and rested his eyes on mine.

'Where is he?' he said quietly, his voice clipped and clear, not suiting his appearance. I didn't respond but held his gaze, trying desperately to make my breathing match his as fear pressed on my diaphragm. He didn't ask again, instead he nodded as if he understood and stepped towards me calmly. Before I could react, he flashed his arm with such speed that I didn't see it coming and he slapped me with the back of his right hand across my face, making me topple onto my left shoulder. The impact sent a white flash before my eyes and I could taste iron in my mouth where I had bit the inside of my cheek, causing it to bleed. As soon as I hit the floor I scrambled to my right, in front of the bed, blocking him from Tom. He started to step towards me and I felt my body prepare itself for another hit. This time I wouldn't fall, there was no way he was coming any closer to my son.

'Move,' he said, clipped again, no sign of anger in his voice.

I didn't and when he asked me again I shot him a look which told him he would need to kill me to get to Tom, and I wouldn't go down without a fight. He raised his hand again, this time in a clenched fist, and I felt my jaw close tightly, preparing to be rattled open when he struck me. Just as he was about to swing, the light from outside the door was blocked by the shape of the large man who forced us into the small room. His presence stopped the tattooed man and he lowered his hand.

'I'll see you later, bitch.' He spat at me before pushing past The Bear on his way out.

Once the tattooed man was gone The Bear turned his attention to me. Then he cocked his head to one side and looked past me and under the bed to where Tom lay with only his hair visible.

'Please,' I said, my voice shaking as I did. I didn't want him to look at him. The man looked again at me. 'Please don't.' The words barely got out through my shallow breathing.

He didn't say anything back, he just put down a tray which I hadn't noticed until that moment and turned, then just before leaving he took something out of his pocket and threw it back towards me. It landed next to the tray he had put down. Then he left, closing and locking the door behind him, putting us back in the dark.

On the floor was some bread, water and beside the tray, the thing he had thrown was a packet of Maltesers. Looking at the two bottles of Evian made me realize how thirsty I was and pulling the tray towards me, I opened a bottle and drank. My pulse thumped in my face where I had been hit. Sticking my finger inside I felt the skin that should be soft on the inside of my cheek had a small tear where I had bitten and as I pulled my finger out, there was blood on it.

'Tom.' My voice sounded scared. I cleared it and tried again. 'Tom, you can come out now.'

'Is The Bear gone?'

'Yes, darling.'

He crawled out from under the bed and sat beside me, leaning into my shoulder. I wrapped my arm around him and pulled a blanket from the bed to cover us.

'Well done, darling. You were brilliant at hiding.'

'Was I?'

'Are you kidding? The best I have ever seen.'

'Did The Bear see me?'

'No way. You were too good at it.'

'Mummy, I've been thinking. Why is The Bear after us anyway? I know why he was after Torak, but why us?'

'Here.' I hesitated. 'Drink some water.'

Tom took the water and drank the rest of the first bottle. Wiping his mouth, he burped and laughed. His giggle was infectious, allowing me to join in and cover the tears that stung the back of my eyes.

'Sorry, Mummy.'

'Don't be. It was a good one.'

'Will that be in the book?'

'Do you want it to be?'

'It was funny.'

'Then yes, it will.'

'Mummy, I need a wee.'

'Okay, darling.' I looked around. There was nothing he could wee in so I told him to use the empty bottle in the corner. He did, half filling it. I screwed the lid on and left it as far away from the bed as possible, not knowing where I would relieve myself when I couldn't hold it anymore.

'Is that better?'

'Yes, Mummy.'

'Good.'

I kissed him on the head before lifting him back onto the bed. As soon as he was lying down his eyes began to lose focus, sleep once more coming to take him to the safe place.

'Did I really hide well? Are you sure The Bear didn't see me?'

'Of course, you're an expert hider.'

'Is that the end of chapter two?'

'Yes, it is.'

'How many chapters are in this book, Mummy?'

I smiled at him and moved some hair off his eyebrow, sweeping it across his forehead to buy me time. I needed to respond as calmly as I could.

'As many as a good story takes.'

My answer seemed to be enough and smiling, he rolled onto his side. After a few minutes of stroking his hair he was sound asleep. I stood and stepped towards the vent to try to see what was outside. I could see an old building. Perhaps a mill of some kind, clearly unused. It told me nothing about where we could be. I wanted to shout, but it was still early, probably too early for anyone to hear me. I would try when the sun was fully up. Returning to my baby I sat on the floor and rested my head beside him. Whereas I was tired before, I was fully awake now, the adrenaline pumping too hard for my heart to manage.

I still knew nothing about what was happening to us and why, but they had delivered food.

It meant we would be here for some time.

Chapter 15

Daniel

Wexham

2nd January 2018, 8.33 a.m.

I had driven around the small borough on the outskirts of Slough several times, trying to get a sense of the place. My initial thoughts were that it was rough growing up in a place like this. Although, that probably had more to do with my state of mind than anything I could see. Yes, some of the town looked tired, and that was what I was drawn to. Other parts of the small place were upper class. I supposed that was like any other place in and around London. I drove aimlessly, trying to pick out anything from my broken mind that might tell me where to go next. It was no use. Nothing came. I was wasting time, but until I had anything more, all I could do was hope for another trigger. To do this, I had to stop.

I parked the car at the end of a cul-de-sac of small houses and decided to walk. I knew I needed to keep my wits about me, my guard up. I got out of the car and thought about taking Katie's notebook with me but decided against it. Then I subconsciously felt the front pocket of my father jeans and the money in it. In the boot that creaked open as I lifted it, I looked for something

I could carry with me, just in case I was confronted. Part of me wished I had kept the knife from my father's house, although I wasn't sure I could use it if I needed to. Rummaging through the boot I found an adjustable spanner, about eight inches and fairly heavy. Perfect.

I locked the car and began walking around the place of my childhood. The footpaths that joined one street with another through tree-lined passages were narrow, houses one on top of the other. The birdsong was loud, perhaps warning me. I had most likely been here before at some point and yet, I felt nothing. I needed something to squeeze its way through the wall in my head and guide me. Around me, lights were on in houses and I looked at one, a modest semi, probably three bedrooms, with a small driveway that backed on to a garden. Could this be the house I grew up in? Could this one, over the thousands of others, be the one where I was a small boy growing up called Michael? I doubted it. But one of these was the house of my childhood and I felt a sadness in the fact that I might not ever know. I didn't even know when I left. Was I still a boy? Or was it just before I had my accident? If it was the later, I probably didn't look much different now to how I did then. I needed to keep a low profile. So, head bowed, I carried on walking as casually as I could.

I turned onto a main road which surprised me as I had expected another small cul-de-sac of houses. On the other side of the road was a man walking his dog, coming in my direction. As we passed one another I glanced back and saw he was watching me. For a moment a voice inside me shouted that he knew everything, and that was why he was staring. I stopped walking, pretending to text, my muscles tensed and flexed as I waited for something to happen. He sensed my hesitation, my preparation and stopped looking. I couldn't help but feel I had won a small victory.

My rational mind took control of my body again and I began to move. The distance between us grew until I could no longer feel the man's presence, and with the moment gone, I realized he was staring because I looked out of place. I was walking around for no reason, in clothes that didn't fit me, my face bruised, my lip split, looking like I hadn't slept all night. I needed a prop. Something that would let people assume all was okay. Up ahead was a small shop. The light outside was dim in the early morning sunshine. Using some of the change in my pocket I bought a pint of milk and a newspaper. Now I was a man out for the morning essentials. Now I could walk around without attracting attention to myself. As long as I walked with my head cast down, hiding my battered face, I was just another man on just another winter morning. Two simple props transformed me into a chameleon. The camouflage meant I could take my time, despite not having time to waste. It was a necessity.

I had to find a thread, grab it and pull it hard to drag my memories into the now. I had made some progress with the picture of France, and in the back of my mind I felt it was a big part of what was happening, but that presented a problem. Soon, if not already, I would be a wanted man. If Sean hadn't been discovered yet, he would be at any moment and then the hunt for me would begin. I felt confident that I could hide in plain sight. But I doubted I could get to France easily, if I needed to. I hoped I didn't, but my instincts couldn't shake the fact that my father wasn't where he lived and France had meant something to him – to us. He had the answers, and I needed them more than anything.

Up ahead I could see a park and as soon as I did I felt the sense of warmth; there was something about it that made me think of summer. I felt drawn to it and as I walked in I thought I could hear laughter being carried on the breeze. It swept through me and vanished. I stepped into the park, the metal gate displaying a 'no dogs allowed' sign, and I was transported to another time. To my right were swings that were painted bright blue. Beyond them were metal climbing frames in yellow and red. I knew what it felt like to be stood at the top of them, looking down at the world like I was a giant. I knew that I could jump from the swings in full flight and land near the bench that was positioned nearby. A bench that I could see my father sat on. This place had once been where we played. I sat on the bench in the same way he would have, facing the swings, looking at the space around me. I could feel movement, lots of it, children running and jumping and squealing with joy. I felt the sense of myself running and climbing, sweat sticking my hair to the side of my face.

Looking behind me, I saw an old football goal, maybe a hundred yards away, on the field that backed on to the park. To the left of it was a row of trees. I felt compelled to walk towards them, so I did just that. As I approached I could see a gap in the evergreens that I couldn't see from the bench and, bending slightly, I stepped inside a sort of cavern made of the foliage that was tough enough to survive the bleak winter.

Walking along, I saw a few dens made out of old pallets, skeletal remains from last summer, and I knew that I would have done the same as a boy. I knew I would have played here. I could feel it. Ahead was an old tree, its leaves gone. It had a wide trunk and low, thick branches. That would have been the tree I would have used. As I approached it I saw markings – something had been carved into it. As I touched the markings a voice made me jump.

'Don't tell your mother we just did that.'

Instinctively, I looked around to see the source before realizing the voice was from inside my head. It was the same voice I'd heard on New Year's Eve; my father's voice. Getting onto my knees, my left one cracking as I did, I looked closer at the markings on the old trunk. It read 'Mikey and Dad, '91'.

It didn't shock me to find the marking, my subconscious told me I would. I closed my eyes, desperately trying to see that moment where my father and I were here carving our names into the tree, but I couldn't.

My knees were beginning to go numb from the cold floor, so

I got up slowly. I didn't know what to think. None of it made sense. I was so frustrated I hit the trunk, my knuckles connecting with the scratches created by my father twenty-seven years before. Somewhere, my family was cold and terrified. Somewhere, my little boy was wondering where I was. Wondering why his father, the man who promised to protect him from all of the monsters in the world, wasn't there. Wondering what he had done to deserve being abandoned. And here I was, in a children's park trying to remember my own childhood, hoping that something would come out of the void. I hated myself for it. Before I could think about my next move I felt the phone that I had been given vibrate in my back pocket.

Pulling it out I saw that the number was listed.

'Katie?' I said desperately, knowing it was impossible as I didn't have my own phone anymore.

'Not quite.'

It was him, the voice, of course.

'I've heard a rumour you've visited a little house in Chalfont. Did you find what you were looking for?'

He knew I was there because of the man I saw outside the house. He must have been working for the voice. Maybe he was the voice. The one who held my family captive. I tried to picture him, but I couldn't.

'No, not yet.'

'But you are on the road?'

I wanted to tell him I didn't have a clue, that I needed more time. That I needed an idea of where to start. But somehow, I knew it would make things worse than they already were. I hoped he didn't hear my fear as I spoke.

'Yes. I'm on the road.'

I heard him move the receiver from his ear – he was about to hang up. I shouted to stop him.

'Wait, I need to know they're safe. I need to hear their voices.'

'They are okay.'

'I need proof.'

'Now, now, Michael. You'll just have to trust me, won't you?'

'Please, let me hear their voices.'

'Friday, you will get your instructions for the drop-off. Get what you took from me back and you'll have them back.'

'And if I get it before Friday, how do I contact you?'

'This attitude is better, Michael,' he said, clearly pleased with my want to get this over quickly. 'Why do you think I didn't block the number this time? Save it in your phone. That way you can update me, can't you? Now, get moving, Michael. You won't find it sat in a park, will you?'

The line went dead and I stood up, looking around. He knew exactly where I was. Somewhere, he was watching, although I couldn't see anyone. Whoever the voice was, he had people following me. First the man in Chalfont, then the dog walker. Were they the same man? I cursed myself for not focusing on the details.

Leaving the milk and paper in the park I stuffed my hands into my pockets, lowered my head and began moving. I needed to get back to the car, get out of this place, and find somewhere busier. Somewhere I could lose whoever was following me. If they found out I didn't know where it was, or even what it was that I had taken, it would be over. Once at my car I drove out of the cul-de-sac and towards the M25. After ten minutes I was sure I wasn't being followed so I came off and found a quiet road to park. A layby outside a place called Denham. Putting my handbrake on I killed the engine and stared at a silver birch, its leafless body shivering in the wind, its limbs groaning through the strain.

I thought about what I knew. A moment in France, the words *this is the place where it all began. This is the place that will change everything*' ringing in my head. I opened Katie's notebook and read and re-read the notes about my dreams, and the accident that consumed most of them. Every now and then something would be underlined, usually when I remembered something new. There was a bridge that appeared in my dreams about three months ago and was there in most of them afterwards. I tried to picture it, wondering if I had been past it today on my drive. I would keep an eye out for it. Maybe I would stumble upon the site of the crash that I recalled most nights. Underlined were also Katie's notes on my moment from New Year's Eve. It seemed she was keeping track of everything I recalled, not just when I was asleep. She noted the comment I made about the smell of sulphur, and the sound of the fireworks, of me being high from the ground looking down. My feeling of fear at being caught. Fast-moving water and a crow cawing. I checked the maps on the phone, and there was no river running through Slough; a canal, but no river. Taking a moment, I wrote down the five things I had learnt, under Katie's last entry, the night before she went down to be with her father. Again, I cursed myself for not remembering her number. I hoped she was oblivious to everything that was happening. I hoped she was still by her father's side. I checked Facebook, still nothing. My list was just as confusing on the page as it was in my head.

1: I am called Michael.
2: My own mother lied to me for as long as I can remember about who I was and where I grew up.
3: My father is missing, clues from his house pointing to France.
4: I stole something a long time ago, before I can remember.
5: Rachael and Thomas have been taken.

Nothing I had remembered or learnt made sense. The only obvious way to understand what I had done, and how I could undo it, was to find my father. He was the only person who I knew could connect them. I needed him to tell me what we did before 2003. Worryingly, I still felt that that would mean a trip to France – something I didn't want to do. Looking at the passenger seat beside me, I saw the three yellow holiday scrapbooks sat waiting to be scanned. With no idea where to move next, at least not in a direction that wasn't the continent, I lifted the top one and opened it.

I tried to focus on my mum's words, read her stories, and look at the holiday snaps and postcards. But, as I looked at the pictures of me as a small child, all I could see was Thomas looking back. Then I thought about him in the van. I tried to shake it but couldn't. Heat rose behind my eyes, forcing its way out like lava from my tear ducts.

My vision was all but gone as I cried long and hard.

Chapter 16

Daniel

Outside Denham

2nd January 2018, 9.30 a.m.

All cried out, I wiped the tears from my eyes and the snot from my lips. The release lifted the air like a thunderstorm after weeks of intense heat. With the close, tight feeling gone I could breathe. Able to think clearer, for the moment at least, it allowed me to slow myself down. I knew being hysterical wouldn't help anyone. Full of hope, I logged back into Facebook and felt my heart skip when I saw I had a new message in my inbox. Katie didn't say much, just left her number with a confused emoji. Katie usually replied in full sentences, unless she was tired, then she said as little as she could. It told me she wasn't sleeping. But it also told me she was safe and oblivious to what was happening. She was being watched, but, so far, they hadn't acted on it. Copying and pasting I dialled. It rang three times and she picked up, her voice sounding panicked and relieved.

'Daniel? Why is your phone switched off?'

'Katie, I can't talk long. I need you to get a new phone, a pay-as-you-go or something and store this number. Then, delete your call log on here and turn this phone off.'

'What? Daniel, what's going on?' Her voice was high and tense. As I spoke I had to stop myself and start again, my words coming out so fast she couldn't understand what I was trying to say.

'Daniel? What's happened? Calm down, you're making me panic. Are you okay?'

'Where are you?'

'I'm at the hospital with my dad.'

'Are there any shops nearby to get a phone?'

'No, I don't think so.'

'Shit,' I said, trying to work out how Katie and I would be able to talk after this call. She couldn't continue to use her phone. Once the police were after me, they would know about her and likely trace her calls.

'My dad's phone is here in his bag? Would that work?' she said, interrupting my thoughts.

'Is it a pay-as-you-go?'

'Yes, he's never been very good with mobiles, his is an old Nokia.'

'Perfect, save my number in his phone and switch yours off after this call.'

I should have asked how her dad was, but I couldn't because in that moment, I didn't care. She, Thomas and Rachael were all I had space to care for. 'Have you noticed anything odd? Anyone hanging around who shouldn't be?'

'What? No. Daniel, what are you talking about? What's going on?'

Taking a deep breath, I spoke, my words almost devoid of emotion, almost. 'Katie, I need to tell you something. I want you to hear it from me rather than anyone else.'

'Daniel?' she replied quietly, mirroring my own tones, the tension unbearable.

'Pretty soon the police are going to be looking for me.'

'What? Why?'

106

'They will think I've done something terrible.'

'Daniel, you're scaring me. What's happened? Where are you?'

I explained as carefully as my racing mind would allow; the phone call and the picture of Rachael and Thomas brought back the squeezing on my chest. I told her about finding Sean's body in their home.

'What? You need to go to the police.' I could hear the shock and disbelief in her voice, the worry etched into her tone.

'I was told if I did they would ...'

I couldn't finish the sentence. I couldn't say out loud that if I failed they would kill them both and then come for her. I could feel the heat behind my eyes again, threatening to spill. I looked at the tree that I was parked in front of, its silvery trunk solid in the wind whilst its arms looked violent and out of control. I focused on the trunk, sitting as low as I could, looking over the dash of the car. How many storms had it survived? How many times had it faced difficulty but stayed firm? Subconsciously I pressed my feet into the car's foot well, every part of the soles of my father's old boots in contact with the faded carpet. Somehow, it calmed me. I told myself to keep focusing on my feet. Keep the ground solid beneath them whilst this storm raged.

'Daniel?'

'Sorry, yes, I'm still here.'

'"They" – who are they?'

'I don't know. Someone from a long time ago. I did something, took something, and whoever it is wants it back.'

'Daniel, you have to go to the police.'

'Haven't you been listening?' I shouted into the phone, immediately regretting it. 'Katie, I'm sorry.' I took a deep breath. 'I can't go to the police. They will think I'm responsible.'

'But you're not. They'll see that.'

'I don't have time for them to work it out though. I need to find out who I was, and what I did, and make it right.'

'What is it you took?'

107

'I don't know.' I paused and focused on my feet, pressing down harder. 'But I'm going to find it.'

'What can I do?'

'Don't believe whatever you hear in the news about me in the coming hours. None of it. I didn't hurt anyone.'

'I know, Daniel.'

'And stay at the hospital. Don't go back to your hotel, even if you have to sleep in a waiting room. I don't want you out anywhere, okay?'

'I don't understand.'

'They told me they were watching you too.'

A heavy silence hung above my head as Katie was stunned into silence. Eventually she replied, jagged, scared.

'Is this a joke?'

'I'm so sorry, Katie. I hate that you're mixed up in this. That all three of you are mixed up in this. And I don't even know what this is.'

She didn't reply.

'Katie. Are you listening?'

'Yes,' she replied quietly.

'I'm going to make this right. I am. But until I do, please, just stay there at the hospital. Katie?'

'Yes, sorry, yes. I'll stay.'

'And if the police want to talk to you … we haven't spoken, you don't know where I am.'

'But …'

'Katie, you don't know where I am.'

'Daniel, I …'

'Say it.'

'I don't know where you are, we've not spoken.'

'I love you, Katie.'

'Dan …' She paused, unsure. 'What the hell did you do?'

'I wish I knew.'

'You sound tired.'

'I am tired.'

'You need to make sure you rest a little.'

'I haven't got time.'

'If you don't, you'll slip up and if …'

She didn't finish her sentence, she didn't need to, and she was right. If I slipped up, one of two things would happen. I would either be arrested, or I would fail. Both meant Rachael and Thomas were likely to be hurt, or worse.

'Even if you only sleep for an hour, get *some*. You need to be able to keep your wits.'

'All right, I promise to rest.'

'You'll feel sharper for it, more likely to make the right decisions.'

'I love you, Katie.'

'I love you too, be careful. And, Daniel, whatever it is, whatever you did, I don't care. Just find it. Save them.'

'I'm going to try. Please be careful, Katie, I need to know you're safe.'

'I will.'

'And text me straight away, so I have your dad's number.'

'Okay, be safe, Dan.'

I hung up the phone and exhaled loudly and within a minute the phone pinged, an unknown number and the message saying 'K xxx'. I saved it into the phone. Speaking with Katie made my body give in to the exhaustion I was feeling. My eyes stung to the point where each blink hurt. I knew I needed to move, keep going, read the scrapbooks and plot my next move. I opened the first one again. I promised myself I would sleep, but only after I knew what my next step was, so that when I woke I had a plan, a direction. A destination. I skimmed the first book. Holidays in the Eighties and early Nineties. Lots of pictures I had never seen before of me as a boy. I wanted to read, to learn. But I was not likely to learn anything that would help from the trips when I was young. I needed to be a teenager, late teens in fact. I needed to be, by definition, a man.

In the second scrapbook I was older, my spot-laden puberty years. I skimmed, but still felt I was too young. In the third I saw me on the other side of the awkward developmental years. My shoulders were broader, my chest bigger. The pictures showed me we visited lots of manor houses and castles, but none that I could see looked anything like the one in my vision on New Year's Eve where I was looking down from the top of a huge building. I flicked further into the journal. Near the back, a few pages from the end was a photo, one I had seen before only this morning, and seeing it again confirmed another flash of memory was entirely true. At the top of the page was a date and a place name.

The year was 1999.

The place was Auvers-sur-Oise, and with dread plucking on my diaphragm, I knew what I had to do.

Chapter 17

Rachael

The Garage

2nd January 2018, 9.52 a.m.

Opening my eyes, I saw that the small vent in the wall had daylight bleeding through. I must have fallen asleep, although I didn't know how long for. My eyes stung. I couldn't have slept long. Beside me Tom lay perfectly still, his little face peeking out from under the piss-stained blankets. It made him look angelic. His soft, fair skin still pristine in this hell we found ourselves. Stroking Tom's hair I stood up, the intention to go and listen at the door. If it was as quiet as I felt it was I would then head towards the vent. See if I could make out anything new.

As I stood I felt entirely drained, the adrenaline now completely gone and replaced with exhaustion. I felt nauseous so crawled to the corner and was sick. As it hit the hard concrete, some splashed back onto my forearms. I was becoming used to the morning sickness, but it hurt more than usual. After being sick I had to shuffle back, and I drank some water, which helped. I sipped a few times and put the cap back on. On the floor there were four pieces of bread on a plate. I picked one up and broke a bit off.

It was still soft, but the surface had started to crisp as it turned stale. Eating half of one slice I put the rest down. Tom would be hungry when he woke.

The water and small amount of food were nowhere near enough, but it acted as a placebo. I had eaten, I had drunk something, so I had tricked myself into thinking I was feeling better. Slowly rising, making sure my knees felt like they could hold me, I carefully walked towards the door and pressed my ear against it. It felt cold to the touch. Somewhere on the other side of the door, I could hear a radio or television playing. It was far away, only the echo of the sound reaching where we were. Turning my attention to the vent I walked over and, on my tiptoes, I looked outside, hoping that there was something that would give me a clue as to where we were. But there was nothing around.

I pressed my cheek to the wall to try to see more of what was outside. The cold surface was soothing on my cheek which still felt hot from being slapped. The air felt fresh against my skin. I would have to lift Tom up so he could breathe it in when he was awake. Straining my eyes, I could make out a pile of something that looked like sand. Frost covered. Swapping cheeks, I looked the other way. There was another building, half of it demolished. But no people. There looked like there hadn't been for quite some time. I suspected that would be the case but knowing it crushed what little hope I had of us being found quickly. Turning my back to the wall I covered my face with my hands and let my body succumb to the emotions I had been forcing myself to contain. My shoulders began to shake as I quietly sobbed.

'Mummy?'

Tom speaking startled me and, wiping my eyes, I moved towards him then wrapped him in my arms.

'Mummy, what's wrong?'

'Nothing, darling, how did you sleep?'

'I don't feel very well.'

'You've not had a lot of sleep, darling, that's all. Why don't

112

you have a drink and close your eyes again?'

'I want to go home.'

'I know you do, darling, I know. But remember, this is part of our story.'

'Is this now chapter three?'

'Yes, Tom. Here, have some water please.'

I handed Tom the bottle and he started to gulp it down. I told him to slow down, saying if he drank too much he might get a tummy ache but really, we had to be frugal. Tom saw the packet of Maltesers and asked if he could have one. I wanted him to have them all, and ice cream and chocolate and as much fizzy drink as he wanted. I wanted him to be bouncing off the walls on E numbers and begging me to take him to a park or fair. I wanted it all, because all of that meant he wouldn't be here.

'But you've not had any breakfast, Tom.'

'Please, Mummy. Just one?'

'Just one, darling.'

I watched him eat it like he would eat a sweet at home. Taking his time to enjoy the flavours. It didn't matter that we didn't know where we were. It didn't matter that he had slept on a damp bed with stained blankets in a cold room with barely any natural light.

Tom was so resilient, so strong, and in that moment I couldn't be more proud of him. A fresh tear came to my eye. He finished his sweet and smiled, chocolate on his teeth, and giggled.

'Can I have another?'

'Maybe, if you eat some bread first.'

'Just bread? Can I have some peanut butter?'

'Bread is all we have, baby. But eat it up and I'll let you have two more sweets, how does that sound?'

'Two more?'

'I know, Mummy is in a good mood.'

Tom tucked into the bread, barely chewing as he swallowed it down. It wasn't a great meal, but he wouldn't be hungry. He ate just over a slice when he asked for the Maltesers again. It left just under two slices of bread. In a few hours it would be completely stale, but would be enough to keep the baby fed and my nutrition levels up – just. I hoped they would bring more food before then.

Tom ate two sweets as agreed, and then took a third, thinking I hadn't noticed. It made me smile. Tom was still Tom – cheeky, fun, a boy who liked to push his luck. I needed him to stay like that for as long as possible. I had no doubt Sean and Daniel and the police were looking for us. But I couldn't afford to wait for them to come. The longer we were here, the more likely Tom would realize it wasn't a make-believe story we were involved in but something far worse. I had to plan an escape. I had to keep Tom's spirits up.

'Right my little angel, are you ready to start chapter three?'

'What's it called?'

As I told him the title I watched his face light up. Tom loved being competitive. 'This one is called "Let the Games Begin".'

Chapter 18

Daniel

Outside Denham

2nd January 2018, 10.17 a.m.

There was no denying it, I had been to Auvers, and the place was, for some reason, important. I read about the trip in Mum's scrapbook. We only stayed for one night, on the way south to Lyon, and Mum had written that my father had fallen in love with the place. He told her that Auvers would be the making of them, though she could never quite fathom why.

For a man so set in his English ways she had written it was nice that he was passionate about somewhere else. But, as far as I could tell, we had never gone back. Messaging Katie, I asked her to ring my mum and get her to call me on the new number. The wait felt like forever in which all I could do was look at that trip to France in June '99 and assess the damage to my face. I applied more glue to try and numb the pain in my tooth, though it did little to help – toothache wasn't like other kinds of pain. The phone buzzed in my hands, making me jump. I quickly lifted it to my ear.

'Mum?'

'Daniel, are you okay?'

'I'm fine. Has anyone been round yet?'

'No, not yet. Where are you?'

'I can't say.'

'Oh,' was all she said in reply.

'Mum, I don't have a lot of time. I'm going to ask you a few things. I need you to be honest with me, regardless of how it makes us both feel.' I heard her take a deep intake of breath.

'I'll try.'

'Don't try, Mum, do. Rachael and Thomas need this.' I could feel my anger begin to spread like a chip in a window exposed to heat, the slow crack working its way through me, making me want to shatter.

'Tell me about France, the trip we took together in 1999.' There was a pause while she thought back, recalling a memory that came to her so easily – something people take for granted.

'Well, it was our last.'

'Our last, why was it our last?'

'It wasn't long after that holiday that your father and I split up.'

'Why did you split up?'

She paused, collecting herself. I knew she still loved my father, I knew talking of it hurt. But I had to know.

'As I've said, your father was into all kinds of things. Things he often involved you in. I couldn't do it anymore.'

'That's not an answer, Mum,' I shouted, regretting it immediately. My stress spilling over on to a person who had only ever tried to protect me. She responded, saying my name defensively. I cut her off. I would apologize for it after this nightmare was over.

'In your scrapbooks, there is no other mention of Auvers? Why?'

'We only went there once. I'm guessing you haven't found him?'

116

'No, Mum, and his place has been empty for some time. I found a book about learning French, is it possible he's there? In Auvers?'

'I don't know. Maybe. He did always talk of retiring there.'

'Why there?'

'I don't know.'

'Isn't it odd that he wanted to retire in the place we had only visited once?'

'Yes.'

'Then why there?'

'He never said. I'm sorry, darling. Your dad was a secretive man.'

I couldn't stop myself thinking that they both were.

'I found another book at his. This one about memory loss. I think he left it for me. And the French book. I think he's trying to tell me where he is.'

'It's possible,' she said after a pause. For a moment neither of us spoke and I jumped as a car sped past my driver's door along the dual carriageway.

'Mum, when did we move to Stamford? When did we leave Slough?'

'When your dad and I split in 1999, I moved up then to be closer to your nan.'

'Just you?'

'Yes, I tried to get you to come but you wouldn't. You wanted to stay because of work and friends.'

'And you let me?'

'You gave me no choice,' she said defensively. My tone was accusing her of being a bad mother without actually saying it.

'And my friends? Why didn't they ever get in touch?'

'You were quite isolated before …'

'What does that mean, Mum?'

'You were like your father, you only kept company with a few people.'

'Why didn't those people get in touch?'

'Because ...' She paused again, struggling to find the words. 'Because, your father told everyone you knew that you had died.'

'What?'

'After your accident your father reappeared after years of being missing. He was panicked, scared. He didn't tell me why, but he said it would be best if everyone thought Michael had died.'

My hand shot to my face to stop myself screaming at her. Yet another lie told to me. Yet another thing I had to try to process in order to save my family. When I spoke, my words were hard, deep. 'And you listened to him?'

Her reply was quick. 'He looked at me like we didn't have a choice. I just wanted to keep you safe.'

This argument would have to wait for a better time. Right now, I needed to learn about what I was doing there in my teen years.

'So, before I was hurt, you left Dad and moved, and I stayed in Slough for another four years?'

She hesitated, catching her words before they came out.

'Mum. Tell me, I don't have time for secrets anymore. Did I stay in Slough or not?'

'I don't know.'

'What do you mean?'

'For a couple of years, we lost touch.'

'What? When?'

'You came to see me just after the millennium, then you were gone.'

'When did we see each other again?'

'When I got the phone call after you were hurt.'

I felt the world spinning again under my feet, the truth too hard to absorb. For years I had not been in contact with my mother at all. I could have been anywhere.

'Do you think I was with Dad?'

'No.'

'How can you be sure?'

'Because at the same time you vanished, he was …' She paused and I heard her stifle a cry. 'He was in jail. Daniel, I didn't mean for any of this.'

I couldn't speak. I could barely breathe. The bait ball of memories started swirling again. Again, I couldn't grab anything.

'You know that, right? You know I'd not do anything to hurt you? I never meant for any of this.'

She was crying into the phone. I didn't have the time or the want to try make her feel better. 'Have you called the police about the car yet?'

'No, I can't do it.'

'You have to, Mum.'

'But they'll know it's you.'

'But it will also tell them that you haven't spoken to me.'

'Daniel.'

'Please, Mum, for me.'

'Fine, I will. Be careful. I love you.'

I hung up the phone without saying goodbye. I couldn't say it, the words would have caught in the back of my throat and only escaped as a sob.

There was no escaping it now. I knew I needed to go to France, and fast. My father was probably there, and he would tell me what I needed to do to get Thomas and Rachael back. I didn't care what I had taken, I didn't care how hard it was to get back. All that mattered was that I did. Another list started to be drawn in my head. This was good. This meant I would detach myself emotionally, even for just a moment and get things moving.

The first two things on my list were obvious, and essential. I needed cash – that wouldn't be a problem, I had ideas on how to get some. I also needed a way to get to France. I didn't have time to make the drive up to Stamford, not when I was so close to London. I also knew I couldn't use my name. Opening up Safari I looked again at where Auvers was. It was about twenty miles north-west of Paris. It would be easy to get there. I then looked when trains ran from St Pancras to Paris. They were frequent enough, and didn't take a lot of time. I just needed to get there.

I needed a passport.

I dialled the number *he* had left me and waited. It rang three times, then he picked up.

'If you want this thing from me, I need you to do something to help.'

Chapter 19

Rachael

The Garage

2nd January 2018, 10.21 a.m.

Sat on the edge of the bed, I hugged myself. Despite it being daytime the temperature inside the room had barely lifted and the cold had crept into my bones. Tom sat opposite me wearing the driest of the blankets like a shroud over his head, his little face the only thing popping out. Smiling at him I pretended to hold a microphone and put on my very best gameshow voice. Standing I addressed the audience.

'Ladies and gentlemen, welcome to *Into the Dark*. A game show about how well you can move around any space without being able to see. This evening—'

'Mummy, it's morning,' Tom said, giggling.

I dropped my gameshow voice. 'I know, darling, it's make-believe.' I kissed him on the head and grabbed the microphone once more. 'This evening we have with us, young Tom. Tell us a little bit about yourself, Tom.'

I pretended to hold a microphone to his lips as he spoke.

'I'm Tom, I'm six and I, um … that's it,' he said with a giggle.

'He's full of mystery, ladies and gentlemen. Okay, so, Tom, are you happy with the rehearsals?'

'Yes.'

'Have you done your counting?'

'Yes!'

'And you remember your numbers?'

'Yes, Mummy!'

'Then let's play *Into the Dark*! Okay. For one Malteser, can you tell me how many steps there are between the bed and the door?'

'Fourteen. No sixteen.'

'Is it fourteen or sixteen?'

'Both, Mummy.'

'Because …'

'Because if I'm walking from the top of the bed it's fourteen and from the bottom it's two steps more.'

'Excellent.'

Tom jumped up and began to bounce on the bed in celebration and I handed him a sweet. He stopped himself, knowing he wasn't allowed to jump on beds at home. I told him to jump as much as he wanted, and he did, and he laughed, and I wanted to cry. He jumped into my arms and, wrapping the blanket around both of us, I lifted the microphone back to my face.

'Now for another. What happens when the door opens again?'

'I hide, pulling the blanket over me so I'm hidden …'

'But …'

'But leaving a little gap so I can see.'

'What are you looking to see?'

'If the lamp goes out!'

'This boy is on fire, ladies and gentlemen!'

'No I'm not, Mummy.'

I whispered. 'I mean you're doing really well, Tom.'

'Oh!'

'Ladies and gentlemen, give this boy a hand.'

I clapped and cheered Tom who seemed really pleased with

himself for getting the answer right, and then he ate his reward.

'For the final spectacular prize, a pizza of your choice when we go home, I have two questions. I need to have the correct answer for both for you to win.'

'I can have anything on it?'

'Anything you want.' I dropped my gameshow voice.

'Even ice cream?'

'Yes, darling, even ice cream.'

I saw Tom sit up straighter, his little tongue on the edge of his lips as he did when he was concentrating. Then I realized he did so, not out of fun for the game, but because he was getting hungry. I looked at the plate on the floor. Only a few crusts of the bread remained – no one had come and replenished our meagre offerings since we got here. My heart hurt. To hide my pain, I put the gameshow voice on once more.

'Wait, before I ask the final questions would you like more sweets for getting them all right so far?'

'Yes! Yes!'

I gave Tom three more sweets from the packet. Looking inside there were maybe half a dozen left. He thanked me and put all three in his mouth, sucking the chocolate off them. I wanted to tell him to slow down, like I did with the stale bread, like I did with the water, but I stopped myself. Little boys should be able to rush from time to time. I watched him wrestle the Maltesers in his mouth, trying to get every last bit of chocolate off them before crunching the middle, his jaw working hard to turn it all to mulch and swallow. Lost in the tastes on his tongue he sat motionless, looking at the space between the edge of his feet and my body. He looked tired. He looked cold. It almost hurt too much to bear. He should be at home, playing games, or on his trampoline, or in front of his favourite film. Not here.

Not here.

I felt a tear begin to escape from my eye, but before it could fully form and drop Tom looked at me and smiled, his teeth covered in chocolate, making it look like some were missing. It made me laugh and he laughed back. He looked pleased with himself for making his mummy smile.

'Right, Tom, final question. Are you ready?'

'Yes, Mummy.'

'You're under the bed, you're watching the lamp. Tell me what you do if it stays on, and if it goes off.'

'If it stays on, I put my fingers in my ears and stay hidden. If it goes off, I listen and wait for you to tell me to crawl out and run to the door.'

'How many steps?'

'Fourteen or sixteen.'

'Ladies and gentlemen, we have a winner! Never before in the history of *Into the Dark* has someone got all of the questions right.'

I started to clap and so did Tom as he jumped up and down on the bed again, shouting that he'd won. A chant that I joined in with, forgetting for a moment where we were, until I heard the bolt slide in the door. I saw fear shoot into Tom's face, and I felt mine getting hotter. Before I could tell him, Tom was already climbing under the bed, dragging the blanket with him. I helped get him under just as the door opened. Turning, I just caught a glimpse of Tom looking towards the lamp. His fingers in his ears. He was doing exactly as I had asked.

The Bear walked in accusingly, his eyes beady and hard. He looked around the room, focusing under the bed before meeting my eye. I had to look away.

'What is going on in here?' His voice was raised, it vibrated in my chest.

'I'm sorry, we were just playing.'

'Playing?'

'I'm trying to stop him from being afraid.' I turned back and fiercely locked eyes with him as I spoke. Trying to show a sense of strength, a bit of dignity.

124

There was a shift in The Bear, his shoulders dropped a little, the tension shifting, just for a moment.

'Well, just keep the noise down, okay?'

'Of course, I'm sorry.'

He looked back under the bed.

'He's hungry,' I said.

He looked at me and I held his eye. My strength doubled by having Tom's fundamental needs as my focus.

'He's hungry,' I said again, this time louder, more forceful. He looked away, towards the floor and his feet, before turning and leaving. He paused at the door, as if he was about to say something but didn't.

Its slamming echoed around us. I called Tom and slowly he climbed from under the bed.

'I hid Mummy, like you told me to.'

'I know you did, darling. You're such a good boy.'

I pulled Tom towards me and sat him on my lap, giving him a cuddle and wrapping the blanket back around us both. His hands were cold through my long-sleeved top. I took them both in mine, cupping around his fingers, and blew on them, hoping my warm breath would help. He flopped his head onto my shoulder and let me warm him. I closed my eyes and rocked gently and for a moment we weren't there.

'Mummy, are we still in the story?'

'Yes, darling.'

'What chapter is this?'

'Four.'

'What's it called?'

'What do you want it to be called?'

'Umm. Can we call it "Thinking About Home"?'

I kissed him on the head. 'That's a great title, darling.'

'Will we get to go home soon?'

I didn't want to lie to Tom. But I didn't want to tell him the truth either. So I told him what I hoped for.

'Yes, we will soon. Just a few more chapters.'

'How many more?'

'Just a few. Some of them might get even scarier than this one.'

'I think it's scary enough, Mummy.'

'I know, but the scarier it is, the better the ending will be. And we want the very best ending for this story, don't we?'

'What will happen at the end?'

'We will be out of here, and we will live happily ever after.'

'I like the sound of that.'

'Me too, darling, me too.'

Chapter 20

Daniel

Outside Denham

2nd January 2018, 10.23 a.m.

'If you want this thing from me, I need you to do something to help.'

'I'm listening,' he said, curiously. Clipped.

'I need a passport.'

'Thinking of running away again, Michael?' His voice dripped with mockery.

It shocked me that he knew I had vanished years ago, although I didn't know why. The man on the phone knew more about me than I did.

'No, I just need to go somewhere. I'm not running from this. I just want to get my family back. Can you help with it? A passport?'

'I know someone. But I'm curious, where are you going?'

'A place called Auvers. It's a small …'

'I know what Auvers is. I wondered if you might need to go there.'

The fact he had heard of the place, and wondered, was another clue to its importance. There was no denying it. France was everything.

'It will take some time. Keep the phone close and wait for further instructions.'

He hung up before I could say another word and, for a while, I stared at the blank screen, expecting something to happen. I wanted to be moving, doing something, but until he called or messaged there was nothing left for me to do except study the scrapbooks and wait for a hint of a memory.

Weariness came over me, my limbs felt weak and my stomach rumbled. If I was going to France soon I needed to try and rest. I needed to eat something, despite having no appetite. When I found my father and confronted him, I needed to have my wits about me, like Katie had said. Turning the phone onto loud I tested the ringtone and was happy that if I dozed, it would wake me.

Closing my eyes, I felt my exhausted body begin to shut down as I went into a fitful slumber.

Chapter 21

Daniel

Outside Denham

2nd January 2018, 11.32 a.m.

I woke with a start and grabbed the phone that rested on my lap, assuming it had rung, confused when the screen was still black. Looking to the car clock I saw that I had dozed for just over an hour. There was a tap on the window and, turning, I jumped at the sight of a police officer who was trying, and succeeding to wake me. I tried to hide the terror I was feeling. I smiled at him, but he didn't smile back. Looking in my rear-view mirror I saw a police car. Another officer was inside, talking into her shoulder. Probably running the plates. I prayed my father had a clean licence.

As I opened the window I was grateful that my split lip and broken tooth was on the left side of my face; it made it easier to hide.

'Hello.'

'Is everything all right, sir?' he asked, looking not at me but around me to see what else was in the car.

'Yes, fine thank you. Just resting for a moment.'

'You realize you are parked blocking an exit slip?' he said, gesturing behind the car.

'Sorry, a what?' I said wiping saliva off my lip and looking in my rear-view mirror to see a small piece of tarmac, which led onto the dual carriageway, that was designed for police cars to sit in.

'Oh God, I'm sorry, I'll move along.'

'Sir, is everything all right?' he asked again, this time with a hint of suspicion in his voice.'

'I've had a long night.'

'Have you been drinking?'

'No, no, nothing like that. I've had a poorly little one at home. You know how it is.'

'I see,' he said again, looking back to his partner. 'Sir, whose car is this?'

I felt my pulse race. I knew I couldn't lie, but if I told the truth and my father's details had a red flag of any kind I would be questioned.

'It's my father's. He lent it to me, so I could drive to Hillingdon Hospital. My partner's father is dying. I'm just resting before going to visit.'

I couldn't believe how easy it was to come up with something convincing in a split second.

'I'm sorry to hear that, sir.'

'Thank you, he's been unwell for quite some time.'

Just then the phone rang on my lap, making me jump. I looked at the screen. It was a withheld number. It was him, the voice. The police officer looked at it, curiously. I let it ring. I didn't want to answer, not with the police stood a matter of feet from me. He could sense my unease. I was sure of it.

'Maybe you should answer it, sir?'

'I'm sure they will ring back.'

'It may be the hospital.'

'Yes, of course.'

Hesitantly I pressed the answer button and held the phone up to my ear, knowing that I would somehow have to tell the voice that the police were here, so he didn't assume I had contacted them myself.

'Hello?'

'Have you got a pen and paper?'

I shot a look to the police officer who had stepped back to talk to his colleague.

'Hello, Katie, are you okay?'

'What?'

'Yes, yes I'm close by. Are you okay? How is he?'

'Michael, are you playing games?'

'I see, I can be there in about – hang on one moment. Excuse me, officer, do you think we will be much longer, sorry?' I said it loud enough for the voice to hear my question.

'You're with the police? What did I tell you, Michael?'

'We'll be done shortly, sir.'

'Thank you,' I said before speaking to the voice once more.

'I think I'll be on my way shortly, darling.'

'What are you doing with them?'

'No, it's nothing to worry about, honey. I was waiting for you to call to tell me when I could visit and I fell asleep. They are just making sure I'm all right.'

'Get rid of them, before they suspect something.'

'I will, I will. Yes, they are very good at what they do. How is he?'

'He's getting increasingly agitated.'

'Okay, darling, well, I'll be quick, I promise. Just hang on.'

I turned my attention back to the officer who looked calmer.

'Is everything okay?' he asked, this time with a little more sympathy.

'I really need to get to the hospital.'

'Are you okay to drive?'

'Yes, I'm fine. Thank you.' I covered the mouthpiece and spoke

131

in a lower tone. 'It's been a long time coming. Still not easy though, is it?'

'No, no it's not. Okay, sir, all checks out. I'm sorry for your circumstances.'

'Thank you, officer. Thank you for checking up on me.'

'Take care.'

The police officer walked back to his car, joined his colleague and drove away, the passenger offering a small wave before they merged on to the road and vanished. I exhaled loudly and let my head slump onto the steering wheel. Once they were out of sight, I lifted the phone to my ear.

'They're gone.'

'What were you doing talking to them?'

'I promise you, I fell sleep. They were just checking on me. They're gone.'

'Were they suspicious?'

'No, no, not at all.'

'Get a pen.'

I did as I was told and, with my hand shaking, I wrote down the address I needed to go to in Katie's notebook. It was a place in central London. There were a lot of cameras in central London. That made me nervous. But a lot of people too. If I was careful, switched on, I could use that to my advantage.

'He is expecting you at 4 p.m. No earlier, no later. Do you understand?'

'Yes.'

'Letting the police talk to you, Michael. I am disappointed.'

'There is one more thing.'

'What?'

'I need cash. I don't think I have enough.'

'You were pretty light-fingered once. I'm sure you'll find a way to get some.'

Chapter 22

Daniel

London

2nd January 2018, 3.58 p.m.

With the address given to me by the man staring at me from the open notebook on the passenger seat, I drove to Uxbridge station, parked the car nearby, grabbed my books, and entered the station, buying a day travel card before hopping on the Metropolitan line that would take me into central London. It was a slow process and with nothing else to do, I looked out of the window and watched the world rush by. At Ruislip station a mother and child boarded and sat opposite me. I turned my head to make sure they couldn't see my swollen jaw and messy cut. I didn't want to attract any more attention to myself than I already had.

I watched them through the glass, the little boy climbing all over his mother and pressing his face to the window. She sat on her phone – ignoring him – and he looked at me. He smiled, and I smiled back, ensuring my broken tooth and damaged face were still turned away. I didn't want to scare him. I raised my eyebrows a few times quickly and his smile widened. He poked out his tongue, the smile turning into a giggle and I covered my mouth, feigning shock. Lowering my hand, I poked my tongue out and he squealed in delight. I could see the young mischievous glint that only the young owned.

His joyful squeak lifted the mother from her phone. She was about to tell him off but saw that he was looking at me. I felt obligated to offer an apology and after doing so quietly, looked away, wanting to, but not daring to, look at the young boy I had just had a fun exchange with. I wanted to tell the mum to ditch the phone, give her little one the time and energy he deserved. I wanted to remind her how lucky she was. But I felt like a hypocrite. I knew I hadn't given Thomas the attention he deserved. I hadn't known how lucky I was to have him in my life.

I had taken him and the title 'Father', for granted.

I would never do it again.

The mother and the boy stood and moved further down the carriage, away from me and, embarrassed, I watched the world rush past out of the window, trying to process what I knew, and see if I could connect anything.

Smoke and rope and explosions. France. A time where I had vanished from my mother. My accident. My obvious link to a criminal world. It gave me a headache but stopped me thinking of Rachael. How I had failed her, first as a partner, then as a friend. It stopped my heart aching with the sound of Thomas's voice playing on a loop. I heard him in the pitch of the door opening. I saw him in the faces of other people. The phone was in my hand on my lap, but it wasn't a phone at all, it was the weight of his little hand in mine. For a moment, I let myself believe it until a tear escaped. I snapped away from the thought before I drew attention to myself.

Once outside the entrance to Euston underground station I typed the address given to me into maps and saw that I had to double back on myself, and wait amongst the hordes of people to cross the road. I hated asking him for help, the man who had taken my family, who had killed Sean and taken Rachael. The man who had drugged my little boy. I wanted to hurt him. I wanted to hurt him badly. But without his help I was never going to discover what it was I took and get it back to him.

The green man appeared, and we moved. Dozens of strangers together, striding in unison. I kept my head low. I was still waiting for them to find Sean and begin hunting for me. Turning left past a Pret, I headed for some gardens that were surrounded by Georgian hotels. A public tennis court in the middle. I could hear the frost on the ground that was still in shade crunch under my feet. Through the gardens I crossed the road and after a few minutes, I found the address. Descending a steep, narrow set of stairs I reached the door and knocked quietly.

'Who is it?' a gravelly London accent asked through it.

'It's, um ... Michael.'

I heard movement on the other side, and then a bolt slid open. The door creaked and then I was face to face with a heavyset man with narrow, bird-like eyes. He looked me up and down. I felt like I knew his face somehow. But not well enough to stop him in the street if I walked past. There was something about the context of this situation that was the link. I almost asked if we knew each other, but with what he did to me next, it meant I didn't need to. He stepped and offered a small hug.

'You look older, but then I guess I do too.'

'It catches up with all of us,' I replied, unsure of what he knew about me or the situation I was in.

'What happened to your face?'

'I fell.'

'You look a fucking mess.' He sighed. 'Makes my job harder. Come on.'

He turned his back and walked into the basement flat, leaving the door open behind him. I saw it as my invitation so stepped inside and closed it after me.

'Lock it behind you,' he shouted back, and I did as I was told. Following him, I walked through the corridor, past two rooms I assumed were bedrooms but looking inside I could see that they were stacked high with boxes. I passed a bathroom and then at the end of the corridor I stepped into a kitchen area that was deceptively big. It led into a courtyard garden that held expensive furniture and an outside pizza oven. It looked more like a bar courtyard than someone's private garden. We didn't go outside, but through another door in the kitchen to a darker room. There was another man there, watching me. His eyes were cold and hard. I looked at him, not wanting to be the one to look away. I wanted to hold my ground.

'This is my associate,' said the fat man. 'Wait here.'

The fat man left the room and it felt as if the temperature dropped. I nodded to the associate in an attempt to break the tension, but he just kept staring, weighing me up, assessing me. It was clear to me he didn't know who I was. After a few moments of uncomfortable silence, the fat man returned with a passport in his hand. He threw it at me and I caught it. Opening it up I saw a picture of me from a few years ago. A brand-new name was underneath. Peter Morales.

'Passport's got three years left on it. He's even been to Mexico and Egypt on it too. I took the photo from your DVLA records.' He took it back from me, threw it to his assessing friend who caught it and dumped it on the coffee table beside him. I didn't know what to say. I was astonished. He could access my DVLA records, create a brand-new passport. What the hell was I mixed up in? It looked real. But, as I looked at it on the coffee table, I felt myself panic. Soon my face would be on the news, I was sure of it. The name was different, but someone might recognize me. I didn't want to take any chances. He could see my anxiety.

'What's wrong? I assure you Customs won't touch you with this.'

'I'm not sure I should look like me at the moment.'

'Oh, I see,' he said, smiling to his associate. 'Been a naughty boy, have we?'

'Something like that.'

'Old habits die hard, don't they mate?'

'I guess,' I said, questioning again what the habits were that people knew me by.

'And you need to look like an entirely different man?'

'If possible.'

'Luckily for you I'm bloody good at this sort of thing. 'Course, it will cost more.'

'I don't have much money.'

'It's okay, I'll take it up with your boss.'

I wanted to say I didn't work for him, but thought it would keep me safer if I played along. There was something about these people that told me not to mess around with them.

'Right then,' he said clapping his hands. 'Come in here. Let's get you looking presentable, shall we?'

I followed him to another room. It had a camera on a tripod in the corner and a white cloth hung behind it. Opposite sat a chair similar to a dentist's chair and hanging from the ceiling, a bright LED light. To the left of it was a red metal toolbox, about four feet tall. He waddled over to it instructing me to sit in the chair. He lowered the back rest until I was practically lying flat and looked closely at my lip, pulling it away from the gum. White heat shot through my face, making me moan despite trying not to.

'Nothing I can do about that tooth, it's well fucked, but I can patch this up. Make-up won't cover the bruising very well, certainly not the swelling.'

He let go of my face and turned his back to me, rifling through the toolbox drawers.

'Will it cause any problems?' I asked.

'Christ, Michael, will it cause any problems?! What kind of question is that? Of course it will. You look like a thug. Customs love thugs.'

'What do you suggest?'

137

He looked closely at the cut on my lip, making small affirming noises to himself for a moment. He didn't avert his gaze from the lower part of my face. I could almost see him creating, using my skull as his canvas.

'I'm going to put a beard on you. It will look real enough, and should help disguise the wound. Just don't smile at anyone,' he said laughing, finding himself funny. 'We'll do your hair too, give you some contacts.'

'Will it take long?'

'It will take as long as it takes. You can't rush art, mate. Besides, what's the hurry?'

Chapter 23

Daniel

London

2nd January 2018, 5.31 p.m.

I had sat in the chair for what felt like an eternity as the fat man worked painstakingly over me. He had started by applying hair dye and brushing it in roughly, the smell making the back of my nostrils itch. My light brown hair was now almost black. After the dye, he cut it shorter using hair clippers, leaving only about an inch on my head. The beard had been glued making my face sweat and finally he added dark contacts. I was allowed to stand and when I did he put a mirror in front of my face. I didn't recognize me at all. My typically English look was entirely gone, replaced with one that was Mediterranean, possibly as far east as Turkey or even Syria.

'What do you think?' he asked. All I could do was nod as I opened my mouth a few times and raised my eyebrows just to make sure it was my reflection I was seeing.

'I know, I'm a fucking genius, right? Come on, over here.'

He ushered me towards the camera on the opposite side of the wall and told me to stand against the white sheet. I looked

139

into the camera and he took a series of pictures. After he had taken three, his associate who, now he was stood up, was a lot bigger than I had first thought, wandered into the room and whispered something in the fat man's ear. I watched as he looked towards the ceiling, concentrating on what was said. Then he looked back at me, his aloof nature gone.

'Well, you have been a naughty boy, haven't you?' he said, smiling but with malice.

'What do you mean?'

'Seems like your little predicament is on the news.'

He chuckled as I moved past him and into the room where a TV played. On the screen was a report coming from the east coast as it prepared for Storm Fionn to batter it with high tides and winds of up to 100 miles an hour. They feared that on Thursday and Friday there would be another surge like the one from a few years back that flooded entire towns. I couldn't hear the reporter talking but I guessed what he would be saying. Overnight disturbances, businesses ruined. There was nothing to suggest a body had been discovered. At the bottom of the screen texts scrolled with other news stories coming in. A footballer was in trouble for drink-driving. Nurses were going on strike over pay conditions, and then I saw it. My heart leapt into my throat. It was only a few words, ones I knew were coming. But it changed everything.

Man found murdered in Stamford, Lincolnshire. Wife and child missing.

The fat man and his tall accomplice stepped into the room. He was no longer chuckling. I didn't get it, there was no mention of my name. Nothing that connected me to the crime yet.

'How do you know I'm involved in this?'

'Whenever I get a rush job I like to find out a few things about who is coming into my house. I knew who you were, what twenty years ago?' He took on a slower tone, knowing. 'But people change, don't they? I got your name – your new one, Daniel Lynch – and from there your records came easy. It's not every day I get someone from Stamford in Lincolnshire knocking on my door, a man who had already changed his identity once, needing to change it again. It's also not every day someone is murdered in the same town. What are the chances?'

'I didn't kill him.'

'Ahh, I don't really care, mate. All that matters is that they want to talk to you. If they find you here, I'm fucked. Time for you to fuck off.'

'What about my passport?'

'Once it's done, we'll call you. Write your number down and get out.'

'How long will that be?'

'A few hours.'

'But I don't have anywhere to go.' I could feel myself start to panic. 'Can't I just stay here until it's ready?' I asked, hoping he would agree. I didn't want to be outside, wandering around London, even with my new look.

'Not a chance in hell. If you get nicked I don't want them coming to my door. No, you leave your number, he'll call you later,' he said, gesturing to the tall man who was looking down at me like he wanted to hurt me.

'Please.'

'Mate, I suggest you go before he gets really pissed off. He don't like men who hurt women and kids.'

'I told you, I haven't done anything.'

'Yeah, well, don't look that way, does it? Go on, leave your number here and get out.'

'Please, I don't want to go until I have that passport in my hands. Without it ...'

I didn't finish my sentence. I didn't want them knowing what I was intending to do and why. If the police did find this place,

141

I knew they would talk and then France would be impossible.

'Come on, mate, don't make a scene.'

The tall man stepped towards me. He took me by the arm and guided me towards the door, his huge hand gripping my upper arm so tight pins and needles shot into my hand. He stopped me near a table with a pad and pen and I quickly opened the iPhone settings and found the number, writing it as neatly as I could so none of the digits could be misread. As we reached the door, he spoke for the first time, his accent from somewhere in Eastern Europe.

'If it were up to me, you'd be dead right now.'

I knew he meant every word.

Opening the door, he pushed me outside and closed it behind him. My fate was entirely in the hands of two men who now thought I'd murdered my ex and my child. I hoped their need for a pay cheque outweighed their morality.

Out on the street I headed towards King's Cross. It was busy. I could hide in plain sight and wait for the call. I kept my head low, the fake beard itching my face. I passed a car and caught my reflection. The man looking back really wasn't Daniel Lynch. Seeing the new me made me feel slightly more confident.

As I walked, I focused on my body, the way I swung my arms when I stepped and my steps themselves. I slowed myself down, stiffening my shoulders a little which made my hips move a little less. I shortened my stride and kept my arms close to my sides. It felt unnatural to walk this way, but it was less like me. More like Peter Morales. I felt sure that I could walk past someone I knew and not be recognized. Or so I hoped.

As I crossed the road near the St Pancras hotel which sat beside King's Cross, the footpaths became flooded with people walking in either direction. I scuttled past mothers with babies in buggies and people who had stopped to photograph the giant hotel near the station. In the distance I could hear sirens. Being London, there was nothing new about that but I listened as they came closer, and pressing myself against the wall, I pretended to text as I watched them fly by. Once gone I continued to walk and then turned into the station. Finding a Pret I ordered a large black coffee, playing with the vowel sounds in each word to change my voice and give me a London accent.

Sitting at a table which allowed me to press my back into a wall, I watched the world go by. People moved quickly, but most looked exhausted from a long day at work. They had no idea how lucky they were.

I checked my watch. It had only been forty minutes since I left the house. I needed to do something to help keep my sanity as I waited. I needed to put my plan into action, to get moving and find my family. Going online I looked at ticket prices for Paris. They were all averaging around £200. I counted my cash. £86.20. I was short, by a lot.

As I looked around at the unassuming people going about their days, it angered me that they were oblivious to the turmoil in which I found myself. Their only concerns were train times or rushing for the underground. I remembered what *he* told me on the phone – I was light-fingered once, and, according to the fat man who was making my passport, it was a habit that had gained me a reputation. I thought of all the magic tricks I had shown Thomas, that I had so easily learnt, and I knew that he was right. Sometime in my hidden but slowly unravelling past, sometime before the accident, I had been a criminal. I could sense it in the way I was scouting everyone out, my eyes following their every movement, so naturally observing their valuables, where they kept their wallets, what pocket a phone was in, a Rolex watch or designer suit. I was once a thief. And I was going to need to become one again.

Looking back at the crowds, I searched out prime targets. Ideally male, middle-aged, smartly dressed, drunk from post-work drinks. There were enough people around that fitted the description. But it was about finding the right one. After a few minutes my eyes rested on my target. His head was down, focused on his phone, texting. An expensive-looking watch sat on his wrist, his suit perfectly cut. He was my man, I could feel it. My eyes drifted to his back pocket. The unmistakable shape of a wallet sat there. No doubt full of cards, debit and credit. My instincts told me so, they also told me he was my mark. A part of me also targeted him because when he realized he had been lifted it would be an inconvenience, but that would be it. He looked like a man with more than enough money and resources. It might ruin his day, but that would be where it ended. Tomorrow, he would be the same as today. Perhaps he'd even assume he lost his wallet rather than knowing he had been robbed. Finishing my coffee, I stood and followed him towards the underground. I would stay close and when the moment was right, I would take his wallet. I didn't know how I would do this. I tried not to think about the details. Trust my body to move accordingly. Use my muscle memory.

I kept him a few paces in front of me as he tapped the back of his phone onto the Oyster reader and passed through the turnstile. It took me three attempts to get my conventional ticket to open the same barrier. I had to walk quickly to catch him up as he headed for the Piccadilly line. On the platform I managed to stand directly behind him in the crowds of people trying to get on to the already packed Tube. There was a press as those getting off the train collided with us getting on. I tried to grab it, but just as I was within touching distance a woman knocked into my arm.

The man stepped onto the carriage and I followed, reluctantly. I didn't want to be on the underground too long in case I missed the call and my chances. I hoped the fat man's timescale of being a few hours was accurate. In the surge of bodies, I was separated from him. Only by the width of two people, but it may as well have been a mile. At the next station, Russell Square, a few people got off and more squeezed on. In the chaos I managed to slide past one of the people blocking me, so I was closer to the man who had now put in some headphones and was looking into nothing.

At Holborn, there was more movement of people and I managed to stand myself next to him, my face almost touching his closed fist as he held on. I held the bar above my head with my right arm, my left by my side, close to his pocket. I had to wait; if I lifted it as we were stationary he'd feel. I needed to wait for the next stop and a distraction. At the sound of the automated voice announcing our imminent arrival into Covent Garden, I knew my chance was coming.

As the train pulled in I could see dozens of people waiting. The train stopped, and the doors opened. With my right hand I let go of the bar above my head and placed it on the bar near my face, intentionally touching him. With his attention focused on our touching hands he didn't notice me lift his wallet with my other. I mumbled an apology and stepped off the train, losing myself in the crowds.

The Tube continued and out of the corner of my eye I looked back. He was completely oblivious to what just happened. I needed to book a ticket and quickly, before he realized and cancelled his cards.

Leaving the station, I headed for Covent Garden Market and found a bench near the Opera House. I opened his wallet, pleased my gut was right. A debit card for Barclays as well as two credit cards. All three contactless. Taking out one of the credit cards I went on to the Eurostar website and looked at train times. Then I checked my watch. It was nearly half past six. There was one at 7.01 p.m. and 8.01 p.m. I wanted to be out of London and on my way to France tonight. But it didn't look like that was going to happen. The next option was tomorrow morning. The first one being at 5.40 a.m. I had a choice. Did I wait and hope I'd get the call and be able to get on the 8 p.m., or did I book tomorrow morning? I knew I had to make the decision soon, before the man discovered he had been robbed.

I hated doing it as it meant I was delaying the journey to France, delaying finding my father to get answers, and delaying the moment when Rachael and Thomas were back in my arms and safe but, not knowing exactly when I would get my new passport left me no choice. I booked the train leaving London at 5.40 a.m., returning the same day at 8 p.m. French time. Whatever was in France, I needed to find it in a day. I daren't let myself be in a different country to Rachael and Thomas any longer, and if I did need to stay, I would get a new ticket home in a similar manner. Using the card that belonged to my victim, a Mr N. Chatsworth, I paid the £338 for a day-return ticket and started to make my way back to the underground and King's Cross to collect it from a machine. The fact I had to delay until tomorrow made me feel like I was failing all over again.

146

Chapter 24

Rachael

The Garage

2nd January 2018, 9.04 p.m.

I didn't want a pink nursery if it was a girl and blue if it was a boy. I wanted something more neutral, a light green perhaps. Fluffy animals or dinosaurs on the walls. He or she would have the same mobile and cot that Tom had when he was a baby and we would fill the room with teddies. New and old. I wanted the walls to be covered in photos too. Photos of Sean and I, and Tom, so the new baby could always see us and know we were all looking out for them. I would even make sure a photo of Daniel and Katie was there too. I couldn't wait, thinking about it almost made me feel warmer, almost. Leaning away from my daydream I watched Tom's little chest rise and fall under the stained blankets. I tried to match my breathing to his, but I noticed Tom's breathing begin to quicken. Sitting up I stroked his back, hoping it would calm him but it didn't. His breathing continued to race. He started to mumble in his sleep. He was having a bad dream.

'It's okay, Tom. Shhh, it's okay, darling.'

Normally my comforting touch and words would settle him,

but this time they didn't. He continued to mumble, and he tossed and turned and then cried out, his scream making my soul ache. Waking, he sat up, tears streaming down his face.

'Mummy, Mummy, The Bear's going to get me.'

I sat up on the bed and wrapped him in my arms as he climbed onto my lap, his legs folded under him and his body curled up against my chest. His ear was on my sternum, listening to my heart.

'Shhhh, it's okay, darling. It was just a dream. It was just a dream.'

I rocked Tom and continued to speak at barely a whisper until his breathing became slow and calm again. After a while my leg started to go to sleep where he was sitting on it, but I didn't care. I wasn't going to move all night. I would sit like this, rocking my baby until daylight came and he was ready to be awake again. I would stay up all night to make sure he slept. Resting my cheek on the top of his head, I continued to rock, taking in his smell. I wouldn't sleep, but feeling his little body curled up on mine and drinking in his smell, I didn't need to. Closing my eyes, I pretended we were at home and I was holding him as Sean was holding me. I hoped he could sense we were okay. I hoped he wasn't losing his mind or blaming himself for us being taken.

I heard footsteps coming towards us from inside the building somewhere, getting louder with each step. Then I heard keys rattle. Instinctively I wanted to put Tom under the bed, but I didn't want him to wake so instead I pulled the blanket higher so only the top of his head was exposed.

The lock snapped, the bolt slid and, creaking on its hinges, the door opened. In its frame stood The Bear. Before he could speak I raised my finger to my lips. He saw Tom sleeping and spoke at a low whisper.

'What's going on?'

'He had a bad dream.'

I watched as he reacted. His powerful frame somehow weakened. His shoulders less rigid.

'I see.'

He came into the room quietly, his hands raised to show he meant no harm. Crouching down he picked up the food tray and started to leave.

'Do you have children?' I couldn't believe the words had come out of my mouth. Neither could he. He looked at me and after a moment he spoke.

'One.'

'Boy or a girl?'

'Girl.'

'What's her name?'

'Sophie.'

'That's a pretty name.'

He paused, struggling to say his words. 'She's a pretty girl.'

I saw pain in his eyes. I wanted to keep him talking, I wanted to befriend him, to make an ally of the man who held us captive, so I could use it to our advantage.

'Do you see her often?'

He didn't respond but looked at Tom who lay fast asleep curled around me. I saw half a sad smile on his face.

'It's never too late to be more involved.'

He looked at me, his eyes showing a fragility that was so raw it hurt to look at him.

'For me it is.'

He turned and began to walk away. I wasn't ready for this conversation to end.

'What would you do if she was in the situation you've put us in? What if she had been drugged and was cold? What if she was hungry and scared right now?'

'I'd move hell and earth to get her free.'

'Then let us go.

'I can't.'

'Why not?'

'I heard you talking, about the story, about The Bear. If you

149

need me to be a part, I'll do it. I'll keep the story alive. I'll say what you want me to say, do what you want me to do. But I can't let you go.'

I didn't respond but turned my attention back to my little boy who luckily hadn't stirred. I started to rock and closed my eyes.

The Bear backed out and closed the door as slowly and as quietly as it would allow. Just before it sealed he told me he was sorry. And I believed him.

Chapter 25

Daniel

London

2nd January 2018, 10.48 p.m.

It had been over five hours since I left the fat man's house and I still hadn't heard anything. In that time I had collected my ticket to Paris, my heart racing as I did, expecting the card to be swallowed. Luckily it wasn't.

With time to kill I spent the hours working on who Peter Morales was. I had to become him. He was going to Paris either on business or pleasure. Business, I decided. That meant I needed some new clothes, something smart. Black trousers and a jacket, a new coat and shoes as well. I walked to the Brunswick Centre, about ten minutes away from King's Cross.

I trailed the sale rails of various shops, paying with contactless, ensuring none of my purchases came to more than the limit. I knew that I needed to get a bag. No one travelled on the Eurostar without one, so I picked one up as well as a diary which I wrote my new name in. I also filled it with appointments throughout the year. Peter needed to be busy and he also needed a phone charger.

151

My battery was down to 38 per cent so in another shop I found a cheap coat and a travel charger, making sure the price came to £27. Stuffing the new clothes inside the bag I walked back to King's Cross and bought 30 euros with the cash I had in my pocket, before settling back in the same Pret with another coffee. Slowly my plan was coming together, and I was taking on my new identity. I told myself it could work, and a small seed of hope germinated.

I knew I should eat something, but I had no appetite. I bought a tuna baguette and knew at some point in the night I needed to force it down me. Once I paid for the coffee and food I threw the bank cards and wallet I had stolen in a bin. They would be cancelled soon, and I didn't want to be tempted to try to use them one more time.

From stealing the cards to purchasing everything I needed, only two hours had passed. So I sat for three more hours in King's Cross, waiting.

Just as I started to panic, thinking they were not going to honour the agreement, my phone rang.

'Hello?'

'Where are you?'

'King's Cross.'

'Good. In fifteen minutes go outside heading towards the British Library. There is a newspaper stand opposite the underground. Go over, buy a newspaper.'

The line went dead and I waited. Fifteen minutes later I stood and walked out of the station towards the stand in question. As I got closer, the man behind the till locked eyes with mine. He knew who I was. I picked up *The Guardian* and handed it over to him. He ducked down for a second and then handed it back. He placed the paper's fold in my hand and in it I could feel something harder than pages. I paid him and walked away. Nothing was said. Putting the paper in my bag I walked towards St Pancras and a toilet.

Once inside a locked cubicle I opened my bag and pulled out the passport. Turning to the back page I looked at the photo of me as Peter Morales. The date of birth was the same except for the year. I was now just forty rather than forty-one. The fat man was right, he was good. If I didn't know already, I'd have no idea it was a fake. Putting the passport in my front pocket I flushed the chain and left, washing my hands in case anyone saw me coming in. Throwing the bag over my shoulder I stepped back into the cold night and headed north of the station, towards the canal. The paths being dimly lit would mean I could hide in plain sight. With a lack of cash, and the cards soon to be flagged as stolen, I knew that sleeping rough was the only way to get some rest tonight. It would be a long, cold night, but it felt safer than hanging around the station, waiting for someone to notice me.

Laying with my left cheek on the frozen ground, the bag strapped on under my coat, I watched the station fall silent in the distance. It was too cold to sleep. So instead, I lay trying not to think until the world became quiet waiting for 4.30 a.m. to arrive. Then I would get up and get ready.

Through chattering teeth and muscles that were so cold they made my lungs rattle in my ribcage I tried to picture the man I once was. Had I experienced something like this before, sleeping rough, hiding from everyone? And would the old version of me be managing this situation better than I was now? Then, leaking forwards from a part of my mind that I wasn't strong enough to stop, Rachael and Thomas came forward. Their image broke my heart and a tear ran from the corner of my eye onto the concrete beneath me. I hoped they were resting. I hoped they were warm. Pulling the phone from my pocket I rang her number and listened to their voices. I must have done so fifty times before I needed to stop to save my battery until I could charge it on the train. The night was one of the longest and loneliest of my life.

WEDNESDAY

Chapter 26

Daniel

London

3rd January 2018, 4.36 a.m.

London fell silent. If only for a moment. The trains had stopped and there was a brief interlude of nothingness before the early morning workers came out in their dribs and drabs. It may have only been for around sixty minutes, but the silence, the total darkness, was somehow comforting. I had assumed all of my life, the life I could remember, that hope was synonymous with light. But those sixty minutes made me see that I had been wrong. It was in the darkness that hope lived, because only in the dark could you see where the light was coming from.

And I was in the dark. I was in the dark as to who Michael was, I was in the dark as to what the crime he'd committed was. I was in the dark as to what I had taken and where it was now. But the darkness was no longer as doomed. My passport sat in my pocket and I was soon going to board a train to find my father. He would tell me what I had taken and where I could find it.

I knew that *he*, the voice on the other end of the phone, needed what I took. He needed it desperately otherwise he wouldn't have

157

gone to such lengths to ensure that I retrieved it. He wouldn't hurt my family, not until he knew for certain that I couldn't get what he wanted. The realization gave me a sort of power. Not over the situation, but how I approached it. I convinced myself they were safe and well. They had to be. Or what motivation would I have?

Looking at my watch I knew I needed to get up and start my journey to France and the nerves started to build. The passport I had been handed looked authentic enough, but I wouldn't know how authentic it was until I tried to use it. If it didn't fool Passport Control, I would be arrested, and my fragile, unfinished plan would collapse like a house of cards. In order to attempt to pass through unnoticed I needed to make myself look, not like a homeless man, but like Peter Morales.

Rising to my feet, the easy task was much harder than it ought to have been due to the cold that had seeped into my bones. I walked through St Pancras and headed to the bathrooms. There were no showers, so stripping down I washed myself in the sink. The barely tepid water made the goose bumps that were already on my body stand up violently. I washed myself quickly, and using my father's top, I dried myself before putting on the new clothes from the bag. Fully dressed, I looked in the mirror. Above my right eye a light-yellow bruise rested where I had hit myself in the moments after this nightmare began. My jaw and lip were still swollen, but the beard covered it well enough for it to go unnoticed if I did my part by not presenting it. I wet my hands and ran them through my short hair to flatten it. I was ready.

Dumping my father's clothes in the bin I headed out of the bathroom, bought myself some deodorant with the cash I had, and grabbed a coffee. Despite being dressed in warm clothes, my core temperature was still very low from my night on the street. I didn't know how people survived being outside night after night. Sipping the hot drink, I felt my insides warm and I looked at my watch. It was just after five. It was time. Taking a deep breath, I started walking towards Passport Control.

Chapter 27

Rachael

The Garage

3rd January 2018, 6.21 a.m.

I couldn't remember the last time Tom sat on my lap, cuddling into me, sound asleep like this. For a moment, I forgot where we were. It was just me and my baby like in the days after he was born and Daniel had to return to work. The silence inside, birdsong out. The quiet contemplation and thoughts of the future. I hadn't realized I missed them. I remembered how Daniel hated having to go back to work, the sad resignation on his face as he would put on his shoes and grab his car keys as I held Tom asleep in my arms. He would try to smile, to appear happy as he walked out of the door, but I could see the sadness in his eyes. He said to me that he was going to put his head down, get the job done so he could get home as fast as possible. Tom was only a few weeks old, and already I knew Daniel was the right kind of man to be a dad.

I hadn't thought of Daniel like that for a long time. Perhaps it was because I knew he was looking for us, him and Sean working together. Sean was resourceful, hardworking. My fantastic and dedicated husband. I knew he would blame himself for not stopping them when they came into our house. But it wouldn't slow him because Daniel would be looking with him and Daniel had something primal deep inside, an animal instinct. He knew when things were about to get dangerous. He knew how to avoid confrontation.

I remember once, before Tom, we were on holiday in Madrid and there was a local derby football match. It got rough and violence spilled onto the streets. People were throwing bottles and chairs, anything they could get their hands on, and our restaurant, where we had been enjoying a romantic meal, was right in the middle. Daniel whisked me up and we fought our way through the crowds. As we did he didn't let go of my hand, and somehow he knew how to get us out. In the chaos people were swinging their arms and things kept flying over our heads. One man ran at us, assuming we were opposition fans and Daniel managed to side step him, trip him and send him falling into others. Somehow, he managed to do this on three occasions, either by tripping, dodging or pulling another fan into the firing line until we were free from the epicentre of the violence. When he needed it, Daniel had something in him that would respond and do whatever it took. That night he pulled me from the crowd without the need for violence, just using his wits to protect me. Then Tom came into the world and I saw that instinct sharpen. I knew he would do whatever he needed to do to find us.

The lock snapped, the bolt slid and I was so lost in thought, I didn't react fast enough. Once I realized he was coming in I lifted Tom off my lap waking him as I did. Before he could hide under the bed The Bear was in the room. Tom saw him and yelped as he scurried under with no blanket to protect him.

The Bear looked at me. In his hands was another plate, this time with a box of Rice Krispies from a multipack, and an apple.

'I couldn't get any milk,' he said. 'Will he eat them dry?'

I nodded, unsure how to respond.

'Good.'

Putting the plate down on the floor he looked under the bed at Tom and sighed before standing and looking at me again.

'Are you warm enough?'

'No.'

'I might be able to get you another blanket, would that help?'

'A little.'

The Bear took off his coat and then removed the cable-knit jumper that was underneath. My first thought was that he was going to undress. But he put his coat back on and handed the jumper to me.

'Here, put this on him. It will pretty much cover him entirely.'

'Thank you.'

'Don't ...'

He turned to leave and as he got to the door he stopped, his back to me, looking over his shoulder not to make eye contact, but to ensure he was heard.

'He doesn't need to hide. I don't want to hurt either of you.'

'It's part of our story.' I look at him, unblinking, unmoving. I want him to know what this is doing to us. What I need to do to make sure my son is safe.

'I see.'

'He asked me how many chapters it was going to be.'

Without turning, without being able to look at me he said five words which filled me with hope.

'Hopefully only a few more.'

Then he was gone and silence returned to the room. I called quietly for Tom to come out, but he didn't respond. I looked under the bed and he was so pale, his eyes were wide with fear. I said again that it was safe, but he just shook his head at me. Crawling under the bed, my back scraping on the cold dusty ground, I lay beside him. It was then that I smelt something and knew why he didn't want to come out.

'Oh, Tom, darling, it's okay.'

He burst into tears and, twisting my body, I fed my arm under his head and nestled him against my breast. His little sobs caused his whole body to shake. I started to shush him, like I did when he fell and grazed his knee but stopped myself. Whether he believed we were in a story or not, he was allowed to be frightened. If I didn't have him with me, I would have sobbed uncontrollably too. So I just held him and let him cry. He pulled on my pyjama top and dragged himself closer. Then he turned so he was in the foetal position his back to me, like he was inside my womb once more. After a few minutes he had all but cried himself out and his breathing had calmed again.

'I'm sorry, Mummy.'

I turned him over and he rested his forehead on mine. I stroked his hair, then wiped the tears and snot off his face with my hand. 'Tom, darling, you have nothing to be sorry for. Shall we get you cleaned up?'

'You promise you're not angry with me?'

'No, of course not. It's okay, baby. It's okay.' I kissed him on the head and began to pull myself from under the bed. He followed behind, looking to make sure we were alone.

'He really scared me, Mummy.'

'I know he did, darling. He scared me too.'

'Will he be back?'

'Maybe, and if he does, you just hide again. Will you do that?'

'Yeah.'

'You're such a good boy. Okay, darling, stand up for me.'

Tom did as I asked and carefully I pulled down his trousers. Luckily, they weren't too soiled. I then took down his pants, careful not to smear the faeces into his legs as I did. I folded them and using the dirtiest of the blankets, I cleaned him up. Then, using some of the bottled water and the edge of my pyjama top, I cleaned him as best I could before putting his pyjama bottoms on again. Folding the pants into the blanket I put them in the far corner of the room near the bottle half filled with wee.

162

I then put The Bear's jumper over his head. The neck was so wide I had to bunch it up so it wouldn't slip over his shoulders. Tom sat on the edge of the bed and wrapped himself up to stay warm. I joined him, cradling him in my arms again.

'I'm so sorry, Mummy.'

'Don't be. It was an accident. It happens when little boys are being very, very brave.'

'Really?'

'Yes, darling.'

'Does that have to go into the story?'

His question caught me off guard and I laughed. In the corner of my eye I saw him smile also.

'We could put it in, but write it like it was me who pooed.'

'Mummy!'

'Or we could say The Bear pooed!'

Tom burst out laughing, his high-pitched giggle warming me. 'Yeah, let's write it so he came in and saw us and pooed in his pants.'

'That's a great idea. Chapter five, "The Bear Poos His Pants".'

Tom and I laughed for a few moments. My emotions were so high I needed the release. I hoped it wasn't the same for Tom. I hoped he laughed because it was funny and nothing else. Once calmed I leant to kiss him on the head and he climbed off the bed and sat down to eat his cereal, his little back to me, goose bumps on his neck and arms. As I watched, I thought of what The Bear said – hopefully only a few more chapters.

If we could keep writing our story and keep laughing, we would get through this. We would be okay.

163

Chapter 28

Daniel

Paris

3rd January 2018, 9.31 a.m.

Thomas was there right in front of me holding out his little hands, stretching as far as he could, asking me to take them, his voice older somehow. All I had to do was wrap them in my own, but I couldn't move the few steps I needed to grab him. He shook his head at me, and turned, walking away into the nothingness. Then Rachael appeared, her eyes as fearful as they were in the picture I had been sent. Her red hair was limp and wet. She told me I had failed. She told me they weren't coming back. Water began forming around our feet and started wrapping around our ankles as it got deeper, the cold stealing my breath. It climbed up to my knees, thighs, groin and stomach. Perfectly black and still, like I was sinking into thick tar.

I looked down, seeing my reflection in it. I was smiling and then Rachael was gone. The water kept rising until it was up and over my head. I started to laugh. Bubbles flooded from my mouth. Each one containing the memoires I cherished. I looked up to watch the water continue to rise. I could see the night sky. Millions of stars looked down at me. One exploded and disappeared, like a firework. Then another, then more until each and every star had gone. The view of stars now just a vast black nothingness. Then I woke. The sound of a trolley cart crashing into an armrest somewhere close by startled me. Sitting up from my slouched position I wiped the dribble from the side of my fake beard and looked out of the window, trying to place where I was now, trying to shake the images. They were not real and yet my body reacted like they were. My heart hurt. My muscles ached like they would if exposed to intense cold. My lungs burnt.

I needed to save them. I needed to remember. More than I needed the clothes on my back and the legs that I walk with. More than air itself. The dream left me rocked but, for the first time, desperation wasn't my controlling emotional state. I was angry. I was angry at myself for whatever and whoever I was before 2003. I was angry at my mum for hiding it and my dad for being in France. I was angry at the voice on the phone. I wanted to find him and beat him until he gave them back.

I had never felt it before, but for the first time I wanted someone dead.

I looked at my phone that was charging in the socket under my table. My service was now with SFR, I would be in Paris soon. The journey was far less eventful than my frayed nerves suggested, with the passport effortlessly doing its job. I breezed through Passport Control and onto the train. It set off on time and the combination of no sleep, warm radiators and the gentle rocking of the carriage as it rattled along the tracks meant that I fell asleep somewhere just south of London.

Realizing my tired body was slouching again I sat up and rubbed my eyes. Unplugging my fully charged phone, I packed my charger into my bag and rang Rachael's number. I just needed to hear them.

'Hey, this is Rachael.'

'And Tom.'

I hung up before it went to the beep and felt myself begin to well up. I would give anything to hear their voices for real. Rachael asking me when I was going to pop the question to Katie. Thomas instructing me on how to build the perfect den. I'd give everything to hear that. Everything. It was only just under two days since I last heard their voices. It felt a lot longer.

For a second, one wonderful second, I could feel him in my arms.

An announcement sounded, first in French, then in English. It robbed the wonderful feeling of Thomas in my arms. It told us that we were arriving into Paris. People around started to put away books and iPads, preparing for the moment they could disembark. I had a few minutes so risked using up vital data to go onto the BBC News website. It felt risky doing so, I wasn't sure if I could be traced or not through it. But I needed to be connected to the world and know what was happening. The headline I had read in the fat man's house hadn't changed but there was now a video. I clicked on it. A young reporter spoke of Sean's body being found. Behind him police tape cordoned off the area and a few uniformed officers stood on guard as forensics in their white suits walked in and out of the house. I panicked, locking the phone and putting it in my bag. As I did, one person caught my attention. An older man three rows down. He was folding a paper and putting it into what looked like a laptop case. Our eyes met just for a moment, but in that moment, I felt like he knew. The same way I had with the man walking the dog, and the man outside my father's house. Looking out of the window I leant so I could see his reflection in the glass. Was it the same man? They were a similar age with a similar style of hair. I couldn't be certain, but then I could say that about everything, couldn't I? I wanted to ask but thought better of it. I would follow, watch. See what he did.

He stood and looked at me again before making his way down

the carriage towards an exit. I pretended it hadn't mattered that I had seen him and slowly got my things together. I stood and walked in the opposite direction going through the doors that joined the carriages. I stood by the exit and watched as the Gare du Nord station came into view, its huge terminal roof impressive and intimidating.

As the train slowed and the platform came into view I could see thousands of people moving, scurrying around with their own problems and worries. If only they knew. Standing in the doorway, my hand hovering over the button to open the door, I couldn't see the man at the other end and when we disembarked I would be a fair distance away. But station traffic only flowed one way, I knew I would set eyes on him again.

Taking the phone out I pretended to email as I alighted, keeping my head low, moving as if it didn't matter. The crowds thickened as more and more people disembarked, from both the train I was on and the other one on the shared platform. The congestion became so thick I struggled to see him. My legs began to move faster. I needed to set eyes on him. Panic began to rise in my chest. I didn't want to lose this guy. If I could find out where he was going, or, if he wasn't going anywhere but following me, I would lead him somewhere quiet and beat answers from him. I wasn't a fighter, but I was a lot younger than him. And I was motivated. I couldn't afford for anyone to alert the police to my whereabouts.

My feet moved faster still, and I felt my hands clench into a fist. So distracted by my building adrenaline, I didn't see him until we were level, three people separating us. Our eyes met and he looked away. Shit, he knew that I knew. He turned right putting more people between us. Not knowing what to do I kept pace, trying to weave my way through people to get closer to him. As we drew closer to the ticket barrier and Passport Control I joined the queue two away from his, keeping my eyes on him. He checked through just before me and hurried away, glancing over his shoulder in my direction. Once I was through, my focus was now entirely on the man. I pushed through people, first mumbling a sorry, then not. He looked over his shoulder and kept up the pace. I was within a few feet of him when I heard a child call out, 'Grand-père'. A boy, a young boy. It stopped me dead. I watched him kiss the boy before standing and kissing the child's mother. He turned and looked at me, judging me before walking away with his family.

My heart started to beat furiously. I needed to get out of the busy terminal. Turning almost the way I had just ran, I fought my way back through the same people I had barged past moments before, this time saying sorry to each one as I passed until I was in the toilets. After splashing my face with cold water, I couldn't help but let my leftover adrenaline take over and before I could stop myself, I'd hit the wall so hard that the sound ricocheted around the room. At the last moment I'd stopped myself from hitting my original target – the mirror. I couldn't do that now, not with a job to do. I had a lifetime ahead of me to punish myself for what had happened. The next few days weren't included. There was something more important to do.

As I left the toilet I seamlessly slipped into the mass of commuters and tourists. I approached the giant destinations board that centred the station, seeing my train to Auvers was on platform four in just under forty minutes and I knew that soon I would be in the place that was at the centre of it all. I would be another step closer to getting them back.

Putting my hands into my pockets I vanished into the Parisian crowd to buy my ticket and wait to board my train.

I was, for now, Peter Morales.

Just another man, going about his ordinary day.

Chapter 29

Rachael

The Garage

3rd January 2018, 9.33 a.m.

The key went into the lock and snapped, the bolt slid and the grinding of the rusty internal mechanics shot into my muscles making me react before I had time to think. Tom scurried back under the bed, his little tummy full with the breakfast The Bear had given him, and pulled the blanket over his head. He left a small gap, I knew he was watching the lamp. It was going to remain on. I needed more time. I needed it to be night. As the door opened I covered my eyes as the light streamed in and my vision adjusted to the change. And when I saw who was before me I couldn't hide my fear. I was expecting The Bear, prepared for him. But it was the tattooed man. The door slammed shut behind him, and the darkness was consuming until once again my eyes could adjust. He stood there, camera in hand and the flash from it blinded me. As he spoke he did so calmly, but I could hear the excitement in his voice.

'How are you?'

'Fine,' I replied quietly.

'I think you're really pretty.' He waited for me to respond, but I didn't. Quietly he walked towards me and lowered himself to my level, resting his hand on my knee as he did.

'I think we should get to know each other, don't you?' I tried to look at him, to show him I wasn't afraid, but I couldn't. I shook my head, a tear escaping from the corner of my eye.

'Don't cry, I'm not going to hurt you,' he whispered, leaning in, his breath hot on my neck. 'I just want to get to know you.'

'Please, don't,' I whispered back.

The tattooed man held his camera up again and took another picture. I raised my hand to block out my face, instantly regretting it as he grabbed me by my throat, crushing my windpipe. Within seconds I could feel the pressure building behind my eyes, my vision blurring. I tried to pull his hand away from me, but he was too strong. As he spoke his breath smelt of coffee.

'If I want to take your picture you don't block me, do you understand?'

I nodded as best I could and he let go. The sudden release made me topple forward, gasping for air. He stood up and held his camera up again, relaxed. Like he was taking a picture on a beach somewhere. 'Now, smile.'

I did as I was told, as best I could with my head swimming, catching a fresh tear that rolled down my face, hoping he didn't see. I didn't want to anger him again.

'You're so pretty,' he said again. 'Pull your top down at the neck line, so I can see your collarbones.'

Fighting back a sob I flashed a glance at the bed. Tom was underneath, hidden. He wasn't about to see what was coming. I hoped he was doing as I asked him to and had his fingers firmly in his ears.

'Now smile.'

I tried to smile. Goose bumps grew on my shoulders as the cold air hit them.

'Good, now pull it down even lower.'

'Please,' I begged.

'Shut up, do it,' he hissed at me. Unable to hold back my tears I pulled the front of my top as low as I could without ripping the neck line, my cleavage exposed. Another flash of the camera.

'Even lower,' he whispered, enjoying himself.

'I can't go even lower,' I pleaded.

Stepping forward at the same speed he did when he hit me, he grabbed the front of my top and pulled, tearing it across a seam. The sudden force of him tearing my pyjama top pulled me forwards, nearly making me fall onto his feet. I steadied myself and once I was sat upright again, my left breast was hanging out.

'Smile!' he said again, this time through a clenched jaw. Another flash, blinding me. When I opened my eyes again he was stood over me, his crotch close to my face. 'You're such a good girl,' he whispered and again I quickly shot a look to the bed. Tom was still hidden. Thank God.

I thought he was going to undo his trousers, expecting me to please him but he didn't. I could see he wanted to, but something stopped him. He noticed before I did; the door was opening.

'Soon you and I are going to have some private time,' he said before taking a step away. I scrambled my top back up and tucked it under my arm then pressed my arm to my body to stop it from falling down, exposing me once more. Looking behind the tattooed man I saw the shape of The Bear, a black mass, his features disguised by the light behind.

'What are you doing in here?' The Bear asked, stepping into the room, leaving the door ajar.

'Nothing, just getting some photos, like I was told.' He turned to face The Bear, and only a few feet from each other they held their ground. The tension between them was evident. These two didn't get along.

'Have you got them?'

'Oh yeah, I've got them.'

'Good, then you should get back to doing your job.'

'I was just leaving.'

The tattooed man brushed his way past The Bear and towards the door. Just before leaving, he turned and smiled at me, a smile that made my skin crawl.

Once the tattooed man had gone, The Bear's body language relaxed. He looked at me sitting in a heap on the floor, trying to hold my top together. He opened his mouth to speak, but stopped himself for a moment, changing the words that came out.

'He shouldn't need to come back in here.'

I couldn't respond, just nodded, wiping yet another tear. The Bear walked towards the bed and I jumped up to challenge him, and as I moved, my top fell once again. He raised his hands in defence and slowly picked up one of the blankets, handing it to me so I could wrap myself in it.

'I'll try to get you something else to wear,' he said, stepping away from the bed. Then, lifting his head, he sniffed.

'What is that smell? Is that …'

'He was scared.'

'Of what?'

'You.'

The Bear looked back at me. A kind of shock in his eyes. He looked towards the bed, then back at me. When he spoke again it was softer. Calmer.

'Me?'

'Yes, you.'

'Oh. You did tell him I won't hurt him?'

'It wouldn't matter if I had. Look at you. I'm frightened of you.'

'Don't be. I mean you no harm. Listen, umm, sorry. I don't even know your name.'

That made no sense to me. Surely he would know who I was, wouldn't he?

'Rachael.'

'Rachael. I'm Sam. Listen, I've got to go and take care of a few things. Someone else is coming here. Don't speak to them.'

172

'Someone other than the man with the tattoos?'

'Yes.'

'How many of you are there?'

He didn't respond quickly, I could see him weighing up whether he should say or not. He looked down at the shoulder I hadn't properly covered and sighed.

'Three. Me, the man who was just in here and our boss. Just keep your head down, okay? I don't want you two to get hurt. This business, it shouldn't involve you.'

'Then why are we here?'

He almost said something but stopped himself, as if he was wrestling with his own morality. Taking a breath, he continued, changing the subject.

'I'll be back later today. I'll bring you and your boy more food. If they come in, either of them, make sure he is really hidden under there, okay?'

'Please don't let them hurt him.'

'They won't, you're too valuable to get hurt.'

'What do you mean, "valuable"?'

'And I'll say that they don't need to come in, that you'll be fine for a few hours.'

'What do you mean, "valuable"?'

'Just try to keep quiet. Don't give them a reason to come in.'

Despite the balaclava I could read in his eyes that he was genuinely worried for me and Tom.

'Okay.'

He looked like he wanted to say something again, and again he stopped himself. He looked to the pile where Tom's soiled pants lay.

'What's his name?'

'Tom.'

'Tom. You're doing really well,' he said looking towards the bed before looking back at me, 'Your story is going to be a really good one.'

The Bear stooped down, picked up the pile and turned to leave. I sat motionless for a moment and he looked back at me.

'I really did this?'

'Yes, Sam. You did.'

He left slowly, closing and locking the door behind him. I was going to heed his warning. Tom and I were in chapter six, waiting for 'The Return of The Bear'.

Chapter 30

Daniel

Auvers-sur-Oise

3rd January 2018, 11.08 a.m.

Pulling into Auvers station, I expected something to happen. Another flash, another memory. But it was just a station. I tried to picture my father arriving here. A bag on his back, or a suitcase in his hand. Ready to start his new life. Was he happy or sad to have left England? Was he here for an adventure, or was he here in hiding? I assumed the latter.

As I alighted from the train, the cold air hit me unexpectedly. Although only twenty miles from Paris, it felt considerably colder. When I left the station I saw that fine sleet held the town in its grasp. It settled on my shoulders and in my hair, frozen only for a moment before returning to water and making me shiver. Despite the time of day, the sun hadn't broken through the thick winter clouds and the street lamps were still on; the footpaths lit by old, dull orange light. Half of them weren't working. I buried my chin into my jacket and, not knowing why, I turned left and began walking away from the station. Only a minute passed when I felt the phone vibrate in my pocket. I hoped it was him, I hoped he would let me talk to Rachael. I hoped to hear Thomas's voice. I couldn't hide my disappointment when I heard it was Katie.

'Daniel, where are you? Why did I get an international connection?'

'I'm in France.'

'What?'

'It's a long story.'

'Daniel, are you okay?'

I wanted to say something, show her that I was handling it, that I was in control, but the words wouldn't come. My whole life had been a lie and I wasn't about to continue. Instead I said nothing. There was something in her voice which allowed me to be still for a second. But in that stillness the wave of fear came again, and I didn't know how to stop it from happening.

'Daniel? Are you still there?'

'Yes.'

'What are you doing in France?'

'I think the thing I'm trying to find is here.'

'What thing? Do you know yet?'

In her voice was a fragility that mirrored my own. I could hear her trying not to get upset, and that broke my heart. I was hurting her, like I had hurt Rachael and Thomas.

'I'd better go, Katie.'

'Daniel ...' She hesitated, the pause making me feel sick. I knew what was coming. 'The police found Sean.'

'Yes, I know. I've seen.'

'What the hell is going on, Daniel?'

'I wish I could tell you.'

'They went to your mum's.'

'Is she all right?'

'She's okay. She sent them away.'

'They'll go back.'

'She said the detective, a woman called Holt, was really hostile. They think you did it.'

176

'Katie, I have to go.'

'Do you think you're close?'

'I hope so.'

'Daniel, I wish I was there with you.'

'I do too.'

'The police will be looking for you everywhere.'

'I'll be careful. Listen, I've got to go now. I'll try to call soon though.'

'Before you go, listen to me. I know you. I know how strong you are. I know how much you love your boy. If I had to bet on anyone in the world to work this out, it would be you.'

'Thanks, Katie.'

'Daniel, I love you. Whatever it is you've done, I don't care, just end it and get home safely. I need you.'

I hung up the phone without saying goodbye, it was too difficult. I didn't want to say that I'd see her later either. In the back of my mind I somehow knew that when I returned, whatever I took, it wouldn't be over. But I didn't care for me. All I cared about was that Rachael and Thomas would be safe.

The wind whipped up around me, blowing the sleet into me horizontally and kicking up dead leaves from the trees that lined the path, covering car windscreens. The effects of winter were visible everywhere. Icicles hung from shop archways. A 'children crossing' sign was almost completely covered in white. Despite it being mid-morning, I'd seen only three cars moving since leaving the station. In all three were solo drivers, wrapped in coats and scarves. They glanced at me but paid me no attention. Their look was only out of curiosity as to why someone would want to be out on such a foul day.

Then came the fourth, its headlights blinding me as it approached. The driver slowed as they got closer. I pretended not to notice but in my peripheral vision I saw two people inside. Both were intently looking at me. As the car passed they were almost at a standstill. In the distance I could see a sign for a café.

I needed to get inside. Inside offered security. I upped my pace. Behind me I heard the car stop entirely. The gears crunched and the car made a high-pitched tone that only a car moving in reverse could make. I wanted to look behind me but thought better of it. I needed to get off the road; turning a corner, I broke into a half-walk, half-run, trying my best to make it look like I was a man who was hurrying to get out of the cold. Crossing the street, I stepped into a puddle by the kerb that was deeper than I thought it would be; it covered my right shoe up to my ankle. I swore out loud and shook my leg before opening the door to the café and stepping in. A little bell that hung above the door rang as I closed it and within seconds a lady, around sixty possibly a touch older, came waddling through a narrow doorway.

'*Bonjour*,' she said.

'Morning, can I have a coffee please?'

'Certainly. Please, sit.'

I did as she said, taking off my coat and hanging it on a stand near the door. I opted for a table in the corner, near the window. It allowed me to put my back to a wall and watch the streets outside. The sleet seemed to be slowing, the wind dropping. With the air now cleared a little, I could start to see more of the opposite side of the road and down towards the town centre. There was nothing remarkable about it from what I could see.

The café was small but clean. Pictures hung on the walls, replicas of famous works, mostly landscapes. On top of the serving counter were several trays. Pastries and cakes were underneath their glass bowl lids. I knew I needed to eat, but I still hadn't eaten the baguette I had bought in London; my appetite was still lost in the void.

I wondered what had drawn my father to such a place and I was sure I would find out soon enough. For now, I needed to sit, have the coffee I ordered, and plan what was next. Perhaps I would speak to the café owner, see if she knew who my father was and where I might find him. A few minutes passed and the lady returned with a small coffee. I was expecting an Americano or something similar, but then remembered the French didn't do such things without it being a request. A coffee here was an espresso first. I didn't mind; the intense level of caffeine would help. I smelt it and felt myself warming.

'Thank you,' I said, meaning it wholeheartedly.

'You're welcome. It's cold, no?'

'Yes. Very.' I looked out of the window again, hoping by doing so that she would understand my polite hints that I wasn't in a talking mood. She didn't.

'Are you visiting Auvers?'

'I'm guessing my English accent gave me away?'

'Yes. Is this your first visit here?'

Looking back at her I could sense her genuine interest, her soft eyes somehow calming, and it relaxed me enough to want to be kind and talk.

'No, I came a very long time ago with my father. In the summer of 1999.'

'This is good. You know how beautiful our town is. Today is a terrible day for the view.'

'The view?'

'The view of Auvers. It's why everyone comes here.'

'Of course.' I noted to myself that something shifted inside. Something connected to my stomach. I felt nervous, a little sick. There was something about the view of Auvers. Something important, not for the town though. There was something important for me.

'Well,' I continued, 'it looks like the weather is improving.'

'Don't let it fool you. This is the calm before the storm.'

'Are you expecting bad weather?'

'Very. Soon the snow will be very heavy.'

'I see, well, it's a good job I'm not here for the view.'

'It is indeed.'

'I'm actually looking for someone. Perhaps you know him. His name is Robbie?'

I watched as she looked towards the ceiling, recalling from her memory.

'No, I don't know anyone by that name. Does he live here?'

'Yes. Well, I think so.' I thought about my father's house in Chalfont, the dust, the translation book. 'He may have moved here about a year ago?'

'No, I'm afraid I cannot think of anyone.'

'I see, thank you anyway.'

'I hope you find him.'

She must have sensed my sadness, my hopelessness because she walked away, leaving me to think and look out of the window. I felt my heart sink. I'd hoped that as soon as I stepped into the town, someone would know him and point me in the right direction. But I wasn't going to get lucky. It meant I would have to walk around the town, ask more people, hope that my luck would change.

I finished my coffee and approached the till. I thanked her, paid with the euros I'd picked up at the train station and put my coat on.

'I hope you find who you are looking for.'

'Thank you,' I replied.

'Your French is very good, sir.'

Confused, I nodded before stepping back into the cold, convinced I'd misheard her. My French was good? I didn't speak French.

Chapter 31

Rachael

The Garage

3rd January 2018, 2.18 p.m.

I must have dozed off again because, for a moment, I thought I was at home in my bed. Then I remembered the nightmare we were in and looked at Thomas. His body was barely visible under the mound of mouldy blankets, his cheeks red through cold. I rubbed my hands together to warm them and then placed them under the covers on his back. It was warm. The blankets may well be dirty, but they were doing their job. Sometimes, life had to be measured by the small victories. Yes, we were in danger, but right now Tom was asleep and warm. Sometimes the small things are all we have.

I, however, was cold, so cold my body ached. I looked to the door and thought I heard someone on the other side. I looked at Tom and was about to wake him and tell him to hide but the noise went. Getting up, I went to the furthest corner of the room to him, pulled down my pyjama bottoms and squatted, my elbows resting on my knees, my head in my hands. Once I finished weeing I looked up and Tom was looking at me, sleepy-eyed and pale. I smiled and he smiled back.

'Mummy, I need to go too.'

'Come over here then, darling.'

'But my toilet is full,' he said, pointing at the bottle he had used a few times and completely filled.

'It's okay. Come and wee on the wall.'

'But I only not wee in a toilet when I'm camping with Daddy.'

'Tom, darling, the rules are different in the story. You can wee right here against the wall.'

Tom came and stood next to me and went to the toilet, he tried to write his name on the wall but didn't quite finish the M.

'Did Daddy teach you to do that?'

'Yes.'

I laughed. 'Remind me to have a word with him when we see him.'

'Is he in trouble?' He looked so concerned that he had told on his dad.

'No, of course not. I just want him to teach me.'

'That's silly, Mummy, you can't learn it,' he said laughing.

'Oh, is it just for boys?'

'Yes, Mummy.'

'Is it because I don't have a willy?'

Tom exploded into laughter, his voice bouncing off the walls, echoing back his joy. He laughed so hard he fell and landed in my arms. I held him tight and tickled under his chin until he wriggled himself free. Then we played the game again to get the blood flowing in his body. How many steps to the door? How many to the wall? He got them right every time. I was so proud.

Behind us the door squeaked again. Tom quickly jumped off my lap and crawled under the bed. I grabbed a blanket and pulled it down, stuffing it under the bed to shield him, and he moved the top so he could see the lamp and the door.

It opened quickly, startling me. I hoped of the three I now knew held us, it was The Bear, but I was expecting the tattooed man. I was shocked to see it was neither. I looked out of my peripheral vision towards the bed. Tom was hidden completely. Thankfully. This man before me was the third; the boss. The small wiry one whose eyes terrified me. Whereas the tattooed one looked at me like a sexual predator, this one looked at me like he wanted me dead. Hard eyes under a black balaclava. I could feel his hatred. He had something in his hand; at first I thought it was a knife and I moved myself closer to Tom, my instinct telling me to put myself between it and him. But, as I moved I saw it wasn't a blade at all, it was an envelope. I looked at the small man and watched as a small smile crept onto his face. He dropped the envelope on the floor, closed the door and locked it again.

As I was crawling over towards it, Tom called out.

'Can I come out, Mummy?'

'Not yet, stay there.'

I picked it up and turned it over. There was no writing on it, the flap not sealed. Inside was a piece of paper. I pulled it out – the texture was like silk and it was firmer than paper, more like a photo. Turning it over I saw something that made me drop it like it was on fire and I covered my mouth trying to fight the sob that was about to escape. Sean. His eyes staring at the ceiling in our bedroom. Blood everywhere. His body mutilated. I had to bite hard on my index finger to stop myself screaming. So hard I could taste blood on my tongue. My body shook, my vision blurred. They had killed him. In the moments when I was fighting to get to my son, they murdered my husband.

Tom was asking me something. But I couldn't hear him through the noise in my own head. A screaming that had no voice. Something that came from the shadows and the coldness that housed us. I couldn't believe they had killed him. I couldn't believe they had shown me. He looked so confused, so frightened. That image would stay with me forever. My poor, poor Sean. I wanted to climb under the bed where I told Tom to hide, and stay there forever. I wanted to give up. I felt, for the first time, hopeless. I couldn't stay strong anymore. I tried but I couldn't, and curling up on the floor, I sobbed. Tom crawled out from under the bed.

'Mummy, what was so funny?' He was confused and I could see why; Tom had never seen me cry before. But I needed a moment, he would have to wait.

'Mummy?'

'Not now, Tom.'

'Mummy ...'

'I said not now!'

My voice came out far louder than I thought it would and when I looked towards Tom, I could see his curious expression turn to one of shock, before he scuttled back under the bed, his quiet sobs breaking the silence I created.

I tried to stop myself but I couldn't, and my eyes went back to the picture of my husband's face, his lifeless eyes looking towards the wall where his blood had sprayed. The bed's duvet was crumpled up in a heap, half covering his legs. The floral pattern that was embroidered into the bottom left corner was covered in crimson. I looked into the dead eyes of the man I loved and thought of the baby inside me that would be fatherless.

I wanted to grieve. I needed to. My body screamed at me to stop, roll onto its side and shake until I passed out. But there was a little boy who needed to continue to believe this was all a story.

I also knew that if I did nothing, Tom and I were going to die here.

There were a million possibilities for Tom's future. We would be close until he hit his teenage years, then he would drift away from me as he tried to find his own way. Then Tom would go to university and drink and party and work out who he was in this world. He would pursue a career, hopefully land the job he wanted and one day, he would fall in love. We would become closer than ever as his relationship blossomed. One day he would have a family of his own. I would be a grandmother and then he would really know how hard and wonderful and frightening being a parent is. He might also really understand what we went through in this place. We wouldn't speak of it. Not out loud. It would be the look we shared that no one else would understand and it would be something that would keep us together until it was my time to die. Tom would be there, with his family, and I would leave life knowing he was happy and loved.

Most of the future, I couldn't impact. But I could change some of how it developed, and I needed to act for there to be any chance of a nice future happening for Tom. Folding the picture and putting it in my waistline of my pyjama bottoms, I took a deep breath and looked towards the bed. His gentle sobs from underneath broke my heart.

It wasn't his fault. It wasn't either of ours. We were the victims. Sean too.

'Tom? Darling?'

'Go away.'

'Baby, I shouldn't have shouted, I'm sorry.'

'I don't want to talk to you anymore.'

'I understand. You're right to be angry. Mummy was being silly. I was sad, I shouldn't have shouted.'

Tom didn't respond straightaway and I didn't speak but waited to let him come to a decision on his own as to whether he would stay angry or not. I looked to the vent. The sun was being blocked out by a passing cloud that looked heavy and ready to burst. I wondered what it would feel like to be up there, in it, waiting to fall? After a minute Tom's little voice carried from under the bed.

'Why were you sad?'

I turned and could see his face poking out from underneath. Looking tired. Looking thinner. His fragility switched something inside me. A wall rose up, locking in the horror of what had happened to my poor Sean behind it. The switch sat me upright and stopped my tears. It made my eyes refocus on my child. I could feel my grief trying to smash through the wall, and it would. Just not now.

'Can I come under?' I asked, and he moved back towards the wall, freeing a gap for me to lie in.

'I'm sorry, Tom.'

'Are you sad now?'

'No,' I lied. Shuffling towards him, I rested my head on his shoulder. 'Are you still angry at Mummy?'

'No.'

'I'm sorry, darling. Mummy shouldn't have shouted.'

'Was that part of the story, Mummy?'

'No. That was Mummy being silly.'

I remembered the half a dozen or so Maltesers that Sam, The Bear, had left us and I offered them to Tom. I could see he wanted them despite refusing so I put them between us. After a moment he took them and quietly ate. I could see him soften as he did. That's what I loved about my baby. He recovered quickly from things. I hoped that would be the case forever, even after this.

I told myself that if we got out of this alive, I would do two things. I would spend more time seeing the smaller things, and I wouldn't shout at my babies, either of them, for as long as I lived. I wanted to say something to him. Tell him what the next adventure in our story would be. Tell him that things were about to change and Mummy would have to do things to make that happen, like in all good stories, but I couldn't. He was having a moment. Him and the chocolate. Who was I to interrupt that? Again, the little victories really mattered in a time like this.

I could feel the photo pressed into my hip and a knot formed in my throat, wanting to be released. But it couldn't be, so I took a deep breath, closed my eyes and forced the love I had for my husband out of my mind. One day I would let it return.

But I couldn't let that day be today. Today, I had to pretend everything was all right. Today I had to think of a way out, or else, I was sure we would follow the same path as my poor husband.

Chapter 32

Daniel

Auvers

3rd January 2018, 2.14 p.m.

After leaving the warm coffee shop I walked around the quiet streets, trying, and failing, to find someone to talk to and ask questions about my father. The town wasn't so big that no one would know him. It wasn't like London or Paris where a person could get lost. The problem I was having was those people weren't around. I had only run into three individuals in two hours; the town was on lockdown for the approaching snow. Each person was too cold or too busy. They were harassed by the elements and didn't want to talk to the lost Englishman. When I showed them the picture of my dad and me in this town in 1999, I noticed that none of them actually looked at the picture but merely cast their eyes towards it for a moment, trying to be polite despite their disinterest. I felt frustrated. I was wasting time I didn't have, and with each rejection for conversation or vague look from a stranger, I thought of Thomas. I wondered if he was warm or as cold as I was. I thought of how frightened he must be.

The brief rest from the bad weather was beginning to pass.

The eye of the storm was moving north, and its tail was beginning to loom over the deserted town. Above me, the clouds were heavy and low, with a hint of purple. Snow was coming, and it was coming soon. I didn't want to be out when it did.

I turned onto another empty street and began walking, unsure if I had already been along it. To me, they all looked so similar. But then again, maybe they weren't, maybe it was my distracted and damaged mind not differentiating between each passing road, door and lane. In the weak light, breaking through the clouds, I could see a man up ahead. He was loading some furniture into a van – a chest of drawers, a coffee table as well as a few other things. His hood was up, protecting his head from the energy-sapping cold. As I approached I tried to appear friendly despite not wanting to smile because of the lightning bolt of pain I felt every time my mouth was open. Waving, I crossed the street. He didn't wave back but looked at me suspiciously. I didn't think much of it, I would have done the same.

'Excuse me,' I said slowly, hoping he understood. I took the photo of me and my father out of my bag and showed it to him.

'I'm looking for this man, he's a lot older now. His name is Robbie. Do you know him?'

The man looked at the picture for a second, his eyes squinting as he tried to focus on the image. I wanted to tell him to take the glasses I could see under his hood and put them on so he could see the picture properly. I wanted to say, 'don't just glance at it to be polite, look at the fucking thing, tell me you know him.' I thought better of it. He considered the image closely for a moment.

'What did you say his name was?' he asked.

I felt my heart skip a beat. The few people I had spoken with hadn't asked anything about him. I told him his name, my voice feeling like it was leaking as I spoke.

'Robbie.'

'English?'

'Yes, English.'

'Yes, I knew of this man. He moved here last winter. I sometimes saw him in the tavern in the square.'

'Tavern? What's the name?'

'Le Balto.'

I felt my adrenaline increase. I was right to trust my instincts and the signs around me. My father lived in the town. My father who was absent but knew things about Michael that were secret to Mum. My father would tell me, one way or another, what I needed to get them back.

'Do you know where I might find him?'

The man paused, looking at his feet. When his words came, they were heavy, sympathetic.

'If it's the man I'm thinking of, he passed away.'

Chapter 33

Rachael

The Garage

3rd January 2018, 2.22 p.m.

I didn't feel the cold anymore, or the hunger, or the fear. I was numb. Tom sat on the bed and played with his fingernails. He had bitten one of them off and was cleaning under his others with it, scraping out bits of dirt that had found their way to that hard to reach place. He had recovered from me shouting at him, but was still quiet. I could almost hear him thinking about how I raised my voice at him, something that was uncharacteristic, and questioning the lie I had told him about the story we were in. He was bored, but I didn't have enough energy or ability to do anything about it. I knew why, I had seen it a thousand times before in the families of dying patients at work. I was in shock. Which meant my blood pressure was low and my heart would be working too hard. I wanted to sleep, I wanted to forget.

Looking to the small vent in the wall, I could still see daylight coming through. I hadn't expected it to be bright outside and a part of me wished it wasn't. I needed the darkness, if only for somewhere to hide from the picture that felt cold against my hip. My Sean, my poor, poor Sean. I couldn't remember what he looked like, and trying only brought the waxy image of his blood-covered skin. I could almost feel the cold coming from him, a clammy deathly cold.

'Mummy?'

'Yes, darling?' I looked at him. He was no longer playing with his fingernails but sat on the edge of the bed, his little legs hanging over and not touching the floor, watching me. His eyes were so much older than they should be.

'Are you all right, Mummy?'

'Yes, baby. I'm just tired.'

'Me too. Mummy, can we go home soon?'

'We can't, not yet.'

'Why not?'

'Because … because we can't, okay?'

'No, it's not okay. I want to go home.'

'Tom, we will, I promise, just not yet.'

'I want to go now!' he shouted. Learnt behaviour from my outburst earlier. Raising my fingers to my lips, I tried to quieten him. I didn't want 'them' to come in.

'Tom, we need to be quiet.'

'I don't want to be quiet.' He threw the blanket from his shoulders and jumped up on the bed, stamping his feet.

'Please, Tom.'

'I'm cold and I'm hungry and I'm tired and I hate this story and I hate you!'

He didn't mean it, I knew that, but it hurt regardless. He was just mirroring my stress and tension, drawing in the energy of the horrible place we were. I wanted him to shout it out, exhaust himself and feel better for the outburst, but he couldn't. It wasn't safe. So I got up, my arms outstretched to try to soothe him but before I could get close, he jumped off the bed and grabbed the frame, shaking it. I hadn't ever seen him so upset and agitated.

191

But, I understood. I wanted to shake the bed frame too. I wanted to shake it until it fell to pieces.

'Tom, we have to stay quiet.'

'I don't want to, I want to go home.'

'I know you do, and we will, I promise. But I need you to be quiet now.'

'No,' he said, slamming the bed frame into the ground. The sound of metal on concrete echoed. I had to stop him, so stepping forward I grabbed him, wrapping him in my arms – part cuddle, part restrain – and fell backwards, sitting heavily on the ground, him on my lap. He screamed for me to let him go but I held on tightly, trying to reassure him with quiet words of comfort. Our heads narrowly missed coming together as he wrestled. After a minute of fighting, I could feel the anger start to leave his body. Exhausted and panting, his harsh words were replaced with the sound of him crying, really crying. It was the worst sound I had ever heard. Turning, he buried his head into my shoulder, his whole body shaking as he sobbed. I stroked his hair, humming gently into his ear until he had no more tears to cry. He looked at me, his eyes puffy and red.

I tried to reassure him that it was almost over. But the way he looked at me as I spoke, I knew he didn't believe me. Truth was, I didn't believe me either, not unless I did something about it.

Chapter 34

Rachael

The Garage

3rd January 2018, 7.18 p.m.

That world had now succumbed to the night. One that carried a wind that every now and then whipped up and roared around the empty buildings outside. I didn't know if it had got dark within the last hour or the last five hours. With each passing moment I felt like I was starting to lose myself. I sat watching the door, waiting for the footsteps, followed by the sound of the keys turning and snapping the lock open, the bolt sliding. Waiting. Thinking. Planning. What I knew I needed to do made me feel sick, more than my usual feeling with my morning sickness, but when the time came, I knew there would be no other choice.

Tom was asleep again, thankfully. Asleep, he wouldn't feel hungry, or afraid or confused. Asleep, he couldn't start to work out that this wasn't a story but something terrible. I hoped he slept until this was over and, I hoped, with what I had planned, it would be over soon.

After so long waiting, I heard what I'd waited for. Footsteps, heavy and with a long stride. It was The Bear – he was back from wherever he had been. As I stood I looked round to see that Tom hadn't moved. Closing my eyes, I listened to his heavy breathing and the approaching steps. They stopped outside the door. It was time to put my plan into action. I wondered, for a brief moment, if I would really go through with it but I quickly pushed the thought from my mind. I didn't have time for second guessing myself now. Then, the key went in, the lock snapped open, making me blink involuntarily, and the bolt slid. I held my breath as the door opened. He was startled to see me looking directly at him. I kept as still as I could and watched him as he stepped through the gateway between captivity and freedom. Through what I was beginning to realize was the gateway between life and death. He closed it behind him and looked at me curiously.

'You all right?'

'Yes, are you?' I asked softly, hoping my nerves didn't resonate in my voice.

'Umm, yeah. I've bought you some food. Sorry it's so late.'

He took another step towards me and handed me a paper bag with food inside and what looked like a new top to replace my torn one. I put the items on the floor by my bare feet, keeping my eyes on his. Then, taking the bottom corners of my pyjama top I lifted it over my head and dropped it beside me. The Bear was stunned, like a rabbit in headlights. Slowly, I grabbed the elastic waistline of my pyjama bottoms and pulled them down, stepping out of them when they dropped to my ankles.

'What are you …' he started to say before I stepped towards him, my naked body covered in goose bumps, and placed my lips on his through the small gap in his balaclava, having to stand on my tiptoes to reach. He smelt of cigarettes and coffee. It made me want to gag but instead I pressed myself into him. I would turn him on, perhaps even pleasure him, and then I would use it to get out. I would make The Bear, through a combination of lust towards me and sympathy towards Tom, set us free. As I moved my tongue inside his mouth I placed my hand on his crotch and began to rub his hardening penis. Using my other hand, I started to undo his trousers. He did something I wasn't expecting. He took a step back.

'What are you doing?'

I ignored him and stepped into his personal space again, and again I pressed myself into him. This time he placed his hands on my shoulders. I waited for them to begin exploring my body, starting with my breasts and working down towards my arse and in between my legs. I wanted to cry but I knew I couldn't. I had to see it through. Looking at him I could see the familiar look men got when they were losing control. I braced myself to feel like I was being violated and committing adultery at the same time when his hands squeezed tighter on my shoulders and he lifted me from him, his strength moving me an arm's distance away. He bent down and picked up my top, handing it to me.

'You don't want to do something you'll regret, trust me. Put your clothes back on.'

'But I want you.'

'No, you don't.'

Stooping down he picked up my pyjama bottoms and handed them to me too, but as he did the picture of Sean fell onto the floor. He looked confused and picked it up, the image facing down.

'What's this?'

He turned it over and I saw resignation sweep over him. His shoulders dropped, his head following.

'Oh shit.'

The Bear looked at me. My naked body unimportant. I felt tears brim in my eyes, but caught them before they could fall. I didn't want to give him the satisfaction. Neither of us spoke; we just stood, looking at one another. Eventually he cracked, his voice weak as if he was fighting to hold his composure.

'I had nothing to do with this.'

'Why did you show me? I can't see my husband's face now without it being like that.'

'I didn't show you. I wouldn't show you.'

'You killed him.' I couldn't keep the rage from bubbling up inside me. The accusation in my tone, the venom in my voice. But I wouldn't cry. I wouldn't show him my weakness.

'I didn't, I promise. I didn't.'

'How can I believe you?'

'The job was only to take you and the boy and keep you somewhere until it was over. There was no talk of anyone getting hurt.'

'But your partner had other ideas.'

'I didn't know your husband was going to get hurt.'

'Are Tom and I going to die too?'

'No, no. I promise you won't.'

'How can you expect me to believe that?'

He started to back away from me, his eyes not leaving mine. I went to say something but as I opened my mouth I choked on my words. He turned to open the door and I felt completely exposed. I tried to cover myself up with the top but it wasn't big enough to cover all of me. So I sat on the edge of the bed and focused on the floor. I had one more thing I could try to get him to let us go. Reluctantly, I had to tell him the thing I hadn't even told Tom yet.

'You know there is more than one child here in this room.'

He turned back towards me, confused.

'I'm pregnant.'

'What?'

'I'm pregnant. It's not just Tom who you are putting at risk, but my unborn baby too.'

'I didn't know.'

'Well, now you do,' I replied looking back at him. 'So what are you going to do about it?' He didn't speak. 'If you won't do anything then get out.'

'Look, just shout if you ...'

'I said get out.'

The Bear turned and left. The door closed, and eventually it locked.

My plan had failed and I was humiliated in the process. I should have dressed, but instead, I buried my face into my top and cried. The cotton stifled my sobs so Tom didn't wake.

Chapter 35

Daniel

Auvers

3rd January 2018, 8.43 p.m.

Since being told my father was dead, I knew I had wasted time by coming to France, so I tried to go back. But the storm had set in, and trains leaving Auvers had been cancelled. With nowhere else to go, I went to the tavern my father drank in and waited for the storm to pass, hoping trains would resume in the evening. But, as the hours passed, I knew I wasn't getting back tonight. I was stuck in France, the place that offered hope but had now become a dead end. If I was going to find answers, I would have to find them back in the UK. I had lost an entire day chasing a man who had passed away.

I hoped that Thomas and Rachael could forgive me for getting it so wrong.

With nothing else to do until the morning I waved at the young barman to bring me another drink. He did as he was asked and tried to make small talk. I dismissed him. I wasn't in the mood to converse. I wasn't in the mood to think. All I wanted to do was let myself succumb to the fact that I had pinned all of my hopes on finding my father and I had failed. I wanted to drink myself into oblivion. The basket that held all the eggs had bottomed out and its contents lay in ruin.

The young barman I had obviously offended walked back towards the till. Then he disappeared through a door that led somewhere I couldn't see, leaving me entirely alone in the tavern. Out of the corner of my eye I watched the narrow gap in the door, trying to see what he was doing. A few moments later he re-emerged, put on his coat and said goodbye politely but curtly, before stepping into the freezing wind, the snow covering his shoulders and lowered head. I watched him until he was lost in the white out. Looking back to where he had been standing I saw an older man, probably the owner of the tavern. He nodded my way.

'*Salut.*'

'*Salut,*' I returned politely before I turned my attention back to my drink, this time sipping it slower. I knew I was going to order a few more, enough to be drunk and fall asleep until I was escorted either to a nearby hotel or the street corner. But I didn't rush – being a less than average drinker, I didn't want to make myself sick. Oblivion would come, but not quickly.

I knew I should have been thinking about the next step, the next move. But, try as I might, I couldn't. All I could do was look out of the window, watching the individual snowflakes fall violently, carried by the ever intensifying wind. My eyes tried to watch each symmetrical pattern, but they were tired and they stung as I tried. It was like I was looking through a window at an old television that had been de-tuned. In the static I saw Thomas's face appear and he was smiling, looking directly at me. When I snapped my focus on his image, he vanished back into the flurry.

I hated that I was powerless to move, like I had been after the first call. Like I had been in London whilst waiting for my new identity. Time was precious, and I had wasted a chunk of it chasing a ghost. All I could do was drink to numb the pain and pray that the storm passed, and the trains were running in the morning.

I tried to take another mouthful of brandy, but my glass was empty so I hauled myself out of my chair and stumbled to the bar. The old man who had flicked between watching a football match on a small TV that was mounted in the corner, and watching me, was nowhere to be seen.

'Hello,' I called, my speech noticeably slurred, like my jaw was numb. There was no response. 'Hello,' I called again, this time louder, banging my hand on the bar counter to get some attention. It worked, and the old man came rushing out from wherever the door led.

'I'm sorry, sir, I was washing up.'

'I want another drink.'

'Sir, it is getting late, the storm is really setting in. Perhaps you should be leaving to get home or to your hotel before it gets worse?'

'I said I want another drink.'

'I'm sorry, sir, but I think you have had enough.'

'What?' I protested, a rage building behind my cheeks, pressing behind my eyes. 'I'm the customer and I want a fucking drink so give me a drink.'

'Sir, please, I really think you've had enough.'

'I'll tell you when I've had enough, okay?'

'I think it's time for you to leave.'

'I'll leave when I'm good and ready. I want my drink.'

I stepped behind the bar, pushing him out of my way to get to the bottle of brandy that I had single-handedly consumed half of – on an empty stomach. I could hear him protesting, his words quick and hard to understand. I could hear an edge in his voice, a shaking beneath the calm appearance. I didn't try to find a glass but drank straight from the bottle, unscrewing the cap and knocking it back.

I felt his hands on me, trying to remove me from the bar, his grip much stronger than his age suggested. He spun me around and as he did, I lost my already failing balance and tumbled into the back counter where the optics hung. I stood and spun, swinging my fist at him, hoping I caught the side of his head. I wanted to knock him out. I wanted to feel the sensation of fist hitting flesh. I *needed* it.

The old man didn't react in time to dodge or to block my swing, but I missed the target anyway and once again fell, this time into the counter that I should have been the other side of. With all of my drunken energy in the end of my fist, I fell hard, hitting my face on the side and fell to the floor. Sat in a heap I saw that blood was dripping onto my lap and, touching my face, I could feel my lip had split open again. The old man grabbed hold of my arm, but the fight had gone out of me. I didn't want to hurt him anymore, I didn't want to hurt anyone. I just wanted my little boy back. My anger turned into sobs as I remained on the floor and let tears stream down my face. Heaving, the old man lifted me up and propped me against the counter. Within seconds a cold wet cloth was pressed into my face.

'Hold this here.'

I did as I was told, suddenly too tired to do anything else. He lowered himself beside me and moved the cloth away to get a look at my cut. I watched as he grimaced.

'Is it bad?' I asked, my words still slurred.

'Nothing that cannot be fixed. Come on, come with me.'

He walked to the entrance and locked it then guided me through the doorway which I had seen him come and go from. Once through, the atmosphere changed dramatically. The country pub feel was replaced with one that felt homely, and for good reason. He led me down a corridor and past what looked like a small office. Turning left, we walked into a kitchen area with a dining table in it. It wasn't a kitchen for customers, but his own. From the kitchen I could see a living room and a bathroom.

There was another door that remain closed, I assumed it was a bedroom. Sitting down on a hard wooden chair, the cloth still on my face to stem the bleeding, I leant against the table to keep me upright. The old man moved past me into the bathroom, emerging moments later with a first-aid kit. He pulled up a chair beside me so we were eye to eye.

'Let me see this.'

He removed the cloth and had a look at the cut and without warning, he placed an antiseptic wipe on it. Despite being blind drunk, it hurt like hell. As he carefully cleaned my cut I wondered why he was helping. I had tried to assault him, and he recipro- cated with kindness.

'It's not so bad,' he said as he started to apply some antibacte- rial cream that reminded me of the one I put on Thomas's grazed knees. I had to close my eyes to stop myself remembering. When I opened them again, the old man was intently focused on applying the cream evenly.

'Why are you helping—?'

He cut me off mid-sentence telling me he couldn't fix my lip if I was talking. After cleaning he pinched my skin together and applied a couple of Steristrips, commenting it was hard to do on a man with a beard. Once he finished he quietly rose and packed away the contents of the first-aid kit before returning it to the bathroom. Now, all of the fight had left me and exhaustion was taking over. I just needed to sleep. Upon his return he told me to stay there whilst he locked up properly for the night. I was too drunk and too tired to argue.

I didn't want to fall asleep, but it was happening regardless so in an attempt to stay awake I stood up. I carefully moved away from the chair and towards the wall directly in front of me, which was covered in pictures. I struggled to focus but could make out the old man with various people smiling in front of the bar. Some were people I recognized from TV and films. It was odd that A-list celebrities would be here in this small French town, but

202

apparently they came. There must have been something special about it. My foggy brain was unable to begin to work out what that might be. Holding on to the wall to keep me steady, I traversed the room and looked at more pictures, most of which were of customers arm in arm with the old man who had a smile that made him look younger.

Then, I saw a picture that took my breath away. In it, the old man was a lot younger, his hair thicker and less grey and he was holding on to someone I had seen before.

I leant in, thinking my eyes were playing tricks on me, but they weren't. What I was seeing was real.

In the picture the old man was hugging Michael. He was hugging me. Before I could turn to speak to him I felt myself become light-headed and the world went black.

THURSDAY

THURSDAY

Chapter 36

Daniel

Auvers

4th January 2018, 11.48 a.m.

I dreamt again and, on trend with recent dreams, there was something different. Something new. After I ran from the car wreck, I saw myself at a great height, on top of the building I had seen on New Year's Eve. I was looking down on to a marble floor. I must have been one hundred feet above. And then I was floating towards it, somehow controlling my descent. As I landed, I heard a voice. The voice. It said, 'tick tock, Michael, tick tock.' I ran up several flights of stairs and back down several others. The world around me was dark, no torch to light my way. And then I stopped. Ahead was a room I knew I was searching for and as I stepped inside, I woke.

I looked to the ceiling, dark wooden beams running across a smooth cream roof. I tried to recall how I'd ended up in this bed but couldn't remember past being sat in the tavern next to the fire, drinking and watching the snow. It had stopped me leaving. I needed to check to see if the storm had passed. As I rolled over, I thought my brain was going to force its way out through my eyes. The pain was so intense I needed to lie back down again. I tried again, this time slowly, and managed to get myself upright with my bare feet on the cold floor. My lip hurt a lot and when I touched it I could feel fresh swelling under the fake beard that luckily was still firmly attached. I ran my tongue along the inside of my lip and tooth. My gum was tender to the touch. It felt like I had been punched.

Looking down at my body, I saw that I was just in my underwear and, confused, I searched the room to see my clothes hanging on a radiator on the other side. My bag was on the floor beside them. Gingerly I made my way to the window to look out. The world was bright which hurt my eyes. Squinting I could see that the snow had stopped but the ground was still covered. It looked thick. I hoped not so thick that the trains weren't running. I grabbed the phone which was placed beside the bed on a small table, plugged into a charger that wasn't mine, the battery reading 100 per cent, and saw I had a missed call from Katie. I wanted to hear her voice. But it would have to wait. I needed to get moving, and quickly. I went online and looked at the train times. The trains were disrupted with some cancellations and delays, but thankfully, they were running. Then I saw the time and my heart sank. It was nearly noon. I had slept most of the morning away. As quickly as I could I walked over to my clothes and put them on, cursing myself as I did. I had to hold on to the wall to step into my trousers but as I was rushing I fell over, and the impact of the hard floor sent a shockwave from my arse through to my head. Once I had my things I opened the door to the next room.

'Hello?' I said quietly. It hurt my head to speak, so I didn't say it again. Instead, I slowly made my way through a narrow passage into a kitchen I vaguely recalled. As I cleared the doorway I was greeted by the old man from the night before.

'You're awake,' he said, smiling.

'Where am I?'

'You are still at the tavern. You were in a bad way last night.'

'I need to get to the train station.'

'In a minute my friend, you look like shit. You need to eat something first.'

'I haven't got time. I need to go.'

'And you will, but eat first and I will drive you to the station.'

I looked at the train app that was still open on my phone. The next one leaving Auvers wasn't for another hour, so I sat. Even if the train was in the next ten minutes I didn't think I was well enough to walk to the station anyway. The old man served me some toast, with jam and butter on the side in small white dishes. I ate the toast dry, not realizing how hungry I was until I swallowed the first mouthful. Beside me was a strong black coffee that I downed in one before quietly asking for another. The old man did as I asked then sat down opposite me.

'How are you feeling?'

'Terrible.'

'You were very drunk.'

I looked up and he was staring at me intently. Like he was trying to work something out. Despite not wanting to, I looked away.

'What happened last night?' I asked.

'You had too much to drink and you slipped, hit your face.'

'Did we talk about anything?' I asked, hoping that in my drunken state I'd not disclosed to a stranger what was happening. I couldn't afford for someone to think they would help by calling the police.

'No, not really. You hit your face and then as I patched you up you passed out.'

'How did I end up in the bed?'

'I carried you in. I undressed you too so your clothes could dry. I hope you don't mind.'

'No, thank you.'

The old man rose and took his cup to the sink to wash it. As he cleaned, a bell sounded and, apologizing, he told me it was a delivery of coffee he was expecting, before leaving me in the kitchen alone. Finishing my cup, I stood and walked around the room. I remembered there was something about it that was important. But I couldn't remember what. I made my way to a row of photos on the wall, and then I saw it. I felt the blood drain from my face and taking the picture from the wall I sat myself down, staring at the image. After a few moments the old man came back in. My shock was clear to see.

'Are you okay?'

'Do you know me?'

'No, well, yes. I don't know. I've been asking myself the same question. There is something familiar about you, but I cannot place it.'

I held the picture out and he took it from me, examining it like it was the first time he had seen it. He snapped his head to look at me again before going back to the picture.

He looked at me like he had seen a ghost.

Chapter 37

Daniel

Auvers

4th January 2018, 12.09 p.m.

'Michael?'

The old man knowing my name, my old name, stunned me into silence. I wasn't sure what I was expecting, but hearing someone other than *the voice* or my mother say the name scared me. I wanted to run. But the neurones that would fire my legs into action were jammed. Cemented, all I could do was try to process whether this old man in front of me was friend or foe.

'Michael, is it really you?'

My voice was trapped. But I managed a guarded nod. The old man laughed which startled me and, embracing me, he kissed me on both cheeks. As he pulled away he was wearing the wide, youthful smile I saw in the photos.

'My old friend. Oh, Michael, I cannot believe this. How is it possible?'

'Possible? What do you mean?'

'It's a miracle. I cannot believe you were here all night and I didn't know it was you!'

'Wait, what do you mean? You thought I had died?'

'After you vanished we got a letter from England saying you had passed away.'

'Vanished? Vanished from where?'

'Here, this town, this pub. Do you not remember?'

'I lived here!?'

'Yes, of course. Michael, do you not remember?' he repeated, his excitement replaced with concern.

Sitting down at his table I told him what had happened, about my memory. He looked at me, unblinking. He started to talk but I couldn't hear his words. I had lived here sometime between 1999 and being in hospital in London in 2003.

He leant over the table and touched my beard. I flinched, not wanting it to be damaged at all. I still had to get home and they were looking for me, so I had to try to stay as Peter Morales long enough to get to my family. He sat back, his expression hurt.

'You really don't remember me?'

'No, I'm afraid I don't.'

'That is such a shame. We had great times here.'

I watched as he shook off the sadness and put on a beaming smile once more.

'My dear friend. You look so much older.'

'It has been a long time.'

'It has. I cannot believe you are back. Are you back to stay?'

'No. I'm here because I've lost something and I think it might be here.' I fought the urge to tell him more. Despite him appearing genuine with his happiness that I was back, I didn't feel like I could trust him.

'That's possible. You left in such a hurry.'

I felt my heart rate increase. Anticipation started to flood into my muscles. I could feel them brace, ready to move. This was it. I was about to find out what I had taken, I was about to be able to make the call that would secure the safety of the two most important people in my life. Two of three. Katie was there, level with Rachael. Both below Thomas.

'Tell me about when I left.'

'There is not much to tell. One day you were here, working in this tavern for me. We locked up together and I watched you walk down the road back to where you lived. There was nothing to suggest it would be the last time I saw you. Then, you were gone. No one knew where. Years later we were told you had died. Michael? What happened?'

'I don't know.'

'But you were in an accident?'

'A car accident.'

'A car accident, yes that was what we were told.'

'When I woke up I couldn't remember my name. I couldn't remember anything.'

'Nothing at all?'

'My family changed my name. I've been living as Daniel Lynch since then. I've no idea who you are or why I am in Auvers or why I feel like I know this place.'

'Michael.'

'Please, it's Daniel.'

'Daniel, I'm so sorry to hear this, my friend. I'm Martin.'

'How long was I here? How long did I work for you?'

'I'm not sure how long you were here, but you worked for me for, let's see, two years.'

'Two years?!'

It was a huge chunk of time, time I couldn't remember. I wondered why my mum hadn't told me this when we were talking about the place. Then I realized. She didn't know. I was in France in that time when we had lost touch. What I didn't understand was why France, and why didn't I tell her?

'Do you know why I came here?'

'That was always a little mystery. But, one thing you used to say was that you were waiting for your father to join you.'

213

'My father?'

'That's what you said.'

My father. I was waiting for him to find me in a remote town we had visited once. The same town he moved back to and, from what I had been told, died in. I wondered if Martin would know him if he saw him? Taking the photo of me and him in 1999 from my pocket, I held it in Martin's direction. He took it from my hand and looked, a smile drawing across his face, as wide and youthful as a smile could be.

'This is how I remember you. You are so young here.'

'The man beside me, he was my father. Did you know him?'

He squinted and brought the picture close to his face. 'Oh my, yes, I knew him. He used to drink here before he died. We often chatted. He was a quiet, kind man.'

With a sad smile he handed the picture back to me.

'Do you know how he died?'

'I was told it was cancer.'

'Martin, my father, did he ever talk of having a family or anything like that?'

'No, nothing like that.'

'I see.'

It made no sense. I had lived here when I was young, waiting for my father to join me and then years later he comes here to die on his own. Auvers had a hold on everything to do with my past, but I couldn't work out what.

I pushed the thousand new questions to one side – about how he died, who was at his funeral, where was he buried. I wasn't here for my father, I was here to protect the right to call myself one. The only title that meant anything. The only one worth fighting, and if need be, dying for.

'I mentioned I think I left things here. Might you know where I could find them? Or where to start looking at least?'

'You don't need to search. I know exactly where your things are.'

214

'Really?'

'Yes, of course. Everything you left is at Madame Etoile's house.'

'Who?'

'You lived with her and her husband.'

'And she has kept my stuff all this time?'

'That's what she has told me.'

'Why?'

'That's for her to tell you.'

I tried to place her in my head. What she looked like, how well we had got on fifteen years ago. Did she look after me? Did she know what I had done?

'She told me she always knew you would come back, despite us all being told you had died. She somehow knew you were alive somewhere.'

'Did we get along?'

'You and Etoile, yes, she was very fond of you, we all were.'

Martin smiled at me and I believed him. It seemed, for a short time, I had a good life here. I still didn't know why I came or why, if it was so good, I left. But that would have to wait. I needed to see those things, my things. I needed to understand why I was here and what it had to do with my son. I looked out of the window and into the street. A car sat parked, its engine idling, maybe fifty feet from the door of the pub. I felt like it was the same car that had followed me the day before. I thought I was being followed still, and I didn't like it. I had two options: confront them or lose them. If I confronted them it might harm Rachael or, God forbid, Thomas. So I had to lose them somehow. Auvers was too small, which meant I was likely to have a tail until I was back in Paris. But first, I needed to go to this Madame Etoile's. I needed my things. I must have looked anxious to leave.

'Mich … Daniel. Is something wrong?'

I could have tried to lie, but I didn't see the point. I was now in my penultimate day to find whatever I had taken, and I was tired.

'Yes, something is wrong.'

'But you cannot talk of it?'

'No, I cannot talk of it.'

'Is there anything I can do to help?'

'That's really kind, but no, Martin. No one can help me. I just need to get to my things.'

'I see. I suppose you don't know how to get to Madame Etoile's, do you?'

'No, no I don't.'

Martin stood, walked to his sink, and opened the drawer beside it then took a pen and a piece of paper. He began writing. I stood to join him. He drew a rough map through the town to her house. Before handing it over he made me promise that once I had found what I needed, I'd come back for a real visit. I agreed. I hoped I meant it.

'Daniel, your French is a little rusty. Perhaps talk slower with her.'

'Sorry?'

'Your French, it's a little fast, she is hard of hearing now.'

I nodded, not knowing what else to do. I hadn't realized, but the entire time I had been speaking in French.

Grabbing my bag I said goodbye and stepped outside. I glanced to my right. The car was gone. That made things a little easier, for now. They were still somewhere, watching. I could feel it. Walking in the direction Martin told me, I looked at the scrap of paper he had drawn the map on. At the bottom were the words, '*Dieu accelere, mon cher ami*'. God speed my old friend.

I knew what it meant without needing to give it a second thought. Like I was reading English. I stopped walking and looked around me. There was a shop to my left, and in the window was a handwritten sign. '*Vente a moitie prix sur tous les pulls hommes.*' Half-price sale on all men's jumpers. I said it out loud, the words flowing from my tongue. I said my name. I said my name and that I was a man who was desperately trying to find something and free his family, and I said it all in a language I didn't think I knew. Every word spoken to the few people I had spoken with, every question I had asked, all in a language I didn't know, that Daniel didn't know. Stuffing my hands into my pockets, I walked towards the address given, hoping I would find what I needed in Michael's old things, praying there would be no more surprises. I'd had a lifetime of them already.

Chapter 38

Daniel

Auvers

4th January 2018, 12.38 p.m.

I knocked on the door lightly and on the third knock it swung open. The old lady before me must have been at least eighty-five. Her tiny, fragile frame was hidden under what could only be described as a house coat. A cigarette hung loosely between brittle fingers. She looked, at any moment, like she might blow away like the ash that bent from the end of her Marlboro. I knew what brand without needing to see it.

'Madame Etoile?'

The old lady stepped out of her doorway and took my hand. She examined it, turning it over before releasing it again. She looked at my shoulders, my face, focusing on my beard. Dropping her cigarette, she placed her tiny jagged hands on my cheeks. They felt cold to the touch. She examined my cut, a questioning look in her cataract-filled eyes. And then she locked on to mine. The quizzical look had gone, turning into one of shock and joy.

She smiled as her eyes brimmed with tears. Her smile was as youthful and wide as Martin's, transforming the image of her

218

before me. It seemed that everyone in Auvers smiled with the same intensity. I felt like I knew her smile well, like I had seen it countless times before, despite having no idea who she was. It filled me with warmth.

'Michael. Oh my dear boy, Michael!'

She wrapped her thin arms around my neck, making me need to either stoop or pick her up. Deciding it was safer to stoop I gently placed an arm on her back, my palm resting against her spine which protruded from her tiny frame. I could feel her crying on my shoulder as she thanked God for saving me.

'I knew you weren't dead. I knew. Oh my dear boy, Michael. It's so good to see you.'

She let me go and, taking my hand, she led me into her house. It was almost as cold inside as it was out. But I was grateful to be inside regardless. She gestured for me to take off my coat and I hung it on a peg before following her down the narrow, dark corridor. We were heading for the kitchen and although I hadn't seen it, I knew exactly how it looked.

A breakfast bar to the right and a range cooker beside it. Pots hanging in size order on a wall near a window that had a blue frame. A table on the opposite side.

A man with a pipe and newspaper. The sound of jazz coming from a small cassette player.

I couldn't believe the image was so clear to me. I could almost smell stew cooking on the stove and freshly ground morning coffee. Stepping into the kitchen it was almost exactly as I pictured it. Although it was more tired-looking than I pictured. The table where I had clearly seen the man reading the paper was empty. Etoile noticed me looking towards the vacant chair.

'He passed, about six years ago.'

'I'm sorry. He was a good man,' I said, knowing somehow it was true.

She smiled again, another that defied her age. 'One person dies, another is brought to life.'

I needed to ask her about where my things were, but didn't want to. I could see she was pleased to see me. I could see I had meant something to her. But I was needed somewhere else more urgently.

'Madame Etoile, I really don't want to sound rude but ...'

'Yes, of course, I know you are in a rush. Martin called before you arrived.'

'I'm sorry.'

'He said you cannot remember your time here?'

'No.'

My head dropped. I was tired. I was sad and something about this woman made me feel like I could be real about it all.

'You are in trouble?'

'Yes.'

I sat down without being offered a seat, and without being able to stop myself, I told her everything I knew. The call in the middle of the night, the picture they had sent. Sean being dead. The police thinking I did it all. Once I started to speak I couldn't stop. I needed it all out of my head. I needed someone else to hold the weight of my turmoil, even for a moment so I could strengthen myself to hold it again. I told her about Thomas, how wonderful he was, how his laugh lit my soul. How he was my best friend. He wasn't just someone I loved, he was most of my heart and it wouldn't beat without him.

'Michael,' she said, stopping me mid-sentence. 'One day you can tell me all about him. But we both know that's not today.'

'I'm running out of time. I don't even know what I took.'

'You came to us from nowhere. You were so young and although you walked and spoke with confidence I could see a boy's fear in your eyes. You were hiding. I saw it. My late husband saw it. But we never asked.'

'Why not?'

'You were a good boy, a kind boy. Whatever it was, we wanted to keep you safe. Over the time you lived here we got to know you.'

'How long was I here?'

'Nearly three years.'

'I don't remember any of it.'

'That is truly a shame. And one day, I will tell you about your time here.'

Madame Etoile walked past me, touching my shoulder on the way back down the corridor and, turning left, she went up the stairs. I followed quietly behind. At the top she turned left again and into a small room.

'This was your room.'

The space was small but pleasant. There was a large window. Outside was white washed.

'We offered you a different room, but you took this one for the view. It's a shame the weather is so terrible. It's quite spectacular.'

'The view of Auvers,' I said to myself quietly.

'Yes.'

Something spun in my mind. Something I couldn't quite connect to. But the view was important. The view was what my father had a photo of. The view was the reason he would know where to find me. The view was the reason I had moved here rather than anywhere else. I felt like all those years ago I was hiding, waiting to be saved.

'Michael.'

I turned from the window and in Madame Etoile's hands was a shoebox.

'Everything you left is in here. In this room, or in this box. I'll give you some time.'

I couldn't take my eyes off the box as she handed it to me.

'I hope what you need is in here.'

Closing the door behind her, I listened as she went downstairs. Once it was silent I looked through the wardrobe and drawers in the room. Still full of Michael's clothes. I found nothing of interest so sitting on the bed, I opened the lid to the shoebox that Etoile suggested was important. Inside were stacks of envelopes. I took them out, hoping for something more. Something obvious. Each one was addressed to Michael Gardner. I had assumed I was still a Lynch, even back then. I counted thirty-three in all. All of them had an ink mark in the corner. HMP Wandsworth. I opened the first. It was dated February 2000.

Michael.

I'm glad you found a way to write. I'm glad you are safe and well. It won't be long till we're together again. I know where you are. As soon as I'm out and away from these long nights, I'll come to you. Until then, work hard, keep your head low.

Is the view up close as beautiful as I imagine it to be? I can't wait to see it. A perfect picture, just for us.

Dad.

I opened another. This one was dated June of the same year.

Michael.

Thank you for your letter. I'm so glad to hear you are settled in your new life. It sounds like you are with good people. Kind people. I wish it had always been that way. Last week was the quarter way mark of my time away from you. I'm keeping quiet. Doing my time. Hoping that it might mean I am out sooner and with you and the view. The days blur, one into another. The nights are long and noisy here, but I just think about the future we planned and I can silence them in my head.

I can't wait to be with you again, my son. Looking at that life-changing view that's just for us.

Dad.

I read five more. October 2000; March 2001; Jan 2002; September 2002 and the Christmas of the same year. Each one was short. Each one talked about the long nights and the view.

I picked up another. The name Michael Gardner was underlined. The first one to do so. Taking out the folded letter I could see it was different straightaway.

Michael.

The days are feeling shorter. Much shorter, and they are starting to feel Bright. I cannot wait to be with you, where you are, with that view. It must be beautiful. I can only imagine other people want to share it with you also.

I hope this reaches you happy and well.

Send my love to Kim.

Dad.

There was nothing particularly troubling about it. In fact, it almost seemed positive – the shorter days, the sharing of a lovely view of the town. And yet, I read it three times. Each time filled me with a sensation of panic. I looked at the date. It was March 2003.

A month before my accident.

I looked through the other envelopes, hoping to find something that would show me what I needed to do next. But there was nothing. I put everything back in the box and went back to the kitchen where Madame Etoile sat patiently waiting.

'When did I leave here?'

'March 2003.'

'Did I take anything with me?'

'You snuck out in the middle of the night. You didn't leave a note, you didn't say goodbye. You just vanished. When we realized you weren't up the next morning we came in to your room. Your bag and telescope were gone.'

'Telescope?'

'It came with you from England and you left here with it.'

'What did it look like?'

'Like a telescope, it was about 3 feet long, white. Fairly old. You kept it close, you hid it under the bed. In all the time you were here I never saw you gaze at the stars, not once.'

'Didn't you think that odd?'

'Of course, but I'm not one to meddle in other people's business. I assumed it belonged to someone you cared for.'

I saw it in pieces. The lenses removed. The empty cylinder lying on a table.

Wrapping it in a plastic bag.

Then it was raining, I was by a tree digging a hole. Covered in wet mud.

A crow crying somewhere close.

A telescope? Could this be happening to my family because I took a telescope? It didn't make sense. No, there was something inside it. Something hidden in its hollow barrel.

'Do you know where I went when I left?'

'No.'

'Did you not want to?'

'Of course I did. We both did. But we couldn't find you. We hoped you were going home to reconnect with your mother. We were heartbroken, but happy that you were mending your relationship.'

'Mending? What do you mean?'

'Oh, Michael, you often talked of how your mother threw you out of the house.'

'She did?'

'When you came to us you'd not spoken in a long time.'

I don't know why I was so shocked. It seemed my mum kept a lot from me, thinking it would do me good. She had always, in the time I can remember, been a rock for me to lean on and now I was learning I had been kicked out, disowned by the woman who cared for me and nursed me back to health after my car accident. The woman who I had always remembered being loving and supportive and patient. What on earth had Michael done to mean she wanted him gone? Who was the boy who had fled to France? I had come all this way, used up all this time, a thing I didn't have

224

much of, and I felt like I was coming away with nothing. A few letters and the knowledge that I once owned a telescope that I never used, yet, when I fled in the middle of the night, I took it with me. And although I couldn't see it, there was something inside that telescope. Looking up at the kitchen clock I saw the time saying 1.16 p.m. I needed to leave soon. On the train home I would read all of the letters again and try to find out more about this Michael Gardner who my mum seemed to dislike.

Leaning over I wrapped my arms around the bony frame of Madame Etoile and thanked her for returning my things. I wanted to thank her for my forgotten time when I lived in her home and shared her life, but I didn't. As I put on my coat I could see her eyes well up.

'Michael, please find a way to tell me when you get your boy back.'

'When I do, I'll bring him here, so you can meet him.'

She smiled, a tear escaping from her smoky eye. I meant it. Once I had found what I needed and got my boy back I was going to take him and Rachael far away from the hurt. Far away from the home we had built and where Sean was killed. Far away from the press which were no doubt beginning to gather into a storm around the house. I would bring them here, so they could heal from their trauma and the loss of Sean and we would quietly learn to live with the events of this week as we looked at the view. I pictured us three in the pub, hot chocolate near the open fire. Thick jumpers hanging loosely on our shoulders. Our smiles meek at first but growing wider and wider until we mirrored the youthful ones of the people I had met in the past twenty-four hours. Thomas would take a big sip of his drink, the chocolate giving him a moustache. Rachael would laugh, so would I. Thomas would join in once he saw what was so funny.

And for a moment I could hear his laugh and it broke my heart all over again. I opened the door to leave, but I remembered there was one more thing I needed to ask.

'Madame Etoile, who's Kim?'

'Kim? I don't know anyone by that name.'

Her answer confused me. I was expecting her to tell me it was a lover I took whilst I stayed.

'My father mentioned someone called Kim in a letter? Was there no one by that name?'

'No, there has never been anyone called Kim that I know of.'

'Could I perhaps have been seeing someone of that name?'

'No, I don't remember. I don't think so, you did like to keep yourself to yourself.'

I had heard that before, but about my father. Perhaps I was more like him than I thought.

'If I kept myself detached why did you let me live with you?'

'You had a kind heart.'

I smiled at her words.

'Michael, how are you getting home? Do you need money?'

I wanted to say no, but that was a lie and my silence spoke volumes. She stepped away from the door to retrieve something that was in the small cupboard which housed her boiler. I could see lots of notes all stuffed into glass jam jars.

'Please, I cannot take this.'

'It's your money, Michael. You insisted on paying us rent to stay, but we didn't have the heart to spend it. We kept it, thinking that one day you would want to get a place of your own. Of course, we had to change it when the Franc was discontinued, but it's all there.'

'And you've kept it all this time?'

'I always hoped this day would come. Only, I wish it was under better circumstances.'

'Me too,' I said, meaning it.

I took some of the money, a fraction of what was in the pot, kissed her on the cheek and stepped into the street closing the door behind me so she didn't have to.

The walk back to the station was hard, the wind battering me, punishing me for my sins. Once I arrived I looked at the board. The train was delayed, but thankfully not by much. I stepped into the waiting room, an old but clean space with dated chairs and built-in ashtrays that still showed the signs of a thousand cigarettes that had been extinguished over the years. On the walls around me were paintings. Some familiar, some not. Under them were the names of the artists. Van Gogh, Daubigny, Cezanne, Pissarro. I knew all of their names. Famous artists who, from what I saw, had been to this small town to paint. I went to sit and as I did I saw a man across the line on the adjacent platform looking at me. Watching. I stepped back into the blizzard and startled him. He turned and left the station. I wanted to follow but decided against it. I knew why they were watching. They wanted to see if I had the item yet. Realizing that scared me. It meant one of two things. They either didn't trust me to deliver, despite them holding something so much more valuable, or they didn't plan to uphold their side of the deal when I did give it back.

Seeing I was alone again, I went back inside and sat next to the small radiator in the corner that blew out a little warmth. I pressed my back into the wall and angled my body towards the door.

Warming my cold body, I waited, watching the departure board and hoping the train wasn't further delayed.

227

Chapter 39

Rachael

The Garage

4th January 2018, 1.08 p.m.

Tom and I had been playing the game again: How many steps to the door, how many to the vent? What he should do when the bolt slid open. He answered, and I could see he tried to be enthusiastic, but he was tired, he was cold. So was I. And I knew he was missing things like TV and warm milk and socks. He didn't say it, I could see it in his face. Now, bored and fed up, he sat on the bed picking at his toenails, both of us on the bed trying to keep warm. Then, I heard shouting from outside the door. It was The Bear's voice. He sounded angry. Rushing to the door I placed my ear on it to try to hear better but the sound of his deep voice bounced off the walls and filtered to me as jumbled echoes. I tried to hear whether whoever he was angry at replied, but it was impossible to make out any other voice than his, although I was sure there were two more. A door slammed and I heard him shout, 'fine, fuck off then.' Tom had stopped picking at his toes and he looked at me afraid.

'It's okay, darling. I think he's just trying to sing.'

'It sounds like he's shouting, Mummy.'

'Well, don't tell him that. He thinks he sounds like Ed Sheeran!'

I smiled at Tom and he smiled back. Then I put my fingers in my ears and made a funny face which made him laugh.

'He wouldn't do well on *X Factor*, would he?' I said, and still laughing, Tom replied saying Louis might like him, and I laughed too.

Footsteps came towards us. I felt panic rise in my chest. Calmly I told Tom to hide, like it was the same as it had been for the last few days. But this time it felt different. The Bear was angry, it was something I didn't want to see. And if it wasn't him it could be The Smiler, or the tattooed one as I didn't know who had left. Of the three, I would want the angry Bear. Pulling the blanket over Tom, I sat on the floor in front of the bed. If they were about to try to do something, they would have to get through me first.

The lock snapped, the bolt slid, the door creaked open and, to my relief, it was The Bear, and he didn't look like the enraged thing I had just been listening to. He looked heartbroken and I couldn't help but feel relieved.

'Sorry.'

'Is everything okay?'

'Yes, fine. Just a disagreement.'

'Should I be worried for us?'

'No, no, not at all. I promise. I brought you some food, warm food. I promise the eggs are thoroughly cooked. They also had the red lion stamp on them, so they are okay for your ...'

I looked at him widening my eyes, asking him to stop. He understood that Tom didn't know.

'Anyway, I hope this warms you up.'

'Thank you.'

The Bear looked like he was about to say something else but stopped himself. He looked down in the direction of where Tom was hiding and slowly backed out of the room.

'Wait. What were you arguing about?'

229

'A few things. You shouldn't have ever been shown that picture.'

'Well, it's too late now, isn't it?'

'And you shouldn't have ever had those pictures taken of you,' he continued quietly. I looked away. Despite what happened earlier. 'So you know, they have been deleted.'

'Thank you, Sam.'

He didn't respond, instead he lowered his gaze to the floor and headed for the door. I stopped him before he left.

'Wait. If they are gone, you can help us. Let us go.'

'I can't do that.'

'Please, you can. You can just walk out and leave the door unlocked and go for a cigarette or something.'

'I can't.'

'It's just a little lock. Just leave it open.'

'No!' he shouted at me, startling me, making me take a few steps backwards. Then, he turned and left and closed the door behind him, the lock snapping shut too. I banged on the door, screaming at him to respond. I needed to know why this was happening to us, what we had done to deserve it. There was no response. When I stopped shouting I heard Tom crying behind me.

'Mummy?'

I turned quickly and watched him jump. My breathing was heavy, hair had fallen over my face. I must have looked like another monster in the story. Sweeping my hair out of my eyes I held my hands up towards him.

'Oh, darling, I'm sorry. I didn't mean to scare you.'

I approached him and he flinched away from me, scared to look me in the eye. Sitting on the floor beside him, I said I was sorry until he leant in and hugged me, filling me with relief.

But enough was enough. I had scared him. It was time to make a break for it. I had tried to beg, tried to seduce. I had tried explaining I was carrying. There was only one more thing to try, when the time was right.

Chapter 40

Daniel

Auvers

4th January 2018, 3.18 p.m.

The terrible weather and warnings not to travel meant the carriages were quieter than I anticipated. I had boarded at the front and walked to the rear. Head low, eyes watching. I counted thirty plus people in the first carriage, twenty-two in the second and only nine in the third so I chose this one to settle for the journey. No one could get behind me and I would have a clear view of anyone coming from the front. I could focus on research without having to dilute too much energy. Taking my seat, I looked out of the window and saw the same person as before watching me pull away. They were too wrapped up in clothing for me to see much, but it was definitely them.

I watched them until they were out of sight, and they watched me, neither of us moving, but I felt we knew each other. Was this possibly the Kim my father wrote of? Turning to face the headrest of the chair in front of me, it took me a moment to remember I was going to try and research my past. I took out the phone, went to Google and started to type my name. My previous search for 'Michael Lynch' filled the search bar. I deleted 'Lynch', and put in 'Gardner', my actual surname before 2003. And there I was, younger, harder, a look in my eyes I had never seen before. It was a stranger in my skin. The first article was from the *Slough Observer*. I had once made the news.

Guilty plea for man behind series of bizarre burglaries. Thief finally given time.

I read on and it told me about how Gardner had been arrested at the scene of a burglary. A silent alarm had notified the police and they caught him 'red handed' at the scene. It said it was suspected that he was connected to more in the area, although there was no evidence. His crimes were almost of a 'professional standard'. It said he was sentenced to six months in jail. The date on it was from February 1998.

I was twenty.

I was a convicted criminal. I wasn't surprised.

I went back to the Google search and read another article from another newspaper. I had twice made the news. My heart squeezed in my chest when I saw the date of it. April 2003. A few weeks before my first memory. I thought I was about to read of when I was nearly killed in the car crash, but the article said something entirely different and yet again, my head starting spinning at the lies that were the foundation of my life. The headline made me feel like I was going to faint.

Man found close to death after savage street attack.

Chapter 41

Daniel

The Train to Paris

4th January 2018, 3.21 p.m.

'Police are looking for any information that can help identify suspects of an attack which has left one man fighting for his life.'

I couldn't read any more. Locking the phone, I rested it on my lap and looked out of the window. I focused on the vast nothingness that the world became post-snow and tried to get my breathing under control. I didn't want to know anything new about me anymore. I didn't want to have surprise after surprise about my life before 2003. I didn't want to learn that my life as I knew it was just a lie. But it couldn't go back to the way it was, the blissful ignorance I once lived in. I had to face the past.

The articles told me two new things: I was once in prison, and my head injury, that I had been told was the result of a car accident, was in fact an attempt on my life. Who the hell was I? A long time ago I had been beaten half to death. I had been beaten half to death just after leaving Auvers and that beating took away my childhood, and more importantly, my crime. I had a headache coming on and I pinched the bridge of my nose, hoping it would help. It didn't. The lack of food, the abundance of alcohol and the fact that my face had been glued together a few times covering my smashed-in tooth, as well as the mental overload of discovering who I was, were all beginning to take their toll. I wanted to sleep and then wake and laugh as it was all just a vivid, horrid dream.

But that was wishful thinking.

This was reality, and frightening. This was more of a reality than the past fourteen, nearly fifteen years had even been. I took a deep breath in. The warm cabin air was still cooler than the inside of my mouth so it caused the nerve in my tooth to send fire into my face. I couldn't think with it causing so much intense pain. It had to come out. Going into the bathroom I opened my mouth and looked at it. More than half the tooth was missing, a hairline fracture going all the way into my gum line. I looked around for something I could use. There was nothing obvious. Part of the mirror's plastic casing was cracked. I hooked my fingers under it and pulled. It hurt my fingertips but it started to come away – enough for me to get my full palm wrapped round it. With one final yank I pulled it off. I now had a splinter of hard plastic frame that felt sharp to the touch. I stuck it in my mouth and pressed the tip into the gum next to the tooth. The pain was intense as I pressed harder, pushing the gum as far back up the tooth as possible. My gum bled as it was forced to expose more of the broken tooth. I could see the colour of it change as it became root. I did the same on the other side, and pulled on the tooth. It wobbled but not enough to get it out. I cut the other side, more blood came. It covered my shaking hands, making them sticky. I cut as far as I could manage the pain. Then, grabbing the tooth, I pulled. It took every fibre of my being for me not to scream out. I hadn't managed to remove it, but it was now longer than the others beside it. I had loosened it. I took a deep breath, preparing myself mentally for what I knew was going to hurt, a lot.

Gripping it as best I could, I pulled hard and fast. A sucking sound came from my mouth as it dislodged from the gum line and came out. More blood. It hurt like hell, forcing me to stumble and sit on the toilet seat. I closed my eyes and held my breath to not scream out. I knew it would die to a dull throb and not rob me of my ability to think. I reached for the loo roll and pressed some hard into my mouth until the blood flow slowed to something I could manage with the occasional swallow. Having washed my face and hands in the sink, I left the bathroom and through blurred vision I sat back in my chair, my legs not wholly trustworthy. My adrenaline was so high my skin itched. I wiped my brow and concentrated on my breathing until the pain began to ease.

The phone buzzed on my lap. It was Katie. The message was short and direct. A warning.

Daniel, you are on the news. Get in touch when you can
X

I knew I would be, but prepared myself anyway. Going to the BBC website I saw that the alert about Sean had become an article. He was named. So were Rachael and Thomas. A picture of them hugging. It was one that was on their mantelpiece. Her smile was wide and all the way to her eyes. Thomas's tongue was sticking out.

The copper who had visited my mum was mentioned – DCI Holt. She was the lead investigator and was gunning for me. A nation was calling for 'men like me' to be punished to the full extent of the law. Then I saw my name. The third time in my life I had been in the news. They wanted to speak to me urgently, not saying I was a suspect but a 'person of interest'. They were appealing for anyone who knew where I was to call a hotline number. I was now a name everyone would know. Closing the app, I rang Rachael's number, the voicemail clicking instantly and their voices breaking my heart.

I messaged Katie back telling her that my train was getting in at about 8 p.m. I said I wanted to see her. It was dangerous, I knew that, but I also knew that a moment with her would give me the strength for what I had to do next.

With Katie by my side I felt strong enough to finish this thing, find what I took, and get them back.

Chapter 42

Rachael

The Garage

4th January 2018, 4.19 p.m.

The Bear hadn't been back since I got angry with him and shouted through the locked door, and now I was angry with myself for not holding my emotions closer. I tried to reason with him, first through sex, then with the truth. A normal person would have responded. But he wasn't a normal man, was he? He was a monster. He didn't feel the same sense of right and wrong that normal people did. And he'd not returned. I started to believe we were going to rot here, or one of the other two would come and kill us. If that was the case, I hoped for The Smiler. I didn't want the tattooed man to touch me again; just the thought of him made me shudder and I wrapped my arms around my chest, the new top The Bear had given me making my skin itch.

Tom was asleep, he was sleeping more in the few days we had been trapped here than he would in an entire week. Maybe it was the side effects of the drugs, maybe it was the lack of stimulation or food. Or maybe, his young subconscious mind was fully aware of what was happening, and it was shutting his body down as a way of protecting him. Regardless, I was, in a strange way, grateful. He didn't have to think whilst he slept. He didn't have to work out that he was living in a nightmare. I periodically checked to make sure he wasn't cold and that his nose and mouth weren't too close to the rancid covers he slept under. I paced. I pressed my face to the small vent, trying to feel the rain that had started an hour before hit my skin. I paced some more and then sat in the corner, hugging my knees, trying to empty my mind. But Sean was there when I closed my eyes, his face barely recognizable under the horrific injuries. His skin was ripped from his face. My husband had beautiful skin. I often teased him that even when he was older he would still be a baby face. I tried to think about that, about his skin. How flawless it was. Barely any wrinkles. But all I saw were the knife wounds.

I wasn't sure I'd ever sleep properly again.

I distracted myself by watching Tom, his back rising and falling gently. I hoped he was having a lovely dream of being somewhere warm. His breathing and the rain lashing against the vent was the only thing I could hear. It was quiet, not just outside, but in my head too. Maybe the quietest it had been in a number of years. I knew the quietness that existed inside me was because I was slipping deeper and deeper into shock. Shock could kill a person. I should have been trying to manage it. Instead, I thought of my life, questioning if it was a good one. Did I love well enough? Had I made the right choices for the people in my life? Was I a good enough mother? Was I a good daughter to my own? Did I mirror her kindness, her patience? Did I tell her enough that I loved her? I tried to think of the last time I made it clear that she was so dear to me, but I couldn't think of a recent time when I had. The only one coming to me was in the early hours of a warm summer evening as I lay in a quiet hospital ward. The silence was like a bubble wrapped around me, Daniel, Tom and her. The sky was beginning to turn from deep blue to amber as the sun rose. I lay in a nighty with a cannula in one arm and a bundle in the other, fresh stitches holding my tummy together, Tom feeding from my breast. My mum stroked my hair. She told me I had done well, she told me she was proud. That may have been the last time I told my mum I loved her.

I would not let it go so long ever again.

I thought of Daniel on that night, how happy he was. How he could barely speak. How he held Thomas against his chest in the chair beside me, an expression on his face I had never seen before. He really was a wonderful father to our little boy. I hoped he was okay. I hoped he was looking for us, using his instincts to save us from this hell hole. And I hoped he would be here soon. I needed him more than ever.

Thinking of them both allowed me to feel tired. Especially my mum – her face in my mind calmed me, reassured me. Like she did the night Tom was born. Like she had done a thousand times when I was a baby. For a brief moment, I could feel her kisses on my forehead. I could feel her arms wrapped around me. I could hear her voice singing the same song I sang to Tom. I closed my eyes, allowing her voice to wash over me. Focusing on her stopped me thinking about anything else just long enough for me to doze.

Chapter 43

Daniel

Paris

4th January 2018, 5.23 p.m.

Finally, over four hours after leaving Madame Etoile's, I had made it to Paris and, disembarking the train, I became acutely aware of flat-screen TVs playing the news. It seemed as if the Gare du Nord had televisions everywhere I looked. High on walls of seated waiting areas. All of them playing the news. Mostly French news stations or world news reports. Some the BBC. I leant against a wall, swallowing some fresh blood and watched one that was to my right, high up on a display board near the entrance. I couldn't hear what was being said by the reporter, but I knew the background. He was stood outside Rachael's house. Police tape lined the footpaths and onlookers were either trying to see inside or laying flowers on the driveway. The camera moved to show some of the people mourning on my old lawn. Heartbroken, without knowing who Sean was or who Rachael and Thomas are. Cards and messages and candles filled the pavement. People stood around waiting. For what, I didn't know. The camera panned back. There were more people than I thought. Dozens of them, maybe more, holding umbrellas that were frequently popping inside out as they tried to shelter themselves and their candles from the winter rain. A night vigil for Rachael, and my beautiful son.

A mother came on to the screen, her son about the same age as mine in her arms. She was speaking and shaking her head. I could almost hear her saying, 'I can't believe something like this would happen here.' The reporter said something else, his expression serious and sullen then the screen cut to a clip of people walking together in a line through Burghley Park. Torches and high visibility jackets. Stepping in unison, throwing the torch light onto the wet ground. I wondered why they were there for a second, but then remembered where I had dumped my car three days before, although it felt like it was weeks since I had done so. I mused that they suspected I had dumped my family there also. I couldn't imagine anything more horrific. In the line I saw faces I recalled. Stamford being small meant everyone was familiar. They all had their eyes to the ground, looking, hoping not to find either Rachel or Thomas. Across the screen a title said, 'A community left shocked. A community searching.'

Then I saw them. Rachael and Thomas. The same picture that was online. I took the phone and dialled her number and listened to their voices as I looked at them until a film of tears blurred them from me. I blinked, quickly catching a tear as it fell, and their picture was gone. It had been replaced by a picture of me. It was from Rachael's 40th birthday the year before. I was drunk and tired. My eyes were dark and hollow. The night was a blast and Sean and I had had a few too many. At the point this picture was taken, he was in the bathroom being sick.

I remembered Rachael, Katie and other friends laughing at me as I protested I wasn't that drunk. Moments after the picture was taken I was up and dancing, the women in my life laughing at me. The picture was to be mocked, something to be teased about. The media had used it to make me look like a monster. They made me look like the kind of man who could hurt his ex and

241

his child. I couldn't look anymore. I glanced around to see if anyone had seen my reaction to the screen, but the station was too busy. People were too desperate to get home. Everyone was keeping to themselves, weaving through one another to go to their next destination. Ties were loosened. Heels had been replaced with trainers for walking. I watched them moving in an almost insect-like fashion. Their days were drawing to an end. Soon they would be sitting down to a good meal or going out for drinks with friends. They would be bathing their children and walking their dogs. Then, they would all go to bed, warm and comfortable with their lovers or wives or husbands. They would wake up tomorrow. A new day, a new beginning.

And I hated them for it.

They were back in the studio. A woman was standing, like she was about to do a weather report, but they weren't talking about the tumbling temperatures and threat of snow. A caption read 'What we know so far.' Bullet points appeared underneath as she spoke. I was beginning to panic. I needed to speak with the voice and tell him that I wouldn't try to clear my name. I would remain the fugitive until I found what was his. Taking the phone out, I was about to dial but could feel someone watching me. I looked up. Ten feet away was a man staring. Once our eyes met he looked away, trying to make it seem as if it was just one of those moments people often had. But I could see him wanting to look at the TV screen. I thought for a moment that I was being paranoid. But, for a split second he looked at me again and began walking away, his phone coming out of his pocket. Somehow, through the disguise I had been noticed. I had been sloppy. He must have watched me watching the screen. I must have given away my connection and made it easy for him to imagine my face without a beard. I followed at a distance as he moved through the crowd, bumping into people, his pace quickening. He veered to the left, heading towards the ticket counters. No doubt trying to alert the station police. I couldn't let him do that.

As I pursued, there was an announcement, a platform altera-
tion for a train going south to Lille. It caused a mass migration
of people all moving in the direction we were travelling. The
crowd got so thick I momentarily lost the top of my mark's head
in it. I had to stop him now. If I didn't and he managed to alert
someone, getting back to England would be impossible, as would
saving my family. I sped up, pushing through people to get closer.
He looked and saw me coming but couldn't move faster than the
crowd dictated. I ducked behind a large man speaking loudly into
his phone and watched as he searched for me amongst the sea
of faces. Doing so slowed him until the large man was beside
him. My mark turned to hurry his pace and as he did, I stepped
out and tripped him, sending him tumbling onto the marble
floor. I made it look like I was trying to catch him, a stranger
whose instincts were to grab, but just as he hit the floor, his arms
outstretched to break his fall, I slammed his head down. The
sound of his skull impacting the hard marble stopped people
nearest to us. It didn't take long for the blood to form into a
small pool beside us. I was hoping that although Paris was busy
and fast moving, people still cared enough to stop and help. They
did, and standing straight, I said I was going to get someone from
the station. I took his phone and backed away. I could see the
man was unconscious, a deep gash on his eyebrow where I had
slammed it into the ground. I knew what it was like to have a
head injury. I wanted to feel bad. Perhaps I would one day.

I walked until I was far enough away from the commotion,
until there was no sign of it at all and glancing towards the board,
I saw that I could start to move to my platform. By the time I
had been through Passport Control the adrenaline caused by
attacking a stranger was gone.

And I was Peter Morales once more. Just another man, coming
home from a meeting in the French capital.

Chapter 44

Rachael

The Garage

4th January 2018, 6.37 p.m.

I felt something tap my leg, making me jump, and opening my eyes I saw Tom. He was stood in front of me, shivering, his eyes looking sunken like those of an old man. I felt guilty for not hearing him wake and being awake myself to comfort him. Getting to my knees, my hip aching from the hard ground I had slept on, I wrapped him in my arms to warm him.

'How long have you been up?'

'A few minutes.'

'You should have woken me straightaway.'

'I didn't want you to lose any more sleep. You look tired, Mummy.'

'I am tired, darling, but it's part of the story.'

He didn't respond but lowered his head and rested it on my shoulder.

'Darling, are you okay?'

'Mummy …' he started, not able to finish what he wanted to say. I thought for a second he'd had another accident. I moved him gently away from me to check, but he was dry and clean. Holding him a foot away from me I looked at his face.

'Tom, darling?'

He looked at the floor, like he had done something wrong. He could do anything in this situation and it wouldn't be wrong, although I didn't want to tell him that, because then he would know how bad it really was.

'I don't want to say.'

'It's okay. You can tell me.'

'You promise not to get mad?'

'Yes, darling. I promise.'

'I don't like this game anymore. I don't want to play in the story. I hate it. I want to go home.'

There was something in the tone of his voice, a delicacy that told me right now he was walking on a tightrope and if he slipped it would mean his innocence would be lost forever. A thin, taut rope. That was all he had to hang on to. That tautness snapped my limbs awake. I felt the blood returning to them, I felt my fingers move like they had been frozen solid up until this moment. Fuck this place. Fuck the wiry man who enjoyed watching us suffer. Fuck The Bear who was too much of a coward to undo what he had done. We were leaving. We were leaving this hell hole.

'Yes, baby, we are going to go home.'

'Really?'

'And it's time to start chapter seven, darling.'

'What's this one called?'

'It's called "Ready to Run".'

'"Ready to Run?"'

I could feel adrenaline start to move though my body. 'Tom, darling. When I tell you, I need you to go under the bed for me, okay?'

'Do I have to?'

'Just one last time. Remember what I told you about the lamp?'

'If it goes dark I have to wait for you to tell me to come out and when I do I must keep my eyes squeezed shut. Like this.'

He screwed up his face as small as he could, making me smile. Somehow, despite the night and day we had endured, the hunger, the fear, the knowledge my husband had been murdered, Tom still managed to make me smile.

'Good boy. How many steps?'

'Fourteen or sixteen.'

'You're so clever. You make Mummy so proud. Now go, under the bed.'

I kissed him on the head and he crawled back under and put the blanket in place, his eyes poking out near the top, watching the lamp.

'Remember, darling, when it goes dark, wait for my voice.'

'I promise.'

'Good boy.'

I got up and pressed my ear to the door, closing my eyes to hear as well as I possibly could. Earlier, after The Bear had been shouting, I'd heard a door open and slam. I hadn't heard it again. I hoped that meant The Bear was alone somewhere in the building. The other two hadn't returned, or so I hoped. I started counting in my head. If after two minutes it was still silent, I was going to act.

Chapter 45

Daniel

The Eurostar

4th January 2018, 6.38 p.m.

Another train, another seat with my back to the exit and a clear view of what could come towards me. Another few hours to wait. Given the context, it was an eternity. If I never went on another train journey for the rest of my life it would be no loss.

But it didn't change the fact that I was coming home empty-handed.

I started to get a rising sick feeling in my stomach. Slowly it crept past my diaphragm and began burning in my throat. I tried taking deep, measured breaths to calm it which caused a fresh lightning strike of pain in my face. My jaw began to feel lax, the acid still climbing. Getting up from my seat I stumbled to the bathroom, barely managing to lift the seat before I heaved into the pan, hot acid that folded me in half as I'd not eaten in a while. It burnt, running freely against the gap where my tooth used to be. With my eyes streaming I looked into the pan and thought that I had vomited blood. It wasn't until I stood and saw myself in the small mirror above the sink that I realized it was just blood from inside my mouth. I splashed my face with cold water and returned to my chair. I needed to eat something. The sudden force of being ill had left me feeling like my legs were hollow. When the trolley came through I would get a hot tea, and a sandwich of some kind. Until then I had to use the time constructively. I still didn't have the item I needed. I argued with myself about whether I was any closer at all. And the panic began to rise inside me again. Don't think about how or why, but when. Focus on the when.

I took out the letters sent by my father and began reading them. It settled my churning insides. I flicked through them and many were of the same nature as the ones I had read. I picked up the last letter in the chronological pile. The last one my father had sent me before I fled Auvers in 2003.

Michael.

The days are feeling shorter. Much shorter, and they are starting to feel Bright. I cannot wait to be with you, where you are, with that view. It must be beautiful. I can only imagine other people want to share it with you also.

I hope this reaches you happy and well.

Send my love to Kim.

Dad.

As with most things in the past few days, it didn't make sense. There was no one called Kim. It wasn't the only thing that was off with the letter. My father had good handwriting and good grammar. In all I had read there wasn't a single mistake. Yet, this letter had a grammatical error on the word bright, the one word that he underlined. The word was important. That, and the name Kim.

My thoughts were interrupted with a BBC News update that pinged on to the phone, its one line causing me to want to vomit again.

Hunt widens for suspected murderer Daniel Lynch.

I wanted to open the app and read the article, but I knew it would do no good. I had to focus on getting Rachael and Thomas back, then the truth would spill. Then it would be over.

Reading the tagline again I had a thought. My name. Lynch. Capitals at the start of the name. Any other context and the l would be lower case. Bright wasn't a mistake. Bright was a name. I Googled 'Bright'. Then 'surname Bright'. There were thousands of references. Looking at the note again I typed in 'Kim Bright'. The first hit was Facebook profiles with that name. I scrolled down a little and saw something that caused a stirring inside me, like in the park at Wexham and when I saw the man I would steal from. An instinctive something that I couldn't ignore. The spelling was different, but there was a story which began talking about the passing of a London gang leader, mildly infamous in the Eighties and Nineties, Kym Bright.

For the first time, things were beginning to fall into place. I clicked on the link and, as the article loaded, the first thing on it was Kym Bright's face. It was a face that I recognized from my youth, and as soon as I saw him, a memory came to me.

Chapter 46

Rachael

The Garage

4th January 2018, 6.39 p.m.

I wanted to wait longer, but waiting longer might mean I missed my opportunity. And I was 50 per cent sure he was alone. I wanted to be 100 per cent sure, but it would have to do. This was it. This was the moment. Tom and I were going to get out of here.

'Baby, not a word. Not a sound, okay?'

'Are we leaving now?'

'Yes, darling, now. Remember, not a sound until the lamp goes out and I say to move, okay?'

'Okay, Mummy.'

Tom peeked at me from under the bed, and I tried to smile reassuringly towards him. My heart was pounding in my chest. My hands tingled. Taking a deep breath, I made a fist and banged the door three times.

'Help! We need help in here!'

'Mummy, what's wrong?'

'It's okay, it's just part of the story.'

I heard the now familiar sound of heavy footsteps echoing

towards me. He was coming. My breathing fell into the same rhythm as his gait. Step. Breathe in. Step. Breathe Out.

'Tom, do not move, okay? Not until I say.'

'Mummy, why is your voice shaky?'

'I'm excited. The story is nearly over. Not a word now, darling.'

Tom nodded and pulled the covers back over him, hiding himself. The footsteps grew louder. Step. In. Step. Out. I heard the keys.

This was it.

I stood behind the door and picked the lamp up, holding it high above my head. The bolt slid, the lock snapped, the door creaked, and light poured in.

I pressed myself against the wall, the porcelain lamp base in my hand, and waited until his large form was fully in the room and the darkness had returned.

Chapter 47

Daniel

The Eurostar

4th January 2018, 6.40 p.m.

I was in a van, sitting between two tall buildings that blocked out the moonlight. A narrow lane designed for horse and carriage. An old city, York perhaps, or London? I was tapping the steering wheel nervously. The van's clock said it was one o'clock in the morning.

The sense of something being wrong?

A bead of sweat running down my back, irritating me. I rubbed it against the chair to smother the life from it. No sooner was it gone than another replaced it.

'Calm the fuck down.' The words echoed in my head.

'Keep the van idling, lights off, be ready to move.' I heard those words but not in that moment, sometime before.

I was doing just that.

The stillness was becoming uncomfortable, like in a horror film when you're waiting for the thing that is going to jump out and scare you. I knew it was nonsense.

I checked the side mirrors, all was quiet.

Nicotine stains in the corners of the roof panelling. I wanted nothing more than a cigarette.

Something caught my eye in the mirror, a shape moving in the darkness. At first I thought I'd imagined it, but the shadow moved again, stepping away from the wall. First one, then two and three coming into the road. All three breathing hard as they moved. One foot in front of the other, knees bent. Feet skimming the floor. Their steps in unison. They moved quickly, but unharassed. Things had gone according to the plan.

Grip tightening on the steering wheel.

The side doors of the van opened. Three in. Their names jumping out.

Robbie. Sam. Kym. Their masks off. Kym nodding to me.

The van was moving.

His voice clear in my head.

'Well done, Robbie. You did well too, Sam.' He paused. I looked into the rear-view mirror, making eye contact.

'Good job, Mikey.'

It was the most detail I had ever remembered from my past. It was something entirely complete. I tried to hold on to it, to remember more, but it faded back into the fog. The man who stared at me – a man who was labelled a gang leader was once someone I worked for.

I read about him, learning he was into organized crime. Money laundering mainly, and robbery. Then in 1999 he was being chased by police after an armed robbery and crashed. He was arrested on site, along with his accomplice and sent down. It didn't say who his accomplice was. For a moment I assumed it was me. But the year was wrong, and the amount of time. Kym Bright was sentenced to twelve years for a series of crimes. His accomplice was sentenced to four.

His funeral was in Slough, his wake at the White Horse pub in the town centre. It was where he operated from before, and drank at after, his conviction. The landlord was his best friend.

I was only a couple of miles from that pub when I was in Wexham a few days ago.

I felt like I knew the place and that told me I needed to go there.

My father's letter was clearly a warning that he was after me, but Kym Bright was still in jail at that time. He must have had someone else come for me on his behalf and now, fifteen years later, someone had come after me again, this time through my family.

I had to summarize what I knew, what information I had to work with. I had stolen something from a criminal. I had hidden it in an old telescope and buried it by a river somewhere. I had names. I had a location I was going to next and a landlord I was going to get some answers from, one way or another.

Resting my head against the window, I knew that I needed to try to sleep, Katie's words coming back to me. If I didn't rest I wouldn't keep my wits and I'd be useless without them. But sleep would come hard, so I took the phone and I went to the news app. The hunt for Daniel Lynch had become the only thing anyone was talking about. The headlines on the BBC were either about the murder, about Rachael and Thomas, or about me. Who I was, where I might be, why I might have done it. The reporters had found ex-girlfriends and work colleagues to talk to. And, worry-ingly, they had been really digging into who I was. Somehow, they had discovered my name, my real name from before. I saw mentions of my criminal past, my attack. They knew I had a dark past and that made me seem more culpable for the crime. A monster who had hidden his identity. I hoped Rachael wasn't seeing these reports. I hated the idea of her thinking of me as that man. Katie on the other hand, she would be reading it all and all I could do was pray once this was over, that she would still love me.

Scrolling through the story, passing over the details they had discovered about who I was, I saw a picture of my mother's house.

The bastards were pitched outside my mother's front door. I felt terrible for putting her in this situation. Below was a short video showing hundreds of people outside in the freezing night air, wrapped up in thick blankets over their coats, holding candles. Praying, hoping. I wasn't sure if I was more horrified than moved. These people didn't know us and most were probably there because it was newsworthy, and they were after their fifteen minutes of fame at my family's expense. But they were there in the pouring rain. A beautiful woman and a gorgeous boy taken by a monster and I could see hope in some of their faces for their safe return.

Locking the phone, I thought about Rachael. I hoped she was still being strong. I hoped she was able to care for our son. I hoped she didn't hate me for what I had done. A huge part of me hoped she didn't know. I wanted to be the one to tell her; I owed her that. I thought about the days before Thomas, and how I loved her dearly. I let those memories wrap around me until my body, tired, depleted and broken, couldn't stay awake any longer.

Chapter 48

Rachael

The Garage

4th January 2018, 6.41 p.m.

'What's going on in here? Is everything alri—'

I didn't let Sam finish his sentence. Instead I crashed the lamp down as hard as I could with both hands onto the back of his head. I was expecting him to have screamed or cried out. But he made no sound as he dropped to the ground at my feet. He started to pull himself up onto his elbows, a groan coming from him as he did. I smashed the base on the back of his head three more times, knocking him out cold. I hit him again just to make sure he was unconscious. The bulb smashed and I was in the dark. I was sure I had just killed a man until he groaned again. A wave of relief flooded over me. I wasn't sure how I would live with being a killer. Putting both of my hands on his side, I had to use all of my strength to roll him into the recovery position before stepping back with my hands outreached trying to find the door.

'Tom, you can come out now.'

I heard him scrape his way from under the bed and count out loud. When he got to fourteen he bumped into me.

'Mummy?'

'Yes, baby, it's me.'

'Are we going now?'

'We are, darling. Now, can you move as quietly as Torak does through the woods when he is running from The Bear?'

'Yes, Mummy.'

'Then let's do it. Let's start the final chapter.'

'We are in the last chapter?'

'Yes, darling. This one's called "The Great Escape". Follow me, keep quiet. Before you know it, we will be home.'

Opening the door, I looked outside. There was no movement. My instincts were right. We were here alone. Just Tom and I, and the unconscious Bear. Grabbing a blanket, I stepped into the corridor, keeping Tom behind me and, quietly, we made our way down it to where I felt they had been arguing earlier. At the end was a door, half open. On the other side the lighting was brighter. We moved slowly. I could feel Tom holding the back of my top. That was good. It was as if he knew that by holding on I didn't need to keep one eye on him. But of course, he didn't do so for that reason. He was scared. So was I.

Before going into the room, I turned and lowered myself to Tom's level. I mouthed to him to stay put and keep quiet and he nodded, understanding my silent request. I smiled, trying to make him feel okay before stepping into the brighter space. It took a moment for my eyes to adjust to the light, and as they grew accustomed I was thankful that the room was empty. If someone had been there I wouldn't have seen them until it was too late to react. The room was small. Maybe fifteen feet squared. In the middle was a table with pizza boxes and empty cans of Coke on them. A small TV sat on a box; it was on, but there was no sound and I didn't look at it, I was just aware of the light movement. Two wooden chairs were up against the table. There was a door further along. It was our exit.

'Tom, darling. Come here.'

Tom stepped into the room shielding his eyes in the same way I had. I picked him up and started towards the door.

'We are going to be okay, Tom. We are going home. Can you be really, really brave for me for a few more minutes?'

He nodded and I opened the door. The cold rain felt hard on my skin. I wrapped Tom head to toe in the blanket I was carrying. He mumbled that he couldn't see, but I didn't respond. Stepping out into the winter night shocked me into a more awake state. The wet ground soaked the hem of my pyjama bottoms, my bare feet going numb almost instantly. But none of that mattered. Squinting through the rain I ran as hard and as fast as I could away from the building that had been our prison. Up ahead I could see a road in the distance, the headlights of cars going past every now and then. One would stop. One would help a woman who was just in thin pyjamas carrying a small boy. I ran faster than I ever had before. I'd be at the road within a minute and we would be saved. I hadn't failed as a mother. I had protected my children. I had stayed brave and pushed my anguish about Sean to one side until I could grieve properly. In my arms was one of my children, in my womb the other. Both warm, both safe. Soon it would be behind us. We were out. We were free.

And the best thing about it, Tom still believed it was all just an adventure story.

Chapter 49

Daniel

London

4th January 2018, 7.44 p.m.

I woke with my shoulder being shook. As my eyes came into focus I saw it was the train conductor. I started to reach for my ticket to show him, but he stopped me.

'No, sir, we are in London.'

Looking out of the window I noticed the train had arrived at St Pancras. Passengers were already alighting and walking with their suitcases and bags towards the exit. The carriage I was in was completely empty. I mumbled a thank you and stood up, my balance not entirely trustworthy.

I realized the conductor was looking at me curiously, so I wished him a good night before I joined the small crowd of people going through Passport Control. As I drew closer I took my phone out. I wanted to look busy, nonchalant. I wanted to keep my head low, my face as hidden as possible. When I looked at the screen I saw a message from Katie. Just two short sentences sent fifteen minutes ago.

I wanted to look up and try to see her through the security checkpoint but stopped myself. Stay on task. Peter Morales wouldn't have anyone meeting him. He'd be just passing through on his way back home.

I handed over my passport to a tired looking young man of about 20, his unshaven face more fine hair than beard. He barely looked at it, or me, before handing it back and sending me through.

And just like that, I was back on UK soil.

I headed in the direction of King's Cross, crossing the street as the rain removed the last of my sleep-induced fog. My eyes scanned the small patches of people who were waiting for late-night trains home. I bought myself a coffee from the Pret inside the station and sipped it casually. The same young man served me the last time I was here. He didn't know, or care. As always in King's Cross there was a police presence, and my prop would help me hide in plain sight. I stood under the departure board pretending to look at my train time, when all I watched was the clock. As soon as it hit eight o'clock, I stepped into the night. I saw a woman standing in the shadows of the entrance. She was looking the other way, a rucksack on her back, hiding most of her profile, but I knew it was Katie. Putting my coffee cup in the bin and stuffing my hands in my pockets, I walked over towards her, aware of the two police officers who were stood at the entrance to the station. They were chatting, relaxed. I stopped five feet from her, she still hadn't noticed me. Before I spoke, I looked around; the voice had told me they were watching her. I wanted to see if anyone was nearby, keeping an eye out, but I couldn't see anyone loitering. The police helped unknowingly.

'Katie.'

She looked around at me, sizing me up before looking away again. She hadn't recognized me.

'Katie.'

She looked again, about to open her mouth to say something but stopped. Her face softened.

'Daniel?'

I nodded, unable to speak. Having someone I cared so much for in front of me allowed the wall that was keeping it all together to fall. Tears began falling. Katie stepped in and wrapped her arms around my waist. I held her close. I closed my eyes. My cheek rested on her head and I quietly sobbed. She didn't try to say anything. She didn't try to stop me, she just held me close and let me feel, holding me up as my legs didn't want to carry me anymore. And I was grateful she didn't try to console me. Nothing she could say, nothing anyone could say would make it right. Not until it was over.

Her silence and understanding somehow snapped the elastic band that had been tight around my chest and I could breathe again. Pulling away I could see in my peripheral vision that the two police officers were looking in our direction. I kissed Katie long and hard. They looked away. When I pulled back, some of my blood was on her top lip. I wiped it off with my thumb.

'Sorry.'

'What happened to your face?' She touched it gingerly, concern etched across her features.

'I fell.'

'I didn't recognize you.'

'Good.'

'Daniel. Did you find the thing that they want?' She looks at me, desperation clouding her face. She knew I was running out of time. She knew what that meant for my family.

'No, but I'm getting closer.'

She took me by the hand and led me away. We crossed the road towards a Premier Inn hotel. Once outside she told me to wait before slipping into the reception. A few minutes later my phone pinged. A message from her saying room 132. I stepped

261

inside and half smiled at the receptionist who was too busy on his phone to care about what I was doing. A sign next to where he sat told me I needed to turn left. Going up a flight of stairs I found room 132. I quietly knocked on the door and Katie opened it, letting me in. Dropping my bag on the floor I tried to smile.

'Sorry, Dan, I thought it was safer for us to come in separately.'

'Yes, of course. Don't be sorry. Are you okay?'

'I'm fine, darling. I'm worried about you. Here.' She handed me a cup of tea. I didn't fancy it but thanked her and held it in my hands, the cup warming them. 'I can't stay long.'

'I know. I'm glad you messaged. I've been desperate to see you, even if it was only for a minute. I've needed to look into your eyes and make sure you're all right.'

'Katie, I'm not all right. I'm scared.'

She put down her mug and wrapped herself around my middle, burying her head into my chest and for a while neither of us spoke. We just held each other for all we were worth, gently rocking like we were both infants being comforted. I had always loved Katie's' embrace, but never more so than in that moment. She gently stroked the back of my neck and gripped on to my coat, keeping me from pulling away, not that I wanted to. Her touch charged me. I felt my battery begin to refill, my empty chest coming back to life.

'You're allowed to be scared.'

'I don't want to be, I want to be stronger. I want to know where I'm going and have a clear plan to end this. And I don't.'

'But you will, I know you will.'

'I've learnt so much about me, the old me. I don't know how I'll ever be normal again.'

'Don't worry about that, Dan. Just focus on ending this, and then, once this is all behind us we can make sure you heal. All three of you.'

Pulling away I looked into her eyes and I could see she truly believed I would end this. Her confidence made me love her even

262

more. Lifting her hand, I kissed the back of it. She had a bruise right next to where I kissed.

'Katie?'

'I got upset. Hit a wall.'

'Shit, your father. Katie, I'm so sorry. I should have asked, I should have—'

'Dan, stop. You have nothing to be sorry for. He isn't suffering now. It's okay.'

I could see it wasn't okay, I could see her heart breaking and it broke mine to know that I couldn't find a way to care properly.

'Katie, I'm so sorry for your loss. I'm so sorry for being too distracted to give you the attention you need. I'm so sorry for dragging you into this.'

'Don't be, for none of it. I want to be here for you.'

I placed my lips on hers and my entire body flooded with warmth. I kissed her like it was the first and last time we would do so. And she kissed me the same way. I could feel her love flowing out of her body and into mine, and in that moment I knew I would save us all. Pulling away, both of us breathing heavier, I looked at my watch. I needed to go. I needed to keep moving. She noticed and spoke, so I didn't have to.

'I've got you some fresh clothes from home.'

Opening the rucksack that was on the bed she pulled out some fresh jeans, a T-shirt, jumper and jacket as well as some deodorant. My body ached terribly and Katie helped me undress. Once naked she led me to the bathroom and stood me in a hot shower. The water running over my face and through the fake beard warmed me through and made me feel more human. Katie wrapped a towel around me and held me until I was dry enough to put on my clothes. Not my father's, not some I had bought from a shop quickly, but my own. It felt like the fabric knew me and soothed my aching muscles. Once dressed I hesitated. Katie looked back at me, her eyes brimming.

'There, good as new,' she said, smiling gently.

263

'Thank you, Katie.' I tried to smile back but couldn't quite get there. She averted her eyes, the sorrow and exhaustion in mine too much for her to see, and she focused on my shoulder, brushing off fibres that weren't there. 'Where are you going next?'

'A pub in Slough. The White Horse.'

'Why?' Her focus was still on my shoulder.

'Because it's the place I have to go next, it's hard to explain.' Her eyes came back up to meet mine and her hand moved from my shoulder on to my cheek. As soon as she touched me, I placed my hand on top, holding hers, and leant my head into her palm.

'I'm worried about you, Daniel.'

'Don't be, be worried for Rachael and Thomas.'

'I'm worried for them too, of course I am. You promise me you'll be careful?'

'I promise.'

'And promise me you'll come back.'

'Yes, of course.'

Her other hand came up, holding my face so I couldn't look away. 'Please, please don't get hurt, Dan. Please make sure you're safe.'

Taking her other hand in mine I lowered them, our fingers intertwining between us. 'Katie, I will do everything in my power to end this so no one gets hurt.' She stepped closer and I let go of her hands, wrapping her in my arms. Her smell was so powerful. I closed my eyes and placed my lips on the top of her head to draw in as much of her scent as I could.

'And then it will be over, and we can get on with our lives.'

'Yeah.'

'And, you and I will go to the coast, we'll get fish and chips and go to that little beach hut we love near my … The blue and white striped one. And our troubles will have melted away.'

She couldn't finish the thought. But I knew where she meant. The hut we love near her father's static caravan by the coast. The place that remained uninhabited throughout 2017, besides us using it on a few occasions. And the hut. A small shed-like structure by the pier. We had seen the owner once, sat outside with a book and a thermos of coffee. And we knew, one day we would invest in one of our own. Just like that one.

'That sounds nice.' I meant it, although it didn't sound that way.

'You can do this, Daniel. I know you can.'

She hugged me and I breathed in her hair. I wanted to stay there for as long as possible. I felt safe there. But I had to move. As I pulled away, she knew I was leaving and didn't try and stop me and I loved her for it.

'I'm sorry to drag you into London for me to leave so soon, Katie. I just had to see you. I needed to see you to stop me losing it.'

'It's okay. I'm glad you did. I want to be with you. Helping you. It's been so hard not knowing if you're okay, if you're safe.'

'I'm fine,' I lied. 'This will all be over soon, I promise. And, Katie, I'm sorry about your dad. Once this nightmare is over, I promise to help you through it, okay?

'I know.'

'Will you do something for me?'

'Anything, Dan.'

'Stay here, at the hotel. Stay in this room, lock the door and keep a low profile. I don't want anything happening to you.'

'Dan ...'

'You've risked enough by coming out to see me. Please, just stay here.' I stepped back from our embrace, my hands going onto her shoulders.

'Promise me?' My voice sounded desperate. Needy. She nodded and I kissed her on the forehead before turning and leaving the hotel room, looking back one final time and then disappearing out of sight. She smiled at me, but I could see she was scared, as scared as I was. Both of us were in way over our heads.

'Bye,' she said in a small voice. She looked like she was about to be abandoned.

'I'll see you soon, my love,' I replied, hoping she didn't hear the crack in my voice as I did. Walking down the corridor I had to wipe a tear from my eye. I hoped I would see her soon, but, with each passing minute, I wasn't sure.

As I crossed the road outside I couldn't look back, it would break my heart. Heading back to King's Cross I took the stairs to the underground. I needed to be in Slough before the landlord locked up for the night.

Chapter 50

Daniel

Slough

4th January 2018, 10.17 p.m.

The White Horse was an eighteenth-century free house that stood proudly in the centre of Slough. Its ancient brickwork, windows and doors seemed otherworldly against the backdrop of high street shops. Before I stepped inside I knew its layout. I would open the door. The bar would be directly in front, to the right would be a fruit machine and to the left, tables – about a dozen of them. Beyond that, a doorway led to a snooker room. It felt familiar. Like returning to a childhood home.

I walked in, a doorway heater blasting onto the top of my head, hurting my cold ears. I took off my coat and shook the rain water from it, holding it away from my body, and walked towards the bar. It was quieter than I thought a Thursday night would be. But the storm was really coming in. Most people were at home, warm and dry. Scanning the room, only hardened drinkers had braved the elements. Tired skin draping tired muscles. I must have been the youngest person in the room by a good twenty years, besides the barman – he looked like a child.

I ordered a pint of Guinness and found a table in the corner, my back to the wall. A view of anything that came my way, as always.

The place had changed cosmetically. I don't know why I was shocked by this. It had been at least fifteen years since I had been here. The fruit machine was gone and the door that led to the snooker room has been removed, the wall widened. I could see restaurant tables instead of the snooker table. The feel of the place though, it was so familiar. You couldn't change the memories that lived in the bricks and mortar, no matter how much money was thrown at it to smarten it up. I sipped my pint and grimaced. Guinness wasn't something I usually drank. I didn't know why I had ordered it. As I lowered the pint an old man walked behind the bar. It was him. Kym's friend. Seeing the old man triggered another memory.

I walked into the pub, it was warm, summer. The barman nodded, as he always did. He washed a glass. I turned left. Picking up a fresh pint. As I walked, people watched.

I was the new kid in a room full of regulars. I had no place here.

A smoky room. A man sat with his back to me. I approached. And sat. It was him. Kym. He was making tea. He didn't drink. He spoke.

Grey eyes that rarely blinked.

'This is a big job,' the voice echoed, distant. 'And you are to be the smoke and mirrors, Michael.'

Smoke and mirrors.

I shook it off, the images not making sense. But it was clear. I was in the right place. Sipping my pint again this time, it tasted different. I took a third sip whilst looking at the man. He was standing close to the young barman, looking down at him to speak. His actions were aggressive despite his words being calm and kind. I guessed he was about seventeen stone. Four inches taller than me. But I had age on my side. I watched him. Little things came to me as I did. His name. Jonesy. He was deemed Kym's brother although I doubted there was a biological connection.

I watched him move around the bar, his age showing, his right knee or hip not as strong as it once was. His arthritic hands were beginning to curl into pincers. He looked over towards me and I looked away, focusing on the rain beating against the window like a coastal tide, surging as the wind rose and dipped. I stayed for as long as I dared until the few people in the pub started to say their goodbyes to Jonesy and 'the kid' before donning their coats and stepping out into the storm. Each time the door opened the wind howled in. Whoever was left in the pub looked towards the door angrily, an expression of annoyance on their faces until it was their turn to drain their pint and leave.

There were only three people left drinking, including me, when I heard the old man tell the young one to start cleaning as he cashed the till. When his back was turned I slipped out of my chair and left the pub.

The rain was coming down so hard it hurt the top of my head as it hit it. Each surge of wind battered my face so hard I thought my top lip was going to split wide open. Across the road was a bus shelter. I would take refuge there and wait. After about fifteen minutes the final few people drifted out, swearing or breaking into a drunken run to get out of the cold. A few minutes later the kid stepped out shouting a goodbye before walking away. Once he was far enough down the road to not care about looking back, I crossed and stepped into the pub once more, flicking the catch on the Yale lock which snapped shut behind me. Quietly I stepped in, careful to place my feet one in front of the other like a cat walking a fence. The old man was in the restaurant area, pushing chairs under the tables. I walked backwards towards the toilets and opened the door. The lights were off. I was confident we were alone.

'Jonesy.'

'What did you forget this time, kid?' he said not paying me any attention. I didn't answer but waited for him to turn and look towards me. He looked around the room, to the door, then back to me. He was scanning like I did. Assessing the situation, seeing the options.

'Have you forgotten something?' he asked. I didn't answer. I just took my coat off and waited for him to come closer. As he did, I could see his guard was up, one foot in front of another. Like I had done. Ready for a fight if need be.

'The cash is all in a drop shoot that goes under the bar. It's on a time release. I couldn't get to it tonight even if I wanted to.'

'I don't want your money.'

'What do you want?'

'Answers.'

'Answers about what?'

'That room behind you, it was a snooker room once, right?'

I could see he was confused. But his guard stayed up. 'That's right.'

'Tell me about Kym.'

He was shocked at the mention of his name. His hands dropped by his side. His confused expression deepened. 'I'm not talking about him. If that's all you want, you're wasting your time.'

I ignored him and pressed on. Although he was dismissive I could see he was also curious as to who I was and why I wanted to know about him. 'Kym once drank here. Worked from here, didn't he?'

'I think you should leave.'

'And he had regular people with him, you, a man named Robbie and a kid called Mikey, right?'

'Yeah, but they are all long dead now so what does it matter? You need to get out of my pub.'

'How did they die?'

'Who are you?'

'I'm just someone who wants to know.'

'Are you a cop?'

'Do I look like one?'

'Who are you then?'

270

I wasn't sure how to respond. I knew that I could beat the truth from him. He was old and I was desperate. But I didn't think I needed to. I couldn't help but think that the old man in front of me and I were once close. If we both worked for Kym like I thought, then we were bonded by the secrets Kym had.

'Jonesy, it's Mikey.'

Chapter 51

Daniel

Slough

4th January 2018, 11.32 p.m.

The old man stepped towards me, his confused expression now a look of concentration. He got to within two feet of me and then stopped.

'Mikey?'

'It's me.'

'You're dead?'

'My father made it look that way.'

'It can't be true?'

Grabbing the beard near the sideburn, I pulled. The glue stretched my skin painfully as it came off. Jonesy just stared blankly at me, his skin grey, in shock. I scratched my face, it felt good to have the beard off. I looked back at the old man who was studying me. He looked at my jaw, my smashed-up lip, my nose. Then he set his gaze on my eyes. A lot can change about a person. But the eyes were constant.

'Fuck me, Mikey, it is you! He was right. The crazy old fool was right!'

He laughed and grabbed me pulling me close, his huge arms almost crushing me. I was glad I decided not to try to beat the truth out of him. I wasn't sure I would have been successful. He kissed me on the head and let me go from his grasp.

'Oh, kid, I cannot believe you are here.'

'Yep, I'm here. Who was right?'

'Kym, he said you weren't dead. He said he knew you were alive. I didn't believe him. Where have you been?'

I told him what had happened to me in 2003. He said he knew all about the attack. He had been told I had died of my injuries, my father being the one to spread the news. I told him about my retrograde amnesia and not remembering anything from before. And then I told him about the phone call. I told him about Thomas.

'Jonesy, I need to know what I took from Kym.'

'You didn't take anything from him.'

'Then why are they after me?'

'You stole something *for* him, not *from* him.'

'What?'

'Just before he went down, you, him, and your dad were working on a job.'

'What job?'

'I didn't know. You didn't ask things of Kym, you waited for him to tell you.'

'I need something or they're going to kill them.'

'I don't know, Mikey, I don't.'

'You were close to Kym, you must know something, Jonesy!' My voice was raised, anger behind the words, which I quickly quelled. Anger wouldn't help. When I spoke next, my voice was softer as I fought to hold myself together. 'I need something.'

He looked away from me. I could see his eyes searching, thinking.

'Jonesy. Did he ever talk about the job we were planning?'

'A bit, but only in his last few months. He had dementia. Not long after he was diagnosed he started talking of you not being dead. I assumed it was the disease. The old fool was right all along.'

'Why didn't you listen?'

'A lot of what he said didn't make much sense towards the end. He spoke of how he missed you. He often said it was the job that would have changed everything.'

'But it didn't happen?'

'Well, it did, according to him anyway. But he didn't do it.'

'Who did then?'

'He always said you pulled it off.'

'Pulled off what? What did I do?' I raised my voice, my frustration taking over.

'Honestly, kid, I don't know. He never said.'

'What else did you two talk about after he was released?'

'Oh, you know, we chatted about being young men. Chatted about his time on the inside. How he had found peace. How he had learnt to let go of the things out of his control. Things like you. Happens to us all as we get older.'

'Like me?'

'I thought it was just the ramblings of a broken mind. But he said about you finishing the biggest job he had ever been involved in. You had the biggest bounty of them all. Then, after he found out you were alive, he said he had learnt from his kid that you didn't remember any of it. He said he didn't want you to know either.'

'What? He didn't want me to remember I was involved in a theft? Why?'

'Like I said, he changed after jail. The money, it didn't matter anymore. He just wanted a peaceful life. I guess, thinking you knew nothing about it all, he would think you would have a peaceful life too. After the attack he was told you were dead. Then he found out you survived.'

'How did he find out when no one else did?'

'He said he found out from your dad. They re-connected when we all knew Kym was on his way out.'

'Did you see my dad?'

'No, Kym and your dad's relationship was always secretive. Your dad used to visit him in the home.'

'I see, and you didn't believe him? Even knowing he had spoken with my father?'

'No, I thought it was just his broken mind plugging gaps in their conversations.'

I understood what he was saying; he thought Kym was confabulating. Like I did.

'Anyway, his time inside made him believe in God or something. He wanted redemption.'

'Redemption?'

'Yeah, redemption.' He paused, holding my eye. 'He was the one who orchestrated the attack on you in 2003.'

His words stunned me. I couldn't make sense of it. The man organized the beating of me, the attempted murder, and then, years later he wanted me left alone.

'I don't understand why he would know I hadn't died and not come after me again?'

'By the time he did, he was too old and too sick to care. He said the past should stay where it was.'

I let myself picture an old man, full of regrets, knowing his time was coming to an end. I would have wanted the same thing for him if our roles were reversed. When I looked back at Jonesy he was watching me intently.

'What was the job?'

'Honestly, kid, I don't know.'

'Were you involved in my attack?'

'No, I was asked to help track you, but I told Kym I couldn't do it.'

'After he came out of jail, what else did you talk about?'

Jonesy smiled to himself. 'He really changed, he went in so

275

angry and came out so much calmer. So much happier. He had taken an interest in painting landscapes. We visited museums, that sort of stuff.'

'Museums?'

'Yeah, we went to Oxford a lot, the ash something or other.'

The Ashmolean. I knew it, another moment like I had when picturing this pub. I had been there too.

'Why?'

'He liked to look around. See the paintings. It's funny, every time we went, he spoke of you.'

I could hear the old man talking but his words sounded distant, like he was on the other side of a thick wall.

I'm alone on a roof, it's cold, clear skies.

Fireworks, lots of fireworks.

Loud and close.

People in the streets. I can hear them singing.

Counting backwards. 5, 4, 3 ...

I'm high in the air. There is a rope.

Smoke, I can smell smoke again.

I swayed on my feet, grabbing a chair to catch my balance. The memory faded and looking at the old man I could see genuine concern for me, a kindness in his eyes conflicting with his large and worn body.

'Who else knows about the job?'

'Only a few of us knew anything about the job. Me, you, Kym, your dad and Kym's kid.'

'And besides me and you, only Kym's kid is alive.'

'Yep.'

'So, Kym's kid is the one who has taken my family.'

'It has to be.'

'Unless it was you?'

'Honestly, kid. It wasn't me.'

I believed him. He was too kind, too open. Now I knew who had taken them, I just had to find what I had taken and get it

276

back. Kym's broken mind wasn't as broken as most people thought. The museum was important.

'Is it still there, the Ashmolean?'

'Of course. Kid, when was the last time you ate something?'

'I'm not sure.'

'When did you last get a good night's sleep?'

'I'm okay.'

'You could have fooled me, kid.'

'Really, I am.'

I thanked him and told him I needed to leave. He wore the same expression Madame Etoile had when I left Auvers. A sadness, but also acceptance. As I opened the door, he called me and I turned back.

'If you need anything, just ring the pub landline, okay? It's on Yell.'

'Thanks.'

I meant it too. I was thankful. He could have not told me anything, instead he was open and honest. Kym had dementia and had decided to let me be right up until the day he died.

Whatever I had taken, I felt it was connected to the Ashmolean. That's why I was there, in France. It was starting to make sense, I was starting to piece together what had happened. It meant I was getting closer to an answer. I stole something and didn't know what to do with it so I fled to France and waited for my dad to be released and then work out what to do. Only, before I could, I had been attacked.

Stepping back into the freezing wind I made my way to a taxi rank. As I walked, a breaking news notification pinged on the phone.

Man left with serious head injuries in Paris, his assailant believed to be wanted man, Daniel Lynch.

They thought I was in Paris, this was a good thing. If I was in Paris the trail would run cold and it would buy me time. I needed to get back to Uxbridge station, back to my father's car and go to the museum.

I looked at my watch. It was just after midnight. It was now Friday. The day that, one way or another, this would end.

FRIDAY

Chapter 52

Thomas

The Garage

4th January 2018, 12.19 a.m.

Mummy is mad at me.

Because when we went outside and Mummy carried me wrapped up like a sausage roll she kept saying we are nearly there but then she stopped, and I hit the ground and my elbow hurt but I didn't want to cry because I wanted to show Mummy I was a big boy. She told me to run. 'Run, Tom, run,' she said. But it was dark and raining and I know that I'm not allowed out in the dark on my own, so I didn't. I could hear her crying. 'Run, Tom, run.' But I couldn't because I would get into trouble. When The Bear grabbed me she shouted 'no' like she did when I was about to do something naughty. She shouted it really loud, the loudest I had ever heard her. The Bear brought me back here, followed by another one who kept smiling at me, and Mummy is so angry with me that she hasn't come back.

But I am angry with her too.

Mummy told me we were at the end of the story, but we weren't because she said the end of the story would be us both at home and I'm not and Mummy has gone. Maybe it was like the Torak stories. Maybe we had finished the first one and now we were in the second and in this story, I had to wait for Mummy to have an adventure all by herself. Then she would come and get me. I wish she had spoken to me first because I would have said no. I wanted to come on the second adventure with her. This one was boring, and I was cold and still hungry and The Bear still scared me.

I heard the door do the sliding noise and I did what Mummy told me to do which was to hide under the bed. I hoped it was her and she would say I was a good boy for doing what I was told. The key jangled and snapped and squeaked as the door opened and I watched through a teeny tiny gap. I saw some feet. They were huge. It was The Bear.

'Kid?'

His voice scared me a lot. It was so deep like a monster's.

'Tom?'

He knew my name. I thought that maybe Mummy had told him and if she had then it was okay to talk to him. But I didn't want to come out from under the bed.

'Where is Mummy?' I said.

'Tom, are you hurt?'

'My elbow.'

'Can I take a look at it?'

'No.'

'Please, I promise to be nice.'

'You're scary.'

'I know. How about if I take my balaclava off?'

'Your what?'

'My mask. Here.'

I saw a big hand reach under the bed. I thought it was going to grab me but it didn't. It came close and it put something black down.

'Is this your mask?'

282

'It is.'

'Do you have a face too?'

I heard him laugh. It was deep, like Father Christmas's ho, ho, ho.

'Don't laugh at me.'

'I'm not, Tom, I promise. And yes, I have a face. Do you want to see it?'

I did want to see it because I was curious like a cat, but I was also scared.

'You promise not to try and eat me?'

'Of course. I've got an idea. What if I went to the other side of the room and then you crawl out? If I look scary you can go back under the bed and I'll leave you alone. How about that?'

I said yes even though I wanted to say no because I was still scared. But I said yes anyway to be brave. Mummy would be watching, and she would see and she wouldn't be mad at me anymore, even though I was still mad at her. I moved the blanket and I could see his legs and tummy but not his head so I crawled a bit on my good elbow, so I could see him. He was looking at me and it didn't scare me as much because I could see he wasn't a bear but a man like Daddy or Sean. Except he had a big beard. So he was still kind of like a bear really.

'Are you okay, Tom?'

I didn't say anything because I wasn't. My elbow hurt and my tummy too because of Mummy being mad.

'Can I take a look at your arm?'

I nodded and crawled out. I held it up in the air.

'Can I come closer?'

I nodded again and he did and he made an 'ouch' sound with his mouth which was strange because I didn't and I was the one with the ouchy. He had a green box with him that I had seen in school before and he opened it up.

'I'm going to clean it and put a plaster on it. Is that okay, Tom?'

283

I nodded again, and The Bear came even closer. So close I could smell him. He smelt like my friend Pavel's dad who smoked even though he knew it was bad for him. I missed Pavel, I even missed school. At school I wasn't cold or hungry or tired. Well, I was tired but a different kind of tired. The Bear put some cream on it which smelt really bad and then a big plaster.

'There we are. All better. Are you okay?'

'I want to go home.'

'I know you do, kid, and you will soon. I promise.'

'I don't believe you. Mummy said we were going and we didn't and now she is angry with me and she has left me here.'

The Bear nodded at me and turned his head towards the door. There were more footsteps outside. I could see a big red patch on the back on his head.

'Tom, you need to get back under the bed.'

'Is it The Smiler?'

'Who?'

'The one that smiles but is scary.'

'Yes, yes The Smiler is coming. Hide back under the bed, okay?'

'Please don't let The Smiler get me.'

'I won't, Tom, I promise.'

I did as he said; I wanted to. The Smiler really scared me and looking through my gap I watched as the door opened and The Smiler's shoes came in. The Bear whispered I was asleep but I wasn't and then The Smiler walked out, The Bear following. I heard the lock go snap and the bolt go squeak and I knew it was safe to come out, I could almost hear Mummy telling me to. I could hear The Bear talking outside and I went over to the door to listen. 'I'm going for something to eat.' And then a door went slam and I knew he was gone.

I just hoped that when he came back it would be the end like he promised, and I could read the story back with Mummy and Daddy.

Chapter 53

Daniel

Uxbridge

4th January 2018, 1.27 a.m.

I was back at my father's old car, glad it was still where I left it. I opened the door, climbed inside and closed it. And I sat there. My mind blank, lost. My breath steamed up the windows quickly as I tried to connect the Ashmolean to me, Auvers and my family. I forced myself to concentrate, remembering the last thing that flashed into my mind.

Being high, fireworks, singing.

There was a fire, I had set one, smoke filled the air, I couldn't see. I was choking, the flames licked at my face, my skin blistered. I tried to leave but I was stuck, tied to the heat. The building burnt around me.

'No, Daniel. That didn't happen. Concentrate,' I said out loud.

I started up the engine and putting the car in reverse, I looked in my mirror to back away. I jumped as I saw someone step out of a parked car behind me. I hadn't noticed him. I hadn't even noticed the car. I stayed in reverse, my foot hovering on the clutch, hoping that because I'd not backed down, he, whoever he was, would get out of my way. When he didn't, I had to assume he was there for me.

The handbrake went up and opening the car door I stood as tall as I could, but still inches shorter than the man before me.

'Michael.'

He knew my name. He knew who I was and wasn't shocked I was alive. That meant he must know what was happening. I looked behind him at the car. Was Rachael in it? Was my son only twenty feet away?

'They're not here,' he said quietly, as if reading my mind.

'Are you the one I've been talking to?'

'No.'

'But you're involved?'

'Yes.'

'How many of you are there?'

'Three.'

'Did you kill Sean?'

'No.'

'Is my boy okay?'

'Yeah, he's okay.' He hesitated, like he was about to say something but stopped himself. I pressed him.

'And Rachael. Have you harmed her?'

'I've not laid a finger on her.'

'What do you want? I've still got time.'

'I never wanted your family involved in this.'

'But you have involved them, you took them, and between the three of you, Sean is dead. His blood is on your hands.'

'I swear, I had nothing to do with him being killed. And I would have stopped it if I could.'

'What do you want?'

'This to be over. I didn't sign up for hurting anyone. I was told that we would threaten you and you would give back the picture and then we would be rich. That was it. We had to keep her and your boy and then we would give them back and disap-

286

pear. There was nothing said about killing someone. Nothing said about your boy being so young.'

'Picture?'

'Yes.'

'This is over a picture?'

A picture, this whole thing is about a picture ... a photograph. Where did you put it, Daniel? Where the fuck did you put it?

'Where are they?'

'Close.'

'Where?'

'Slough Trading Estate.'

'Take me there.'

'I can't. If for a second it's known we've spoken, then ...'

He didn't finish his sentence, he didn't need to. We both know what he couldn't say. If it was known we had spoken, they would be killed.

'How can I trust you?'

He looked at me. He looked as tired and beaten as I felt. 'You can't.'

'Then why should I listen?'

'I've got a little girl, about Tom's age. I can't do this anymore.'

I felt a squeezing in my chest again. Thomas's first steps popped into my head, how he walked from me to Rachael and then turned to make sure I was watching before he fell. His first day at pre-school. Walking away, leaving him in the middle of a room surrounded by other kids with a wooden block in his hand and me crying in my car because I knew he didn't need me as much anymore. But he needed me now. I couldn't trust the man in front of me. But I needed to try. I needed my son back.

'What do I need to do?'

'Carry on with what you are doing. You need to make it look like we've not spoken. I'll get him and bring him to you.'

'How will you know where I will be?'

'We've been tracking you this whole time.'

'How?'

'Your phone, the one we gave you.'

I couldn't believe I hadn't seen it. The whole time I had been thinking they had eyes on the ground watching me, following me and they hadn't needed to. I thought of the dog walker, the man outside my father's house and the two in Paris, one I had followed and not hurt, the other whose head I'd smashed into the ground.

'So carry on, for a few more hours. I'll find you and I'll give you them back.' He hesitated as he spoke, unable to keep my eye, looking around him.

'What about the picture?'

'I've already got blood on my hands. I'm not having a little boy's too. No amount of money is worth that.'

'You promise to keep them safe?'

'Yes.' He covered his mouth, disguising it as him wiping his lips with his coat sleeve. It told me he was lying.

'And after?'

'I'll disappear like I planned. You'll never see me again.'

Stepping forward, I locked my eyes on his. Although he was far bigger than me, I felt like a giant, powered by my willingness to do whatever it took to save my son.

'If you hurt them, I'll kill you.'

He nodded, understanding I meant every word, but he wasn't afraid regardless. Quickly he stepped back towards his car. As he walked away, I could see the back of his head had been bandaged up, fresh blood showing through. I wanted to ask him what had happened but before I processed the image he had started his engine and disappeared.

I watched his tail-lights until they were lost into the night. Once sure he was gone, I texted Katie. I wanted her to know this nightmare might be over soon. I told her one of his captors would bring them to me.

Until he did, I had to continue with my journey, so reluctantly

I fired up the engine. I had to drive further away from Slough where I knew they were. It went against what every fibre of my being wanted me to do, but I did it anyway.

Chapter 54

Thomas

The Garage

4th January 2018, 2.18 a.m.

I didn't know if The Bear was going to come back. He said he was but so did Mummy and she hadn't come back yet. I wanted to lie on the bed because the floor under it was cold and hard and not like a bed, but Mummy said I should hide so I did. I needed a wee so badly my tummy hurt. So I looked to make sure The Bear or The Smiler weren't there and got up and had a wee in the corner where I had with Mummy before. I tried to write my name again but only managed the T. I really needed it but there was only a little and it was orange. I'd not had orange wee before. And then I thought that it might taste like orange juice even though it was wee and because I was so thirsty I tried a bit that was on my finger and it was yucky, and now I was really thirsty.

I was starting to worry about Mummy. It was still dark and it was still cold and she didn't have a coat on and it was still raining which meant she would be soaking wet. It was silly for her to be out still. She would get poorly. I wanted her back here with me. I was tired. It was at least ten at night which is really late and I wanted to sleep but sleeping on the floor was difficult because it was hard, so I climbed on top and pulled the blanket over my head. It made a den, a rubbish one anyway. Not like the dens I make with Daddy. Those dens are the best.

I wish he were here right now to help me make one. He would know what to do.

I closed my eyes and thought about the zoo, the one closest to my house that used to have a white tiger. But it was now gone. And then I heard noises. I thought it was barking at first like a dog but then I realized it was people and they were speaking really loudly to each other.

I was too scared to get up and try to hear more at the door.

It went on for about a minute and then I heard someone shout really loud, like Daddy does when he stubs his toe, and then it went quiet again, really quiet. Really, really quiet, and somehow that was scarier. I closed my eyes and tried to sleep but I couldn't help feeling like I was being watched. I tried to remember the sound of Mummy singing to me, hoping that it would make me feel better.

The bolt squeaked, and the keys snapped, and the door opened and someone came into the room. I could hear their footsteps. Pad, pad, pad. They were light. It wasn't The Bear, it was The Smiler. I squeezed my eyes closed so tightly it hurt and hoped that he would leave me alone. It went really quiet again and I thought for a moment he was gone, but then the covers were pulled off my head and he was there, smiling. Up close it was even more scary. It wasn't a happy smile. He had a cloth in his hand and he pressed it on my face. I thought he was trying to give me a wash like Mummy did every night before bed, but he pressed it hard into my mouth and nose. I couldn't breathe through it. I tried to shout 'stop you're hurting me' but I couldn't speak. He had his other hand on the back of my head, squishing it into the cloth that tasted sweet on my lips. I started to get really scared, then I felt funny, like I was falling asleep, but too quickly.

Chapter 55

Daniel

En route to Oxford

4th January 2018, 3.31 a.m.

I drove in silence, the hum of wheel against tarmac strangely calming. It reminded me of Thomas's first nightlight when he was a baby. It threw stars onto his ceiling and could play lullabies or 'womb' sounds. We spent the first six months of our lives with these sounds playing every night. For a brief, wonderful moment I was there again. Leaning over Rachael, fast asleep facing Thomas, who was beside her in the Moses basket. His arms up above his head like he was mid Mexican wave. His tiny chest rising and falling. Rising and falling. The whole house quiet besides the womb noise playing, and their calm, peaceful breathing.

I stopped myself. I didn't have time to escape into my own head. He needed me to be strong, to be a father who didn't abandon him when he needed him the most. But I was driving away from where I now knew them to be, hoping that the man who took him was honest.

I felt powerless. I felt powerless to protect my own boy.

I needed noise. The hum that was calming was now making

me feel an anxiety climbing on my diaphragm, its icy hands clawing at me as it fought to pull its way out, so I turned on the radio and listened to a stranger's voice until its icy grip let go a little.

Winding through the countryside south of Oxford I wished I had taken the main roads. The night was dark, the cloud thick and, although it had stopped raining, the wind was beginning to whip up as the storm came inland blowing dead leaves and small twigs from the trees that lined the road. Some gusts were strong enough to move the car as I drove. It was hard driving with my exhausted eyes.

On the radio they talked about the incoming Storm Fionn, the winds looking to hit over 100 miles an hour and coastal areas were to be vigilant as the wind on top of the tidal surge would create very dangerous conditions. Then they spoke about Rachael and Thomas again. How the hunt was still on. How the police, led by DCI Holt, were investigating leads in Paris with Interpol, to find their prime suspect: me. Reports confirmed blood was found on the inside of my abandoned car. They spoke about Stamford and how the vigil was still going despite the weather turning for the worse. They cut to the reporter who had been there throughout:

'I've spoken with several of the residents of Stamford and asked them when they were going to take shelter from the incoming storm.'

It cut to another voice, one I recognized. It was Sharon, the annoying mother from Tom's school who insisted on being the voice of Year 1 students so she could push her own poor child into the centre of things. I could almost picture her standing on a milk crate with a placard:

'The people of Stamford will not rest until Rachael and Tom are found and the man responsible is brought to justice.'

It may have been the first thing she had ever said that I agreed with. And in a strange way, I was grateful for her persistence.

I couldn't hear any more and switched it off again. They didn't know I was back in the UK. The police must have identified my movements by now. I couldn't work out why that wasn't in the public's interest to know.

I looked at the phone's satnav that was on my lap and it said I was eight miles away from the Ashmolean. I needed it to give up some secrets and help me end this. Although the big man had told me he would free my son, I needed to make sure I still found the picture I took. Just in case.

Chapter 56

Daniel

The Ashmolean, Oxford

4th January 2018, 3.43 a.m.

I climbed the steps that led up to the main entrance of the museum two at a time, the wind battering my left side with its icy cold gusts. I took shelter under one of its pillars that stretched up forty or fifty feet, so tall they swallowed me whole. Sheltering from the wind by pressing my back into one of the pillars, I looked at the main entrance door. I felt as if I had been through it, a few times perhaps. But I could feel the sense of daylight, of other people. I remembered my flashback. I was high, looking down on the Oxford streets. I was on the roof.

Pulling my coat as high as I could under my chin I braced and stepped into the wind once more, this time to walk around the building to see if there was an obvious way to the roof. I headed back down the steps and turned right, then right again onto St John Street. Then again right onto Pusey Place. I didn't know why I had chosen to come this way. It was instinctive. The Khalili Research Centre was on my right, in front of me a narrow, secluded alley that the side of the Ashmolean ran along. As I got to the end of the lane I turned and looked back where I had walked.

I was alone in a van. Waiting.

A clock read 11.52 p.m. 'Just three more minutes, Mikey.'

A watch alarm sounded. I turned it off. Climbed out. Closed the door. The streets empty.

There was scaffolding. I began to climb.

The memory was gone. But I could still see its imprint. I had climbed scaffolding that was once here where I stood. We knew about this, it was part of the planning. It was a perfect place to do it. Quiet. Secluded. I could see why I had picked this location to start the break-in. Only, I wasn't the one supposed to be doing it. I was supposed to provide smoke and mirrors. Yet, I remembered me, not anyone else, but me, climbing up.

Looking up I wondered, if I climbed up on the roof, as I had done all those years before, would it trigger something? There was a drainpipe that ran up the side of the building. One that was metal and fixed to the wall with the same materials. I wrapped my hands around it and shook. It felt secure. Checking that I couldn't see anyone, I began to climb. It was harder than I thought. The cold metal was making my fingers feel numb and the sleep deprivation was sapping what little strength I had. I only made it up about six feet when I slipped and crashed hard onto the ground, my left ankle taking most of my weight and failing. I heard a tearing sound and felt sharp pain instantly. I cursed myself for being so clumsy and wrestled off my boot to look at my foot. It was tender across the top travelling towards the outside ball of my ankle. I pressed firmly on it, trying to feel if there was a break, but I couldn't feel anything. It hurt like hell but I didn't think it was broken. I stood and pressed my weight on it. Pain shot up into my calf.

I sat on the cold floor and took off my other boot and sock. I put both socks on my damaged foot, then I put my boots back on, tying my left one as tight as I could. The action made a compression boot of sorts. I could feel throbbing in my toes, but I could also stand on it a little. Grabbing the drain pipe once more I climbed, threading my whole right arm in the gap between wall and metal, anchoring me. It took longer to climb, but there was less chance of me slipping. I assumed on a night so horrid, no one would be out to catch me in the act.

After a few minutes I pulled myself onto the roof, gasping as I rolled on, flat on my back, grabbing at air. Once my lungs stopped burning, I walked along the roof to see if I could get a look at where I may have broken in. Recalling my flashes, I was higher than I was now. As soon as I looked up I saw it. High on the Ashmolean was a wall that ran the length of the roof. I couldn't see from where I stood, but I knew there was a hatch that allowed people onto it from the inside. It was from there that I watched fireworks exploding, heard people singing. It was from there that I broke into the museum. I could see it as clear as day.

I'm alone on a roof, it's a cold, clear sky.

Fireworks, lots of fireworks.

Loud and close.

People in the streets. I can hear them singing.

Counting backwards. 5, 4, 3 …

I'm high in the air. There is a rope.

Smoke, I can smell smoke again. It's me, the smoke is coming from me, a canister in my hand. I drop it and wait. It crashes to the ground as the smoke rises. I slide down the rope. I'm only after one thing, one item. I know I am. Strict instructions to get one thing.

I felt my body begin to shake. My vision was blurring. Images swirled into my head. I saw the room I climbed into the museum to enter. The walls were covered in paintings. Masterpieces. I ignored them and found the one I needed, one by Paul Cezanne.

That's why France was so important. That's why I hid in a small town for years waiting for my father. He knew where to find me. It's why we stopped for a day on our way south for our holiday in the summer of '99. I thought of the picture, us posing. I had been looking at the wrong thing. I should have been looking at what was behind us.

This is it, Mikey, this is the place where it all began. This is the place that will change everything.

His words now made perfect sense.

On New Year's Eve 1999 as fireworks exploded over Oxford, I stole a picture, a Cezanne painting.

One called 'View of Auvers-sur-Oise'.

Chapter 57

Daniel

The Ashmolean, Oxford

4th January 2018, 3.57 a.m.

I had discovered what it was. I had discovered what I was searching for – a rare and expensive painting. A masterpiece. It made sense. It would fit inside a telescope if I rolled it. I just had to find it now.

There was a noise, a buzzing. It took me a moment to understand it was coming from me. The phone was ringing in my pocket. I hoped it was the large man calling me, telling me where my son was. It was Katie. I sat down, sheltering myself from the wind.

'Daniel?'

I didn't speak, as a car drove past slowly. I watched it until it was gone.

'Dan? Are you there? Tell me what happened. You said one of them met you?'

'Yes. He came to me and told me he was going to release them,' I replied in hushed tones, keeping low in the shadows cast by the ancient roof.

'What did he say?'

299

'He said he didn't sign up for killing anyone and Thomas was lovely. He said he was going to call me soon and arrange to meet and give them back. No strings attached. Until then I've been told to carry on. Make it look like I'm trying to find what I took.'

'Can you trust him?'

'Yes, no, I don't know. I'm still going to search for it, but hopefully it will all be over soon.'

'Thank God. Where are you?'

'On a roof.'

'What? Daniel, what are you doing on a roof?'

'Nothing. I'm getting down. I have to go.'

'Be careful. I love you.'

I hung up. I couldn't say it back. I didn't have enough love in that moment for anything other than my son and, truth be told, my son's mother. I looked at the black screen of the phone, willing it to ring. Willing the big man to say he was on his way to meet me. But it didn't. I climbed off the roof, slowly, my right arm wrapping around the pipe once again as I did. A few feet from the ground I slipped and landed heavily again, this time causing no damage to myself. Slowly I stood and made my way back towards my father's car, my left foot hurting so much I limped a little. As I turned the corner I could see my father's car and there was someone sitting on the bonnet looking my way. Someone I knew. Someone who had recently been on TV. I thought about running but she shouted over the wind that she was alone, she wanted to talk. I looked, there was no one else there. It was just her. Cautiously I approached.

When I was only a few feet away she lifted her hands up into the air, palms showing. I carefully padded towards her, one foot in front of the other. Looking not at her but around her, in the shadows of the buildings.

'Are you sure you're alone?'

'Yes, Daniel. My name is—'

'I know who you are. How did you find me?'

Chapter 58

Thomas

Location unknown

4th January 2018, 4.04 a.m.

I had a dream. Mummy and Daddy were there, and we were at the seaside. Mummy was reading while Daddy and I built sandcastles with buckets and spades. I had a bright red one, like a fire engine, Daddy's was blue. We filled them with wet sand and patted down the tops of our buckets before lifting and showing our sandcastles. As the sandcastles slid out they were much bigger than the bucket. Each one nearly as big as me. And we built lots. One on top of the other, stretching high into the air, so high and so big it blocked the sunshine out. I watched as Daddy climbed and climbed and climbed. Each time putting a new sandcastle on the top taking him higher and higher. I stood at the bottom. Mummy sat in the shadow of them. I shouted his name, but he couldn't hear me. He just kept building and building, and I shouted at him, 'Daddy, if you keep going up it will fall down.' But he couldn't hear me. So he kept going up, up, up. I asked Mummy to move, but she wouldn't. She just lay there. And then it fell. And Mummy was buried, and Daddy was broken.

I didn't like bad dreams.

I woke up and my arm had gone to sleep and my head felt funny. Like I was dizzy and falling over even though I was lying down. I looked at the ceiling. Only it wasn't the ceiling in the cold room. Or my bedroom ceiling. It was metal. And the bed I was in wasn't a bed but metal too. Like I was in a metal bubble. I tried to sit up but couldn't, so instead I rolled onto my side. I could hear a car noise going 'brum bruuum', and I felt like I was being juggled around. I was in a van again, this time without Mummy. And then I got excited because maybe I was going home, and she was there waiting for me. I hoped so, I wanted to go to bed, and I wanted to eat some yummy foods like cereal or yogurt with a glass of milk that would give me a moustache and make Mummy laugh. And I would ask for a straw so I could blow bubbles.

I wanted to put new pyjamas on, straight from the radiator so they were nice and warm on my body. I wanted to watch *Toy Story 2*, the one with Jessie as she was my favourite, and eat popcorn and have a blanket on. I wanted to hear Daddy's voice on the phone. He would tell me he was looking forward to the weekend and I would say I was too and we would go ice-skating with Katie like he said. And we would laugh at Daddy as he fell on his bum because he can't skate. Mummy would be at home when we got back, and she would kiss the top of my head and I would go and see Sean in the kitchen who would make us all a drink. Daddy and Katie would come in and I would show them how good I was with my remote-controlled car and they would talk grown-up talk but it would still make me laugh, even though I didn't really know what they were saying. And I would go to bed and Daddy would kiss me, his stubble tickling my cheek. Sean would too, Katie would wave bye bye and then Mummy would come and tuck me in. Kissing me, telling me she loved me.

'Dream sweet dreams, Tom. I love you.'

'I love you too, Mummy.'

She would put on my nightlight and go downstairs and I would listen to them talking in the kitchen. Laughing at one of Daddy's jokes that Mummy always said were bad but she always laughed anyway. I would hear them having a nice time. It would help me go to sleep.

Mummy always said I had a good imagination, so I used it and I pretended to be there. For a little while I could hear their voices.

The van turned and I rolled across the floor and hit the other side. It didn't hurt, and I sort of found it funny but it wasn't really because I didn't have anyone to laugh with. I decided I would call this chapter 'Laughing on My Own'. I hadn't named the last one so thought about it. That one would be 'The Weird Sleep'.

My chapter titles weren't as good as Mummy's were, but she could help make them better when I saw her.

The van stopped and I heard someone get out of the front. The door went slam behind them. It made me jump. Then the back door opened. I thought it was going to be morning. It was strange that it was still dark. How long was I asleep for? The Smiler looked at me. His eyes were like a snake's. He lifted his finger to his lips and made a shhhh noise. I nodded, too scared to talk. He grabbed a bag that I hadn't noticed was by my feet at the back of the van. It was really big and really heavy and he dragged it out making heaving noises as he did. The bag fell on the floor with a thud. He then slammed the door, making me jump again. I lay down again and closed my eyes. My head still felt funny, like I might be sick.

And then the van started moving again.

Chapter 59

Daniel

Oxford

4th January 2018, 4.08 a.m.

'You're not an easy man to find.' Her hands were in her pockets, she was being battered by the wind, yet her eyes didn't leave me.

'And yet, here you are, DCI Holt.' I paused a little way away from her, not wanting to get too near.

I looked around, searching for her backup, for the people coming to haul me away and blame me for a crime I didn't commit.

'Daniel, I'm alone.'

'Why?'

'I don't really know.'

'If you want to talk, make it quick.'

'I should arrest you.'

'And yet, you haven't, so you're here for a chat. Start talking, I don't have time. I have to keep moving.'

'Where are you going, Daniel?'

'I don't know.' I try to move past her, but her next words stop me.

'I don't think you did it.'

304

'Did what?'

'Any of it.'

'Good, because I didn't.'

'But you are involved in something.'

'Yes, I am. Why don't they know I'm back in England?'

'I wanted to buy some time.'

'To do what?'

'Investigate. I've done some digging, discovered who you really are and made the assumption you would be retracing your steps. Can you really not remember anything before 2003?'

I let myself sigh, resigned to the fact that I was now talking with the police and I shouldn't be. 'I get bits, like dreams. Nothing concrete.'

'And you know more about who you were.'

'A little.'

'And is your son and ex being taken connected?'

'Yes.'

'I thought so.'

'You haven't explained how you found me.'

'I looked in to what you were up to in your previous life. When you were Michael. I found that you worked for Kym Bright. It was easy to find the pub in Slough. He was famous for operating from it. I spoke with the old man. He told me about this museum.'

'Just like that.' I clicked my fingers. 'He told you.'

'No, at first he denied knowing who you were. But when I told him I thought you were innocent and I was trying to help, he relaxed.'

'What else did he say?'

'Not a lot. I was hoping you could fill in the gaps.'

'I didn't kill Sean.'

'I believe you. Daniel, you have to tell me what's going on.'

'I – I don't know how.'

'Here's what I know. Sean was killed in Rachael's house, your old house. She and your son Tom—'

'Please, don't talk about them.'

'They have been taken. Naturally you became the suspect when we found your car with blood in it. But that alone didn't make sense. Why would you ditch a car near Stamford and then walk back into the town to steal another from your mum's house. Blood was found in the downstairs toilet. Assumed to be yours or the victim's.'

'It was mine, I split my lip.'

'Your mother's stolen car was found in Chalfont. From there you're speculated to have been seen in Paris. A man who rang us was assaulted by someone he believed to be you and his phone was stolen. That was you, wasn't it?'

'Yes.'

'What is going on?'

'I don't know if I can trust you.'

'If I thought you were a murderer and kidnapper, I would have brought the whole force in. The force that are still looking at Paris right now. Daniel, please, just tell me what you know.'

She was right, she had taken a leap of faith, I needed to do the same. I sat on the car next to her, looking at my feet.

'I was attacked, nearly killed in 2003. I sustained massive head injuries, there was swelling to my temporal lobe. I spent some time in a coma. Then I woke up with my mum by my side, although I didn't know who she was. She told me I was Daniel Lynch. Everything before the attack was gone. My childhood. My first kiss. My school days. Gone. And I was okay with that. Until Monday night, when I got the phone call.'

'What phone call?'

I told her about the call I had received late at night. And the photos sent to me of Rachael and Thomas tied in a van. I told her how I drove to their house and found Sean and then I spoke to the man, the conversation in which he told me I had until Friday, today.

'What did you do?'

'That's what I'm trying to find out. From what I've pieced together. Michael was involved in a big crime. A robbery at the Ashmolean.'

'There've been several over the years.'

'I stole "View of Auvers-sur-Oise".'

'What?' She couldn't hide the shock from her face. She clearly knew what it was and how expensive it was.

'I don't know for sure.' I paused, tired of telling lies when I had lived through them for so long. 'Sod it. I do know for sure. I can feel it. That's the thing I took for Kym Bright all those years ago. I think he was supposed to do the job, but was arrested before he could and I stepped up to do it for him. He's now dead and someone wants it back. That's why Sean was killed, that's why they were taken. They've given me until today to deliver it. A straight swap. But I still don't know where it is.'

'What *do* you know?'

'I know that I had it when I lived in France. Sometime after the theft and before I was attacked. I was hiding it inside a telescope. I think I was hiding it and waiting for my father.'

'Your father?'

'Robbie Gardner. He worked for Kym too.'

'Daniel, you said you had to keep moving. Why?'

'They are watching me. They know my every movement. If I stay still for too long they'll know I've either found it or run out of options. If I keep moving it looks like I'm tracking it down. Please, I have to go. If you want to carry on talking, you have to get in the car.'

I unlocked the old beast and stepped past her to get in. Through the glass I watched her as I fired up the engine. She sighed and walked around the bonnet climbing in to the seat next to me. The car rocked gently as I put it into reverse and backed out of the parking space. Slipping into first, I began to drive away, watching the Ashmolean roof until I couldn't see it anymore. I didn't know where to go. All I could do was wait for him to call me back. Until then, I needed to stay accessible. With no idea what was next I began to make my way back to London.

'Where are you going to look for the painting?'

'I don't know, hopefully it won't matter anyway.'

'What do you mean?'

'One of them found me. He said he was going to get them out. He said he was going to bring them to me.'

'When?'

'I don't know. I just had to keep going, make it look like I'm searching and wait for him to call.'

'And you trust him to do as he said?'

'No, but what choice do I have?'

I fell silent and drove. Holt beside me took out her phone.

'What are you doing?'

'I'm not calling anyone. I'm just looking for something.'

I merged with the A4144 heading north. It would lead me to the M40 and back towards London. I knew they would be watching and I also knew that as a kid I was always in or around London. By heading back, it would look like I was doing what I said. Going to collect. But really, it would get me closer to Slough for when he called back. Holt sat beside me quietly tapping her phone. I wanted to look at what she was doing, but didn't. She was a police officer, and I was wanted by the police, yet she had turned up alone and I had to try to trust her. With less than twenty-four hours to go, I needed all the help I could get.

My phone pinged in my pocket, making me jump. I dug it out as quickly as I could.

'I think it's him. The one who said he'd bring Thomas back to me.'

'Put him on loudspeaker.'

I nodded, took a deep breath, and answered the phone, my voice giving away my anxiety.

'Hello?'

'Do you think I am stupid, Michael?'

308

The voice wasn't of the man I met only a few hours ago. It was *the voice*.

'Did you think I wouldn't find out? Do you think you and him meeting to arrange your family's release wouldn't go unnoticed? I see you everywhere, Michael.'

I could feel the blood draining from my face. I looked at Holt but she gave away nothing.

'Please, it wasn't my idea. He came to me. He said he was going to get them out. I didn't ask him.'

'But you agreed.'

'Yes, no. I mean, I just want them back.'

'There are consequences for your actions.'

'Please, please don't hurt them.'

'New rules, Michael. When you have it you call and I'll tell you where you can deliver it. Once I have it, I will then tell you where to pick up your family.'

'Please, we agreed we would swap at the same time.'

'That was before you decided to test me.'

Holt typed something into her phone and held it up. 'Proof of life.'

'Let me speak to them. Please, let me speak to Thomas. He will be scared.'

'He's asleep right now.'

'Wake him up.'

There was no response.

'Wake him up. Let me talk to my son!'

'I suggest you calm down.'

'Let me talk to my fucking son!'

'You are on thin ice, Michael. Can you hear it cracking?'

The line went dead. Immediately I regretted shouting at him. He was right, I had to stay calm, and I had to work out the problem like I could vaguely remember my father teaching me when working out a puzzle. Thomas was alive, he had to be. If not, then Kym's son would never get back 'View of Auvers-sur-

309

Oise' that he desperately wanted. We still had our agreement, even with the change of details. I took deep, measured breaths. Holt didn't say anything. I guess she was used to seeing people at their weakest. I was grateful for her silence.

A few moments later a message came through. I opened it and gasped. It was a photo of the man I had met, lying on his back, his eyes looking up to the ceiling in a pool of his own blood. His throat slit. Beside him, Thomas, my beautiful, innocent little boy. He looked so tiny. So delicate. He was laying on his side. Unconscious. I couldn't see Rachael anywhere in the picture. Under it was a short message. A warning.

No more fucking around, Michael.

I hoped Thomas didn't see the murder happen. I prayed he didn't know how much danger he was facing. I wished I could die so he wouldn't be there. I felt my soul bleed through my pores.

'Daniel, what is it? Daniel?'

I handed Holt the phone.

'Jesus.'

I began to cry. I knew I didn't have time to, I knew I needed to keep moving but I couldn't. My body needed a release. I felt paralysed. I felt weak. I was still failing.

'I don't know what to do. Please, you have to help me.'

Holt grabbed the back of my neck. Her grip was strong. The pressure somehow reassuring.

'That's why I'm here, Daniel.'

'But if he finds out the police are involved ...'

'I'm off duty.'

'You mean?'

'Right now, we are looking for you in France. Soon they will know you're not there anymore. I can keep them in London. I can keep them away. You just find the painting.'

'Why are you doing this?'

'When I discovered you had amnesia I questioned your motives. You had none and that told me you were a victim in all this.'

'Thank you, DCI Holt.'

'Karen.'

'I'm worried I'm not going to ever find what I stole.'

'Then let's not waste time trying.'

'But …'

'Let's just find your family. Let's find the bastards who took them.'

I felt a rush of something flood through my body. Hope. Holt seemed resourceful, inspired. With her now as an ally, my only one. I felt this nightmare would soon end. I drove in silence as Holt made calls in the seat beside me to old friends that owed her favours. I had told her about the man saying Thomas was on Slough Trading Estate and that became the subject of her conversations to persons unknown. It didn't take long for a few potential places to be identified. Most of the industrial estate was used and busy. But one site, where ICI used to be based, was mostly closed and it was a big site with lots of unused and unsecured areas. For the first time since the nightmare began, I felt close to Thomas and Rachael. However, it was fragile, like a butterfly's wings, there, beating, but very easily smeared into nothing. Holt said she would go to ICI first. She said it felt like the best fit. I wanted to go with her but she was right. They were only keeping their eyes on me and didn't know Karen Holt was helping.

Driving in a loop I dropped her off near the Ashmolean again, beside her car. She put her private mobile number into my phone but didn't say anything. We were about to head in different directions, but hoped to end in the same place. No sooner had she climbed into her car and driven away than the phone rang.

'Michael?'

'I'm here.'

'Did you get my picture message?'

'Yes.'

'Get to the Grand Union Canal in Slough.'

'Why?'

'There is something I want to show you.'

Chapter 60

Daniel

Slough

4th January 2018, 5.16 a.m.

I arrived at the Grand Union an hour after the call and walked
along its path with the canal on my left. My tired eyes stung and
played tricks on me. Shadows on the water took on a human
form and looked like they were walking as the surface current
moved. I passed the ruin of what used to be a bridge, its archway
support all that was left of something that had once joined on
to the adjacent one that I could just about see across the water.
On the other side of it I stopped and pressed my back into the
crumbling wall and waited.

It was still dark, but not so dark that I couldn't see the water
a few feet away from me. It looked more like a black carpet that
stretched off into the pre-dawn in both directions, reminding me
of the dream I had on my way to Paris. I watched the path waiting
to see the outline of a person approaching, straining my ears to
hear their footsteps. The leafless trees and constant hammering
of rain making me hear things and see things that were not there.
To my left I could see the road that went over the canal that I

had walked along before climbing over a barrier and down the slope. Every now and then a car would pass, its headlights picking up the rain drops that were coming in sideways.

I felt like I was wasting time. Holt told me to get back to my father's, retrace my steps and find new things. I thought about walking away; it seemed I had been sent here for no reason. But he could trace my moves. If I left without saying, he might make me pay. He held all the cards, he had all the power. Part of me hoped he would come in person so I could meet him eye to eye. I wanted to see what kind of man could do such horrific things to Sean and then to the giant man who tried to help. Then, I wanted to beat him until his face was broken before drowning him in the canal. Only after he told me where they were.

Something caught my eye in the water. A large black thing that floated towards me before nestling into the tree limbs that overhung. It looked like a sleeping bag of some kind. Walking towards it I focused on its shape. I couldn't process the image for a moment.

Then I did, and the world stopped working.

I was looking at a body bag.

I took off my coat and shoes and jumped into the canal, the water slapping me hard as I entered. I tried to swim towards it but for a moment I didn't move. It was so cold I could only suck in small amounts of air, my diaphragm not letting me breathe out again. I fought forwards, my arms numbing from the freezing temperatures. Reaching the bag, I grabbed hold and struggled to find a way in. I managed to make a small hole and with all of the strength my numbing arms could manage I tore it open. I wished I hadn't. I heard screaming, like a monster being vanquished. It took me a moment to realize it was coming from me.

In the low light I could see her face, her beautiful face. Swollen and broken. Her nose was sharply facing left, her right eye swollen shut. Her lips were split. I could see that teeth were missing. She had a blood stain coming from her ear.

Holding her I kicked my legs as hard as I could. They were beginning to feel like they weren't mine anymore. Reaching the side, I ducked under the water line to get under her. Then using my shoulders and back I lifted her out of the water and she fell heavily onto the concrete bank beside. It took me three attempts to climb out myself. My muscles had stopped working. I managed to get my chest flat on the floor with my legs still in the water and then I rolled my limbs out. Crawling over I rolled her on to her back, ripped open the rest of the bag and pressed my ear to her chest. I couldn't feel her breathing. I checked for a pulse, first in her wrist, then neck. Nothing. Opening her mouth, I placed my lips on hers and blew into her cheeks. Then pressed on her sternum. Trying to pump her heart. Breathe, pump. I did it for as long as my tired body would allow. Then I stopped to check her pulse again. A car went past, briefly lighting us both. My hands were covered in blood. I couldn't work out how. Before I could check we were in the dark again. Another car passed, another flash of light. Her top, one I didn't recognize, was dyed crimson. Tearing it open I could see a dark mark under her ribs. Another car passed. Another flash of light. The mark was a knife wound. It was deep.

She would have been dead within minutes.

I sat down heavily and looked at the starless sky, the rain hitting me in the face. Then I heard a sound, a rage-filled grief that echoed off the low winter clouds. I cried until the tips of my fingers hurt. The woman who I had loved once, who I still loved, was dead, because of me. A woman who was to be a mother again. Murdered. And I didn't know if my little boy had followed the same fate.

I scooped up Rachael's head and held it in my lap. Her face was covered in her limp, wet, red hair, I carefully moved it off and arranged it neatly. I didn't want to look at her as she was. I didn't want to remember this image but couldn't look anywhere else.

Leaning forward I kissed her lips and remembered our first kiss, sat in the middle of a cinema like a couple of teenagers. The kiss I gave her when we found out we were having Thomas. The kiss we had after he was born and placed in her arms. A thousand more that I treasured without knowing how much so. Hers was the mouth I should have kissed for my whole life. I just hadn't realized.

I didn't want to leave her on the concrete. It was hard, cold, and lifeless. In the water she would be weightless, free, and that mattered. So gently I dragged her back in. She was on her back, her head close to me. I gave her one final kiss before letting her drift away in the slow-moving water.

Watching her drift away I felt a rage build. They had done this. *He* had done this. I couldn't let it happen to my son. I took off my top, putting my coat on my bare skin and felt the phone in the coat pocket. I rang Rachael's mobile number and listened to the sound of her voice as I watched her float away from me. I wanted nothing more than to find the fuckers and kill them all. But with no guarantee of Thomas's safety I had no choice but to carry on, assuming he was still alive. Then, I could grieve as much as I needed. I started walking. My legs like lead, my stomach in knots. I had to stop to be sick. Hot bile spilled from me and folded me in half. The phone rang in my numb hand. I could barely hold it as I hit the receive button. My voice was trapped under the violent shaking.

'Michael?'

'You didn't have to kill her.'

'She left me no choice. She tried to do something stupid. I wanted you to see, just in case you were planning on doing something similar.'

'I need to know Thomas is alive.'

'He's fine.'

'But you won't let me hear his voice?'

'No.'

'Have you killed my son? If he's dead, what incentive have I got to carry on?'

'The hope that he isn't.'

The line went dead.

'Hello? Hello?'

I rang back frantically. It rang and rang without reply.

I tried again, and again it rang and rang. I tried to get up, I tried to move again but I couldn't. Rachael was dead and my little boy was in the care of a murderer. Making a fist I hit the floor. I did it again, and again. I hit the floor with everything I had. My knuckles were swelling quickly, making it hard to bend the fingers of my right hand. I had to stop myself from smashing my own head in. With trembling hands I scrolled the phone book for Holt's number. She picked it up on the second ring.

'Daniel?'

'Rachael is dead.' Saying the words out loud opened a fresh floodgate to my grief and fear. I began to sob, really sob. Rachael was dead. She was gone. And I was powerless to stop it from happening.

'I couldn't save her. I couldn't save her.' I started to sob again, unable to control myself.

'Daniel, listen to me. Did they mention Thomas?'

'I said I wanted to talk to him, but they wouldn't let me. He's dead. My baby is dead.'

'Daniel, did they say that? Did they say that explicitly?'

'They wouldn't prove he was alive, they told me to carry on and hope.'

'But did they say explicitly that Thomas was dead?'

'No.'

'Then he's not dead. We are at Slough Trading Estate now. We think we know where he is. Where are you?'

'At the Grand Union Canal in Slough.' I paused. My eyes brimming, my body convulsing. 'I can't believe she is dead. The things they did to her.'

'I'll send people to Rachael. Get out of there.'

'But …'

'Get out of there, find somewhere to hide. When we have him, I'll call.'

Chapter 61

Thomas

Location unknown

4th January 2018, 6.07 a.m.

I woke up facing the floor and it was moving and I couldn't work out what was happening. Everything was upside down, like it would be if I was in Australia, but I couldn't be because I was in a van and you can't drive all the way to Australia. It was about a thousand miles away and across a sea. I felt pushing on my tummy and realized I was upside down because I was being carried by a man. He had drawings on his hand of a bird. I could see the feet of someone else and looking, I saw it was The Smiler behind us. He was looking away so didn't see I was awake. As the man with drawings carried me, his shoulder dug into my stomach. I wanted to say it hurt but I was too scared, so I pretended I was asleep again and hoped he, or The Smiler, didn't notice. I watched his feet and the back of his legs as he walked really quickly. The van was there too. Behind that, I couldn't see anything. It was pitch black. Blacker than any bad dream. There were no street lights or buildings or fields or houses. Just blackness as far as I could see. Like I was looking at the edge of the world. The place

319

where dragons lived. That's where I was and that was my chapter title: 'Dragon Land'.

Although I couldn't see anything, it was really noisy, the wind growling loudly and whooshing past. It was so hard that I saw The Smiler was pushed sideways sometimes. And I could hear something else. Something even angrier than the growling wind. It was a dragon taking deep breaths. In and out. It gave off a smell too, a bit like salty animal fur. It really frightened me.

The man stopped and I heard keys rattle as The Smiler opened a door, then we were inside. I was dropped on the floor. It really hurt my leg but I didn't cry out. I bit my lip instead. He stepped over me and I watched as he went down a small corridor, opening doors and looking inside. Then he came back and I closed my eyes. He grabbed my ankle and dragged me into a small room. I hit my head on the doorframe on the way in. But he didn't care. Then he closed the door behind me and I was alone again. Outside the wind was so strong I could feel the room moving. I didn't want to be in the stupid story anymore. I wanted Mummy to stop messing around and take me home. I was upset that Mummy had finished the story without me and I started to cry. I didn't want to, I wanted to be a brave boy. But I did it anyway because when I cry at home Mummy comes and gives me a cuddle and Daddy would stroke my hair and tell me a story and I wanted that.

I cried and cried but they didn't come. And outside, the dragon kept breathing.

Chapter 62

Daniel

Slough Trading Estate

4th January 2018, 6.18 a.m.

Holt didn't call but she texted me an address and, putting it into maps, I saw I was only half a mile away. Leaving the car, I ran. After ten agonizing minutes of blind running, the tears still falling, I turned onto Leigh Road. On my right was the sign for ICI Paint. As I jumped the barrier a sleepy security guard came out of his cabin and tried to stop me. I dropped my shoulder and barged into him, knocking him to the ground, barely breaking my stride. I ran, my left foot slowing me down and forcing me to run awkwardly. After a few minutes I saw an unused building. Inside, torch light. I pushed myself harder, practically taking the door off its hinges as I crashed into it.

'Thomas? Thomas?'

'Daniel?'

'Holt? Where are you, where is Thomas?'

I followed where the sound of her voice came from and could see her torch lighting the corridor I was in. I came into a small room. A TV played. BBC News 24. The sound on mute. There was a table, three chairs. Empty pizza boxes. In the corner was the body of the man I had seen in the photo, his face covered with a coat. Thomas had been in this room at some point recently. Holt stood in the opposite doorway, her face grey. She stood like she was guarding it. Beside her were two others, one man, one woman. They held my gaze but didn't speak.

'Holt? What's down there?'

'Daniel.'

'Where's Thomas?'

She didn't respond but looked at her feet. It was bad. Whatever was behind her was really bad.

'Is he there?

'No.'

'Where's my son?'

I walked around the table and tried to get through the door. She wasn't budging.

'Get out of my way!'

'Daniel, stop. He's not here.'

'What do you mean? What do you mean? Where's Thomas? Where is he?'

I pushed again and her accomplices stepped in to grab me but she stopped them, telling them to step back before letting me through. At the end of the corridor was another room. As I approached it the smell coming from inside hit me before I could see. The smell of excrement, vomit. The smell of ammonia consistent with piss was overpowering and as I stepped into the space, the smell intensified. In the corner I could see the source. Urine stained the walls, vomit splashed the floor. Using my phone I lit the small space. A single bed sat pressed against the opposite wall to the sick, several damp blankets on top. To my right, a lamp lay smashed on the floor. A small amount of blood beside it. A plate, two empty water bottles. At the foot of the bed was another blanket. It was covered in fresh, wet mud. There was also a black stain and as I stepped closer I could see it wasn't black at all but dark red. Dried blood. A lot of it. Holt was stood in the doorway. Her voice was softer.

'Daniel?'

I turned and looked at something she held in her grasp. I couldn't make out what it was, or maybe I did, and my mind wasn't letting me process it.

'What's that?'

'I'm so sorry, Daniel.'

In her hand was Thomas's underwear. Covered in faeces. My boy had been stripped, and now he was gone. I dialled *the voice*. It rang and rang before disconnecting. I tried again, nothing. The third time it didn't even ring. Just an automated message telling me the caller wasn't available.

It was over. I had failed him.

'Daniel?'

'I need a minute.'

'Sure. I'll be out here. I've got to call it in.'

Holt tapped the wall before turning and leaving. Her soft compassionate voice was gone as she barked orders into her mobile. I suspected there would be a dozen cars here within minutes. Forensics. Wouldn't take the press long to get wind of it. Not that any of that mattered. I sat on the edge of the bed, a broken spring digging into the back of my thigh. The police would want to take me in, question me, find out what happened and see if I was accountable for any of it, which I was. They would eventually let me home, the press waiting to photograph the monster who got away with it. I wanted Katie to find out before the press storm started. Dialling her number I waited for her to pick up. My phone beeped in my ear, letting me know I was down to my final 5 per cent of battery. As soon as I heard her voice, I cracked wide open.

'Daniel?!' The reception was terrible, her voice cracking. Interference on the line made it difficult to hear her. Storm Fionn was disrupting phone lines. It took me three attempts to form

323

the words, the vowel sounds catching in my throat. When they came, they carried like dead weight.

'It's over.'

'What? What do you mean? Have you found it, is Tom okay?'

'No. It's over.' I looked up through a small vent to the sky, the clouds moving quickly, morphing as they were carried by the strong winds high above. From up there, I must have appeared so insignificant. And for a moment I tried to visualize myself up there, looking down. It didn't help. 'I failed him.'

'What do you mean?'

'I didn't find it in time.' My words came as sobs, the tension I had been holding across my diaphragm releasing, allowing my emotions to spill. A cascade of fire and pain and hurt and hate flowing from me, a waterfall I couldn't slow. I lowered my phone, unable to fathom the strength to keep it to my ear.

'You've still got a few hours,' she said loudly over the interference and my own broken sobs. 'Daniel? Daniel? Are you there?'

Bringing the phone back to my face, I spoke. A numbness replaced the pain. One I welcomed. I hoped it would numb me until my body shut down entirely. 'They killed Rachael, Katie. They killed her and dumped her in a canal. Now Thomas is gone.'

'Oh God, Daniel.'

'Katie, I've got to go. The police are coming to talk to me.'

'He might still be alive, they might have moved him or something. You've still got time. You've got to carry on. Don't go to the police. If you do then it really will be over. Get up.'

'I can't.'

'Get up. Get on your feet, keep looking. Thomas can't be dead. They want whatever it is you took. He has to be alive. You haven't delivered yet. Tell me, list off to me what you know.'

'Katie, there is—'

'Do it, Daniel. I'm not asking you, I'm telling you! This is not over. List off what you know.' Her voice was forceful, hard, and I needed it. Her strength forcing me to be stronger.'

324

'Okay,' I said, wiping tears from my cheeks. 'Okay. I left Auvers with it in a telescope. I got home to the UK. I hid it somewhere. It's here, somewhere.'

'Good. That's it, calm yourself, and get moving, there is still time.'

'Time for what, Katie? I'm never going to find it. I still don't know where to even look. I've failed.'

'You have to keep moving.' The line was full of static, her words cutting out as she spoke.

'No, it's over. I'm going to the station with the police.'

'Don't, Daniel. Can you hear me? Don't do that. Find the painting. Find th—'

The line went dead. My battery drained. Holt stepped back into the room, her hands in her pockets. I couldn't look at her. I thought of Monday, only the beginning of the week and yet so long ago. I thought of my last hug with Thomas. How it was just like any other hug. I didn't take the time to feel his arms around me, I didn't take the time to smell his hair and give him a kiss that would last forever. I wished I told him that he was the light in the dark skies of my life. That he had become the horizon from which the world came. And now he was gone. I focused on a small crack on the floor. I wished it would open up and swallow me whole.

'My battery died.'

'I can get you a charger, don't worry about it. Let's just get you in, so we can talk officially. We'll get a doctor to see to you as well, okay?'

I nodded.

'When they interview me, who do I say I am?'

'You're Daniel Lynch.'

'But I'm also Michael Gardner.'

Holt came over and crouched down, trying to draw my eye. 'You are Daniel Lynch. Michael Gardner, and what he did, doesn't matter to me. No one knows what he did back in 1999 besides you, me and those bastards. No one.'

Then it hit me. She was right. Only a few people knew the crime Michael had committed.

A memory slipped into my mind. It was as clear as day. If I didn't know better, I would say it was confabulation, but it definitely wasn't.

'Karen, I need some air.'

'You want me to come with you?'

'No, I need a minute.'

'Of course. Shout me if you need me.'

'Thanks, I'll just be outside,' I lied.

I walked back through the corridor, past the small room with the TV and out into the storm. Turning right I walked quickly towards the entrance. The security guard must have run into Holt because when he saw me, he nodded. Then, breaking into a run I headed back to my father's car. Aside from Holt, there was only one person besides me who wasn't dead that knew what Michael had stolen.

One. Kym's kid.

Firing up my engine, I knew where my last spiral in the circle would take me. I knew who had taken my family. I knew who they were. Things had not gone as they had planned, their control was gone. And I knew where they would want to go, somewhere to clear their head and be secluded. I knew a lot about them and knowing that meant there was only one place left they could be. It was about a three-hour drive. Enough time to plan my revenge. Every part of me wanted to die and be with Rachael and Thomas again, every part but one. The one that needed revenge. After I had fulfilled that part I would let my heart stop beating.

Chapter 63

Thomas

Location unknown

4th January 2018, 6.31 a.m.

I had fallen asleep, but then there was crashing and banging and I wasn't asleep anymore. There was a smashing noise and I could hear lots of naughty words being said that were so naughty I'm not allowed to say. It was really scary so I pretended to be asleep again. They left me alone when I was asleep. But they didn't this time. The door went crash as it opened and The Smiler came in. Behind him the other man sat with his head in his hands, I could see drawings on both of them. I could hear him saying 'it's over, it's over' again and again. He looked sad. It was strange to see a man upset.

The Smiler grabbed me by my hair and started dragging me. I tried to hold on to his wrists but it didn't help.

'It hurts,' I cried but he didn't listen. In fact, he held tighter. I could feel my hair falling off. I cried, 'It hurts, please stop it.' But he didn't. This wasn't supposed to happen. This wasn't part of my story. I was really scared and he was hurting me a lot and the words I had heard were not words that should be in a story. 'I want my mummy. Please, I want Mummy.'

He didn't say anything, instead he threw me on the floor. I crashed into a wall. I closed my eyes tight and it went really quiet. Like he was gone. I wanted to look but I didn't do it because maybe he would come back. But I did it anyway. And he was there. He was breathing hard, his back turned. He wasn't wearing his mask. I hoped that if he looked at me he wouldn't be so scary like when I saw The Bear from under the bed.

'Please, I want my mummy.'

'Shut up, Thomas, I need to think.'

I knew the voice, but I must have been dreaming or imagining it because the voice I heard didn't make sense to me. I started to cry loudly screaming for someone to help. Screaming for Mummy or Daddy. There was something shiny. I looked. It was a knife, a big one, and it was pointing at me.

I saw their face, and the voice did belong to who I thought it did. They came towards me, the knife getting closer and closer and I lost the way to speak words.

Chapter 64

Daniel

Somewhere on the A10

4th January 2018, 8.04 a.m.

I had been driving for ninety minutes, give or take, including stopping at services for petrol and a car lighter phone charger, a newspaper with my picture on the front, and two tubs of Pringles. I was worried the cashier would recognize me, but he barely acknowledged my existence as I paid in cash. I had emptied the Pringles and wrapped the tubes in a few sheets of the paper. It looked like a crude poster tube, but it would do. I would show it and they would be distracted and I would kill them in that moment. Thinking of it drove me forward. I might get hurt during the fight. I might even die. But I didn't care. I didn't care one bit.

Once my phone had fired up again it had rung twice, both times Holt. She had left a voicemail but I hadn't listened.

I had pictured that at this point, I would have the painting and they would still be alive. I had pictured a straight swap. Rachael sobbing in my arms as I kissed Thomas on the head.

I could almost smell him.

My phone rang again. This time it was Katie.

'Dan? Are you okay?'

'Do you want to know where it was, all this time?'

'Sorry?'

'It was in the pub we used to drink in remember? The White Horse?'

My question was again greeted with silence.

'We used to play snooker there. Me, you, my dad, your dad, of course. You were on the soft drinks. Too young back then. You sometimes wanted to sit in our meetings, and your dad let you until the Ashmolean job came up. Then you were told to go away, get a drink, and play some snooker or something. I can remember your face, how put out you were. Still, they were good times, weren't they?' There was a heavy silence, I could almost hear her panicking. As she spoke, there was an uncertainty in her words.

'You've gained some memory, I see.'

'Not all, but enough. You gave yourself away.'

'What?'

'You told me to keep looking for the picture, just before my phone died. You told me to find the picture. Only a few people knew what I stole in 1999. My dad, Kym, and Kym's kid.'

'It doesn't change a thing.'

'I'm coming to you.'

'That's not what was agreed.'

'I don't give a fuck. I'm coming to you. I have the painting.' I lied, looking at my improvised poster tube made of the Pringles containers wrapped in newspaper, knowing she would believe it was inside when she saw it, because she was desperate. 'At twelve o'clock, I will be there.'

'You don't know where to find—'

I cut her off. 'I know exactly where you are.'

I could hear her voice panicking. For the first time she wasn't pulling the strings.

'This is not what we—'

I cut her off again, knowing I could, knowing she wouldn't threaten to punish me. 'Do you want it or not?'

My question was greeted by silence.

I focused on the road ahead, now busy with lorries and people who were brave enough to battle the weather. Branches from trees lined the road. People were stopping to move them. I drove on.

'Twelve o'clock, Katie. I'll be outside the little blue beach hut we love so much.'

I hung up the phone before she could say anything back, and drove on quietly.

I had just under four hours – plenty of time to picture the way I was going to kill my girlfriend.

Chapter 65

Daniel

Sheringham

4th January 2018, 11.41 a.m.

Storm Fionn was in full force as I walked the final leg of my journey. The wind tore at my clothes, tried to remove the skin from my bones. It tried in vain to push me away from the coast-line. I watched a seagull flying, hanging onto the air with all of its strength until it landed heavily on a rooftop, almost falling off.

Sheringham was a ghost town, the shop doors were all closed where they would usually be open and inviting. The footpaths that were usually full of dog walkers and charming pensioners, completely deserted. Bunting that swept from one side of the road to the other buffeted in the wind. Several of them, having snapped, dangled like they were swinging from a noose. It was perfect. If the usually busy town centre was empty, where I was going would be even more so.

As I approached the end of the town I could hear the sea. It was angry. Signs were placed warning people to stay away from the coastline. Dangerously high tides and winds. It would help keep people away. But not me, or her. I had nothing to lose, she still wanted what I had. What I had told her I had, anyway. We would be the only two people out. It was perfect. With my improvised poster tube under my arm I turned onto the pedestrian walkway that lined the coast and felt fine droplets of sea spray on my face. The tide was high. Powerful cresting waves smashed into the defence wall that lined the footpath and spilled over, like a giant hand coming to grab what it could before crawling back into the sea. When the waves went out I could see the giant blocks of concrete at the bottom of the wall, designed to help slow its force. A job they were failing at.

I walked until I came to a line of small beach huts painted brightly. I pictured the times Katie and I came here; the sun would always be shining. We would get a coffee and pretend the blue one was ours whenever someone walked by. Those days we held hands, we kissed and then we would walk back along the coast to Beeston Regis where we ate dinner outside on the veranda and drank too much red wine. The evenings drew on. The stars came out. She told me she loved it there. Being at the coast made her troubles seem to melt away.

And they would today. Her troubles would soon be over, forever.

I stood, at the end of the long line of huts, and looked towards Beeston. Mud cliffs hugged the coastline. The pathway sloped down to sea level, and the sea itself was almost kissing the cliffs. When the tide was low there were hundreds of metres of soft sand, all of it under water. A small path along the rocks was all that remained. I leant on the blue and white striped hut and waited.

I thought about how we met, our 'chance' meetings in Stamford town after Rachael and I split. I thought about how, when I told her about my retrograde amnesia, she didn't freak out, or ask questions. She accepted it, she accepted it not out of kindness, but because she knew. She had known all along, and she used her charm to get into my world, my bed, my family. It explained how I had a phone in my glove box of my car and how there was no sign of a break-in at Rachael's. I didn't check to see if my spare key for Rachael's was there. I suspected it wasn't.

I thought about how it all came to be. She was there when I first remembered Auvers again, I told her all of my dreams, my flashes, she knew I was going to get it all back, and she had waited for the right moment to strike.

The only thing that didn't make sense was her dying father; Kym Bright died years ago.

And only a week ago she'd played with Thomas in the park on their own as I visited Will. Him laughing, her smiling. It was all part of her plan. Now, he was dead, and she would die too.

All I had to do was wait.

Chapter 66

Daniel

Sheringham

4th January 2018, 11.57 a.m.

I knew that very soon her shape would be seen as she walked along the line between cliff and shore. I was a big cat, a tiger, hiding in the long grass waiting to pounce. The cold was gone, the wind was lost on me. The heavens had opened but I didn't feel it hit my skin. None of those things could affect me now. Then I saw her. She was walking towards me, her right arm up trying to shield herself from the rain. Her left out, helping her with her balance. I watched her slip and fall into the cliff side. Only this morning I would have rushed down to help her. Now I enjoyed seeing her tiny frame be battered by the storm. When she eventually reached the ramp that led to the beach huts she was soaked through and her dirty hair was matted across her forehead. She still looked like Katie, she still looked like the woman I had fallen in love with, but when she saw me and stopped, she wasn't Katie anymore. She had to shout for her voice to be heard over the deafening wind and crashing waves.

'Is that it?' she said gesturing to the tube under my arm.

'Yeah.'

'Hand it over.'

'Come and get it.'

'Michael, now is not the time to fuck around. Hand it over and I'll tell you where he is.'

'I found where you were keeping him in Slough. I know what you've done. So if you want this, you need to come and pry it out of my hands.'

'No, no, this is not how it's working. If you want your boy back, you play by my rules. Mine. I'm not being overlooked again. I'm not being pushed out because my dad always liked you more than me.' She was angry, hysterical. I could see it in her eyes, the way she fidgeted from foot to foot. This was not how her plan was meant to happen and she was left flailing.

'Is this what it's all about? Daddy issues?'

'My father was weak, he was pathetic.'

'He died years ago!'

'I used him as an excuse to get out of your fucking house and away from that fucking child.' Her hair is flying all over the place, her eyes bloodshot, hands shaking. If anyone were to see us she would look demented.

'I thought you loved us, Katie?'

'That was the idea.'

'Why didn't your dad try to get it from me?'

'He said he needed redemption for all of the things he had done. He said he needed redemption from what I did to you. That we both needed to let it go.'

'What you did to me?'

'We were told to give you a beating, a warning. But you know, I just can't help myself sometimes.'

I saw it. The moment when I was attacked, the moment I lost everything. There were a lot of them, young and hungry for blood. A boot was coming down on the top of my head, smashing it into the tarmac, I was begging them to stop. I looked up. The

336

boot was small, a woman's. It was her, she had stamped and stamped on my head until I woke in a hospital bed. Katie had been the one who robbed me of my past.

I remember seeing her face. Smiling, enjoying herself as she stamped on me until the lights went out. I looked at Katie. She was smiling at me now.

'Yes, you remember now, don't you? Hand it over, Michael.'

I looked at the tube of Pringles, wrapped in newspaper. 'Why did they have to die for it?'

'Sean was trying to be a hero. Rachael tried to run. She left me no choice. You know, Michael, just before I met you in London and helped you wash and get dressed, I had been beating the teeth out of her pretty little head. Then, when you left to go to Slough I drove the same way, back to finish her off.'

'Shut up.'

'She screamed like a little bitch as I slid the knife into her chest. I took my time too, enjoying her suffering. She was always too pristine, too together. I always fucking hated her.'

'She was going to be a mum again!' I screamed at her, our voices getting lost on the wind.

'Like I care.' She shrugged her petite shoulders, as though a life were nothing.

'What about Thomas?'

'Hand it to me, let me see it, and I'll tell you where he is.'

Her words slapped me into focusing on more than killing her and dying myself. Thomas was still alive. She'd not killed him. But he would be killed when she found that the tube I had under my arm was empty. I needed to stall, I needed to think. I looked over her head, towards the cliffs. On the top I could just make out the white shape of a static caravan. Thomas was up there. Probably being watched by the third one the big man spoke of. He was so close and only Katie was in my way. She was small, I could barge my way past. I could throw her into the sea. Then, I could surprise the other one, who wouldn't be ready to be

337

attacked and get Thomas back. But she had managed to kill Sean and the big man who wanted to help. She had killed Rachael. Even if I had slept and my body was working properly I wasn't sure I could take her. I had to use the prop. I held the tube high above my head.

'What are you doing?'

'If you want it so bad, catch.'

I threw it as hard as I could and watched as she ran towards it. Somehow she managed to catch it before it went over the storm breaker and into the violent sea. But it didn't matter. The path was clear. I ran as hard as I could towards the cliffs. Just the other side of the bend in the rock was a set of steps that would take me up to Thomas. As I ran, my left leg suddenly stopped working and I fell. I tried desperately to get back up but I couldn't keep control of my limb. It shook violently but I couldn't work out why, until I looked down and saw a knife sticking into my calf.

Somehow she had managed to catch the tube and then turn and put a knife in me before I could pass. I tried to stand and failed. This time when I looked, she was over me, the knife being pulled from my leg. It hurt so much that I screamed. I started to crawl from her, biting back the pain. Her legs were over me, following, toying like a jaguar would with its prey before finishing it off. My only thought was of getting Thomas when I felt heat in my leg again, my thigh this time where she plunged the blade in. I rolled onto my back, a pool of blood forming quickly. I tried to move but couldn't get up. Standing over me, smiling, Katie unwrapped the tube and discovered it was empty.

She screamed before lunging at me again. I stuck up my arms to block her. The knife drove into my hand, it cut into my forearms, bouncing off bone. I couldn't count how many times she swung it at me. Somehow she hadn't managed to get through to my face or chest. She was screaming at me, most of it I couldn't understand. What I did understand though was if I didn't stop her, my son would die.

The knife came down again and I stuck up my palm to block it. The tip of the blade came all the way through and I closed my hand as much as I could. It wasn't enough to pull it from her grasp. But enough to stop her pulling it out of me. Just enough for me to act. I swung my left arm, and hit her in the ear. She tumbled off me, the knife sliding out of me once more. I tried to get up. Blood loss made it difficult but I managed to pulled myself onto my good leg using the railing that stopped people falling over the edge.

A wave came in and water swept over my head, the weight of it making my knees buckle. It tried to pull me in with it, but I held on. I was blinded by sea water. I didn't know where Katie was. I saw an arm coming towards me and I grabbed it. The knife inches from my face, I used my weight to spin, pushing Katie on the railing with me stood an arm's reach away. My breathing was heavy. I was struggling to stand. Blood dripped from my arms and leg onto the floor. I knew I would pass out soon and then I would die. But it didn't matter. I had to stop her getting back to Thomas. With the remaining strength I threw myself at her, shoulder first. She thrust with the knife, but I kept pushing her. The blade went into my side but I didn't stop myself. Digging deep I dropped my weight and forced it up. I felt my shoulder impact the side of her face. It lifted her off her feet and, grabbing her legs, I threw her over the barrier. A wave crested, swallowing her. When it receded, she was on the rocks, her head split open. Another wave came in, burying her from sight and when that left, she was gone.

Dropping to the floor I lay on my back and felt the rain hitting my face. The sky was just a vast grey sheet. The wound in my side was deep. I strained to twist my head and look at it. I could see blood bubbling, the air in my lung leaking onto the floor. I told myself to breathe, but it was impossible to do so. My blood continued to flow. I needed to go to sleep but wanted to fight it. I wanted to see my son one last time. To tell him he was all that mattered, and he would always be loved, in this life and the next. But it wasn't going to happen. And it didn't matter. Someone would find Thomas soon, he would be okay. I gave in and closed my eyes, focusing on a moment of him as a baby in my arms. Me rocking him to sleep after giving a night-time feed, the world calm and still, pre-dawn outside our bedroom window. It made what was to come okay. For some reason, I thought of the park only a week ago, when things were wonderful. How quickly a life can change.

I once read that the moments that were truly important in life, the moments we all carried forward and recalled on our deathbeds, we subconsciously recognized as they were happening, and because of this, our own subconscious made sure we stopped to take it in. All we had to do was ensure that when our bodies told us to stop, to breathe, to use our senses to their fullest, we listened.

I did, and I could swear that Thomas was calling my name.

Epilogue

Daniel

Auvers

Six months later

Limping through the canola field that ran as far as I could see, I had to stop and rest. My thigh muscle burnt like I had run a marathon rather than walked for ten minutes. Catching my breath, I watched the warm wind dance across the yellow tops of the pungent plant, listening to the noise it made and, in the distance, a river.

It had been six months since that day on the coastline of the North Sea where Katie and I fought, but my body still hadn't fully recovered. My limp, although less prominent, was still with me, as it always would be. I still couldn't make a fist with the hand that Katie had plunged the knife into. But I was lucky, for a short while I was sure I'd lose it altogether.

I still couldn't remember what happened after Katie fell into the sea and I lay watching the clouds, waiting for death to come. Perhaps I never would. Perhaps I didn't need to. All I did know was I had been saved.

* * *

My first recollection was days after in a small room, my arms and chest and leg bound tightly in bandages, a drip running into my left arm. But it wasn't a hospital room. I had no idea where I was. Outside, the sun was shining faintly and in the distance I could see hills. At the foot of my bed was someone I was sure I'd never see again. Thomas. As I struggled to sit up, he woke, and upon seeing me, my beautiful little boy jumped into my arms. It hurt like hell, but I didn't care. We sobbed until we had no more tears and then we just lay there, holding on to each other for dear life, both of us watching the clouds float by. Me stroking his hair with my good hand and kissing his head, taking in his smell until my lungs were full and he fell asleep. Then the door opened and Karen Holt came in, a smile spreading across her face as soon as she saw us together. I wiped the tears that had freely fallen from my eyes, not out of shame, just so I could focus once more.

'Nice to see you awake, Daniel.'

'Nice to be awake. How—'

Before I could continue, she stopped me, saying she'd tell me later. I needed my rest, so closing my eyes I let myself drift. When I awoke it was dark and Thomas was still sound asleep lying next to me, Karen was at the foot of my bed.

'Hey,' I whispered, careful not to wake him.

'Hey.'

'Where are we?'

'Somewhere safe.'

'I don't understand. Why are we not in a hospital?'

'You've been all over the news, Daniel. Everyone knows about what really happened, why it happened.'

If the world knew everything about what happened to Sean and Rachael, then I had no reason to hide. I'd be questioned and be away from Thomas who would likely stay with my mum until I was released.

'I don't understand why we are hiding?'

'Because, they also know about Michael Gardner. And suspect that he was involved in the theft of the Cezanne painting. Gardner's wanted for questioning.'

'I see,' was all I could say, taking my eye from Holt to look at my little boy sleeping beside me. 'I'll never forgive myself for what's happened. They're dead, his mother is dead because of me.'

'Because of him. You are not Michael Gardner.'

'Aren't I?'

She couldn't answer, and it was unfair of me to expect her too.

'I was sure I was going to die.'

'You very nearly did. After you took off, we ran your plates through number plate recognition and after a while it was clear you were heading to the east coast. We looked more at Kym and discovered he didn't have a son, but a daughter, Catherine Bright. It wasn't hard to find out that she had a place on the coast. We found Thomas first, with another man who was expecting Katie. He tried to bolt when he realized the police were there.'

'Who was he?'

'He was the voice you had been speaking with. A known accomplice within the Bright Gang. You may have known him in your previous life.'

'Was Thomas hurt when you found him?' I tried to sit up but my body didn't let me, so I leant back against the pillow.

'Scared, a few knocks and bangs. But he was okay. I told him I was a friend of yours. He was really brave.'

'When you say we found him, what do you mean by "we"?'

'Not "the police" we, just the same two work colleagues who believed you were innocent as well.'

'Thank them for me.'

'Of course.'

'I'm so sorry, Daniel, about Rachael, about all of it.'

'Me too.'

She nodded towards me before continuing. 'Then I found you.

343

I thought you were already dead. I couldn't believe you were still breathing.'

I stayed in that room for another three weeks, healing and helping my son come to terms with what had happened. I dreamt of my life before 2003 and the more recent events, seeing Rachael's face in most as I found her in the canal. I would wake up sweating and Thomas would comfort me. I would do the same for him as he dreamt of a monster who smiled at him, trying to take his soul. Thomas thought the whole thing was a game, right up until his mother died and I fell in love with her all over again. Even in the darkest of moments she was strong, far stronger than I was being. I owed her his future. A bright one where he was happy and living in a safe place. One night whilst watching him sleep, I knew where that place was.

With help from Holt, and a fat man who was good at forging documents and didn't want to face a lengthy jail sentence, Thomas and I had new passports and were on our way out of the country. Holt had told me that after what we had been through, she couldn't bear the idea of us being separated again by a police investigation. I could only think of one place to go. The place that on my short visit told me I was happy there, and that Thomas would be safe. Holt said she didn't want to know where we were going. So we said our goodbyes at King's Cross. And I thanked her for saving my life. I hoped, one day, when the world had forgotten about me again, I would see her.

And we had been here ever since. Quietly rebuilding our lives.

'Daddy, come on.'

Thomas shouting my name was him clearly saying I had rested for long enough, so I continued limping through the field, following the sound of his voice as he kept calling. I saw him up ahead, his net and pole resting on his shoulder; he hoped to catch minnows in the river. He dipped in and out of my sightline. Each time he disappeared I felt panic rise in my stomach, but I had to push it down. I owed it to Rachael. I had to take over the story, and in it I was okay, we were okay, we would have a happy ending.

Clearing the line of canola, I was greeted by the river bank, the water softly moving through. Thomas was already sitting down, taking his shoes and socks off to wade in with his net. I hobbled over, and using a tree, I lowered myself to the ground to take off mine and join him.

He came running over to me and into my arms, kissing me on the cheek.

'Hurry up, Daddy.'

'I'm hurrying, I'm an old man.'

'No, you're not.'

Looking at him, the sun lighting his pale skin, I smiled.

Placing my shoes on a small hole that had been carved into the bank by high tides I slowly pulled myself to my feet. As I walked to the edge I heard a crow cawing from the tree above where I sat. It stopped me in my tracks as I was struck between the eyes with an image, a memory. It was so clear. So precise. I was in the rain, burying something. Covered in mud. The same image I saw on New Year's Eve, which felt like a lifetime ago. But this time I was remembering something where I was currently standing. Spinning around I looked to the tree, to my shoes. It was the wrong tree, but the right place.

Scanning the banks, I saw it. A giant willow hanging into the water. I looked to its base and smiled. There was a telescope resting there, waiting for the day Thomas and I would dig it up.

'Daddy? Are you okay?'

I looked at Thomas, and in that moment he looked just like his mother, his eyes so much older and wiser than a six-year-old's should be. I smiled at him and he smiled back.

'Yes, darling, I'm fine.'

Walking into the cool water, I let myself close my eyes and tilt my head towards the warm sun, its glow filtering through my eyelids, bathing my vision in yellow. Having my eyes closed heightened my hearing and I heard birds chirping various tones, and the breeze sweeping through the trees. I heard Tom singing to himself as he played, filling my entire body with warmth.

And in the distance, behind all of it, I heard the sound of sirens.

Acknowledgements

Writing a second novel is never easy. All of a sudden, I have gone from writing whenever I want and crafting a book on my own time scale (a scale that was 5 years long) to writing to a tight deadline. The transition has been wonderful and weird and hard and liberating all at once. It's been a wonderful adventure, but one I wouldn't have been able to complete alone.

So, first and foremost, I would like to thank HQ Digital and my editor, Hannah Smith, for always believing in my writing (even when I couldn't) and always being on the end of a phone to answer the questions raised when writing *Close Your Eyes*. Without your input this book wouldn't be a book at all. I hope you know how much I value your ideas and suggestions.

To the people around me in my day to day life, thank you for being there. A special thank you is needed for John Shields, my wonderful mate who has helped me with the challenge of creating believable characters. Another thank you is needed for the talented fellow authors Louise Jensen and John Marrs. After the whirlwind of *Our Little Secret* you have helped me stay connected to the thing I love, which is writing words.

To Kelly-Ann Gordon and the team at Eastern School of Performing Arts as well as the students, thank you for understanding the road I've been walking down and supporting it, allowing me to continue to teach as well as write this book.

To you readers. The support you have shown and kind words you have shared have been overwhelming and wonderful. Without the retweets, posts in book clubs and word of mouth discussions I wouldn't be in the place where I am now. And this place is the dream!

Finally, to Ben. You deserve all of the praise. Without you there would be no motivation, no determination and no inspiration. And I will forever try to repay you for this.

If you loved *Close Your Eyes* then read on for a sneak peek of
Closer Than You Think …

Prologue

28th August 2018
Bethesda, North Wales

The eighth

He once read somewhere that people become who they are based on their environment and experiences. Their childhood memories, the interactions with friends and profound moments, good and bad, experiences create the building blocks of existence, and once those blocks are set, they are solid, like a castle wall. Some people are kind, some passionate, some victors, some victims. Some are violent. He knew that more than most. And although people couldn't fundamentally change, he knew, from personal experience, they could evolve. Transform. A switch could be thrown, showing a different way to be, without really being any different at all. It happened in nature: the caterpillar doesn't change its DNA when it becomes a butterfly, but unlocks a part of itself that has lain dormant, patiently waiting for the right moment to create a cocoon. He had experienced several evolutions which had altered the direction of his thoughts and actions. But these didn't change who he was. He would always be someone who killed.

And it wouldn't be long before he would kill again. A matter of an hour or so. He wanted to fulfil his purpose now, but knew he had to wait, be patient, and watch. Standing in the shadow of a wide tree, he looked into the eighth's bedroom window, waiting to see her enter, and he thought about when he would be in that room with her just before he ended her life. He knew she would panic and cry and scream before he sedated and killed her, because they always did.

He had planned to be outside her house after dark. But, with it being such a long time since he had done the one thing that made him feel alive, the thing that made him feel like he was flying, he arrived early and took time to enjoy that forgotten sense of anticipation. This also gave him a moment to reflect on the last person he'd failed to kill in this manner. A woman named Claire Moore. She played on his mind more than she should. The one that got away, so to speak.

Before coming to Bethesda, he'd felt compelled to write a letter to Claire. He wanted to explain the reasons for his absence from the world. He revealed to her that after their eventful night a decade before, he needed to regroup, re-evaluate. After her, he never intended to kill in the same manner as he would tonight. But then he discovered she was moving on, leaving that night, their night, in May of 2008 behind. He wrote that he had learnt she was becoming the same person he felt the need to visit before. Which told him she was forgetting him, and he didn't want his last survivor to forget him, because if she did, everyone else would.

He knew, one day, she would read his letter. Perhaps, before then, he would write more. If so, he would let her read them all, right before he ended her life. He could have killed Claire Moore several times in the past few months but decided not to. He wanted to wait, savour the moment. He wanted her to know him as well as he knew her, and to understand his reasons.

He wanted to be able to taste the connection they once shared on the tip of his tongue, as the light in her eyes faded. Claire Moore would die, as she nearly did by his hand all those years ago, but not yet, not until he was in buried in the centre of her soul once more. He wanted every voice to sound like his, every shadow to be one cast by his frame blocking the light. It was the reason he was in Bethesda, and why the woman whose window he looked into would die.

The knowledge of what would happen within the next hour, and what would follow over the coming weeks – the speculation, the fear – coursed through his veins so hard his skin itched. He knew he needed to focus, to contain his excitement, until night staked its claim over the day. He centred on his breathing, regulated his heart rate. He pushed thoughts of what he would do to the woman in the house opposite him out of his head.

Then she, the eighth, walked into her bedroom. He watched her step out of her work clothes, her light skirt falling effortlessly around her ankles. He enjoyed the sight of her slim frame in just her underwear, and the tingle that carried from behind his eyes to his crotch. It was a feeling he hadn't felt in a very long time. There had been plenty of kills since 2008, but not one reignited the fire he remembered from a decade before. For the past ten years, when the itch had been unbearable, he had scratched it discreetly, and taken those no one cared for. The old and alone, the homeless, the migrant. But this one was to be a spectacle, like in those wonderful days in Ireland, putting him back where he belonged, in people's minds, in Claire's mind – a destructive force touching everyone like cancer.

He missed being someone who was feared. In the days when a simple power outage caused widespread terror, he would often kill the electricity to a street, just to watch people panic, thinking they would be next. He especially enjoyed one occasion, three months after that night with Claire Moore, when a storm swept off the Atlantic and cut the power in Shannon. It caused the whole town to descend into terror, thinking he had visited. Police took to the streets, people locked their doors. News helicopters circled, expecting to see a house fire in the aftermath – his other calling card. But there was no fire, no death as he was in Greece on that day, on the island of Rhodes, enjoying the sunshine without a care in the world. He intended that trip to be one in which he learnt to be the man he would become, the man he had evolved into. But, seeing the news, the terror coming out of Ireland, drove the desire to kill once more. It was there, on the sun-bleached Aegean coast, that his metamorphosis began, as he felt a more primal calling. He needed to kill, not because it was his purpose, but for the thrill of it. After a brief search he found his victim, an unaccompanied male who had survived the Mediterranean Sea to start a new life in Europe, and he ended his life, luxuriating in the power he felt while doing so.

But the power didn't last long, because no one cared about this man's death. And upon returning home to Ireland, he could sense he was being forgotten. Over time, only the areas he had visited remembered the horror of those months between April 2006 and May 2008. To try and cling on to his power, he would still toy with their memories, killing the electricity from time to time, just to see the panic unfold. He would walk through the town and watch as whole families squashed together in one candlelit room. But time heals all wounds, and their outright terror diminished to a quiet readiness. Eventually, a power cut became just an annoyance once more.

The eighth hadn't closed her bathroom door and he could see as she unclipped her bra and dropped it on the floor. He glimpsed her breasts, and the tingle intensified. But he didn't want to fuck her; the very idea was repugnant to him. His pleasure came from somewhere else.

He visualised his approach as he waited for the sun to set. Once darkness held, he would go to the single distribution substation. It was less than two hundred metres away, and he knew it supplied the power to her house, along with a few hundred others. The enclosed five-metre wall containing the substation was built in the Nineties, along with the houses it supplied, and was secured

354

with a padlock on its front gates. The bolt cutters that sat heavy in his rucksack would make light work of that. Then it was a case of isolating the switch gear and using a rewired portable generator that would intentionally overheat and blow. This simple and well-practised task would black out the entire street and beyond.

He pictured the walk from the substation to her back door, and then breaking in. He knew he would find her stumbling around upstairs with her phone as a torch. He suspected she would be in her nightwear. He thought about what he would do to her. The fun he would have. The joy he would feel feeding off her fear.

Then, once satisfied, he would place her body in the bathtub, douse her with petrol and ignite her. He would leave before the heat cracked the windows and smoke billowed into the sky. He would go home and cook himself a meal, a pasta dish to replenish the burnt carbohydrates from his evening's work, as he knew from experience work drove his appetite. Then, full and content, he would watch the news, waiting to see what he did featured on it, and the assumptions they would make. And he knew he would get away with it, because he'd gotten away with it before.

His kills in Ireland landed in the lap of a brute of a man named Tommy Kay. Kay was a drug dealer with a reputation for being heavy-handed if a favour or loan hadn't been repaid. He was sent to prison for running down a man in his Range Rover, nearly killing him over a hundred-pound debt. Kay's arrest and that night with Claire Moore were a few months apart, and although Kay was never charged with the murders in Ireland, he was widely believed to be the serial killer that haunted the country, never saying otherwise. Perhaps he enjoyed the notoriety it gave him?

But Kay's motivations for tacitly claiming his kills weren't his concern, because one day they would know how wrong they had been. Until then, he would play on what the media would no doubt suggest: because Kay was now dead, tonight was a copycat.

355

After ten minutes the eighth came out of her bathroom, a towel around her body, another wrapped around her hair. She turned on her TV, then stepped towards the window, her arm outstretched to close her bedroom curtains. She couldn't see him. He knew it. The fading sun directly behind him was low. The trees tall. She wouldn't be able to see anything beyond the dusty orange skyline. But still he pressed himself further into the tree's shadow. She paused before drawing the curtains, her eyes looking out above his head. The last line of sun painted colours in the evening sky. A perfect disguise for him. Hide the ugly thing that he had become in something equally beautiful.

It was almost time. Another thirty minutes and it would be dark enough to work. He smiled, knowing how tomorrow's newspapers would read.

Chapter 1

6th May 2018
St Ives, Cambridgeshire

As I lay on my right side, left arm under the pillow that my head rested on, I fiddled with my necklace, counting the keys that hung from the thick silver chain. Four keys. Front door, back door and two smaller window keys, one up, one down. I watched the alarm clock flick from one minute to the next. I had done so for the last hour, waiting for it to say 05:05, then the alarm would sound, and I could get up. I'd wanted to get up at three minutes to four, a dream of fire waking me, but forced myself not to. By doing so, I hoped I could present myself as a woman who wasn't struggling to sleep. Although, I don't know who I was trying to kid. I *was* struggling to sleep, I always do at this time of year.

I watched the minutes turn into hours and waited for my alarm before rising, because it felt like a victory over myself. It was me telling myself I could be normal if I worked hard at it. And that was important, to be as normal as I could be. This daily victory was one of the few things I liked about the month of May. It seemed small, maybe even pointless, but the small things mattered more than I could have possibly foreseen. I had no choice but to enjoy the little things. Like the morning sunshine and the sound of the breeze in the trees; the buzz of bees in my

357

garden collecting nectar from one of the many flowers I grew. If I focused on these details, I would get through the month I dreaded. Then June would come, and I would survive another year.

Rolling over to face the window, I looked through the small gap in my curtains to see pale blue sky outside. Not a cloud in sight. It made me smile. A cloudless morning was another victory. Stretching, I uncurled my arms and straightened my legs groaning as my muscles pulled, and blood flowed in my limbs. A feeling I liked. Reaching over, I turned off my bedside light and picked up my phone, checking the date. I didn't know why I did that. I knew exactly what day it was. I had been checking and counting down for weeks now. The date that was the source of my sleepless nights, the date that ruined the month for me was only thirteen days away. Thirteen long days until I could reclaim the night for its intended purpose. I couldn't help but feel a rising trepidation that started just below my belly button and slowly oozed up through my stomach and chest. I sat upright and tricked myself into thinking gravity would stem the flow. With a few deep breaths, it worked.

This year marked ten years since it happened. My mother had somehow convinced me it would be healthy to go back to Ireland, back home. I didn't like flying; I didn't like the idea of going back there again. But Mum stressed it would be good for me. It would cleanse me, and, she said, would help me remove the guilt I was feeling for enjoying the time I was spending with my new friend, Paul. She was right, of course, but it didn't make me feel any better about it.

The red digital display flicked to 05:05, and the buzz made me jump. Gently, I hit the off button with my left hand. I looked at my emails on my phone. There wasn't much going on aside from some spam emails from Groupon, trying to sell me unmissable deals on spa weekends. This was exactly what I needed, and yet another thing I couldn't do.

There was also one unread Facebook message. Sighing, I opened the app and I saw who had sent it. Killian. He had messaged at 03:19. I shouldn't have read it. But I did anyway.

Hi, Claire, how are you? Is everything OK? We keep missing each other. I've been thinking about you, being May and all… I hope you are all right. I am here to talk if you need a friend.

I went to reply but stopped myself. Instead I clicked on his profile, seeing his photo hadn't been changed in all the years I had known him. The same lopsided smile, same thumbs-up gesture. The same mountain range behind him. I scrolled down to see the group page he was an administrator for: the Claire Moore Support Page. Tapping the bold letters, the next image I saw was a picture of me. I couldn't bring myself to read things from the past written there, as kind as the words were. I just wanted to see if there was anything new. The last post was from January.

Claire, on behalf of everyone here at CMSP, we want to wish you a Happy New Year. 2018 will be a good one.

I hadn't responded to the message, but remembered that shortly after a cheque came through the post from the support group, with a note attached saying I should go away somewhere nice.

I didn't spend it, I never did.

I threw the phone on my bed and rolled onto my back. I regretted reading the message. The group have always been supportive, but recently, Killian unnerved me in a way I couldn't put my finger on. To stop myself overthinking and ruining the day before it had begun, I looked towards the window. Lazy dawn light filtered through the thin curtains, casting beams of honey across the ceiling. I focused on the colours, letting myself enjoy the softness for a moment. Owen would have loved me observing this; he would tell me to enjoy the moment for as long as possible, as all things are short-lived. If only he knew how right he had been. I could almost hear him saying it, his voice light and melodic. I stopped myself. Perhaps one day it wouldn't hurt so much.

Lifting myself out of bed I slowly placed my feet on the cool wooden floor and walked quietly into my bathroom, careful not to disrupt Mum and Geoff who were asleep in the room next to me. I hadn't intended to stay the night at Mum's. I'd only wanted to come for a quick cuppa and book the online tickets for our flight to Ireland, tickets she insisted she paid for. But a quick cuppa ended in me staying for dinner and then it was late. Going home by myself was too daunting. Mum knew this, and once it had crept past eight and the daylight had faded, she offered the spare room so I didn't have to ask.

Closing the bathroom door behind me I switched on the light and waited as my eyes adjusted. Then, stretching again, feeling the blood move around my body, I considered how much I hurt. I did most mornings. Sometimes it was excruciating, sometimes tolerable. This morning I was OK. The only part of me that felt discomfort was my right foot – it always seemed to ache more in May than at any other time in the year, suggesting my pain was more psychological than physical. I popped a codeine tablet, just to be safe. Considering the mirror, I noticed that my eyes looked dark and heavy. Age was doing its dance on my face. Not that age really mattered anyway, it was all just borrowed time I would have to give back. I realised that getting older and watching a face wrinkle was a gift some didn't receive.

I heard footsteps in the hallway, followed by my mum's sleepy voice.

'I'm outside.'

'Thanks, Mum.'

She knew I was in the bathroom and had gotten out of bed, so I knew she had an eye on me. It meant I could have a shower. Something I cannot do unless I know I am safe, even after all this time. Removing my necklace, I hung it on the back of the door before stepping into the shower and turning the water on.

After the initial shock of cold water hitting me, it quickly warmed until it was so hot my skin turned pink as I washed the night away. Another night survived. Another night in the countdown completed.

As the hot water poured over my head, I focused on the heat on my scalp. I couldn't help wondering, as with most mornings recently, what I had been doing exactly ten years ago when my life had been so very different. Owen and I were probably still in bed, his heavy arm draped over me, our bedroom windows wide open, letting the cool breeze waft our net curtains, making them float like ghosts. We would get up, shower, maybe together, and then have breakfast before going our separate ways to work. He would kiss me goodbye at the door before jumping into his car and driving down the lane towards Cork. He might have been back that day, or he might have been going off-site for a few days in another part of the country. With his car out of view, I would climb into mine and drive to the pre-school where I worked. The children would arrive, and I would spend the next six hours playing, reading, cooking and helping with toilet breaks, giving gold stars to the little ones who went all by themselves. I would then come home, cook for us both, and go to bed with the windows wide open once more – oblivious to pain, heartbreak. Evil.

I knew it wasn't healthy to reminisce; that wasn't my life anymore and nothing would bring it back. I turned my attention to the torrent of hot water that ran over my forehead and into my eyes, sticking my lashes together. It stung a little, but that was good. It stopped my dark memories pushing forwards. I stayed there, head against the tiles, until thoughts of what my life had been like a decade ago washed down the plughole.

Wrapping myself in my dressing gown that I'd brought round to Mum's a few months ago and left here, I put my necklace back on, comforted by the weight of the four keys, and walked down the narrow corridor of Mum's bungalow into the kitchen. As I passed her room I could hear Geoff snoring. No sooner had I flicked on the kettle, the cat, Baloo, greeted me. He was named after the bear in *The Jungle Book* because of his colour and the huge paws he'd had as a kitten. He meowed and stared at me, unblinking.

'Are you hungry, little man?'

He rubbed himself up against my shin to tell me yes, and acting on cue I rolled up my dressing gown sleeves and took out a pouch of his food from the cupboard beside the bin. As soon as I'd emptied the pouch into his bowl, he dismissed me. The bloody cat didn't like anyone.

I made a cup of green tea, adding a slice of lemon, and walked to the back door, needing to take some measured breaths before opening it. With my heart beating faster than before, the door creaked open, letting the rousing spring morning flood in. The air was clean and fresh, making goose bumps rise on my exposed forearms.

Dawn was my favourite time of the day. The world was still asleep, and felt somehow different. The air smelt cleaner, richer, as if the lack of cars and noise and bustle of people wrapped up in their own sense of importance allowed the trees to sigh. Dawn brought a sense of peace and magic that didn't exist at any other time in the day and, for a short while every morning, I felt like I had it all to myself. I drank it in, the peace. Again, it was in the small things, things I had only let myself see in recent years.

I stepped barefoot onto the lawn. The morning had not warmed the dew enough to evaporate it. As I walked towards the bench in the middle of the lawn, I felt the cold creep through my feet, soothing them. Broken blades of grass from yesterday's cut stuck to my soles. I couldn't look; the grass cuttings served as a powerful reminder of something I longed to forget.

I looked back towards the bungalow to see if Mum had come into the kitchen to make sure I was all right. The kitchen was empty. But I could see my footprints in the dew, perfect shapes that caught a glimmer from the rising sun. My eye was drawn to the impressions of my right foot. I had to look away. Then, sitting on the bench under a maple tree, I allowed myself to momentarily forget where I was, letting my thoughts and anxieties dissolve like sugar in hot water. This feeling of serenity wouldn't last long, so I let myself be wrapped up in it. Although the sun was weak, I could feel it warm my skin. Undoing my dressing gown, I let it touch my neck and collarbones. I focused on what I had been taught by my doctor a long time ago: enjoy the sunshine on your skin. I took a deep breath and focused on my neck which was gently warming, and drew in the smell of morning dew.

After about five minutes the moment faltered, and without warning my mind drifted back to the thoughts of flying home with Mum in ten days' time. It had been a long time since I'd last travelled any distance, and I wasn't sure how I would cope. I felt the small ice-cold hand I'd housed for a decade pluck my diaphragm like a guitar string, making the next few breaths hard to draw. I didn't want to go, but I knew I needed to. It was the right thing to do. I owed it to him, at the very least. But really, I owed him more than I could ever repay. Sighing, I sipped my now-cool tea and waited for the noise of the day to start. I heard a dog barking a few doors down, then a front door somewhere along the row of houses attached to mine opened and closed.

The world was awake, and it wasn't mine anymore. Going back into the bungalow I tried and failed to not look at my footprints.

If you enjoyed *Close Your Eyes*, then why not try another gripping from HQ Digital?